ROSE & THUNDER

ROSE & THUNDER

LILITH SAINTCROW

www.lilithsaintcrow.com

DEDICATION

To Skyla, who believes.

Acknowledgments

Thanks are due to Mel Sterling, who kept me (reasonably) sane; to Miriam Kriss, who always has something good to say, and to Skyla Dawn Cameron, for making things pretty and the occasional stabbing.

Last of all, dear Reader, let me thank you as well, the best way I know how, by telling you a story.

Chapter One

It started with the rosebushes. The stupid, silly rosebushes. And my big mouth.

Actually, it all started with Jimmy Cassidy. He stole my entire stash—the money I kept taped inside the toilet tank so he wouldn't find it. (Once you start hiding money in the toilet tank because of your main squeeze's general reliability issues, you might as well consider yourself single again anyway.) He found it and went to visit his dealer while I was telling fortunes on Salk Avenue. I couldn't pay the rent, I couldn't even eat. Three thousand dollars, gone on one of his benders. This time I couldn't chalk it up to his sweet lazy smile and the way his black hair tangled over one eye, the way he hummed sometimes when he went down on me like he was having a great time. The sex was good, but the monkey on his back was better for him, I suppose.

It always is. We'd looked good together, black hair and blue eyes, a matched set.

I'd been thinking it was almost time anyway; the itch in the soles of my feet had gotten a little intense no matter how many pedicures I gave myself. The wind had started to moan, too. Not calling with its high plaintive voice: *Isabella, Isabella.* No, instead it had just started to make that lowdown hungry noise a wind can make when it touches the corners of a cheap apartment building. The noise that tells you to get ready, because the time of traveling is coming 'round faster than a landlord three weeks after the first of the month.

That's where it started, back to the same old song. I had my Oldsmobile packed to the gills with stuff—I couldn't think very well, I was too busy crying—clothes, and some books. He'd taken the rest, little bit by little bit, any book that was worth any money at the secondhand stores, anything he could pawn. My mother always used to say that when you woke up from a bad man you always did it in one jump, like a nightmare in the early-morning time. I woke up from this one with three thousand dollars, my books, my music, and my carnival glass candy-dish gone.

I packed anything edible in the car too, which came down to cigarettes, bread, peanut butter, and pickles. So I'd diet for a while.

I actually had a hundred and fifty dollars, because I'd broken down and started telling fortunes on the street again. My cards were safe, because they were tucked in my messenger bag; I never went anywhere without them. I had my ID and my bankcard too, but an account without anything in it isn't any good either. I don't really trust banks. My mother had trusted hers, and look where it got her. Her estate had gone to a particularly rapacious banker, leaving her only daughter a beggar too crippled with grief to even fight him.

I let him have the money. It choked him in the end. You don't mess with a witch's daughter, even when the witch is dead.

I left the city in a cloud of dust, cursing. Cassidy would be lucky to find a girl that would tolerate him like I did, especially after the fourth or fifth repetition of a curse to take the starch out his Mr. Spunky. I'd never find out if the curse worked, but I could dream, couldn't I? Besides, the wind was up, singing at me to keep moving on.

I made good time all the way towards the Rockies, telling fortunes and singing songs in the big cities to scrape together enough gas and munchies to get to the next town. I worked with a carnival again, until they wanted to go south and the wind told me to go north. I heard on the radio before it faded it out in static that there had been a fire in their big top one night; fourteen people had died. Again, I'd jumped before the ship sank.

So I was in the mountains, driving through podunk towns and running out of cash, when the radiator cracked.

I'll say this much for that blue Oldsmobile: it did me well. I put a good hundred thousand miles on it over six years before it clunked to a hissing stop, and it was no spring chicken to begin with. I pulled over to the edge of the cracked and fading two-lane blacktop and came to a stop with my car directly under a huge weeping willow tree, whose branches draped down and scraped across the car roof as I rolled onto the grass. I'd over-adjusted, steering too far onto the shoulder. Didn't matter, the car was dead anyway. Steam billowed out, and I saw low fluid shapes with teeth in the shifting mist before the wind sprang up again, blowing it away and whipping the willow branches against the car's panels. It was a sound like hundreds of tiny fingernails scraping the painted metal. I ground my teeth and rolled down the window. I lit a cigarette while I watched the steam billow from under the hood. The cards hadn't lied; they had been predicting disaster for the last four hundred miles.

I smoked in silence. There was a gentle green slope down to the river on my right; the road had been tucking itself neatly into a green valley between two mountains, coming down from the last big pass, when the blue Cutlass finally stopped running. Really pretty, in a Rocky Mountain High sort of way. On my left, across the road, rock faces climbed up toward heaven, and on the other side of the river was another hunk of sharp stone. The water chuckled and the wind whistled, and it was cold in the shade.

A hawk cried out in the distance. I finished smoking and sat there for a minute. My head throbbed, the headache retreating because the worst had happened. I took a swallow of cold coffee left over from the morning's starchy breakfast in a backwoods cafe where the loggers and truckers stared at me. Rinsed my mouth, spat out the open window.

"Okay," I said.

I got out of the car, my messenger bag bumping against my hip, and went to the trunk. I had two clean pairs of jeans, a black cashmere sweater and a sundress—I stuffed those in my canvas duffel. Three black T-shirts, one white shirt, and the knife my mother had given me. The pearl necklace she'd left me as well, and the sapphire ring—Cassidy never pawned those because I never wore them, always kept them in my messenger bag. My copy of *Strange Stories Amazing Facts*. My dog-eared copy of *Les Fleurs du Mal*. The last pack of cigarettes I had, the loaf of wheat bread I'd bought, the jar of peanut butter, and my copy of Gibbon's *Decline and Fall*, abridged. I couldn't let that go. My tiger's eye necklace, which I fastened at the back of my neck and let dangle between my breasts. The turquoise bracelet—it brought me luck—I slid on too. There was enough room for another pair of jeans and a white button-down shirt, as well as a pocketknife, the small cedar box I had carried everywhere for years with its cargo of ashes, and the three-by-five velvet-covered notebook that held photographs. Then I zipped it up, hefted it experimentally, and jammed two pairs of socks into it after a moment's careful consideration. I closed the trunk and stood looking at the river for a minute. It glittered in the sun, and I thought I heard harsh, subliminal laughter on the wind.

"Get a hold on yourself, Isabella." The sudden hush made me wish I hadn't spoken. The valley watched me, stone rising up on either side considering me with the ageless patience of the near-eternal. Being acutely aware of one's surroundings can be a curse, especially when you're recovering from crying your heart out over a bad man and running blindly into another disaster.

I walked carefully around the car to the willow tree and laid my hand on the trunk, rough bark supple and lively under my palm. Willows were good trees; they weren't haughty like oaks or secretive like elms, or as flighty as cherry trees. A willow could be counted on, like a mountain ash or a birch, to help a witch in trouble.

"Hi," I said, softly. "I'm sorry, but I can't push the car away. I would if I could. I'm going to have to leave it here. I *am* really sorry, but someone'll probably tow it or strip it down soon. I hope you don't mind."

I waited a second. The wind kicked up again, whistling over rocks and brushing the branches back and forth with a soughing, gentle sound. The willow nodded, its branches sliding against the car, almost...well, caressing.

I shrugged, snugged my messenger bag's strap across my body, picked up my duffel, and started to walk.

CHAPTER TWO

I COULD HAVE GONE BACK toward where I'd taken the nameless highway away from the interstate and found the last town I'd flashed through, or I could strike out for new territory on the theory that I was closer to another town. I picked striking out, and wouldn't you know, it was the wrong way to go. I've often wondered since then if the shape of events to come was already unreeling under my feet, wondering if I wasn't quite my own master even then. I've even wondered if the hands of my mother's gods reached out and caressed my radiator.

Thinking like that can drive a person crazy, even if it's a witch who's blown through just about every major city in America and quite a few that aren't. You learn to have a high weirdness tolerance as a witch. Some luck isn't bad or good, it's just *luck*, the way the pebble falls or the coin flips, the way the cue ball rides. Luck or gods, it didn't matter. There I was, walking down the road, that's all that counts.

The highway followed the valley and the looping river, then the river vanished down a gorge and the highway turned down another valley. I kept walking until dusk and then backtracked a bit to a campground, and I lit a fire in a little picnic barbecue thing with my Zippo. The blisters on my hands from switching the duffel back and forth stung until I could whisper to them. Then they only ached.

The temperature dropped even more, and I found myself wishing I'd brought a coat. The sweater was soft but it wasn't enough, and I managed only a few hours' worth of broken sleep on a wooden picnic table between nightmares and the cold.

Darkness is complete once you get away from cities, and I know why people used to bar their doors with two-by-fours at night. It's not so much the wet-bandage blackness even though there's rivers of starshine overhead, but the feeling of being naked and vulnerable, the thought of what *could* be lurking in the darkness on the ground, ready to rend you with sharp teeth while you inhaled its meaty breath for your last scream.

The monster you can't see is the most fearsome of all.

The dreams were bad—snarling, dripping teeth and wrinkled muzzles, big dogs fighting. I didn't wait for dawn, just for the fire to burn down to a punky glow in the stillness of early-morning. There wasn't anything that could burn, it was all concrete around the picnic-barbecue-thing, so I left it and trekked back out toward the road. Sometimes there's nothing to do but walk forward.

I walked. And walked. I was going to get blisters on my *feet*, too, I could feel it, and I hadn't stopped to read the cards. When I finally came across a sign that told me Tremont—the next town—was five miles away, I celebrated with a cigarette and a peanut butter sandwich, as well as another session of whispering to my raw, aching palms. There was another campground with a water fountain that hadn't been turned off, and I had an empty Evian bottle, so I filled that and continued on until I found myself on the outskirts of a largish town-smallish city under a bunch of glowering mountains by the time noon came around.

Welcome to Tremont, the sign said, white-painted, with primroses planted around its solid feet. How welcoming it was remained to be seen.

I walked past quiet little homes and made my way to the northern part of downtown (just follow the freeway in most places, you know, and you can find something to eat with little hassle) and found a Barb's Cafe that promised *All the Pancakes You Can Eat*. I still had a little over a hundred dollars left, so I stopped for a lunch, and knew as soon as I'd stepped in the door I'd made a mistake

Silence. Locals only, and I was heaving all my worldly possessions in a bag half my size.

I caught the waitress's eye. She was short, dumpy, and bottle-blonde, with baggy pantyhose and thick-soled white nurse's shoes. I took a deep breath. There was a radio playing some country-and-western song back in the kitchen, and the hiss of bacon frying. My stomach growled quietly, reminding me that I didn't want to skip another meal unless I wanted real trouble. I brushed a mass of tangled black hair back, wishing I'd thought to get a handkerchief or something to tie it up with.

So I decided to brazen it out. "Hi. Are you guys open for lunch?" Pretty soon even whispering into my cupped hands wouldn't be enough; the skin would break and bleed.

I'd lost a few calluses, I guess.

It was a stupid thing to say, but I had to say *something*. A couple of truckers at the breakfast bar turned in their stools to look at me, and there was a pair of county sheriffs sitting in the window, watching me. Assorted other people gave me the eye, and the waitress wiped her hands on her stained apron.

"Hi there." Her face set, flat and neutral. "Come on in. You sit down here—" She pulled a menu out and indicated a seat in the very back of the smoking section. I followed her, grateful, and made sure to sit with my back to the wall. I was already digging in my pocket and had a twenty-dollar bill out by the time she laid my menu down.

"I've got money," I said. "I probably look pretty bad, huh?"

She glanced at the twenty, and her face became infinitely friendlier. I felt like I'd won one.

"Naw, honey. You just ain't from around here, 'sall. You want coffee?"

"Please. With cream." I didn't slide the strap of my messenger bag off just yet, though. "Do you have the local paper here, ma'am?"

That won her over almost completely. "Shore do. Quarter a copy, but if you stay here an' read it, 'sfree. We just fold it back up. You want one?"

I dug a quarter out of the front of my bag and handed it to her. "If you wouldn't mind. Thank you, ma'am."

She lit up and beamed at me, and I suddenly felt sorry for her. She had a heart condition that would kill her in under a year. The knowledge slid whole and complete into my consciousness; I shut my eyes as soon as she left me, willing the flashes to stop. I had to eat, or I'd start telling complete strangers what their spouses were doing. The gift always got stronger when I was hungry. Mom said it was because I was already half in the next world, tethered to this one only by my body's hunger. *Food's the ballast that will keep you here, Bella my love,* she would half-chant, reminding me to eat.

When I got myself back under control, I lit a cigarette and studied the menu. Pancake special. French toast special. Denver omelet special. Like every other small-town menu I'd ever seen. I could have read it in the dark.

When she came back with a cup, a coffee pot, and the paper, I looked up at her and smiled, determined to be charming. "Thank you."

"Aw, you're welcome, honey. You know what you want?" She poured my coffee, stacked five creamers on the table, and slid the paper across to me. I handed her the menu.

"May I have the spinach-and-mushroom omelet special, with hash browns and bacon please? And some orange juice?" I gave her my 'innocent waif' smile and watched her melt.

"You're a real nice girl." Fresh lipstick smeared bright red across her teeth, and for a moment I was sure her mouth was bleeding. "Course you can, honey. You want some toast or a biscuit with that?"

My back was cold and prickling. "Toast please. Wheat."

"All right then." She clicked her tongue at me, and I widened the smile. *Look at me, fucking great at winning over the locals.* The name tag on her pink sweater said *Darlene.*

Oh, gods. I'm trapped in Mayberry.

She moved ponderously away on her too-thick legs, and I added cream and sugar to my coffee. Stirred with the regulation spoon, and opened up the paper to the classifieds. Evidently Darlene had pronounced in my favor, because everyone stopped looking at me and went back to their food. Mom had always told me that people like us had some sort of smell—maybe pheromones—that regular folks were uneasy with. They didn't know why they were uncomfortable, but they were, and apprehensive people can turn into violent people at the drop of a hat.

The fact that I could tell fortunes with a deck of cards most people had never seen before or whisper a car accident into happening probably had something to do with it. The fact that I could, if I wanted to, tell a stranger what they were thinking...or what their spouse was doing...or *who* their spouse was doing probably didn't help either. I have given up wondering why people always come to fortunetellers wanting to know about infidelity and then get so angry when the card-reader or crystal-gazer confirms it. After all, if they already *suspected*, why get angry at Madam Zelda the Precognitive Wonder when she tells you it's true?

I sighed, the newsprint turning to little squiggles in front of my watering eyes. Looking for work was never my favorite thing to do, but I knew a town this size probably wouldn't like me reading cards on the street. They'd throw me in jail if they didn't ride me out of town on a rail; I'd been in enough dicey situations in not-so-small-anymore-but-not-big-enough-yet towns to know. I blinked away tears and gave myself a sharp mental scolding. Self-pity would do me no good.

I had two or three possibilities circled when Darlene came back with steaming plate of food. She set it down, I thanked her, and her bright little eyes slid across the paper. "You lookin' for work, honey?"

You think I like being virtually homeless all my life? "I guess so."

"What are you lookin' for?" Bright and interested, I was good gossip waiting to happen.

"Anything, really." It was the truth. "I can waitress, and work a cocktail slot, and I can clean houses. I'm good with kids, I have a clean record, I can type. I'm just looking for a place to settle down." That was the gods' own truth, too. The only problem was, the wind would start calling my name soon enough—how soon I didn't know—and something would happen to drive me out of every safe haven. I couldn't put down roots here or anywhere else, nosirree. Wherever I was needed, there I was sent, willingly or not.

Her teeth were still smeared with crimson lipstick, though there was none on her lips. It gave her the distinct appearance of being bloody-toothed and older than her years. The laboring thuds of her heart hurt a little to hear. I wondered if it was a birth defect, or if she literally had a broken heart, broken enough to kill. Sometimes my gift wasn't too specific between the physical and the spiritual.

"Well, there's work here, for those that can get it. You're real polite, won't have no trouble I hope. Go get your toast." With that, she shambled away. I wasn't interesting enough to warrant more help than that, I guess.

The food was okay, and she came back with my toast and some strawberry jam. Refilled my coffee cup. Then she left me alone, which was okay by me.

One of the classifieds caught my eye as I was finishing the hash browns. I brushed my hair back again and twisted it into a sloppy chignon as I read, wishing I had something to hold it with. I'd stop in a drugstore and get some elastic bands.

Outside, the sky was gray, and rain started to speckle the pavement. Great.

Housekeeper needed, light work only. Salary and benefits. Must be able to read. Apply in person, 4444 Tremont Avenue. Terse even for a classified ad, and since when was literacy a requirement for scrubbing toilets? And "light work only" was usually a danger sign. Still, it looked good, and my fingers tingled as I read it. I could check a phone book for a map, a town this size shouldn't have many confusing streets.

I finished breakfast and had another cup of coffee while I smoked another cigarette. Outside, the rain played fitfully, sometimes misting down, sometimes stopping. I watched the cars crawl by on the street and wondered if anyone had found my Oldsmobile yet. The pass had probably been the kicker, a couple of thousand feet is hard on any car.

Yes, I actually thought that.

When I finished, I paid Darlene and left her a good tip. She had little enough time to enjoy it. I did use the restroom to relieve myself and wash my face. Wonder of wonders, I found a scrunchie in my messenger bag. With my hair braided back I felt much more like myself. Curly hair is both a curse and a blessing, like everything else in my life.

On my way out, I stopped at the ancient cash register. "Excuse me, ma'am." I tucked the newspaper under my arm. Darlene looked up, a flash of something—was it fear?—darting out from her little eyes. "I was wondering if you could tell me where Tremont Avenue is."

"Got something out there?" Her mouth turned down at the corners, like she was sucking on something bitter. I was relieved—at least she didn't flash her horsey, painted-red teeth at me.

"I think so," I said. "That's where I'll start, anyway."

"Out the door, turn left, and go about five blocks. There's a KwikMart and a liquor store there. That's Tremont." She glanced around. Nobody was near us—the county sheriffs had left, and the truckers were still at the breakfast bar. "If you ain't got a job by nightfall, best be out of town, miss."

Now what in hell did that mean? Her mouth was drawn tight, a pursed little pucker. I nodded slowly, trying to decide if she was honestly warning me or just pulling a stranger's chain. "Okay. I get it. I will."

"All right then, honey. Left and five blocks."

"KwikMart and liquor store," I said. "Thank you, ma'am." *You're going to die soon. I wish it wasn't so.*

"Name's Darlene." As if I couldn't read her nametag. "You remember what I tell you. After dark, don't stay here 'less you got a place to hide."

Land of the free, home of the brave. Huddled masses need not apply. "All right." I had to work for a pleasant tone. I turned around and walked for the door, and noticed that the glass door had a padlock hanging from an iron grille, rolled up under the sidewalk awning. So when Main Street closed down at night, it *really* closed down. Wow.

"Thank you," I said again before I left.

She didn't reply.

Chapter Three

Darlene's directions were good. I turned left, smelling the good greenness of rain, and followed Main Street (aka the infamous two-lane highway) for five blocks until I saw the KwikMart and the L'il Drop Liquor Store. (Both fine business establishments, no doubt.) The street sign said Tremont, and I walked a few doors down to my right and checked the addresses.

Shit.

The addresses were in the 1800's and going down. I backtracked, crossed Main Street again, and started walking.

The town was nice, in an unremarkable way. It was a little odd that pretty much all the houses had heavy-duty screen doors—the kind with iron bars and maybe some decorative scrollwork on them. It was *really* odd that once I got off the main drag, the houses all had bars on the windows. You usually didn't see those in the smaller cities, they belonged mostly in ghettos and barrios. In some cities, the rich had them, trapped just as surely as the poor, and they learned nothing from the experience either. *The highest walls are those we build ourselves,* my mother used to say.

I walked, and walked, and walked.

By the time I was in the 2900's the rain stopped flirting and started coming down in earnest. My sweater was quickly soaked, and my hair was cold and heavy against my back. It was down to my waist, braided, so it took a while for it to get thoroughly wet, but it did. By the time I reached the 3500's I was cursing to myself in a low steady monotone. Water poured in black buckets from an iron-dark sky, and thunder grumbled to the west, and the duffel was getting heavier by the second.

If my stupid fingers hadn't kept tingling even through the pain, I might have bagged the whole thing and hitched a ride out of town. My digits had never led me wrong before, so I kept slogging through the rain and noticed that the sidewalk was better mended out here. The houses were bigger, and the lawns were well-kept. Gardens were in style. I saw irises and hydrangeas, lavender and peonies, a monkey tree and several kinds of pansies and petunias. The rain kept coming down, and thunder rumbled even louder by the time I found the 4000's, and I had to cross the street (jumping over a small river masquerading as a gutter and storm drain) to get to 4444.

Which proved to be a three-story gray stone affair, done up in Victorian style, with a four-car garage and enough driveway to park five RVs on. The place was massive, and I could see a slice of manicured lawn through the gate.

Or rather, "Gates," capitalized and underlined. Big, wrought-iron, set in a big stone wall. Highly unfriendly, but my fingers kept tingling irresistibly, a sure sign of something I was supposed to do. *How in the hell am I going to do this?*

The back of my neck crawled with water and gooseflesh. I stood looking at the gate for a good two minutes before I saw the next lightning flash up in the mountains somewhere, getting closer. That did it.

I cast around and found—glory hallelujah—an intercom box on the left-hand side of the gate.

I girded myself, forded the driveway, and pressed the big red button. Rewarded with a muffled beeping sound, I stood there with my nape crawling and my fingers itching like crazy while the rain drove down like it wanted to drown the entire town.

Finally, the intercom crackled into life. "What?" A passionless electric voice, I couldn't even tell if it was male or female.

I pressed the red button again. "I've come about the ad in the paper," I said, and let go.

"...Press the black button to talk." Now the voice sounded annoyed.

Well, I was too, come to think about it. I dutifully pressed the black button. "I've come about the ad in the paper." I let go again.

Pause. Thunder again. More thunder. The rain intensified, if that was possible.

"Who are you?" the intercom crackled at me.

I shrugged, forgetting the voice couldn't see me unless it had cameras. Pressed the black button again. "Isabella Harpe. I saw your ad in the paper. Housekeeper."

There was another long pause, and the intercom beeped. "Come in," the electric voice said, then the gates buzzed and clicked. The left half of the gate swung halfway inwards and stopped.

I splashed through, my boots almost slipping on slick, pristine black paving. I was halfway to the house when the gate clanged shut behind me. I jumped and glanced back, a shudder ruffling through me, continued on because I'd come this far I might as well.

The front door was mahogany, big enough for three of me, and one-half of it stood slightly open. I hopped the steps to the porch, enjoying the sudden relief from rain pounding at me, and glanced over the lawn.

The rosebushes.

Not just one or two, but rows of them, set to one side. Dripping green leaves and tightly-closed buds showing just a few tinges of color, indistinct and watery through the rain. They were planted on either side of the front walk, too, and massed under every window. *The smell must be deafening in summer.* I shivered a little more. It was fucking *cold* with the rain—and now the wind started to get into the act. The wooden boards of the wraparound porch creaked under my weight, and the open door groaned inward a little, pushed by invisible storm-fingers.

The hall inside was a dark cave.

"Hello?" I called tentatively, into that dimness. The bulk of the house would mute the thunder. Rain rang on the roof of the porch. The gutters would be spouting.

Now's the part in the movie where the big bad wolf comes out of the shadows and eats me in one gulp. My, Grandma, what a lovely spooky house you have. I suppressed the urge to giggle like an idiot. My breakfast was a cold lump in my stomach.

"Come in." From inside. Male, low voice, very good. *Very good.* Like caramel, deep and rich. I would have paid, even out of my limited funds, to hear it recite Shakespeare on the stage. "If you like."

That voice went a long way toward dispelling my unease. It was, for all its beauty, a human sound.

"I saw your ad in the paper." I kept peering through the door, unwilling to step over the threshold just yet. "Housekeeper. It said to apply in person."

"You didn't expect the rain." His tone was flat, careful.

Is it that obvious, asshole? Good luck getting hired, I shouldn't have done this. When will I ever learn to act like a normal person? "No. I didn't." I refrained from adding *dumbass* onto the end of it, but only just.

Thunder crashed overhead, getting closer. They made storms big out here. "Come in, if you like."

"I don't know if you want me to. I'm soaked." *And I've got all my worldly possessions in two bags.*

"You'll catch a cold." Now he sounded…what? Regretful? Amused?

I didn't have anywhere else to be, and the idea of drying off was a powerful temptation. My fingers kept tingling, so I shrugged and stepped forward. The foyer was floored with marble, black and white squares fit for Fred and Ginger. *Dear gods.*

A sudden, intense urge to sneeze loudly was firmly repressed. I tented my fingers and pushed the door open a little more, then decided to go for it and stepped inside.

I stood dripping on a slick stone floor, cautious and cold. It smelled like beeswax and lemon polish. I had to wait for my eyes to adjust to the dimness, and as soon as they had, the door swung shut behind me. It closed with a click, then the deadbolt slid home.

Now *that* was something new. Was the house electric or something?

The first feeling was creeping dread—the door had just shut behind me like the jaws of a trap. The second feeling, hard on its heels, was an almost comforting sense of being enclosed. Almost *safe*, as if the house had folded a warm towel around me and clucked, *there there dear, come in; we're so happy you've arrived!*

The feeling wasn't very sane, but it was familiar enough. I was safe for the time being.

There was an indistinct figure at the end of the foyer, on the steps that could have been in a Hollywood musical. If any place needed domestic help, this was it. Whoever he was, he looked tall. I waited for my eyes to adjust even more, blinking, and heard the thunder again, muted by the bulk of the house. Immediately after that, a lightning flash sizzled through the windows and thunder almost immediately followed again.

I decided to make the best of it, waiting for the ringing in my ears to stop. "Hi," I said brightly, to the motionless figure on the stairs. "I'm Isabella Harpe. Nice to meet you."

"Tremont." There was a huge chandelier, dark and tinkling, hung a story or two above the marble. I had a brief vision of it falling down and had to repress a mad giggle. I couldn't concentrate on that. If I thought about it too hard it just might happen, and there would go my chances of getting a job.

"Is this the right house? Forty-four forty-four Tremont, right?" I peered up at him. "It's pretty dark in here. Did you lose your electricity because of the storm?" *If he did, then why did the intercom work? Don't be stupid.*

"No. I can see quite well in the dark, and I forget other...people can't." He took a step down, and I was relieved to see him move. "I'd forgotten I placed an ad in the paper. Desperation, I suppose." His laugh was a bitter little chuckle, like he was chewing on something awful. Then, "Close your eyes, I'll turn the light on."

I obeyed, not wanting to be blinded. There was a moment's worth of waiting before light bloomed painfully even through my eyelids. I waited a second or two, blinked furiously. He'd turned the chandelier on; golden light drenched every surface. It changed the whole front hall from a dusty cave into a very grand, if a little overdone, musical-movie foyer.

"Wow." I dripped onto the crisp marble squares, repressed another sneeze. "That's...wow."

I had to look around to locate him again; he moved very quietly. He'd ended up off to my right, in the shadow of a doorway. Probably a grand little parlor, I guessed, and turned slowly. I could make out a black sweater and a pair of khakis with a sharp crease, and he was wearing black socks.

Not only that, but he was big. Taller than me—almost everyone is—very tall, topping six feet. And broad-shouldered. His face was an indistinct blur.

"Too bright?" he asked.

"No, it's okay. I probably shouldn't have asked for any light, I feel like a drowned rat. Guess it's not a good first impression."

"You're polite, at least." Noncommittal in the extreme.

I got the feeling he was about to dismiss me. I did *not* look forward to walking some more in the downpour.

"I saw the rosebushes." I searched for something more, anything that might sound appropriate. "It must be beautiful, when they bloom."

The stupid, silly rosebushes. All I could think of then was that he had so many, he must like them, and people always liked talking about their hobbies. It was why they had them. Right?

Maybe I could have left right then, if I just hadn't opened my mouth about the roses. Once I said that, it was already too late. Maybe it was too late the moment I walked up to the door, maybe it was too late the moment he spoke, or I did...but I really think it was the rosebushes that clinched the deal. Made the bargain, so to speak.

Of course, it might not have been that. He would have let me go, anyway. I was just supposed to be there, that was all.

Like I said, a person can go crazy thinking about it.

He went very still again, and the back of my neck was really crawling now. Maybe I'd made a mistake. My fingers had never led me wrong before. Oh, well, first time for everything, like Mom always said.

"The roses," he said, and I could tell from the flat tone in his voice that I'd done something wrong.

Okay. Let's get gracefully out of here and find a cheap motel for the night. At least you'll be able to wash your hair. "I'm probably bothering you." I hadn't even set my bag down. "I'm sorry to disturb you, I really am. Excuse me." I turned halfway around, meaning to head for the door.

"No!"

The force of it took me by surprise; I jerked back around and stared at him. He hadn't moved from the doorway, but he had thrown his hand out, fingers outstretched, as if to stop me.

"No," he repeated, a little less loudly. "It's no disturbance. Please, come in. Would you like some tea? Coffee? Hot cocoa? You must be chilled."

"I just had breakfast." I turned on the polite tone that kept a man at arm's length. "I really didn't mean to bother you, sir. I saw your ad in the paper and I need work, so I walked out here and I—" I was already planning on how to get out the door and to a warm dry hotel room. This place was out of the rain, but the vast luxury of it was beginning to make me uneasy.

Almost frightened.

"You're not from this town." It wasn't a question. "Please come in. You're not disturbing me. Quite the...quite the opposite. I just didn't expect any response from the ad. I'm the one who should be apologizing."

"I'm just passing through," I took a nervous step sideways, almost regretted it because of the way my boots squished. "I have a clean record, I have ID, and I'm not afraid of hard work. Housekeeping, it said."

He nodded. His face was still indistinct. I saw the color of his hair now—blond. Golden blond, shaggy and thick, like he hadn't had a trim for a while. "You're the only person who came. You can have the job. It's yours. If you want it."

"What does it pay?" That was only the first important question.

"Negotiable. Name a price."

This was more familiar ground; unlike most women I have no compunction about bargaining. Guess it comes from being a poor homeless wandering witch whose mama trained her to be no fool. "What kind of cleaning?"

He gave that bitter little laugh again. "Mostly the library. Alphabetizing, dusting and watering the plants. Maybe some cooking if you feel like it, I keep odd hours. The house mostly takes care of itself. Can you read?"

"I wasn't raised by wolves. Of course I can read."

That mirthless little chuckle again. Either I was amusing him or he was poking himself with a needle. "You can read to me." It wasn't a question. "That's all."

I ticked it off on my fingers. "Dusting and alphabetizing the library, watering the plants, maybe occasional cooking, and reading to you. What are the hours?"

"No more than six a day, all told. Room and board too."

"Eight hundred a week. But I'm not a good cook, I'll warn you." It was a long shot, but I was betting that he would want other errands done too. A house this big? You bet. I still hadn't decided if he was the type of man I could be around without getting propositioned. Eight hundred a week was preposterous, and I was half hoping he'd refuse so I could get the hell out of there, tingling fingers or not.

"Done. I don't care about the cooking, really, just the library. Cash or checks?"

Now do you think I'm an idiot? I shrugged. "I don't trust banks."

White teeth gleamed. He was smiling. "I don't blame you. The local credit union will give you an account, as long as you're not a felon."

"Not last time I checked." I peered at him, trying to see past the shadows. Why was he hiding? "You're saying I've got the job?"

"If you want it."

I shrugged again, feeling my shirt stick to wet skin on my shoulders. "Sure." What did I have to lose? The highway would take me out of town the next time the wind blew anyway. There wasn't a house on earth I couldn't escape. One good thing about being a witch: you find out early you can whisper locks into opening.

He paused. "There's one more thing you should know." His voice was still even and wonderful, caramel-toned. Except for that bitter little laugh, and the sudden feeling that he was gathering himself to say something offensive and filthy.

I tensed. "And that is?"

He stepped forward into the light. I gazed at him, not understanding, until I saw.

His face would have been even and regular, except for the mass of scar tissue eating three-quarters of it. It started under his shaggy hair and went diagonally down, and two blue eyes looked out. His nose was a ruin, but his mouth had been left alone, and it was chiseled and perfect. Somehow that made it worse, the perfect lips and the white teeth. And that voice. Gods.

So that's why he's so weird. I was a fine one to talk about weirdness. But the scarring explained a lot, it really did. I'm lucky that I can pass for normal most of the time; he couldn't. Not with that face. If I knew anything about human nature, he probably wasn't the town favorite. If he was slightly eccentric as well as rich and scarred, he probably couldn't get much in the way of conversation or companionship.

I waited. He waited. Thunder rattled in the tense silence.

Finally his mouth twitched, quirked downward. "Aren't you going to ask me what happened?"

I looked steadily at him. "I'm waiting for the 'one more thing'."

He indicated his face with one sharp movement, his hand a stiff blade. "This. Does it bother you?" His tone plainly said, *or are you blind?*

My eyebrows went up, my mother's patented *oh, is that all?* expression. "Lots of people have scars. Sometimes inside, sometimes outside. Doesn't bother me."

"Easy for you to say. You're a very pretty girl."

My fingers were still tingling, but the goosebumps on my nape had vanished. Maybe I'd just been cold. The world snapped back into its accustomed dimensions, settling with a thud. A welcome feeling, telling me everything was back to normal. "That's a bad thing when you're looking for work sometimes. People make all sorts of assumptions."

"Do you want the job?" He said it like it didn't matter to him, but his hand clenched into a fist. He wasn't dangerous—I could tell that much, it was the same way I could tell who *not* to hitch a ride from—but he did look slightly...what was the word? Skittish, maybe. High-strung.

Nervous.

"If it's open." Casually, off-hand. The territory kept getting more and more familiar. This, I could deal with.

"You have the job. I'm Tremont. You're Miss Harpe."

"Okay." I shivered a little. I was soaked to the skin, and my duffel was wet too.

"Come into the kitchen." He turned on his heel and glided away.

What else did I have to do? I followed.

Chapter Four

THE KITCHEN TURNED OUT TO be nice and cozy, done in Delft blue and cream. There was a blue enamel kettle on the stove, and two mugs set out. I took this in while I set my duffel down beside the wooden stool he motioned me toward. That put me up against the breakfast bar, done in some light wood, and I could look out the bay window over the sink and across what should be the backyard. There were more rosebushes, an expanse of lawn, and what looked like a solid wall of green— maybe junipers, maybe cedars, maybe ivy against the wall, I couldn't tell with the water blurring everything.

In the distance, the mountains rose. The sky was black with clouds pouring down from their heights. My hair dripped, and diamond lances of lightning stabbed down on the peaks twice in quick succession. Good to be out of the rain; I almost shuddered to think of going back outside.

"Tea?" he asked. "Coffee? Apple cider? Hot cocoa?" Here, in the brightly-lit kitchen, he seemed to forget his ruined face, his broad back to me, as he turned the stove on.

"Tea will be fine." My fingers gave one last painful tingling squeeze, then the sensation faded. Mission accomplished, apparently. It was as close to a pat on the back as I ever got nowadays.

"What kind?"

Gods above, anything warm will do. I rallied myself to make an effort. After all, he'd just hired me. "What do you have?" The floor was tiled, the countertops bluish granite, everything neat and clean. There was a cheerful robin's egg mat in front of the stove, and another one at the sink. All the mod cons. A telephone hung on the wall to my right, a sleek cordless thing, and a plain pad of paper lay on the counter underneath it. There was a silver pen set at a precise angle across the paper.

"Chamomile, Earl Gray, Irish Breakfast, Moroccan Mint..." He trailed off. "An herbal tea sampler..."

"The Moroccan Mint sounds divine. Do you smoke?"

He shook his golden head. "I don't, but you do. Feel free."

"It's your house." The kettle began to click as the heat began. It was nice and warm in here; I rubbed at my face and wished for a towel.

He set a fluffy blue hand-towel on the counter, and a crystal dish. "Here. There are more towels, and you can use that as an ashtray."

"It's your house," I repeated. A little foolish, but you never presumed on the first day.

"I don't mind. I actually kind of like it." Those blue eyes came up to meet mine. Something swam through the bottom of those eyes, there and gone in a flash like goldfish at the bottom of a pool. "I can open the window a little."

I decided against smoking, took the towel. "Thank you. This is lovely." It was nice to dry my face off, and the bottom half of my braid. That about finished the towel, but at least I felt better, and my hair wasn't quite so cold. He took the towel back and tossed it into a small wicker hamper set between the kitchen and the hall.

There was a glass-covered extension behind me, full of palms and hanging ferns, with a small table and four chairs set in it. That would be nice on sunny mornings. Now it was gray, and the ferns looked a little out of place.

The kettle chirped, and he poured, handed me a mug. "I live here," he said, finally. "It's lonely."

No shit, Sherlock. I blew across the top of the tea to cool it, folded my hands around the blue ceramic mug, and soaked up the blessed warmth. My sweater might begin to steam soon. "So I see. Do you have other domestic help?"

Of course, the idea of him cleaning this whole thing by himself was vaguely amusing, but wrong. Like imagining the Queen of England cleaning her own toilet. He was just too upper-crust.

"The house takes care of itself." A vague movement of one broad hand. "One can't advertise for a companion anymore. It used to be that you could place an advert for someone to talk to—there were people trained in the art of conversation, reading, singing. Ladies' companions, mostly, for travel. That's been forgotten. I couldn't think of what to put in the ad."

I took this in, looked over the kitchen again. *A 'ladies' companion', like in some Gothic novel.* "So you're just looking for someone to be social with. I guess this town isn't a very social place."

He found that halfway funny. "You've already found this out?" At least, he laughed, that same bitter sound I'd already heard. I decided I didn't like it nearly as much as I'd like some honest amusement from him.

I shrugged, wished I hadn't because my sweater was beginning to creep and stick. "I've traveled a lot. You can usually tell what places are friendly and which aren't. This place seems a bit...strange."

Thunder rattled again, as if underscoring my words.

"It is," he said. "Believe me, it is."

"Everyone has bars on their windows," I continued. "And the cafe downtown was distinctly Locals Only, if you know what I mean."

"You're very perceptive." He stood on the other side of the counter, watching me. He wasn't dangerous, just odd.

Okay, a *lot* odd. But my fingers had led me to good prospects before. The last had been the old fat woman who ran a herd of professional child thieves out of her house. She'd been jolly and good-natured, unless you were one of the pros. I did housecleaning and errands for her and read her cards until she died of a massive heart attack and the kids drifted away. That had been another walk-in-off-the-street event.

My life was full of them.

I looked out the window, and he moved, restive. Maybe he was even shy.

Well, when in doubt, talk about the weather. "It's a big storm," I said. "Do those happen a lot?"

"It's the season for them." He laid something on the counter.

I looked down. Sixteen hundred-dollar bills, fanned in a neat row. They were genuine.

"Two weeks advance," he said. "To prove I'm serious."

I stared at him. Faint alarms ringing in my head, desperation and intuition warring with common sense. "For dusting and reading? What's the catch?"

"You have to commit to staying, for at least as long as I pay you."

I shook my wet head. *I knew there was something.* "I drift around. When the wind changes, I might have to go."

"Stay as long as you can, then." Not presumptuous or commanding. A little wistful. I tried to imagine what it was like—had he been scarred in adulthood? No, it had to be when he was young.

My sweater rubbed wetly on my shoulders. I was glad I was wearing a couple of layers, I was pretty sure my nipples would be poking out like searchlights otherwise. "Okay. I'll stay as long as I can." *That I can promise.*

"Good." The tension leached out of him. His shoulders went down, one corner of his perfect mouth curled up fractionally. "Good enough. That's all I can really ask for."

I took a sip; it had cooled down rapidly. "The tea's nice. And the house is beautiful."

"I'm glad you think so." Now he was bored. It was hard to read his face, because of the scarring; I had to rely on his body language. "Drink up, and I'll show you your room and tell you the house rules."

Rules. Okay. I gathered the money up into a neat pile. That kind of made it official that I was employed here, with all the obligations and rights that presupposed. "You're sure? I could be anyone."

"So could I. I'm sure."

"All right." I folded up the bills, plunged them into the depths of my bag. My cards were there. I wanted to have a quiet moment and ask them what they thought of this guy. "So what do I call you? Mr. Tremont?"

"Just Tremont," he said. "My family built this town."

"Oh." I absorbed this. "So why did you put an ad in the paper? You should have been able to find anyone in the town to do this for you. Some high school student or something."

He didn't think much of the notion. "Nobody from the town would want to spend that much time with me," he said. "I'm considered dangerous." Those blue eyes cooled again. They were darker than mine, and without the dark ring around the edge of the iris. Not witch-eyes, my mother would have said.

"Oh." *From where I'm at, you look like a kitten. All meow and no claw.*

Still, men were bigger, and they had funny ideas about ownership.

"A wolf in sheep's clothing." He might have been smiling. It was hard to tell. Staring at his mouth might have been misinterpreted as a come-on.

"Well." I tossed my braid back over my shoulder. "Are you?"

There was a long pause. I took another drink of tea. He looked away, out the window, where another strike of lightning crackled down. Thunder reverberated. "Not at all. I'm a wolf in wolf's clothing."

"Well, at least you're as advertised." I didn't mean to sound flippant, but I was tired and had walked miles in the rain and cold and probably still upset over my beautiful blue Olds dying. And this morning's meal in a cafe where every eye was on me. And the carnival bigtop burning down. Disaster and death dogging me.

No wonder Jimmy Cassidy had chosen smack.

"Indeed." Now he was smiling. "I think you'll do very well, Miss Harpe."

"Thank you, Mr. Tremont."

"Just Tremont. How's your tea?"

I looked down. Staring would be impolite. "I'm done, thank you."

"I'll show you your rooms, then." He set his own cup down. I didn't see what he'd had to drink. "You must forgive me, I have great difficulty dealing with people."

"Me too," I said, sliding off the stool. "Guess we might get along after all."

CHAPTER FIVE

HE LED ME UP STAIRS and down halls until I was almost lost, but eventually we came to a door at the end of a red-carpeted hall, oak carved with mermaids and covered with gilt. I actually let out a half-snort of laughter. "Wow." I tried not to sound horrified and failed, dismally.

He gave me a look I could only classify as apologetic. "It's the safest room in the house, Miss Harpe. I'm sure you've noticed we're safety-conscious, in this town."

"That's one word for it," I muttered as he opened the door.

I was greeted with a vision of antique maple and cream silk and dark blue velvet. There was a four-post bed, a nightstand, and a fireplace with a brass screen that had Art Deco peacocks complete with blue glass eyes on their tails. The fireplace housed a roaring fire that smelled like applewood. Tiffany lamps— maybe even not fakes—and two big, comfy-looking chairs, a maple armoire, and a vanity with a mirror clear as a placid lake.

My fingers tingled again. I took in the hardwood floor and priceless, threadbare Persian rug. "No." I shook my soggy head. "You've *got* to be joking."

His shoulders stiffened. "All the other rooms are worse than this one." Did he sound diffident? He certainly did. "I don't have a garret with a tin cup, but I can make one for you if you'd like." He sounded as sarcastic as I supposed a man could sound while trying to sound embarrassed at the same time.

A sudden feeling of camaraderie bolted through my middle. It was just the sort of thing I might have said.

There's a mystery here. "You ran an ad in the paper for *this* and nobody showed up?"

"There are people who wouldn't step on this property to save their lives. I'm a pariah. An outcast."

"I know what pariah means," I said, maybe a little tartly. "I happen to be one myself. Are you really serious, you want me to stay here?"

"Of course. If you would. If you want to."

Let's get this straight. "Let me just repeat the terms, right? Six hours a day. Reading, dusting, alphabetizing, watering the plants."

"Yes. And staying as long as you can."

I gave him a hard look, but his face was unreadable under the wrinkles and pleats of seamed flesh. This close, I could see the thin threads of indigo in his irises, and crinkles at the corners of his eyes. He sometimes smiled, if those wrinkles were any indication.

There was something else there, too. Something I recognized.

"Okay." To prove it, I shouldered past him into the room, so close I could smell his cologne. Something dark and musky, I didn't really like it but I could see getting accustomed. I dropped my duffel on bare hardwood. It would probably leave a wet mark. "Is there a place I could wash some clothes?"

He pointed. "The laundry chute's right there."

"I'd rather do it myself." *I don't trust my panties to anyone.*

He shrugged. "Rules of the house." He paused. "Humor me."

"I'd better get my clothes back," I said darkly. *And you'd better not sniff them.*

"You will. I'll leave you to freshen up. Dinner is at six. I hope you'll join me. I'll explain the rules and show you the library afterwards."

I would've preferred rules first, but my jeans were beginning to itch. "Thank you. You won't regret this."

"And I hope you won't," he said, and closed the door.

Thunder crackled above. The windows were huge—there would be good light on a sunny day. I was on the second floor, and the window gazed over more rosebushes. There were also some laurel hedges, and a small garden full of some other plants I couldn't identify from this high up.

I found out the room had a bathroom attached, an empty walk-in closet scented vaguely with rose sachet, and a little sitting room that had windows and an actual fainting couch done in blue velvet, with empty bookshelves. "Wow," I said again, to nobody. There were more chairs and a pale ashwood writing desk.

I've seen a lot of poverty, enough to make me appreciate a warm dry room with a fire going. I'd *also* seen enough antiques and priceless little doodads to know that Tremont was family money, and didn't skimp.

First things first, though. I opened my messenger bag and dug out the cards, wrapped in a frayed black bandanna I had worn on my sixteenth birthday. I untied them, shuffled, and dropped down onto the floor in front of the fireplace. My hair dripped, and so did my shirt.

The cards are old and faded; my mother had them from her grandmother, the Witch of Cold Mountain. Yes, Great-Grandma settled in the Appalachians; she spent most of her life telling fortunes for people who would come for miles to sit at her worn kitchen table and hear her thready voice through the purple veils of mountain sunset. She sent her daughter away to school in New York with pockets stuffed full of dollar bills and the talent for being irresistible to rich men; my mother was a product of the richest boarding schools in Europe, shipped off by her courtesan parent.

Me? All I got was the talent that ran in our blood like madness and a peripatetic childhood, wandering around as my mother evaded every place that might tell her she belonged, ending up dying poorer than her mountain grandma who had, at least, never wanted for food. Mostly because some of her clients were too poor to pay in anything but pigfat or potatoes.

The cards are rectangular, the pattern on the back is red, and they are faintly greasy from so many years of travel and handling. The art is old, medieval, and many months of patient tutoring had to go by before I began to see the shifting patterns under the surface of each card's bright color, learned how to read the faces of the queens and the body language of the kings, learned how to smile back at the jacks and tell the aces what I wanted to know. Reading cards is like reading dice or crystal; the tool doesn't matter. All you have to do is...connect. The talent for telling the future projects onto the screen of whatever tool you use, you just have to figure out how to look deep enough to see the image.

I shuffled again, cut, and threw five of them down in a line.

Three blank white cards, *Le Chevalier de Epee,* and *l'As de Coupe.* I sat there in front of the roaring fire; my skin was too cold.

I had never seen *three* blank cards before. Neither had my mother. One blank card meant that the future was so uncertain as to be impossible to predict, even for my gifts. Two meant that there was certain trouble on the horizon.

Three? I was screwed for sure. But at least I was meant to be here. Faint comfort indeed.

"Well," I said out loud. "That answers that." Knight of Swords and Ace of Cups. The heart, and a stranger with...a sword? This was a weird one. Thunder boomed and rattled.

I put the cards away, gently and respectfully. Then I unpacked my canvas duffel and laid my few clothes out. Thankfully the books weren't soaked, and I could wear a black T-shirt and a fresh pair of jeans. I bundled the rest of the clothes up, including the ones I had been wearing, and took them over to the laundry chute. I opened it up and eyed the dark well of silence. "Take good care of my clothes, please." I whispered into the darkness. "They're the only ones I have. I'm a bit thin right now."

I dumped my clothes down. They vanished. I tried to imagine Tremont laundering them. Failed completely. He didn't seem the panty-sniffing type either. Repressed, but not repressed enough.

I padded naked across the room, my clean clothes swaying from one wrinkled fist. The bathroom was just as lush as the bedroom, almond and light blue with gold accents. It was Art Deco, and good Art Deco at that, none of the knockoff stuff. Two fluffy blue towels, an old cast-iron bathtub with a shower curtain fixed to a ring above the tub, and I examined myself in the lovely oval mirror over the pedestal sink.

Drowned rat. Black hair plastered to my head, my eyes were huge, bloodshot, and bright blue in the pitiless glare. Thunder banged outside, a padded hammer.

This room is the safest in the house, Miss Harpe. I untangled my hair from the braid, wincing, and hoped that the shower had some shampoo. The shower steam fogged the mirror in short order.

You're a very pretty girl.

"People assume too goddamn much," I muttered, and stepped into the incredible comfort of hot water.

Glory be, there was shampoo-with-conditioner, expensive stuff. And French hand-milled soap.

He seriously had trouble getting people to apply? Maybe they all knew what I did: too good to be true usually is.

A wolf in wolf's clothing. My fingers wouldn't lead me wrong.

No reason not to use the hot water while it was there. Living rough for a while, you appreciate the little luxuries.

I was cautiously beginning to feel optimistic for the first time since the blue Oldsmobile had blown up. My fingers had once again led me to the right place at the right time, and this job might prove to be what he said it was. If it wasn't, there was no reason why I couldn't slip out of the house and hit the road. I'd done it before.

There was one time I'd been trapped in a lovely chateau in Martha's Vineyard, suckered into an au pair job where the husband kept trying to get me alone in a room. He had been one slimy piece of work. I'd escaped that after a week, whispering the locks on the bedroom door into opening. Really, I felt sorry for the little boy I'd been caring for; no wonder they couldn't keep a nanny. The mother was a distant alcoholic, and the dad the worst I'd seen in five years. I'd left whatever luck I could for the boy, hoping he'd turn out all right.

I toweled off and got dressed, dried my hair with a fresh towel, found a tortoiseshell comb in the bathroom cabinet. I hadn't been this clean since leaving Jimmy Cassidy. Thunder retreating, no longer a hammer on an anvil.

The storm was almost spent.

I hung up the towels and French-braided my hair, mopped the end of the braid after tying it off with the abused scrunchie.

The fire was still burning, marvelous glorious warmth after the cold of the last few days. So I sank down on the bed, my messenger bag beside me. The mattress cradled me, soft and springy, and I didn't have more than ten minutes before I fell fast asleep.

CHAPTER SIX

I WOKE UP, AFTER BLANK unconsciousness deep and soft as cat's fur, to sunlight striping the room and the smell of cinnamon rolls. Curled on my side, holding my bag to my chest like a teddy bear, I'd zonked out but good. I sat up, yawning hugely, and the fireplace had been cleaned out. There was a neat pile of clean clothing on the chair next to the bed.

My own clothes, fresh and dry. The thought that I'd been sleeping so soundly I hadn't noticed someone creeping into my room was disturbing, to say the least.

I rubbed my face, yawned again, and smelled coffee as well as cinnamon.

A knock on the bedroom door. Two light, authoritative taps

I gained my feet, crossed the room in a happy little dance, twisted the doorknob—and it refused to open.

There was a deadbolt, and it was clicked home. *How the hell...* I glanced back at the pile of clean laundry and the empty fireplace.

Another knock, a single this time. I unlocked and opened the door to see my employer, holding a breakfast tray.

My surprise must have painted itself across my entire face, because he laughed. This one was a great deal more natural than the bitter snort he had used yesterday, and his eyes actually lit up. It was nice to see, even with the ruin it made of his cheeks.

"You slept all night. The storm was awful."

"I didn't hear it." I rubbed the sleep out of my eyes. *Did someone lock me in? Who? The deadbolt opens on my side.* "I was supposed to come down for dinner, wasn't I. I'm sorry."

"No." I got the idea he would have waved it away, if he could have grown another hand. *Poof,* don't trouble yourself, it's all right. "Don't worry. You were tired. I was glad you were resting. Would you care to have breakfast with me?"

You'd better not turn out to be an asshole. I stood aside, eyeing the tray. "That looks heavy. Come on in."

He did so, with an ease that told me he was stronger than he looked. "It's not so heavy." He set it down on the carefully on a rosewood table between the two fireside chairs. "Coffee? Cream, sugar?"

"Cream, please." This was a little outside my normal range. "Um, look. I don't really know what to do here."

"Just sit down and eat. We'll discuss it later, your schedule and duties. For right now, consider yourself a guest here."

I folded myself down in one of the chairs, and pulled my legs up, crossing them Indian-style. "A paid guest. You really should have had more people answer that ad." *Who the hell locked my door last night?* It didn't seem an appropriate time to ask.

"I never said I didn't."

"Yes, you did," I corrected him, and he handed me a hand-thrown blue mug. I smelled fresh-ground caffeine berries, not like the usual slop passing for coffee in restaurants and truck stops. "This is good stuff."

"It is. You're right on both counts, I haven't had any other responses to the ad." He settled himself stiffly in the chair across from me, as if his bones ached.

"How long have you been running it?" Mom always said that would be my curse. Curiosity.

Another quirk of those perfect lips. What could have scarred him that badly? It didn't look like fire or acid, though I'd only seen the latter once. "Three months."

"So I didn't cut anyone local out of a job. Good." I nodded, and took a sip. Blessed caffeine. I always felt woolly-headed in the mornings before a jolt. There was something else I was curious about, wasn't there? "Are you okay?"

A startled glance, his shoulders tensing as if he expected a punch. "Why do you ask?"

"You look like you're in some pain. The way you're moving." I tossed my braid back over my shoulder and regarded him steadily. "I'm sorry."

"You're right. I didn't sleep well, last night. No need to be sorry. Usually people don't bother looking at me, they can't stand it."

It was the flat tone of truth that made me pity him a little. Sad, but matter-of-fact as well. Like he had stopped caring, he'd just accepted it. Would it ever be the right time to ask when it had happened, and how? Was it just on his face, or anywhere else? He seemed about my age, though that wasn't any indication.

It could be that he wasn't at all. My senses weren't tingling the way they would if he was just people-shaped instead of actual person. "Does it upset you, to have someone look at you?"

A shrug, settling himself stiffly even further into the chair. "Sometimes people stare."

"What I meant was, do you want me to look away?" I persisted. The locked door was mostly forgotten in the face of this new, fascinating puzzle.

"No. Look if you like. You're probably used to people staring, too."

"Not so much, but yeah." There was a long pause, not quite uncomfortable, and I decided to come clean. "I'm not exactly...normal. As if you couldn't guess."

"Hm." It was a brief, not very expressive noise.

"I go across the country telling fortunes and working at menial jobs until the wind calls again, then I'm off and running." I looked down into my coffee cup, saw the steam rising from it take the shape of a toothy animal head. What *that* meant was anyone's guess. Maybe I was still disarranged from walking into town and getting half-drowned in the rain. "I'm good at telling the future, I always know when to jump. I've scared a lot of people."

"You tell fortunes?" His tone wasn't the usual half-uneasy laughter of regular people, the *how many fingers am I holding up* or *what number am I thinking of?* Instead, it was interested and polite, as if he knew exactly what I was talking about. "Do you use runes, or crystals, or cards, or...what?"

Well, look at this. Wariness rose in me—maybe he was one of those Bible-thumping small-town types who research 'the occult' so they can unravel Satanist 'conspiracies'.

I hoped not. I already liked his wry sense of humor.

"Tarot. I read them every day. In a town like this, I wouldn't do it on the street, they'd run me out of town on a rail if I was lucky. But in the cities, I can make a good living. Or traveling with a carnival." I waited. Would he tell me to get out, or try to convert me to Christianity, or tell me the devil had my soul?

"Fascinating." Sharp intelligence in his blue gaze, a flicker of the real person behind his mask peering out. "I would never have guessed."

Sooner or later you might have. "It makes people nervous."

"I'm not. Not about that. Here, have a cinnamon roll." He deftly transferred one to a plate, using two forks; his fingers were callused. He had a catlike economy of motion that I only saw in dancers or fighters, for all his stiffness.

That was either comforting or really bad. He was big, and I'd been on the receiving end of male violence before. He handed me the plate and a fork, and I watched him carefully as he separated another roll from the ceramic dish they were in. "I pegged you as the hippie type, if you want the truth."

It surprised me into a laugh. Mom had often remarked I'd been born a few decades too late. "I suppose I am. Is that a problem?"

"No." He set his plate down, regarded me. The sunburst of his hair almost matched the light coming in through the windows. I would have to close the blue velvet curtains tonight, unless I wanted to wake up at dawn. There was another pause, his gaze on me. I tore a bit off the cinnamon roll and tasted it. Gooey cinnamon melted in my mouth, heavily laced with cream-cheese frosting, and I decided then and there this was a good place.

Anyone who can make cinnamon rolls well can't be all bad. Just like that bookstore I worked at, where the owner would only accept checks if you had a current library card.

Tremont didn't seem too hungry. "I have the paperwork for health insurance, if you're interested. And we can discuss other benefits as well."

I had to chew and swallow before I could reply. "I don't usually get sick. But I'll do it. Who knows how long I'll be here?"

There went all his good humor, drained away and a sheer blank stone wall replacing it. "You've promised, and I've paid you. Is that enough?"

Well, now I felt like a mercenary. And if this kept up, I'd start overlooking how tall he was. "I told you I would, for as long as I can."

That got through. He smiled, or tried to. His face drew up in pleats and seams of flesh. So much better, because I could see *him* in there behind the ravaged flesh. Not like Cassidy, whose eyes had been as flat and surface as his beauty.

I should have seen Jimmy Cassidy coming six miles away. Instead, I'd hoodwinked myself.

Again.

Nobody to blame but me. Why did I have a thing for bad-news men? It was one of the great mysteries of human life, a witch talented enough to tell the future and I managed to date every loser within a fifty-mile radius.

Cassidy's past. Come back to here and now. I took another bite, making a small sound of approval, and he relaxed a little more.

Yep. Definitely no trouble from his quarter. Maybe he was one of those gentle giant types, though he wasn't nearly hairy enough.

"All right." That rich voice, when he let go a little, got even deeper. "That's good enough."

Silence fell. I ate, and after a few minutes of watching me, he did too. Thank the gods, because it was proof that he was really people inside his people-shape, so to speak.

I listened to the house, its creaks and whispers and silence. It needed some music. Some Grateful Dead, maybe, some Janis Joplin. Definitely some Led Zeppelin. And some Beethoven.

When I set my plate down he offered me more, and I shook my head. "No, I'm okay. I usually don't need a lot of sweets. I'm more of a wheat-germ, oat-groat sort of girl."

The sunlight burned in his hair. It was really amazing, that hair and those eyes; I almost felt sorry for him being scarred. "You'll have to make a list of what you'd like. Vegetarian, vegan, whatever you want."

"Are you vegetarian?" I had a faint ringing sense that I'd forgotten something important, chalked it up to pre-caffeination nerves.

"No. I'm a complete carnivore." His face fell, and he looked away, at the fireplace. There was a long pause, and he surprised me again. "Would you read the cards for me, Miss Harpe?"

"If you want." Stray tendrils of black hair had worked loose and fell in my face, corkscrewing crazily, I tucked one behind my ear. His gaze rested on my hand for a moment. "I'm not sure you want me to."

And that would be the end of a nice place to rest, if I scared him with that now.

"Maybe not. You're right. I don't want to know. Finish your coffee, I'll show you the library."

"You're smart." I tried to sound light and amused. "Most people don't realize that they don't want to know."

"I'm more afraid of what you would see for yourself. I know *my* future. Are you done?"

You know your own future, huh? That's not usual. "Thank you." I got to my feet. "My boots are still wet. Mind if I go barefoot?"

"Not at all." That blue, blue gaze flickered down to my feet. "I'll just watch out for anything sharp." He flowed upright. The stiffness was only temporary—or maybe he was trying to hide it since I'd noticed it. "The library's just down the hall. Bring some more coffee, if you like."

"Good idea. How about you?" Getting a headshake from him, I poured myself more and followed him out the door, wrapping my hands around the mug.

Maybe I was dreaming this. Coffee, a library, divine baked goods...it was as close to heaven as a girl could get.

Be careful, my Bella. I heard my mother's voice. *Too good to be true always is.*

Maybe if she'd been a little less cautious we could have settled somewhere. Maybe if she'd been a little *more* cautious that oily ferret bastard of a banker wouldn't have stolen everything.

Down the quiet, beeswax-scented hall, there was a huge set of double doors on the left. Tremont turned both knobs and pushed them open with a dramatic little flourish that made me laugh. The laugh soon turned to a gasp.

Holy hell, he wasn't kidding. The library was huge, three full stories tall, wrought-iron staircases going from level to level. We were, of course, on the second level. I filled my lungs with the spicy scent of paper and binding glue, the safe, wonderful, dusty smell of books.

On the first floor, there were writing desks and comfortable chairs; jewel-green ferns hung from the ceiling and the staircases. A card file crouched in one corner, with plenty of little drawers, all neatly labeled.

It was more books than I had ever seen outside of a major-city library. "My gods." Every other thought was driven clean out of my head. "You weren't kidding. Six hours a day won't be enough."

Three stories' worth of books. This house was a lot bigger than it looked from the outside. No wonder he needed help.

"You'll have to stay, then." He sounded relieved. I was too busy gawking to check his expression.

Good gods above. "Why didn't you ask for a real librarian? This could keep someone busy for months."

"Do you think anyone in this town desperate enough to work for me has a library science degree?" His tone took my attention away from the books for a moment. His mouth was a straight line, he gazed up and to the side at a particular fern, his ruined profile presented to me. "Housekeeper was the only label I could think of that might conceivably fit the bill."

"Wow." I was saying that a lot. "Is this a research library or something? What's the theme?" *Gods above and below, look at all this! Just look at it!* I won't deny it, I was *exulting*. This was beautiful, the kind of thing I'd always dreamed of.

"There are people that come from all over the globe to look at the books. I needed someone who could be discreet, and who could read to me...and who wouldn't gawk at the people that came here. You happened along. You're perfect."

I stepped up to the railing, curled one hand around it, and looked up, then down. "Jesus," I breathed. "This is *huge*."

"Do you want a raise?" His tone was so even and flat it took me a moment to realize he had actually unbent enough to joke with me, and I laughed. It was a free sound, here in this hushed world of dust and paper. I could even see more study carrels placed between bookshelves. *How many people use this place?* "Just dusting all this is a job in and of itself."

"Why isn't this place more famous? This many books—seriously, come on. Spill."

"I'm a private person," he said. "And the texts are... esoteric."

"This is odd." I'd seen stranger things, like the summer I'd spent in Chicago running messages for a *santero*. Once I'd even delivered a shrunken goat's head in a jar, floating in formaldehyde, to the richest clutch of lawyers in the city. They hadn't even batted an eye, and I'd wondered—never out loud—what they'd needed it for before I figured out I didn't want to know.

Six months after, I'd left Chicago when Luis closed up his store—and I'd heard later that several powerful, prominent lawyers had taken swan dives off the fiftieth floor. "Now I'm not just curious, I'm outright intrigued."

"Are you ready to start?"

I nodded. "All right. Lay it on me."

CHAPTER SEVEN

EVERYTHING WAS PRETTY SIMPLE. IF I needed anything, I only had to ask Tremont. My duties were to dust, alphabetize, and water. There was no computer—*the books don't like* them, Tremont said. Every afternoon, from five to six, I would read to him. I could leave the house in the mornings or afternoons, as long as I was back by dusk. If I was outside the house after dusk, I was to call the house, collect if I had to, and ask for Tremont. He gave me business cards with the address and a phone number printed on high-quality card stock. Anyone in the town was supposed to let me call him. I would be paid in cash or check every week, and the local credit union would give me an account as long as I wasn't a felon.

I didn't protest at the "back by dusk" thing. I was too busy.

The books themselves were marvelous. Some of them I knew—*Astrology for Beginners, Ephemeris 1950-2200 Rosicrucian Fellowship, Necromantica Alba, The Nine Portals of Hell.* I'd either read, used as reference texts, or heard of them, all while hanging out in occult shops and honing my own gifts.

The rest of them were similar, but titles I'd never heard, most wrapped in supple leather, editions dating from the 1500s to the very latest. The occult, magick, alchemy, witchcraft, astrology, astronomy, physics (these were newer books), mathematics, the history of occult societies.

I could see why he didn't want publicity. Small-town Bible-thumping America would've loved to hold a fundie barbecue in there.

My fingers were tingling nonstop. I could take any of the books I wanted to my room to read them at my leisure. There was a collection of folios of loose papers with handwritten notes, and dictionaries for almost every language I'd ever heard of. And that wasn't even half of it.

I'd heard whispers that places like this existed, but I'd never thought I'd ever actually *see* one, let alone end up working in it. The occult shop and carnival circles are notoriously untrustworthy. I thought it was just another urban legend. The occult library watched over by a rich, mysterious owner? Oh, yes, everyone's heard that story.

Here it was, right in front of me.

I was supposed to give a list to Tremont of any items I needed—paper clips, glue, or even personal items. Those I'd pick up on my own, but I wouldn't tell him that to his face. I have never yet had to ask a man to buy me tampons. A list of the food I liked, so that he could have 'the house' cook for me.

"Anything you need," he said. "Anything at all, tell me." His tone was oddly serious.

I finished my second cup of coffee, and I was itching to get started. "Wow," I said for the fiftieth time. "You were serious. Really serious."

"I am rarely anything else."

I tossed him a grin over my shoulder. "Yeah, so I noticed. So what do I do first?"

"I would suggest you make your shopping lists. I, um, almost hate to ask, but do you need more clothes? You seem to travel light."

I was in such a good mood it barely even made a dent. I didn't even think about the sudden diffidence in his tone. "I guess so. I had to leave a lot behind. My car died on me, you know."

"Mmh." A short expression, maybe agreement, maybe just expressing he'd heard me. "I suppose they'll have your measurements, if you put anything down the laundry chute."

They? That reminded me, I hadn't seen anyone other than him all day. I didn't even get the sense anyone else was in the house, which was weird. Usually I can feel other people, a kind of animal instinct 'hearing' the breathing, living silence of other people. Without the constant sense of others around me, the place felt a little empty. "I'll buy my own, thanks." I ran a finger along the shelf, noticing the disarray of the books. "These aren't really in any order, are they?"

"They're grouped mostly by subject. New acquisitions arrive every month. It's only recently that it's become...well. As you see it."

"Huh." I laughed then, delighted. "You know, I might not get a lot of work done, with all this to read."

He made noise, though, of the living and breathing variety. Shoes against the floor, a slight sound when he brushed against the shelves. "I expected as much. Maybe I'm just lonely."

"Maybe you are." I turned my back on the books and looked at him, sitting in a wingback chair behind the biggest desk, a mahogany monstrosity that wouldn't be out of place in any Victorian gentleman's study. Papers scattered over it, and a collection of pens and paperweights. There were files, and different books stacked up and opened to different pages. He looked loads more comfortable now.

I wanted to ask why nobody—from the town or from the world outside—had come to take the job. Surely he had placed the ad elsewhere, if so many people from around the world came to study here?

Who was I to ask? I'd wanted a job, and I had one. Maybe it was because I'd mentioned the rosebushes. My fingers had led me straight to it. Maybe I was supposed to be here.

I wouldn't put it past my mother's gods to stick me in an occult library run by some scarred millionaire. They had a weird and twisted sense of humor. I had only once in my younger years seriously asked for some excitement in my life and ended up seventy-five thousand in debt to a card shark and almost getting shot before I could play him for it and get the hell out of town in the back of a rickety, oil-burning El Camino driven by one of the craziest Mexicans north of El Paso. That was the first *and* last time I ever asked for anything from Mom's gods. "Shopping lists. Okay. Can I have a desk?"

He didn't miss a beat. "Pick any one you like."

I eyed the monstrosity he was sitting at. "Maybe something a little smaller."

He pointed. There was a smaller, much more restrained maplewood number empty in front of a lovely bay window that looked out on a tiny garden space. No roses, thank the gods. I saw lavender, rosemary, hyssop—an herb garden. Perhaps a witch's garden, I saw some silvery rue. The desk had a comfortable chair, and plenty of paper. I looked it over.

That wasn't there before. Maybe it was a test. I contented myself with a single long look.

Yep. It definitely hadn't been there before. I couldn't quite think of what *had*, though. "The garden's beautiful."

There were only a couple of places I've ever run across capable of doing that now-you-see-now-you-don't trick, and it made me want to sneeze every time.

"I like it." Did Tremont look worried now? Maybe he should. You couldn't just ask a normal person to come in and deal with this, although sheer obliviousness might work in their favor. By the time they realized something else was going on…but no. Normals were dangerous when they had those sorts of realizations. Fear does ugly things to people.

I lowered myself into the chair and viewed the desk. *You just produced this out of thin air for me, house?* "Looks okay. All right." I found paper, and a high-quality fountain pen. "Shopping lists." I vaporlocked for a second or two—so much to do, the entire thing whirling inside my head.

Lucky, lucky me.

Tremont looked almost surprised to find himself smiling, and his mouth hurriedly turned down as soon as I caught sight of it.

It was a day for humor, and my own laugh didn't seem so out of place now. "I'm an idiot. I need my bag, and some music. You've got a CD player? I'll be right back." And with that, I waltzed over to the stairs and ran up, ducked out the second-floor door, and ran down to my room. I did a little happy-dance, scooped my bag up off the bed, and ran back down to the library.

I found him silently sitting in the same chair, watching the door. He didn't appear to have moved, but there was a small open cabinet next to the maplewood desk, revealing a CD player and a stack of discs. I took a closer look.

Janis Joplin, Beethoven, and the Eagles. The Rolling Stones, some Shostakovich, Rod Stewart, Stevie Ray Vaughn,

Fleetwood Mac, and some Nina Simone. Most of them were the kind of discs I'd lost to Jimmy Cassidy, or scratches and scuffs as I bumped around. An iPod would have been nice, but personal electronics aren't my thing, and loading music into one is more trouble than it was worth when you don't have a laptop or a stable address. "Okay." I restrained myself from the fifty-first *wow* with an effort. "We have the same taste in music, it seems."

He didn't agree or disagree. "Play what you like."

I selected some Beethoven—the Appassionata—and put it in, waited for the first notes to adjust the volume. Lovely Bose speakers, the notes melted like candy in the air. I settled myself at the desk and got out three piles of paper, hung my bag on the back of the chair.

I am going to need paper clips. It was a good place to start.

CHAPTER EIGHT

I FINISHED THE LISTS AND handed them to Tremont, who didn't even glance at me, and made a circuit of the library to determine the extent of the mess. It was considerable. I was glad I'd worked in so many little occult bookstores, I had an idea of where to start.

There was a little trolley that could be wheeled around on each floor. Thankfully not too many of the books had to be taken between floors.

All the same, I was grateful when Tremont called "Lunch, Miss Harpe," from the bottom of the well.

I came down the stairs with a pair of books—*Basic Spells* and *True Clairvoyance*. "Well," I said to his bright blue, hopeful gaze and ruined face, "congratulations. It's not hopeless. It'll take some time, though. What's for lunch?"

"Soup." Was it my imagination, or did he have to clear his throat before he could talk? Maybe he had allergies. "Tomato, I believe, and sandwiches. Ham, or grilled eggplant?"

"Oh, my. Just what the doctor ordered. " I set the books down on the desk. The wood glowed from within, burnished to a high gloss. Just the sort of furniture I liked. "Should we be eating in here?" I made a helpless gesture, encompassing paper, shelves, the whole mess.

"It's fine. What do you have there?"

"Books, what else?" I dropped into the chair across from him. "I'll take some soup. Hey, I have a few more things I'd like."

"Give me the list, and I'll make sure it happens. Which books?"

What, you're going to censor my reading? Good luck with that. I handed them over, though. Maybe he was just interested. I'd opened the window behind my desk, and the smell of rain-washed garden came rolling into the library, ruffling my hair. *Aida* played softly on the stereo, robbed of most of its elemental power but still pretty. My fingers touched his, and he moved quickly away; almost as if my skin had burned him, the touch was so brief I got nothing from it. He glanced over the books, handed them back, careful not to touch me, his respiration shortening slightly.

Okay. So he was skittish, not a playboy. Hard to be a playboy with that face, I supposed, even if the money would do all the talking.

I gave him the list. Again, he didn't even look at it. "Can I?" I said, indicating the fresh carafe of coffee. At least, I hoped it was coffee. "It's coffee, right?"

"Indeed it is. Please, do." He was also spooning me a mug's worth of soup. He didn't seem the type to stand on ceremony, and didn't expect me to do the pouring and serving. "Eat something solid, Miss Harpe. You'll need it for the afternoon."

I sipped at my coffee, made myself comfortable, and began to alternate coffee and soup. It was nice to just sit, to feel the warmth spreading through my stomach. I finished half the soup and decided to chance a sandwich, took one from the pile set on a silver platter on the priceless little table between us. We lapsed into silence again. I ate with my eyes half-closed, savoring the food.

He wasn't one of those people that had to chatter and fill up every spare bit of airspace. I liked that. Alone in here, he probably didn't talk for days.

When I was finished, I set my cups neatly aside, dabbed at my mouth with a linen napkin.

"Back to the salt mines," I said.

Tremont looked up at me from his own coffee. He looked a bit more relaxed now. "Don't you want a break?" The sentence stopped abruptly, as if he wanted to say more. Or as if he was afraid he'd said too much.

"I'm in the mood. I want to get the third floor mostly organized in a couple days. And after that—"

"Don't forget I have your time from five to six today. Tea's at four, and afterward you'll read to me. It will work better that way." He inclined his head slightly, and I got up, stretching. Time to get back into yoga, I wasn't getting any younger.

Tea. Honest to gods tea. He'd do very well in an English castle, he's so prim. That little headshake, like dismissing the servants. I was amused, inclined to be charitable, and enchanted all at once. "I won't forget. Call me down at four, okay?" He probably could have turned blue by holding his breath and I wouldn't have given it a second thought, I couldn't wait to get back to the books.

"Certainly." He sounded...relieved? And sad. "Don't tire yourself too badly, Miss Harpe."

I restrained the urge to point out that I'd just driven halfway across the country *and* walked into town, I could handle lifting a book or two. "Oh, for God's sake, it's Isabella. Kids used to call me Izzie for short, but I don't recommend *that.* Isabella will do just fine."

That brought out something amazing—first truly open smile, unshadowed by any bitterness at all, that I ever saw from him. It made his face scrunch up into pleated valleys and gullies, but his eyes were sparkling, and I could see someone shy hiding in there. "Isabella, then," he said softly. "Thank you."

He really was shy. No wonder. I waited a beat, turned to head for the stairs. *Just Tremont,* he kept saying. The name of the town and the name of the street. *My family built this town.*

I was halfway there when he spoke. "Miss Ha—um, Isabella. It's Jeremy. Jeremy Tremont. Call me what you like."

"As long as it's not *late for dinner,* right? Thanks." I smiled back over my shoulder at him and took the stairs up to the third floor. My thighs were burning by the time I got there. This would be a workout and a half.

I went on through the afternoon, doing preliminary sorting. Once I stopped and came down the stairs for a drink of water. Tremont was nowhere in sight, but there were plain paper grocery bags set by what was now my desk, full of almost everything I'd written on the list. *That was fast. Almost, ha ha, like magic.*

I poured myself a cup of water from the crystal pitcher set neatly where the lunch tray had been. There was a plate of cookies, which I didn't touch, but I did take a few baby carrots from a dish set beside the water tray. A container of trail mix in the grocery bags, too. I wasn't about to gorge myself when there was work to be done.

Since I was alone, I put on some Fleetwood Mac—a Greatest Hits CD—and turned it up a little. Then I went back upstairs. The CD was about an hour long, by the time it was done it would be time to read to Just-Tremont.

Jeremy. I wondered what he would want me to read. Maybe something pornographic? No, he was a nice guy. A bit of a prude, really.

I was sorting a stack of philosophy books that had somehow gotten into the Astrology section when, at the end of the CD, I heard the library door on the first floor open. There was a distinctive squeak of hinges, then I heard voices.

"—dangerous," someone said. "Looks like they're going to bloom this year."

"Be quiet, if you please," Tremont replied, so low I could only hear every other word after that. "...time. The curse...here during a storm."

"Oh, really? Good luck for you then, you old son-of-a-bitch. I thought you'd lost your hope." This voice was male, unfamiliar, with a slight breathy rasp to it. Someone smoking too many cigarettes, I guessed.

I'd probably sound like that someday.

"I asked you...your voice," Tremont said. "...still the Protector."

The music stopped, and silence filled the library. "You might be," the other man said. "But what if she's the curse—"

"*Enough!*" Tremont snapped, and that velvety voice turned into something harsh. "I will *not* have you cause any mischief right now."

There was a brief, crackling pause. I was on my knees in front of a pile of books, my mouth hanging open. I didn't like to eavesdrop, but this was...interesting.

"I just want to see you happy, my friend." The other man had lost his levity, and sounded much more serious. "You know, it's about time. The curse can't last forever."

What curse? I doubt either of them have ever had a period. I rose, dusted my knees off, and started to whistle a few bars of *Dreams*. Thunder doesn't only happen when it's raining, but who could complain?

I tripped down the stairs with perhaps more noise than was strictly necessary and found my employer, standing near the first floor door with the guest.

He was a thin, dark man wearing a red sweater and torn jeans, a pair of well-used boots and a silver flute hung on a cord around his neck. A long nose, long spidery fingers, and the messiness of his hair all worked together to give him a thin, hungry, unkempt look.

"Oh." I hoped I sounded surprised. "Hey, Mr. Tremont. I thought I heard someone come in."

"Just Tremont, Miss Harpe," he said, inclining his golden head. "This is Calamus. He's here to do some research."

The idea brought me up short. The theoretical possibility of someone coming here to use the books was one thing, but the logical extension of what *kind* of person would do so was quite another.

A life spent in high weirdness of one sort or another means that sort of question makes you cautious as all fuck.

I took refuge in a kind of cheerfulness based on hundreds of normal retail jobs. "Well, the place is a mess, and I just started, so I don't know where everything is." I gave a bright, sunny smile. "But I'll do my best to help." *Isabelle Harpe, cheerful shopgirl. Customer is always right, etc., etc.*

Was Tremont trying not to smile? I thought I saw his mouth twitch.

"That's most kind of you." Calamus examined me from top to toe, his forehead wrinkling. It did nothing for his lean, weathered face. "I'm glad Tremont finally has some...help. He's been looking long enough."

The smile dropped, and Tremont gave him a blue-eyed glance that could cut steel. "It's time for your reading, Miss Harpe. I have the book."

56

For a moment I thought he meant reading the cards, but the rest of me caught up with my body just in time to keep me from opening my mouth like an idiot. "Great. Let me get some water. Where, ah, do you want me to do it?"

"I thought on the second floor gallery, overlooking the garden." Did he look uneasy? It was hard to tell. "If that's acceptable."

"It's your house, Mr. Tremont." I manfully restrained from studying the new arrival. He wasn't outright ogling me, but it was close.

"Just Tremont." They both watched me as I drank a small glass of water from the crystal carafe, sitting proudly next to a couple bottles of Evian. "Bring your water."

Being waited on by invisible people was beginning to feel a little eerie. I hadn't heard a single footstep yet. "I was planning on it." I snagged a bottle, and gave him an extremely sunny grin. "Lead on, Macduff."

One of those rare genuine smiles turned his face into a crinkled mess again, and the new guy had the grace to look away.

Good. I was beginning to feel a little…well, protective. Scarred and all alone in this big house, with the silence in every corner didn't seem like a good time.

I followed Tremont's broad back up the stairs, Calamus drifting along behind me. My back prickled, and I did my best to keep ahead of him. We threaded through rows of bookshelves, until we came to the 'gallery', wide windows on one side and the blank ends of bookshelves on the other. Da Vinci's *Madonna of the Rocks* watched us from a framed print on one bookshelf, ferns in hanging pots dangling gracefully from wrought-iron arms on the others, and a bust of Beethoven on a pedestal snugged up against yet another bookcase. It would have looked empty and chill except for the two leather couches, a lectern, and a comfortable-looking papasan chair with a black cushion. I was already hoping neither of them would take the papasan.

Calamus dropped onto one couch with a sigh, swinging his scarred, dusty engineer boots up too. He proceeded to stretch out and make himself comfortable, and I longed to glare at him.

Instead, I looked to Tremont, my eyebrows lifted so high they practically nested in my hairline. "Should I sit or stand?"

His expression didn't change, back to unreadable. He stood stock-still, holding out a leather-bound book. "Either, Miss Harpe."

"I told you, Isabella." I took it, his fingers avoiding mine. A faint tremor running through him, or was I just imagining his hand shaking a little? I studied the embossed leather cover. "Propertius. In Latin." *My goodness, aren't you a scholar.* "Mind if I take the papasan?"

That made him move, a slight graceful movement indicating the cushioned bowl. "Please. Whatever you wish."

I folded myself down cross-legged, set the bottle of water on a convenient table, and flipped through the book. Nicely-bound, the type crisp and clear, the pages a little worn. Someone had read this before.

I twisted the water open, took a sip, and looked over at Tremont, who had lowered himself stiffly onto the second leather couch. Instead of watching me, he gazed at Calamus's boot-toes.

"My accent's a little rusty." I began cautiously.

Tremont paused, like he hadn't considered it might be. "Just approximate. I trust you've had some Latin?"

What else does a witch pick up? Most of the ceremonial magic texts are in bastard Latin, and Mom always sent me to Catholic schools when she could. "I've hung around a few nuns," I cracked.

Calamus snorted, and Tremont gave him another quelling look. Or, more precisely, Calamus's toes got the look, and they seemed unconcerned.

I hoped Tremont wouldn't look at me like that. It was, quite frankly, forbidding. I decided my Sister Perpetual Hemorrhoid impersonation would *not* be appreciated, cleared my throat. "Do you want me to start from the beginning?"

He nodded, his eyes were bright with something unidentifiable. He began studying the carpet instead of glaring at his friend's feet.

I paged past the table of contents, and found the first poem.

"All right." *Just like school talent shows.* "Propertius. *Martyr caritatum.*" And I began to read.

My accent wasn't bad, though I did stumble over a few passages. It had been years since I'd read aloud, or been near a Latin text. I read for an hour, stopping only to take sips of water between poems, occasionally varying pitch and tone. Warming to my work, choosing my inflections, remembering more and more of Masses sung in cathedrals or intoned in drab English, black and white nunbirds pecking away at pronunciation, the way they moved. Swaying penguins, and the clacking of rosary beads. Heavy incense, and my mother's gentle smile. *They have their own way, and we have ours, Bella my love.*

Finally, Tremont sighed. "That's enough. Thank you."

His voice jolted me out of the dream. I looked up, owlish. Clouds had moved over the sun, and gray light filled the library. The lamps burned with rich golden electric light, though, and the entire library took a hushed breath.

"Was that all right?" My throat was a little sore.

He nodded. "Well done. You're a natural."

You're the one with the good voice. "I haven't read Latin aloud since twelfth grade." *Mom insisted, said it was a tongue of power. Tongue of bloody impossibility, more like it. No wonder the Romans were so warlike. I would be too if I had to listen to that all day.*

Calamus sprawled on the leather sofa, eyes closed, fast asleep. His fingers still played with the silver pipe, a slow, somnolent, almost obscene caress. I frowned at his boots, again. You just shouldn't do that with leather.

Tremont saw my look, and a half-smothered chuckle escaped him, not bitter at all. "He's had a hard wandering road to get here. He'll sleep all night, it's how he is. Come on, let's go have dinner. I'm hungry, and you must be too." He made no effort to keep his voice down.

"Starving," I said, and I was. "Where should I put the book?"

"Just leave it there." He got up, moving more gracefully now. The stiffness I'd noticed that morning had evaporated. "Bring your cards, if you want to. I'd enjoy hearing what you think."

"About what?" My tongue almost tripped over the syllables. An afternoon of hexameters and *quids* and *illes* will do that to you.

"About your cards. I didn't bring a tea-tray today, I was busy greeting Cal. I'll have to make sure you get your tea tomorrow." He stretched lithely, catlike, muscle moving under his crisp white button-down.

I'd have to keep my ears open. Maybe he'd talk about the scars before I left.

Don't ask. The library was quiet, and my sudden sharp unease had no definable source. Alone in a house with two strange men, Tremont's wide shoulders and suppleness not bothering me as much as Calamus's dreamy strangler's hands.

As if he heard me thinking about him, Calamus snorted in his sleep, sliding deeper into the cushions.

Funny, Tremont was bigger, but he didn't make my alarms go off. In fact, I hurried after him down the stairs. He kept glancing back, checking like a mama hen with a straggler.

It was kind of cute.

"I do apologize for missing tea," he said, and did he sound a little tentative?

"It's okay." I scooped up my messenger bag—maybe that was the uneasiness, I'd been out of arm's reach of my cards. "I'm American, tea isn't a huge thing. I usually get so involved with what I'm doing that I forget. Or, you know, I can't afford to."

He halted at the library door, his hand tensing on the knob. "How often is that? That you can't afford it, I mean. If you don't mind my asking."

"Only sometimes." It was easy to say, for once. "Sometimes I try to be normal. I end up picking bad boyfriends who like to smoke my earnings. Or shoot them up the arm. It's a failing of mine. When I go back to reading the cards, the money comes in, and I'm okay. I never get too far down."

"Hmm." His back was straight and rigid as he led me through the house. Plush red carpet, a few more of those pretty Persians, a door half-open showing a wall of paintings I wanted to take a closer look at, a marble statue of a nymph tucked in a niche. "Perhaps you're meant to be a card-reader." Even with longer legs, he didn't make me trot to keep up, measuring his stride.

"Maybe." I hugged my bag to my chest. "I just don't like to frighten people."

"I see." He stopped in front of a set of double doors. "This is the study. I spend quite a lot of time here, it's more of a sanctum than the library. Please, feel free to come here whenever you like."

Ooooh, the study. It was like a gothic novel—the all-holy study, the male preserve. "Thanks," I said, hopefully not very sarcastically, to his broad back. "Are you sure?"

"You're good company. Restful." He opened the doors.

It was a nice room. They were all nice rooms. This one was definitely masculine, though. I didn't even need the weapons hung on the walls (including a very plain, probably genuine broadsword accorded a place of honor on the wood-paneled wall) or the shabby red velvet to tell me that. Not to mention the fireplace and the scuffed leather chairs, or the decanters set on a sideboard. All it needed was Basil Rathbone in a smoking jacket.

"I try to be good company." I lost the battle with my inner snark. "So…this is your mancave." There was a set of dueling-pistols in a case on the mantel, and something that looked like a mace hanging next to the door.

That almost annoyed him, I could tell from the restrained eyeroll. "It's comfortable. My father liked antique weapons." He indicated the fireplace, where a welcome blaze was burning. It didn't smell like applewood, and even though the house was warm enough, the warmth contrasted well with the grayness outside. "Have a seat, if you like. Would you like a drink?"

Why, I might take a mint julep out on the patio, Scarlett. "Do you have any cognac?" *Tell me you don't.*

"Of course." He still had his back to me.

I stepped cautiously away and backed up toward the fireplace. He was beginning to sound a little miffed. Maybe I hadn't enthused enough over the antiques.

"What are you doing?" he asked, almost incuriously, as he walked over to the sideboard and picked up a decanter. Cut-crystal, unless I missed my guess. This wasn't just old money, it wasn't just rich. It was *wealth*, and it reminded me of my mother's horror of anything resembling a gilded cage. Grandma had wanted *security*, Mom had always wanted *freedom*, and I wondered what I wanted, sometimes.

Seemed like I was too busy jumping around from place to place to figure out.

"Backing up." No reason to lie. "You sound annoyed."

"I'm going to have to remember that you are unusually perceptive." He said it to the fireplace, instead of to me. He poured two drinks, turned on his heel, and his expression—what I could see of it—was merely set. "If I seem harsh...or annoyed, it's simply because I'm not used to people. I am painfully aware of my lack of manners, especially in the presence of pretty women." He approached me cautiously, held out a snifter with two inches of cognac in it. "Forgive me?" A half-wistful, half-joking request.

Now that I can believe. I dropped my bag into a chair and accepted the glass, making a point to step closer to him than I needed to. His shoulders hunched a little, as if he was the one afraid. "Sure. No offense, but with a place like this, you should be receiving at least some mercenary female attention, you dig? I can't believe you don't."

"Well." A soft smile, those perfect lips curving just a little. I was getting used to his face, and looking at his eyes instead of the rest of him. *That* was where to find the real Tremont. Maybe because he wasn't used to anyone looking at him, his gaze spoke louder than most people. "There aren't many women willing to come here. I think you're the first to visit willingly, without needing something desperately, in five years. Feeling special yet?"

That's either really comforting or not comforting at all. "I'm feeling hungry." That earned me a smile, white teeth flashing in his ruined face.

There was a muffled knock at the door. He set his glass down, went to answer it; I turned to the fireplace, blazing merrily away. There were no voices in the flames, just ordinary fire.

Tremont returned, set a crystal dish on the table next to me. "Here. If you'd like to smoke, that is."

I lit up gratefully. Books could only hold off nicotine addiction for so long.

Maybe I should cut back. I was down to a half a pack, would have to go shopping soon.

Besides, I wanted to think, and getting out of the house is always a good way to do that. "I need to go into town tomorrow. Drop by the credit union, get some clothes, I'm pretty thin in the fabric department, pick up some smokes, that sort of thing. So can I start early in the morning and go during lunch or something?"

"Of course. Go when you like, as long as you're back before dark. That's very important." He took the chair across from mine.

Oh, yes. I've been meaning to ask about that. "That's the second time—no, third time I've heard that. What happens at dark around here?" *Since there's a millionaire and a library of occult books, something else has to be going on, right? That doesn't happen in a vacuum.*

"The town is simply not safe for you after dark." Evidently that was all he was prepared to tell me, because his face shut like one of his books, with almost the same crisp snap. "Humor me."

I took down half the cognac. It was smooth, and detonated in my stomach like a nice warm bomb. I couldn't taste much of it through the smoke. Sweet blessed relief washed through me; I ashed in the crystal dish and began to relax. I almost felt like I'd gotten all the way over Jimmy Cassidy.

I felt worse about my car dying, now. Finally.

That did not, however, mean I was prepared to let anyone put me under a curfew, for God's sake. However, I chose some diplomacy, for once. "This is one of the weirdest jobs I've ever had, and that's saying something. I never thought a library like this existed. I mean, there's rumors, but not very solid ones."

"This town is a little more congenial than most, and my family has been here for two hundred years or so, but still... Maybe I'll move to the city eventually, I don't know." He looked away, toward the fire, his gaze haunted. You could see a shadow of what he'd look like underneath the scarring when he was pensive and in profile like this.

"You can stay under the radar in cities." I knew from long experience. "Tomorrow, my first stop's the public library, so I can find out about the bus system, how to get around. I'm assuming they have internet there?" I waited, but he just looked baffled. "You know, computers? Public terminals?"

He shook his golden head. "I wouldn't know. I'll have a car and driver for you by tomorrow. That will ease my mind about your safety."

Well. "I *could* just walk." I took down the rest of the cognac—it's really meant for sipping, but to hell with moderation.

There was another knock on the heavy wooden door, and he flowed upright. He went between stiffness and grace at odd times. Maybe he had a football injury from his prep-school days? I filed that away to ask later and forced myself not to smile.

He came back with another one of those heavy silver trays. I wasn't sure how I felt about constantly being fed like this. Then again, left to my own devices, I usually lived on peanut butter or yoghurt for weeks at a time. Maybe it wasn't so bad.

"It's brown rice stir-fry, with tofu and peanuts. I, um, you're not allergic to peanuts?"

"Nope." I shook my head. "I smell garlic."

"Garlic bread. I wonder who dreamed that up."

"Italians?" It took me a second to catch up. He meant the invisible staff. *I've heard of the class divide, but this is really something.* "It sounds good. Yeah, I'm not allergic. I'd bathe in peanut sauce if I could. Pad Thai is a religion."

"Again, I wouldn't know. As long as it pleases you, I'm happy." He set the tray down on a small, restrained ebony table, just big enough for its cargo. "Tonight we can be informal. Tomorrow Cal will dine with us, and we might have other guests. You aren't required to do anything but attend to the library, Miss Harpe, otherwise you'll be treated as one of the guests here."

Was that a speech? It didn't sound rote, but it sounded like he'd been rehearsing it for a bit. Plus, he made it sound like he'd never had pad Thai before.

That was a crying shame.

He uncovered the tray, handed me a plate. There was heavy silverware, polished to a mirrorshine. He served me as if he was used to it, ladies first and all that, but he wasn't done with the speech. "If any of the guests are rude to you," he said, "simply walk away. Tell me, and I will eject that person from the house. Clear?"

I nodded, took a bite. It needed more chili flakes, but was otherwise perfect. It was faintly comforting to find something "the house" hadn't done right the first time. "Nice to know," I said, once I finished chewing. "People assume too much about me."

"I know the feeling." His gaze traveled down, rested briefly on my bag, the crumpled cigarette packet on top.

"I bet you do." A glass of milk sat demurely on the tray; Tremont saw my inquiring glance and handed it to me. "Thanks. Hey, when do the roses bloom?"

His gaze snapped aside, and he tensed. It was subtle, but I was getting very good at reading him. "As often as roses usually do, I suppose. Why?"

Huh. Were they a leftover from an old girlfriend? Was he allergic? "I like roses. I thought you would too, since you have so many of them."

He shrugged, his face that locked door again. Even his eyes went dark. "They go with the house, and the library. I don't particularly like or dislike them. I do like the garden behind your desk. It's useful and beautiful."

For a change of subject, that's a pretty graceful one. The meal passed mostly in silence, and when I set aside my half-finished plate, my stomach full to bursting, I lacked only some white wine and a smoke to make my contentment complete.

"You don't eat much." Tremont sounded uncertain. "Is it not acceptable?"

"I'm *stuffed.* You'll have to roll me out of here before long. Besides, there are more important things to do. I should get back to the library."

"Not at all." His own plate was barely touched, but at least he took down solid food. That was comforting. "You've done enough today. Perhaps you should arrange your suite to your liking, or walk in the garden, or simply stay and keep me company. Dessert should be along any moment, with coffee."

Sounded like it was time to play the let's-get-beyond-uncomfortable-acquaintances game. "After dessert, you could just talk to me. So I know more of what I'm dealing with."

He brightened visibly, straightening in his chair like a drought-stricken plant after a real watering. "That's an excellent idea." Almost pathetically grateful, that lovely voice shaded with…what? Had he expected me to run screaming?

Right on cue, another one of those weird muffled knocks reverberated on the door. I was almost on my feet before Tremont was up and across the room, so quickly I barely even saw him move. Shaking his hair down over his face, he crossed the room yet again. He'd make a hell of a waiter.

"Poltergeist maids." A shot in the dark. "Is that why I never see them?"

Another shadow crossed his face. Had I violated some Emily Post commandment?

"They don't like to be seen. And it's just as well, I like my employees to be discreet." He bit off the end of each word. So hard to find good help these days, and all that, uppity servants not knowing their place.

"Discreet." I contemplated lighting another cigarette. "I'm maybe not the best choice in that department." *Like, at all. And they're not just discreet, they're* invisible. *I haven't even heard a cough or a whisper.*

"I'm not paying *you* to be do linens and cook, just to work in the library and read to me. I don't care if you're discreet or not, but my domestics, yes. I am old enough to be eccentric, you see."

Lord of the manor born. "Okay." *You'd be really nice if you just loosened up a little.* "I get it. Thanks for explaining." *Explaining absolutely nothing at all.* My nose twitched, and the crawling up my back was uncomfortably, vividly familiar.

There was a mystery. I hadn't been led here just to stack books and enjoy myself.

Dammit. I should have known. The Harpe name meant *no vacations.*

He set the tray down on his chair and made a few deft movements. At the end of it, hey presto, he had everything stacked neatly on the dinner tray, and the cover back on. Then he whisked that away to perch on top of the desk and replaced it with the new tray, which turned out to hold strawberry cheesecake and a fresh carafe of coffee.

Lord, it's like they know me. "Cheesecake."

"Do you like it?" He settled himself in his chair, regarding me with those bright baby blues, nervous again. I wasn't going to get used to these moods of his anytime soon.

He was interesting. You don't often find a man with something pleasant under an ugly surface.

"Do I..." I paused for dramatic effect, staring at him. "Good heavens, man! Cheesecake is a *religion*." I pointed at him, a playfully accusing jab of index finger. "Don't tell me you 'don't particularly care' for cheesecake, or I'll have to catch the first train out."

Did I imagine it, or did he actually flinch?

"I happen to like it quite a bit." Grave and quiet, but with a twinkle in his gaze. "Rest easy on that account. Take a slice, there's plenty."

"You know," I said, making myself good and comfortable in the chair while miraculously finding some room in my overstretched tummy for the food of the gods, "you're spoiling me."

"Really." He sounded amused, and poured two cups of coffee. He added a dollop of cream to mine.

I set the cup aside, thanking him with a nod, and proceeded to close my eyes and turn my entire attention towards sampling the cheesecake.

Rich and velvety and subtle, balanced against the tang of fresh strawberries. How they found strawberries this early in the season was beyond me. I sighed, a soft noise of approval deep in my throat. The fire crackled, and I have to admit I didn't care if the help was poltergeists or Fitzark's Demon Helpers. "That does it," I said without opening my eyes. "I'm staying. You'll have to carry me out on my shield. This is *so* good."

"I'm glad it pleases you." That soft, rich voice roughened just slightly. A pleasant, hoarse rasp. Sounded like he had something stuck in his throat.

It was probably cheesecake.

I opened my eyes, but he studied the fire as if he hadn't seen one in a long, long time. "Aren't you going to eat?"

"I don't have much appetite for sugar. I am, as I've said, a carnivore."

"Great." He seemed too polite and repressed to be a real he-man steak tartare guy, but I could be wrong. "More for me, then."

That broke the ice, and another one of those un-bitter laughs finished melting it. We were safely past acquaintanceship and slipping into the first stages of "friend," those shallow warm waters where you get to point out distant shapes on the horizon.

The Latin wasn't just to impress me. He had the benefit of a classical education. Ovid to Seneca, who he happened to know a great deal about. We found each other both conversant with Baudelaire, Rimbaud, the derangement of the senses, absinthe, Wilde, and able to comfortably philosophize the existence of God—or gods. He'd done his homework and knew his history, and appreciated the drugs and delirium parts.

Jeremy Tremont wasn't a delirium sort of guy, but he appreciated it. For someone with such a scarred face and bitter laugh, he was surprisingly optimistic about life. I was actually more of a cynic, which is always a pleasant surprise.

Look, I've been accused of an almost Pollyanna-like faith in the ability of things to work themselves out just fine, inherited from the steadfast faith my mother had in her gods and her intuition. Well-founded faith, for the most part, with only a few notable lapses.

Those lapses had been doozies.

I didn't want to think about that. I wanted to enjoy myself, and set to talking books and philosophy with a will. We argued for a good half-hour about Marlowe versus Shakespeare. He, amazingly enough, took Marlowe's part, mostly on the strength of *Tamburlaine*; we quoted enough Elizabethan to each other to choke a PhD and I ended up dissolving into laughter after he bungled Mercutio's Queen Mab bit. I think I'd had entirely too much booze by then, very nice whiskey I didn't bother soiling with ice cubes.

Dusk came, purple velvet pressing the windows, the firelight brighter. I began yawning through giggles and apologizing. He poured more amber alcohol into two tumblers, and I found my cards in my hands without any real idea how they'd gotten there. I do that sometimes, shuffling and playing with them while occupied with chatting.

Tremont eased his shoes off, pushing them neatly back under his chair. "Use your cards," he said, the third time I yawned. "Ask them how long you'll stay."

I was just tipsy enough to agree. "If you like." Without further ado, I slid down to sit cross-legged on the floor in front of the fire, took another mouthful of whiskey, and laid out three cards.

Le Chevalier d'Epees, l'As de Coupe, le Homme de les Quatrepeds. Thin faces gazed steadily up at me. You can use any deck, really, but Grandmama's Ettiella worked best for me.

"Huh." I spread my hand over them, feeling for the warmth. "Knight of Swords, Ace of Cups, and the World. A nice trio."

"Maybe I shouldn't have asked—" he began, the crease between his melted eyebrows deepening. The neat red lines across the toes of his socks matched each other.

My gift took over.

I opened my mouth. "The heart of a stranger, open for the asking. A heart covered and blind, denied for too long. The World—change, destiny's wheel, and an end of a curse passed down in blood and torment..." The words came from very far away, through a roaring. It was always that way, when I foretold. Whatever spoke through me then was harsh and grating, a voice my mother had called 'colder than Joan Crawford.'

I came back in soft stages, the lump of warm food in my stomach a tether, though the alcohol made the connection more tenuous than it should have been. "There." I shook my hand out, aware of the world around me again. "Does that answer you?"

He was on his feet, staring at me, his blue eyes wide. His jaw had dropped. "You're a true Sibyl." His scar-roped cheeks blushed, his expression almost unreadable but I tried anyway. Hopefully he wasn't about to get scared of me.

"Great." I swayed a little. The booze was *really* beginning to get to me. I hadn't had a drink in a while, and I was particularly susceptible. Sometimes drinking was the only thing that shut down some of my more...well, embarrassing talents. "What did that mean to you? Anything?"

He paused. "No," he said. "Nothing at all." Too quick, too definite. I'd hit paydirt, I just couldn't tell where.

Liar. It always means something. "Oh, well." I scooped the cards together, tied them in their black bandanna. "I'd better go to bed. That's enough fun and games for one day." He froze, looming over me; I packed my bag back up and looked up at him. "Give me a hand up, will you?" I raised my arm, spreading my fingers, making a little beckoning movement. *You're not going to be afraid of me, are you, Tremont? I hope not. Come on.*

He actually *flinched*. I stayed where I was, determined. Either I was going to prove I wasn't disgusted by his scarring, or he was going to have to look ridiculous by being afraid of one little girl and her habit of telling the future.

What had I said? I couldn't even remember it, something about hearts and wheels.

Great. My talent was a country singer.

He slowly bent, closed his warm, hard fingers around mine. A quick pull hauled me up and I nearly stumbled into him—he didn't know his own strength. He caught my elbow as I overbalanced—he could easily have tossed me across the room. "Easy there."

"Wow. You lift weights or something?" I was right inside his personal space, and thank the gods I didn't get that old familiar feeling from him. The shaky, explosive, buried terror of a normal human being given a peek behind Time's great curtain—and willing to bludgeon the holder of said curtain to make the fear go away.

"Something." Hoarse again, Tremont uncurled his fingers from my elbow.

My head barely reached his collarbone; I that musky cologne of his enfolded me. A dark scent, flavored with night, and vaguely familiar. I was right, I could get to like it. At least it wasn't perfume or Brylcreem.

"Are you all right?" He sounded honestly worried.

"Just tired." And I was. Had it only been yesterday that I'd been slogging down mountain roads, getting as far as I could before some other disaster took over my life? "It's been a long month or two." *Or year.*

"So I see." He stepped back, twice, pulling his hand away, as if I'd burned him. "Go to bed, Miss Harpe. You can find your way to your room?"

"You call me that one more time I'm going to scream. It's Isabella, and yes, I think I can handle it. I got here, didn't I?"

"All right. Go to bed, Isabella. Rest." He crossed his arms and tried glowering at me, mock-commanding.

As long as it was only mock, we'd get along just fine. I snorted, settling my bag across my body. "Go to bed yourself, Jeremy Tremont. You look pretty hashed too."

"I won't be retiring for a few hours," he said, and backed up another step. "Go. Sleep well."

I left him in the study and rolled away in a cloud of whiskey and good food. I only got lost once, and managed to backtrack as soon as I realized I'd passed the same bronze figurine of a Minotaur on a marble plinth. When I finally found the gilt mermaid door guarding the cream and indigo room, I tossed my bag down near the bed and tacked my way across to the window.

The window seat, covered with crushed dark blue velvet, was big enough for two. I dropped down, looked over the new nightfall of yet another town. Up here on the second floor I could survey the garden and see the high wall, earthly stars of human habitation glimmering beyond. There wasn't much of an orange stain of citylight in the sky, and I found I kind of liked the idea of being able to see the stars once in a while.

I opened the window as far as it would go, curled up with my half-pack of cigarettes and a crystal ashtray, and decided to do some heavy thinking.

This was a nice enough place, but something was off. The air was crawling with something I hadn't felt since my last meeting with a coven of real witches. Call it magick, call it power—*something* was crackling in between the visible and not-so-visible. Tremont, town, street, and man, were all part and parcel.

The roses. The library. Servants that didn't ever appear, just knocked the door and handed through trays of mouthwatering food. They also crept into my room and left folded clothes, cleaning out the fireplace while I slept and locking the door behind them.

I hadn't asked Tremont about *that*. Some things a girl just has to chew on by herself.

Lovely. The alcohol haze began to fade a little. *Invisible Oompa-Loompas waiting on a scarred millionaire with an occult library. This could only happen to you, Isabella.*

It was better than cocktail waitressing or cleaning toilets, that was for damn sure. Whatever else Tremont was, he didn't seem the type to force himself on a girl. He was too painfully shy, even if he sometimes forgot and practiced that razor deadpan wit of his.

I smoked in silence. The night breathed up from warming earth, I smelled cut grass and incipient rain. It would be nice to have some more sun, I decided.

My mother had never liked roses. *They'll drain the love and care right out of you*, she'd say. *They're selfish flowers.*

I was just about to pack it up and go to bed when my peripheral vision caught a flicker of motion. I peered down out of the window, glad I'd turned the lights off.

The shape was long and low, fluid, its outline blurred and broken. It paced back and forth among the roses and lavender, and I caught a flash of night-glowing eyes.

An animal.

A big one.

I squinted. I have great vision, but this was just too far, too dark, and I'd done too much drinking for me to make anything out...other than the fact that it seemed catlike. Catlike and pretty big. Here in the mountains? It could only be a cougar.

"Goddamn," I breathed. I took another drag off my cigarette. No wonder everyone had bars on their windows, if cougars were running around. Weren't they dangerous?

Everything I knew about cougars could be summed up in the words *kittycat* and *hunts*. I was glad I was on the second floor. "A real cougar."

It stopped, and I could swear it looked up at me. There was a flash of light—animal eyes at night, that funny blue-gold-green color they get. Rods and cones reflecting differently, or so high school science had taught me.

I took a deep breath. "Hi," I said, not yelling, but speaking low and distinct. Cats have great hearing, it's always impolite to shout. "I'm glad to see you."

The cougar just stood and stared. It was a big one, too, but my sense of proportion or perception must have been misfiring through the alcohol because there was no *way* a cat could be that big. Its coat looked strangely shaggy, but I was frankly too buzzed to care. The cat-eyes shone, regarding me steadily.

I decided to explain. "I mean, I've just blown into town and I don't know anyone. You don't look like the welcoming committee, but I'm glad to meet you anyway."

The cougar made a graceful movement and sat down, its white-ruffled face tipped up toward my window. "I'd come down and greet you," I continued, "but you might be hungry, and I'm supposed to be resting. So..." I took another drag, the familiar comforting burn of smoke. Let it out. "It's nice here. A little weird, but nice."

There was no reply, of course. Did it have too wide a face to be a cougar? I was sadly behind on my taxonomies. There weren't any other big cats in this part of the country.

Not unless one escaped from the circus. Ha ha.

Not funny, Bella. I could imagine all too well what could happen inside a bigtent when fire broke out. The screams, and the panic...and if I was so good at predicting shit, why couldn't I have saved some lives instead of just blithely haring off because I'd heard the wind moan my name? *Isabellllla....Issssabelllla...come away, come away....*

I shivered. The wind wasn't speaking, I was safe to stay at least one more night in this place of quiet and food and books. Was there anything more to want? We sat there, the cat watching me, me smoking and watching the cat.

Finally, I stretched and yawned, a pantomime princess patting at my mouth. "I think I'll turn in. Just be careful out there, you're a very pretty cat." *Even though you probably have huge teeth and big claws and wouldn't think twice about eating a stringy little witch as a snack.*

The cougar twitched its whiskers at me, looped back on itself and was gone, just like that. Its coat, blended with the uncertain light, was...striped? That was ridiculous, cougars weren't striped. Were they?

"Be careful," I repeated to the dark, rain-smelling night. "It's a hard world out there. I know from experience."

Then I closed the window—well, mostly, I just left it open a crack—brushed my teeth, and curled up in bed in the dark room, happy and just a little sore, especially in the glutes.

This job would definitely be a workout.

CHAPTER NINE

THE NEXT MORNING I WAS in the library by six o'clock, while it was still dark. Tremont brought a tray with oat groats, orange juice, and coffee at about eight. "Isabella," he said from behind me as I bent over the desk, putting a stack of herbals carefully on one corner. I had to carry them up to the second floor in a bit. "You're up early."

I didn't jump; I'd heard his footsteps, comfortingly loud. He was too heavily muscled to move with sneaky silence.

"Well, if I'm going to town today, I want to get some things done first." I gave a glance over my shoulder, and saw with some satisfaction that he'd relaxed a little.

Today Tremont was in a black sweater and jeans, a pair of nondescript heavy boots. A gold watch—Rolex if I didn't miss my guess, I've stolen enough of them to know—and his sunburst of hair was freshly combed.

So not quite casual. Partially snazzied up today. For all I knew it could be habitual. "Then I'll have time to take care of some errands. The credit union, maybe a thrift store, a drugstore... I'll see what you've got out here."

"Good." He nodded, set the tray down. "Just make sure that you're home—"

"—before dark," I finished for him. "Mmmmh." I contented myself with a noncommittal noise. "I filled out the paper for health insurance, it's right on your desk." *Probably won't be here long enough to matter.*

"I'll take care of filing it." His golden hair was dark with water. I wondered again how far the scars went down his neck, if they spilled down that broad chest to his narrow waist.

Business first, Bella. "And taxes," I continued. "I haven't ever paid taxes, I always get a return, but who knows? This year might be my lucky one."

Did he smile very slightly? Hard to tell. "It might. Care for some coffee?"

I accepted a cup. Barefoot, in a black T-shirt and jeans, with my jewelry on, I felt more like myself than I had in a while. I'd decided to look for some candles and some incense while I was in town. I was almost never without incense.

"Sleep well?" A five-minute break to talk to him wouldn't hurt. Maybe he made the effort to be pleasant for guests? He didn't seem the type to be into empty socialization.

Or gossip. What would he have to gossip about, though? The habits of rosebushes? The Dewey decimal system?

"Well enough." His eyes were dark today, and that fluidity was back. No stiffness. "You?"

I'm not hungover, if that's what you're asking. "I slept okay. Hey, I saw a cougar last night."

He was so still I had to check to see if he'd blinked. I almost wanted to check him for a pulse. "A cougar?"

"A big cat, under my window. It sat around for a while and then left. Very polite feline. Well-mannered." I gave him a wide grin and watched him go tense, muscle by muscle.

His teeth showed too. It was an attempt at a smile, but not a very good one. "Really. You didn't go downstairs, or open your door, did you?"

"No." My eyebrows pulled together, the grin fading. The house was absolutely silent. Not even a creak or a whisper of a domestic's foot. We might as well have been on a desert isle, Tremont and me. "Of course not. Why?"

"It could have been dangerous." He turned away so abruptly coffee splashed against the rim of his cup. I stared at his broad back under the black sweater. "You must never be outside after dark."

My forehead was going to be permanently tattooed with lines of puzzlement. *All right, everyone out of the pool. I can deal with weird, but this is Too Far.* "I slept outside the night before I got here," I said, a little sharply. "Nothing happened to me. I think

I can handle a late curfew, you know, I'm an adult. Besides, I just won't walk under trees, if it's a cougar."

"The danger may not be from the animal." His shoulders were stiff. "Or at least, the danger from that animal is so slight as to be negligible. It's the...people...I'm worried about. I simply want you to be safe, Isabella." It sounded as if he was gritting his teeth. Was he shaking? A fine, almost-imperceptible tremor?

Good one, girl. You go. Alienate your boss on your third day.

"What's up with the people around here?" I found myself stepping a bit closer. I wanted to drink my coffee, but even more, I wanted answers. "What's the big secret? I mean, it's better if you tell me now, and I'll know enough to be safe. If I find out later, I might decide to haul ass and all you'll see will be the taillights." *Except my car's dead. That metaphor doesn't fly.*

Well, metaphors never did. I scrutinized his quarter-profile, ruined with scarring. It didn't look like burns, or like claws. Thick ropes, like webbing, almost silken. Had he been born with them?

Gods, I hoped not. Kids could be savage, I almost shuddered to think of this shy, ironic man in a younger skin, enduring childhood taunts and cruelty.

Whoa, Isabelle. Can the white-knight routine, he's twice your size and pretty capable of looking after himself. Don't get involved.

"People around here go mad after dark." *Now* we got a flash of Mr. Serious, his tone grim and his eyes pale and flinty. "You're not from the town, you're an outsider, and you're working here. With the Pro—ah, the pariah. That might be enough to protect you, but I don't want to risk it."

"A bunch of redneck hooligans." I waved a hand to dismiss it, just like he might have. "I've handled worse."

Living in a city, you can hardly escape violence—at least, ending up in the neighborhoods I was likely to live in. I'd convinced a homicidal drug dealer not to shoot me once, I'd talked a serial rapist into turning himself in to the cops; I'd once even talked a whole gang of Skinheads out of beating me or a Sikh shopkeeper up.

I was a flat-out pro at taking care of crazy people. Hell, most of my boyfriends qualified as insane, not to mention my own sweet self. Madness was never a problem, as far as I was concerned.

"Please." Gritting his teeth even harder. "You promised, Isabella."

I hadn't promised to stay in at night, but I had promised to stay as long as I could. So it was like a technical promise.

Normally I might have just smiled and gone my merry way, but my good friend Darlene the waitress had warned me specifically against nightfall too. I'd thought she was just being nasty, but hearing it from two different ends of the spectrum was...thought-provoking.

"Tell me why." The feeling—that there was a mystery here, that something was truly Going On instead of just the normal A1 Steak Sauce Weirdness that permeated my life—returned, raising gooseflesh on my upper arms and causing a squirrely little wiggle in my chest that I could have passed off for indigestion if I hadn't been possessed of an empty stomach.

Here I was, plunked in front of a puzzle to put together. Just call me Nancy Drew.

"It's not safe." He didn't even sound like he expected that to satisfy me.

Fair enough. It didn't. "That's not a reason."

"It's all the reason I can give." His back was absolutely rigid. I didn't think my own face could get any more squinched-up with puzzlement—or any hotter, the blush coming from nowhere.

Something was coming off him in waves, some kind of desperation I couldn't decipher like my clients' needs, like my boyfriends' wants. No, he might as well have been speaking a foreign language.

"*Please*, Isabella."

I thought about it some more, and sipped at my coffee. My cheeks refused to cool down. I hadn't blushed this hard since third grade at Sacred Heart in Brooklyn. "What if I decide to go out for a drink, or something?"

Another tiny movement, almost like a flinch. "Someone will go with you."

"Oh, hey, now." I was beginning to get slightly tweaked. Slightly? No. *Really* tweaked. "I don't need a *chaperone*, for God's sake. I didn't sign on here to be locked up once the sun goes down—" My voice hit the pitch right before *harpy* and I winced. This was a stellar way to start the day.

"Isabella." Just on the edge of pleading, he still wouldn't look at me. "I *can't* explain. Not right now. You promised."

I sighed. "I did kind of technically promise, I guess. Thanks *so* much for reminding me. Fine. For right now, you're off the hook. But I'm going to find out, and when I do, we're going to have a little talk—if I'm still here at all, that is. You dig me?"

"I see your meaning." He wasn't relieved—pulled his shoulders up, his back still iron-tight. The library, a hushed oyster closing around both of us, almost rippled with invisible tension. "If I thought you would believe me about this place, I'd tell you. Can you trust me, just a little? Haven't I earned at least that?"

"I guess so." I didn't have to work to sound grudging. "You've been nicer than I expected." I took another sip of coffee, and he unbent enough to take a drink from his own cup. *God knows I need some caffeine to deal with this. I would ask for a little help, but I think that would only cause more chaos.* "I'll exercise a great deal of caution and think twice before going out after dark. Okay?"

"That's all I can ask." Did he sound relieved? Of course. Wonderful. Good for him. "Thank you. Believe me, as soon as I can, as soon as you'll understand it, you'll hear all the specific reasons. For right now, please, just do what you can to stay inside this house after dark, or call me to send someone for you if you're outside after sunset."

I made a little, dissatisfied sound. My curiosity was heading into high gear, and that always meant trouble. "I guess. Jesus. I can't believe this. Two days into the job and I've already had a fight with you."

"Was that a fight?" His blue gaze swung around, met mine. "Really?" He sounded baffled and pleased at the same time. I rolled my eyes, again with the theatrics for his benefit, and a genuine laugh, full of merriment burst out between his perfect lips.

I almost forgave him outright. "You act like you've never had a good old fashioned fight."

He laughed harder. I gave him an aggrieved look and he was off again, almost wheezing. It took me about five seconds to start laughing as well. I almost forgot how serious I was. I actually *giggled* until I could calm myself down. Then I waited for him to stop. It took a while, but he finally wiped at his eyes with, of all things, a snow-white, precisely folded handkerchief rescued from his back pocket.

Silence. He regarded me with a twitching mouth, the handkerchief folded into his capable palms.

"Okay," I said. "Seriously—" But that started him again, and I started to laugh again too, and I gave it up for a while.

When I could speak, I wiped at my own eyes with the flat of my hand and regarded him with what I hoped was a serious expression. "Jeremy," I said, trying to keep my voice level and not ruin the effect by sniggering. "I *am serious.*"

His mouth twitched again, but he managed not to guffaw. "I know you are. I'm sorry—you literally will not believe me until you see it for yourself, but gods willing that day is far away. Now, please, eat some breakfast. You've been working very hard."

"I know I have." I took a bowl of oat groats. More fresh strawberries, too, I helped myself to plenty of those. He handed me a glass of orange juice; I had everything settled on the table and looked up at him. "Aren't you going to eat?"

His mouth turned down at the corners. "I already had breakfast." Very softly. "Thank you."

"What the *hell* was that?" Calamus demanded from the second floor. "Shouting! Laughing like loons! Do you know what time it is?"

I immediately glanced at Tremont, who waved his hand at me as if to say, *don't worry.* "Stop your moaning, old man. If you'd sleep in a bed like a reasonable man, you wouldn't be awakened by laughter." A slight pause. "Or maybe you might," he added, thoughtfully, his eyes full of wicked glee. I choked on a mouthful of orange juice and had to tilt my head back, waiting for the burning in my nose and eyes to go away. *Thank the gods it wasn't coffee.* I swallowed a giggle.

Tremont looked at me, briefly, and surprised pleasure shone from his scars.

Boys always like it when you get their jokes.

"You're a fine one to talk, you old monk," Calamus grumbled. "Is that coffee?"

"Mind you leave some of that for me," Tremont cautioned, as he headed for the door. "I'm going to bring more strawberries." He paused. "Your manners, Cal."

"I know, I know." The other man sighed.

I pulled my legs up into the chair and focused on the oat groats, my nose still burning from the sudden application of orange juice. Calamus hopped the stairs, light as a bird, scratching at his ribs like guys do in the morning, and I nodded.

"Good morning, Mr. Calamus."

"Cal," he corrected me, half-growling. His dark eyes were half-lidded, sleepy. "And how did you get here, fairy princess?"

That almost managed to make me shudder. Even Grandmama had steered clear of the Good Folk, and she was a woman who feared absolutely nothing. "I walked."

He scowled, but Tremont had shown me how to handle him. I just gave him a sunny smile and picked up my coffee cup, taking a scalding gulp I immediately regretted. "How about you?"

"Walked too. Where are you from?"

You think I'd tell you right off the bat? "All over," I said. My burned tongue throbbed, but it served me right. "How long have you known Tremont?"

"Probably longer than you've been alive." Those long fingers tipped and tapped, pouring a cup of coffee with spidery grace. He set the silver carafe down, picked up his green china mug, and tossed almost-boiling coffee down all in one gulp.

I'm no longer on the sunny side of thirty, my friend. Watch your mouth. "Wooooow." I drew the word out, my stoned surfer chick imitation doing me good service for once. "Do you do that to impress all the girls?"

He snorted, poured himself another cup. His clothes were more artfully disarranged than really ragged, and someone had gotten the dust and mud off his boots. I wondered if the invisible servants were responsible.

So he was capable of taking a joke. "Well, you can tell me. Is Tremont a nice guy?"

Calamus laughed. It was a merry sound, edged with broken glass. "I don't know if I'd go that far. He'd take a bullet for a friend, if that's what you mean, but he's harsh and very cynical. Not had the sort of life that makes for *niceness*. That face, and that monklike disposition. Gods must have been playing a joke." He fixed me with one dark, baleful eye and took another gulp. "Not that you have to worry," he added, visibly more alert now that the caffeine was in his system. "He wouldn't do anything to *you*."

Well. Isn't that illuminating. I nodded, ate more oat groats. Chewy and satisfying, thicker than oatmeal, and just the thing to keep you going all through a morning.

Calamus studied me intently, his lean face vaguely familiar. "Funny. You don't look like a cursebreaker. You're too little."

Cursebreaker? "I can swear like a sailor, buddy. I learned from the best." Had I ever seen him before, or did he just have one of those faces? Some people are like that, built to blend in.

Some predators are, too.

He gave me a baffled look, as if I was too dense to be believed, and his free hand crept up to touch the silver flute hanging against his chest. "How did you get this job? He's turned down more librarians than you can imagine."

And now he's fishing for information in return. Nothing ever changed. "I answered the ad. I walked out here in the middle of a storm, maybe he felt sorry for me. I complimented the roses, too."

Calamus let out a high-pitched, nasal wheezing laugh that instantly irritated me. "He probably hates those fucking roses."

The door creaked, and Tremont reappeared with a bowl of strawberries, sliced and topped. He also carried a fresh carafe of coffee, brushed silver just like the other one.

Calamus's eyes bugged a little. "No eggs?" he said, sarcastically enough that I cringed inwardly.

Tremont simply glanced at him, the way you'd look at a slightly malfunctioning appliance. "You know where the kitchen is. Take your coffee cup with you, put it in the sink. *And* the empty pot, thank you very much."

"Am I a guest or a slave?" Calamus demanded dramatically. He looked about ready to stamp his feet and fly into a Rumpelstiltskin rage.

Tremont made a slight sound of annoyance, put the strawberries down next to my empty bowl, and poured himself a fresh cup of coffee. "Mind your manners, old sod," he said, mildly. "Or I'll throw you out."

Cal grumbled the entire way out the door. I watched this exchange with a great deal of interest. "Am I supposed to be getting my own breakfast? I'm more than willing."

"No." He turned to face me, ducking his head a little—it must be habitual, to make his hair hide some of the scarring. For such a pressed-and-laundered man, his hair was certainly a mess. "I *like* having breakfast with you. Cal's a grump, and a nasty one at that. He'll be in a better mood in a few hours. You're a delight in the mornings."

"Just wait," I said, reaching over to find an ashtray. "Can I smoke, or would it be rude?"

He waved a hand, that lordly manner managing to be a little charming instead of rude and entitled. "Do as you like. I don't mind."

I lit up, and sighed with contentment. "This is so nice. I really shouldn't smoke in here, you know."

"Huh." He made a small sound, not quite a word. "You may do as you please, Isabella."

"I asked Calamus if you were a nice guy."

Tremont laughed. He had a variety of unamused laughter, one for every occasion. "And what did he say?"

I wished I could make those kinds of ironic little sounds. "He said you were harsh and cynical, but I had nothing to worry about." I managed to deliver it with a straight face, even. When he stopped to glance at me, as if to gauge my expression, I stuck my tongue out.

That made him laugh again, *real* laughter, and I found out I liked the sound of it. "See? You feel better already. Thank the gods I work here."

"Indeed." The merriment was gone as if it had never occurred; his eyes going dark again and his face shutting like a dusty book. And I thought *my* moods were quick. "Indeed. What else did he say?"

"He said you'd take a bullet for a friend." I wished my imagination didn't work so well. It didn't make his scarred face change in the slightest, though. "Right before he started talking about your disposition," I added. Sooner or later I'd get a reaction.

I was beginning to like getting reactions from him.

"And what do *you* think of my disposition?"

I almost missed the telltale flicker of muscle as he set his jaw. Ready for the worst, it would seem. *Aha. We have a way in.*

"I think you're the weirdest man I've ever met." *Well, except for that old dragon in Seattle. What was his name?* "But that's okay. You're good. I trust you."

"You trust me?" Definitely surprised. I liked that, he didn't sound so shy or so sadly determined. I even liked the way his shoulders came up a little, straightening.

"Yeah. My intuition's excellent, and it tells me you're a nice guy." *Not to mention the fact that I'm a dyed in the wool witch, and I think I'm supposed to do something here. Something that includes taking a look around this big pile of a house and asking a few quiet questions in town.*

"Really." His jaw twitched again, and he visibly stopped himself from commenting further down that road. "I'll endeavor to prove you right."

"Just be who you are. Pretending never made anyone better."

He didn't reply. Maybe he was wise enough to know that wasn't quite true.

CHAPTER TEN

AFTER I FINISHED BREAKFAST AND worked for another three hours, I decided it was time to stretch my legs. I hopped down the stairs to the first floor—Calamus was poring over a stack of music books on the second floor, I had been talking to him while I worked at sorting the shelves—and told Tremont that I had some stuff to do. "I'll be back before dark," I added, feeling very magnanimous indeed.

Tremont didn't look up, his back to me as he examined papers on his desk. "There is a car and driver waiting for you at the front door. The driver—Lewis—is mute, so please don't expect him to make conversation."

His golden head dipped, fractionally. Highlights in his hair almost layered, like stripes, and I'd've thought it was an expensive salon job if I didn't know he probably hadn't set foot in a barber shop for a while.

Maybe that's why he was so shaggy-headed. "Thanks for telling me. You'll be okay here alone?"

I don't know why I asked. His shoulders straightened but his head dropped a little lower. Framed against the sunny window, a stained-glass saint in a black sweater.

"I will endure until you return," he said, and I thought he was joking. So I just patted him on the shoulder—hard muscle—and went on my merry way, snagging my bag from my own desk.

I was getting to feel a little proprietary. Maybe it would make the gods yank this away from me all the sooner.

The 'car and driver' turned out to be a very old glossy black number, the kind you see in foreign movies about the fifties. I could have walked, or called a cab, but he'd gone to so much trouble...but this wasn't going to be very inconspicuous. At all.

I stood there, my arms folded, staring at the thing, its paint and chrome gleaming. The 'and driver' portion appeared in the form of a nice young man, thin and brown-haired, with big sad brown eyes. He looked like a puppy, truth be told, and I immediately stuck out my hand to shake his. His grasp was warm, and he beamed at me.

"Hi," I said. "I'm Isabella. Tremont told me that you have trouble talking—I can talk enough for both of us."

He smiled, the gentle smile of a maybe-fool, and I had a moment's worth of unease about trusting my life to him in a vehicle, especially one so old. Then he let go of my hand and motioned toward the car with brisk assurance.

"Thanks," I said. "I need to go to the credit union, I guess, and to a drugstore. And then, if you have a Goodwill or Salvation Army, just any kind of thrift store. I need clothes. Then I guess we'll be done, unless there's anything interesting in this town."

He nodded again, and opened the back door for me. It was kind of weird, talking to him; his body language was so eloquent it was like a conversation anyway. I settled against vintage leather, missing my blue Oldsmobile suddenly very much. I wouldn't have even stopped in this town if I'd been driving, I'd have turned up the radio and slid right on through.

I'd've kept going until I found something bigger, maybe on the coast. Maybe I'd have finally arrived in California, like everyone told me to. There were a lot of witches and other things there on the coast, I'd blend right in.

Though I was having trouble believing LA could be weirder than Tremont town. It was feeling more and more like thirteen o'clock all the time here.

Lewis piloted the car smoothly, which was a relief since there wasn't anything resembling a seatbelt. I contented myself with looking out the window. It was nice and clean. Hardly even looked like an antique.

Tremont was well-kept, and bigger than I thought. It wasn't a city, but it wasn't a podunk either. I watched the streets flow by until I had a good idea of the geography, then settled back into the novel luxury of being driven. It was nice to look out the window, something I never got a chance to do unless I was in a cab. But I couldn't stretch out my legs in a cab, or have control of my window in a bus.

I cautiously decided I kind of liked being chauffeured around.

Lewis finally pulled the car into a well-maintained parking lot. This would be the Tremont City Credit Union, a proud little brick building with well-watered hedges.

My family built this town. I was beginning to feel more and more charitable towards him. Growing up rich, scarred, and alone here must have been no picnic.

He never spoke about his parents. Of course, neither did I.

Lewis appeared at the door to open it for me while I was still working up the courage to get out. I thanked him, feeling a little conspicuous—there was nobody visible but I could bet that someone would see me. Smaller towns were gossip factories, I knew this. And this town was maybe not big enough to escape that fate. I *hated* being talked about; it was only one short step from *talked about* to *ran out of town*. It's an even shorter hop from there to *burnt at the stake*.

The building's interior greeted me with murmuring, paper-shuffling silence. People were waiting in a line, next to potted ferns and palms. There was a Customer Service desk, and the entire place felt like a lie and a trap. I hesitated.

"Hi there!" a cheerful blonde blue-eyed ponytail cheerleader greeted me from behind the service desk. Her blue blazer looked tailored, she was fresh-faced and professional enough to be in a glossy magazine. Probably even wearing *nylons*, for God's sake.

Say what you will for my lifestyle, at least I never have to wear those sausage-casings of uncomfortableness. My hesitation bloomed afresh. This was a *bank*. They could dress it up however they wanted, but places like this were bad for people like me.

Isabella. You're thirty blessed years old. Calm down.

"What can I do for you today?" Actually, the ponytail blonde was a little too thin, as if her bones were twigs. There was something odd about the shape of her face, too.

Now or never, Izzie. Carpe financials, and all that. "I'd like to open an account, please." ID all ready, as well as my battered Social Security card. Dealing with any bureaucracy makes me nervous, queasy, like I've done something wrong even when I haven't.

I suppose that's what they're built for, bureaucracies. I reminded myself that I was in charge, and I was going to go through with opening this account.

"Okay." She produced a sheaf of paper. "What's your name? I'm Donna."

Sure you are. And you'll marry Wally and birth the Beav any day now, when you can fit it into your career in high finance. Sarcasm would probably not help here. "It's nice to meet you, Donna. I'm Isabella. Isabella Harpe, harp with an 'E'."

I didn't expect what happened next. Donna the cheerful ponytail turned into Donna the big-blue-quivering-eyes. "Oh." Her smile vanished like a small woodland animal. "Oh, yeah. Tremont called about you. Come this way, please."

Tremont? Not Mr. Tremont, not even 'the' Tremont. Just Tremont. I blinked. "Is there a problem?"

She actually turned cheesy-pale, leaning over the counter to whisper. "Oh, no. No, we just want to make sure there aren't any mistakes. Tremont doesn't like mistakes."

I half-expected Rod Serling to come out with a cue card to tell me my next line. I needed it, too. I didn't have the faintest. "What?"

She was already out from behind the counter, motioning me toward the offices. "Come this way, Miss Harpe."

"It's Isabella," I corrected, faintly. The fear coming off her in waves was awful to see, shimmers of puce and sick yellow; it was even more awful to *feel.* My empathic ability is mostly touch-based, it has to be pretty strong for me to feel someone else from any distance. "Look, I don't want to be a problem."

"No problem," she assured me, setting off down a narrow yellow-carpeted hall. "Mr. Blake will personally handle it. He's the president of the credit union. Come this way."

I don't think I want to. "Good gods, what are you scared of?"

She actually unbent enough to shush me, finger to her thin, glossed lips. "It's okay, Miss Harpe." She opened a door and put her head into a dark cave of an office. "...—Tremont," she said, and stood aside. "He'll see you now. Pleasuretomeetyou."

Just like that, Donna the blonde ponytail was gone, striding back down the yellow hall with her hair bouncing. Either withdrawing to fight another day or beating a hasty retreat, I couldn't tell.

Well, this is interesting. I stepped into the office. "Hello?"

The oily Mr. Blake, a round little man with quivering pale cheeks, nearly levitated from his chair. "Hello, Miss Harpe!"

He looked, in fact, just as freaked out as Donna, if a little more greasy. Beads of sweat stood out on his pasty forehead, and his bulbous brown eyes blinked, moist and wary. "Come in, please, sit down. What can I do for you? We are *so* happy to have you here."

The office smelled wet and mossy, with the sharp tang of rotting wood right underneath. I took a deep cautious breath, and the smell remained. It was also damp, my shirt immediately sticking to my skin, and the blinds were shut against the daylight.

I lowered myself gingerly into the offered chair. His desk gleamed a little, the kind of sticky patina you on restaurant counters that haven't been cleaned in a while.

Much more about this started to make sense. "I just wanted an account so I could cash my paychecks without a hassle. I didn't expect the red-carpet treatment."

"Oh, we like to take care of our customers." His tongue, shocking pink, dabbed out to touch his lower lip. A glimmering trickle of sweat eased down the side of his face. "Mr. Tremont is a very good customer, his employees are *most* welcome. Here—" He offered me a sheet of paper. "If you'll just give me your name and Social Security number, I can take care of all the details in a few moments."

I complied, using my bag to write on instead of his desk. I didn't want to touch that tacky-wet looking surface. *An actual goblin. Working at a bank. Now I've seen everything.*

He took the paper, tapped on his computer with his long spidery fingers, and gave me a nervous look. "So." A long uncomfortable pause. "How do you like our town?"

For a moment the vision of a pale, unhealthy frog sitting in the chair, stroking at the keyboard with slim padded fingers and blinking first one eye, then the other, filled my head. I looked hurriedly down at my own hands, blessedly human. I hadn't had flashes like this since...well, the first time I'd met that gypsy woman in her dusty little shop in Saint City. I'd had persistent crawling thoughts of spiders the whole time I was in her store, and been *really* glad to get away.

Those happened in the presence of something not quite human—the world is a lot more crowded than anyone thinks. But meeting a one of the fabled gold-squatters in a bank office was a new one even for me.

I couldn't remember if goblins were carnivorous. Of course, there were different types, and this one seemed scared of Tremont, so...maybe I was safe? "It's very nice, and very clean," I said diplomatically, through the lump in my throat. "I can't complain."

He finished tapping at his computer, and a printer whirred into life. He produced a temporary checkbook and a few brochures, and we made small talk while he finished up and explained the intricacies of savings-and-checking in Tremont City. He was soaked with mossy-smelling sweat by the time we finished, it rolled in thin rivulets down his face. I was feeling a little sick, so I just took the paperwork—they would send me an ATM card within a few days—and escaped to the parking lot, ignoring Donna's gasp at seeing me again. I made it to the car; Lewis was already holding the door open.

I'd deposited a mere three hundred dollars. The rest of it I'd keep safely on me. Baby steps.

Holy crap. An actual goblin. It was a relief to soak in the sunlight. Their fear was enough to suffocate me.

Empathy is a curse.

That's not what's bothering you, Isabella. What's bothering you is the fact that you just got your checking account from a very large frog in man's clothing. That was a gosh-for-sure goblin, and this place might be too weird even for you. Do they have Kine or shapeshifters at the local café?

The vision of Darlene with her lipstick-smeared teeth rose in front of me again. It was distinctly *not* comforting. The prohibition against going out after dusk began to make a lot more sense, now.

Tremont was right. I might not have believed him.

Lewis, thank every god that ever was, still looked human. I studied him over the back of the front seat, was relieved when I had no creeping, funky little visions. "Lewis," I managed through a dry throat, "can you find me a drugstore here, but one that isn't on the main drag?"

Lewis shrugged, his dark eyes examining me in the rearview mirror. I got the idea there might not be one off the beaten path, or that he might be politely wondering why I'd requested such a thing.

"I don't feel like being stared at." *Although I'm not a goblin. Wow.* "Hey, can I smoke in here?"

He nodded, smiling, and I rolled down the window a little and lit up. I needed the nicotine.

CHAPTER ELEVEN

I DUMPED THE BAGS ON my bed, got out my new carton of smokes, and set that on the nightstand. A hundred and fifty dollars at Goodwill, a big deal for me—and picked up assorted drugstore items as well as a collection of candles and some Nag Champa incense. Nag Champa shows up in headshops all across the U.S., and you can find good quality almost anywhere.

I broke open a box, smiling at the memory of the headshop—glass pipes and disdainful teenagers with greasy hair. Thankfully, they were *human* teenagers, none of them turned into weird animals while I watched. They hadn't muttered or sweated, just stared at me as I selected my candles and incense, paid in cash, and went on my way.

Gods bless America. You could find hippies almost anywhere these days. Back in my great-grandmother's day, she'd had to make her own candles. Now *there* was a punishing chore. If I never smelled bubbling tallow again it would be too soon.

I lit a stick of incense and set it to smolder on the windowsill. The window was wide open, catching a rainy breeze from the gardens, and I'd found a CD player sitting outside my bedroom door, the same beautiful little Bose kind as the one in the library.

Tremont must have had a few lying around. I plugged it in and found a classic-rock station from another town over. Pink Floyd began warbling. *Up...and down...*

I sang along, unpacking. Bellbottom jeans and paisley tops, crochet and black velvet, sixties drag, cheap and looked great on me. My hips were earth-mother, I'd often wished I was as lithe as my mother.

I could probably even score some pot from the greasy-haired disdainful teenagers, if I wanted to. I laughed at the thought, and at that moment, someone knocked on my door.

"Hey," I called, lighting a patchouli candle. "Come on in, baby, it's the Summer of Love all over again."

I was almost beginning to believe I was sane.

The door opened, revealing Jeremy Tremont, his scarred face unreadable. "I see you found the CD player," he shouted over the Rolling Stones.

Maybe it was a bit loud.

I turned it down while I lit a cigarette from the patchouli candle. "Hey, boss. Thanks for the tunes. Look, I'm back before dark like a good little girl."

"And in fine form, I see." He examined the room with great care, looking everywhere except at me. "Would you join Cal and me for tea?"

"Sure. Let me get my stuff into the laundry chute and I'll be right there." *And if I can find a quiet moment, I have a couple of questions. Like about this whole Twilight Zone of a town.*

"I can wait." Then he just stood there, his hands loose at his sides. The black sweater didn't quite cling to him, but he filled it out nicely. "It smells good in here. Different. Young."

There he went, sounding wistful again. The house was so quiet even with me in it, I almost shuddered to think of him closed in here all alone.

What about the household help, Isabella? Lewis is all you've seen, and he's not even household. He just drove away. Not to mention the idea that maybe the driver hadn't been, well, *people*-people.

"Patchouli and Nag Champa. Lots of people don't like either." I tore a price tag off a pair of Levi bellbottoms, picked up a white peasant shirt, sniffed it, and made a face. "Definitely needing some laundry here. I have a little question for you too, Tremont." *More like fifty thousand questions.*

"What?" He looked amused. How I could know that without any discernable change in his face was beyond me. Maybe the changes were just so subtle they weren't conscious.

I picked up a black crocheted vest and examined it, critically. "I got my account from a frog-goblin at the local credit union who sweated enough to fill up a gallon jug. Why is everyone here so goddamn scared of you?"

"You are indeed unusually perceptive."

I waited for more, but he just stood there, his hands empty and his boot-toes placed nice and level, watching me.

"That's not an answer." I tapped my ash into the same crystal dish I'd been using for an ashtray. It kept showing up sparkling-clean.

He finally nodded slightly. "You're right."

I kept ripping off price tags, with perhaps a little more force than strictly necessary. My best find was a silk Chinese-collared tunic in a shade of pigeon's-throat gray that would look really good on me. I was a little wary of trusting it to the laundry. Also, washing my own panties was a point of pride, so resolved to find the laundry room as soon as possible.

I stripped the final price tag and tipped the whole pile of clothes down the laundry chute. Tremont just stood there, his eyebrows lifted quizzically.

The effect on his ruined, scar-veined face was a little startling, and I stared at his eyes very hard for a moment or two, looking for what he was feeling. There was amusement, and something else I'd seen too many times, in the eyes of too many men. Desire.

Dammit. Just when I was getting comfortable, too.

"Are you going to answer me?"

He made a slight movement, shoulders lifting and dropping, not quite a shrug. "Because I'm rich, and different, and I'm ugly, and my family built this place in its own image. Because I reflect them, and because I don't reflect them enough. They fear power and crave it in equal measures. Does that answer you?"

Well. You get a prize for fortune-cookie philosophy, at least. Thanks for giving me a nice long answer that explains exactly jackshit. "I suppose it might," I conceded finally, picking up the paper bag that held my drugstore purchases—scrunchies, a new comb, elastics, headbands, tampons, some makeup.

And a blue cardboard container of iodized salt. My mother's voice echoed in my head when I saw the stacked cartons, a warning heard too many times not to heed. "I get the feeling I'm not here by coincidence." *Which, you know, I never am.*

"Do you believe in coincidence?"

I set the paper bag inside the bathroom door. "My mother didn't. She said that coincidence was just the fool's way of explaining fate."

"She sounds very wise."

"She was a witch." I watched him for a reaction. If this town was half as strange as I thought it might be, a witch would hardly be news.

"That would make you one, by blood." Smiling, his face riven and crinkled. "No wonder you came here."

I'm here because I dated a junkie and my car blew up. It was comforting to think those were the only reasons. "Well. I'm supposed to be here for now. Anything else I can't answer for." *I think I'm handling this really well.*

I could already tell I was going to have a little trouble sleeping that night.

He nodded. "Are you coming to tea?"

"I guess so." It wasn't like I could refuse.

I followed him down to the kitchen. Calamus was already at the table in the breakfast nook, pouring tea from a silver teapot. "Nice to see you," he said, sounding snide enough for two. "And the fairy princess has returned."

"Hi, Cal," I returned. "What crawled up your ass and died?" I didn't care if he was a "guest". I'd just shook hands with a sweating frog-goblin who had talked to me about checking account balances and interest compounded monthly.

Jeremy surprised us both by laughing. "I knew you were the right one." He actually pulled a chair out for me. I didn't argue with him—maybe I had time later to disabuse him of some of those exquisite manners.

But I kind of liked them, too. Useless to deny it.

Calamus snorted. "Cream? Sugar? Lemon? Screw you?" He looked like an imp from a storybook when he sneered.

Tremont glanced at him, almost anxiously. Funny how I preferred the scars to Calamus's lean, weatherbeaten face.

I had to laugh. Calamus was my type of guy after all. I get along really well with dockworkers, maybe because I've been poor enough to understand them; Cal struck me as the blue-collar type. "Cream, you nasty boy, you. Watch your mouth, I'm a lady."

"You certainly are." Calamus added a splash to my cup. His ragged sleeve flapped a little—the shirt had seen hard use, and looked hand-sewn, repaired in places with small clumsy stitches. All his clothes were older than they looked, worn into pieces, even his dun T-shirt, under a chambray button-down and his red sweater, had holes near the collar.

I surveyed the tea-table. Tiny sandwiches arranged on platters—watercress, cream cheese, cucumber. And sugar cookies. I accepted the cup from Calamus and toasted Tremont.

"*Salut,*" I said, and took a sip. Calamus slurped at his, waggling his thin dark eyebrows, and I choked on a tea-soaked laugh.

Tremont glanced from me to Cal and shook his head. A faraway look came into his blue, blue eyes, but he said nothing. Cal sobered, glanced at Tremont, sneered at me. It was such a cartoonish expression that I laughed again, and that made Tremont smile.

We were all getting along so *very* well. "So, Cal, maybe you can dispel some mystery for me. I went into town today, and the funniest things happened." I indicated Tremont with my teacup. "Why are they so scared of our friend Jeremy here?"

Calamus blinked. "He told you his Christian name?"

Why, you're jealous. I sniffed. And what an awful expression, *'Christian' name.* "No, I just kept guessing until he blushed like a pagan, and then I knew I had it. Come on, Cal, give."

"I don't—" Tremont began, his eyebrows coming together.

Was this going to piss him off? Maybe.

"Long story," Calamus interrupted. "It started with his family, a long time ago. They practically built this town and people settled here; this town is—*was*—their private preserve. They've protected it ever since it started. That makes people nervous, I guess." Calamus took a more mannerly drink of his tea, a couth little sip. All levity fled his tone. "Though I guess the scars have something to do with it."

Tremont studied Cal with narrow-eyed intensity. His free hand, settled on his knee, had curled into a fist.

I leaned forward slightly, touched his wrist. "I'm sorry. That was kind of rude, but I like to know. This is *weird.*"

Jeremy shook his head, golden hair falling over his forehead again. I might have done the same thing if I'd been him. "Forgiven. It doesn't bother me so much, said out loud. It's the whispers I mind, the little sidelong looks."

"I get it." My fingers softened on his wrist. I got a confused, blurred impression of sadness before I took my hand away. It wasn't right to spy on what he was feeling. I decided to swallow my curiosity for the time being. "Okay. I'm done with that. What's for dinner?"

"Anything but that vegetarian slop," Calamus snapped. "Steak. Potatoes. *Real* food."

Well, he sucked in the tact department. I was beginning to think it was intrinsic. On the other hand, I was now hungry, and teensy sandwiches wouldn't cut it. "I could go for steak. I've been running on nerves and caffeine for a long time. Haven't had red meat in a year or so."

Tremont nodded, sipped at his tea. His blue eyes hooded, the scarring even made fine veins on his eyelids. "Whatever you want, Isabella. Calamus should thank you."

"Oh for God's sake," Cal burst out, "You live like a monk."

Jeremy shrugged. "I have books," he said, flatly, and that struck me as so funny I had to set my teacup down before I dropped it, shaking with laughter.

I've met a lot of people with mordant wits, but his was something else entirely. I was beginning to feel like the Good Witch Lollipop around this guy.

"You know what I mean," Cal grumbled. "No wine, no women, no song—"

"I do occasionally have a glass of wine, women don't like me, and I can't sing." Tremont didn't elevate his pinkie when he sipped his tea, but you got the idea he wanted to. "*Must* we talk about this?"

Guys can cordially despise each other and still get along, and it sounded like these two were professionals at it. "What am

I reading today?" I asked, diplomatically enough. "More Propertius?"

"Maybe." Tremont gave me what could be termed a measuring look. Hot sunshine gilded his hair. "Maybe some Shakespeare."

"I don't know if I'm that snazzy with the iambic pentameter."

Cal's laugh had the same husking quality I'd noticed in his voice, as if something in his throat was permanently roughened. "I thought fairy princesses spoke in nothing else."

"And as for women," I continued, ignoring Cal, "I like you just fine, but then again, I'm strange. So we'll have to call that one a draw."

Jeremy nodded. "Certainly." He gave Calamus a sharp glance, and the thin dark man pulled down his baggy red sweater sleeves.

I settled back in my chair, bringing my knees up and wrapping my arms around them—one of the maneuvers you can't ever really pull off in a skirt "You guys have this weird anti-friend thing going on."

Tremont was back to the bitter little bites of laugher, his scarred face twisted into something that could be mistaken for a smile. "Calamus is no man's friend, and he thinks I'm too old and stodgy."

"And Tremont thinks I'm irresponsible," Calamus added. "I don't see why we can't live like lords."

"We're not going to talk about this." Tremont's tone brooked little argument, and the tea-table almost rattled. "I'm a Protector. Those things simply aren't done."

"Oh, they're done," Calamus muttered darkly. "They're easy in the doing, too, young man."

I watched this, expecting another volley from Jeremy's side. He glanced sidelong at me, and his face…softened, somehow. "Calamus, we will address our philosophical differences later. For right now, Isabella, will you tell me how you came to be here? I still haven't heard the whole story."

As a subject change, it wasn't very graceful, but then, he didn't have to be. This was still his house.

I took a deep breath. "Well, I left my boyfriend after he blew our rent money on dope and packed up my Oldsmobile. Was moving across the country—you know, I'd tell fortunes until I saved up enough to move on, sleep in my car or in a motel—then I came over the pass and my car died under a willow tree. I hiked from there, spent the night in a campground. Just inside the city limits, maybe. Can't recall." Had it been?

"Yes, you mentioned that. You slept outside? Did you…did anyone bother you?"

Calamus gave him a look that could only be classified as alarmed. I didn't blame him—Tremont had shifted to bolt-upright, his blue gaze sharp. He actually quivered with alertness while remaining completely still. It was a nice trick.

Aww, that's cute. Is he worried about me or my honor? I had to restrain the urge to ask. "I was fine. It was too cold to really sleep, so I was pretty hashed when I came on down the mountains and had breakfast in your fair town. Babe's, downtown, you know—they have an okay omelet. I looked through the paper, saw the ad, and my fingers tingled so I knew it was a good prospect. I hiked out here just as it started to rain, and you know the rest."

Tremont nodded. His hand, holding his mug of tea, was shaking just a little.

Calamus's dark eyes were wide and disbelieving. "You just walked up to the door? And—"

"Good God," Tremont sighed, set his tea-mug down. He appeared to have mastered himself. "You could have been seriously hurt."

I looked over at him. "You wanted to know, Jeremy. Is the Inquisition over or am I fired?"

He shook his golden head, took a deep breath, and settled back into his chair. "You would have to do a great deal to be 'fired.' I don't mean to pry. Forgive me."

Cal's eyes were as big as dinner plates. He looked like he'd just swallowed a bag of flies and was just now conscious of the fact.

Quit thinking about flies. You'll start thinking about frogs. Don't think about frogs either. It was like trying not to think of a pink elephant.

"Forgiven and forgotten. You asked, I told you, it's done. Okay?"

Tremont nodded, staring into his teacup. "I think that's the first time in my life anyone has ever forgiven me outright."

Even if he was weird, he was still sad and lonely. I reached over, picked up a cream-cheese and cucumber sandwich, and took a bite. "I'm the forgiving sort—or so my mother told me." *And every boyfriend I've ever had has proved it, I guess.*

That halted conversation for a full sixty seconds. Cal finally blew out a breath between pursed lips. "Well. This has been a *most* fascinating tea," he said primly. "I can't wait to see what we discuss next. Politics? Religion?"

Yeah, that would be about right. "Let's talk about books. What are you here for, Cal?"

"Sheet music. I'm searching for something special to mark a...an anniversary." He blinked, a slow, nasty smile spreading over that thin, graven face. "Since Tremont has such a *fabulous* library, I thought he'd have something appropriate."

I nodded. Took a deep breath. "What's your favorite book?" This was taking all my tact, and I think Jeremy saw that. He should—he was busy stealing little glances at me when he thought I wasn't looking.

The question seemed offensive—at least, Cal's upper lip wrinkled. "I'm passing fond of Browning," he muttered, and stuffed a whole sandwich quarter into his mouth.

Tremont sighed, a sharp, adult sound.

Welp, I just failed miserably at small talk. Again. "Okay." I set my teacup down. I stood, my chair scraping back from the table, and Tremont rose hastily. I picked up my bag. "Sorry, guys. Got to get to work. Excuse me. See you later."

With that, I strode out of the kitchen and headed for the library. This had to be the strangest place I'd ever set down in. I wasn't sure I wanted to stay. It took a lot of tact to deal with both him and Calamus, and there was something funky happening. It made my neck itch. My nape, to be absolutely precise; the spot of skin that warns everyone of trouble, whether they listen or not.

I had gone from really liking Calamus to being unable to stand him in less than half an hour. Why was that? I still didn't want to think about the frog-goblin. Tried not to think about that *or* Darlene's red teeth, and failed miserably.

How many other not-people people were in this town?

I went up to the library and lost myself in alphabetizing to some Beethoven—the *Eroica*. It was good music to think to, even if I didn't like what I was thinking.

About the end of the symphony I was busily shelving a stack of sorted ephemerae, and didn't hear Tremont until he stopped right behind me and cleared his throat.

I jumped and whirled, dropping four books and letting out an undignified squeak. The Beethoven just kept going, *molto allegro*, my hair tumbling free of its scrunchie. I stood there, my palm flat against my chest, my pulse pounding all through me, and Tremont's hand dropped. Had he been intending to touch my shoulder? My hair?

"*Jesus!*" I gasped in a breath, let it out, and made my shoulders relax. My entire chest thudded like John Bonham doing a rattling solo in an empty room. "You scared me. Hi. Look, I'm sorry about tea—"

"No," he said. "Don't be. Cal isn't fit for company most days. He's not a nice person, Isabella. I've spoken with him, and he will watch his manners. Please..." He struggled with something for a moment, then shrugged, his own shoulders dropping helplessly. "I'm sorry."

"Well, I wasn't very polite either. You have too many questions and not enough answers here, Mr. Tremont."

He gave that bitter little laugh again. "Don't I know it," he said. "I really am sorry."

We were back to that brittle formality of his. He wasn't a dope fiend or fast with his fists—at least I didn't think he was—but I was beginning to be rather fond of him, in my own special little way.

It was at that precise moment that I figured out I wasn't going anywhere. I was in this for at least the foreseeable future. The puzzle of scarred, repressed Jeremy Tremont and a town full of weird was just too interesting.

This is going to be fun. My pulse began to come down out of redline, and I batted at my hair, trying to get it back out of my way. "What are we reading today?"

He held up a red leather book, gold-edged pages winking at me. "Juvenal. I thought we would try some satire today. This is a translation, and quite a good one."

Good, I don't think my Latin made either of us happy. I nodded, my hair tight in one hand, the other massaging my aching nape. One of the things I missed about the city was clubbing, I was always so limp and exhausted from dancing I couldn't be stressed. If this kept up I was going to come down with a migraine.

"Satire sounds good." I found the scrunchie, and had the mass up out of the way in short order. He kept watching, just standing there with the book, like he had nothing better to do.

Did he?

He didn't move, just stood there, like a stag staring at headlights.

"Lead the way, boss." I stepped close enough to smell that musky cologne of his, subtracted the book from his tense fingers.

That broke the trance. He cleared his throat, stiffly. "Anything you say, Isabella."

CHAPTER TWELVE

PURPLE DUSK FILLED THE WINDOWS behind the papasan. Tremont stopped me at the end of a chapter. "That's enough, Isabella. Thank you." Softly, his voice stroking every surface. On the couch, in the same place he'd been the day before, but this time his eyes were closed, his head tipped back.

He looked relaxed. Almost...happy.

And yet...there was something dark in his aura. It was a subtle change; I was hungry, or I might not have seen it. A heavy, sharptoothed cloak over him, shaggy textures sliding like fur, claws where hands should be.

I swallowed dryly. His eyes opened, heavy bright blue, dilated pupils. For a moment they had the strange reflective shine of an animal's eyes at night, and my heart slammed against my ribs for the second time that day.

"Jeremy?" Squeaky breathlessness turned the word into a broken croak. "Um..."

He blinked slowly, straightening with that fluid, scary grace. "You've gone pale."

Too much fun for one day, I tasted copper adrenaline, sweat springing up under my arms.

Get out of here. "Um." My fingers tingled for the cards. I set the book aside with finicky care, everything turned nightmare-slow. Struggled up out of the papasan chair, grabbing at my bag, my entire body stiff. "Excuse me."

I fled.

"Isabella? *Isabella!*" His voice pursued me, surprised and worried.

Frightened.

That made two of us.

I locked the bedroom door, my fingers fumbling in my messenger bag. The patchouli candles were still burning— something told me he didn't worry much about fire hazards; I lit a cigarette with trembling fingers. I dropped down on the floor beside the empty fireplace and tore my cards free of the bag's innards, spilling a pot of cinnamon lip-gloss and empty chewing-gum wrappers. I shuffled, snap-gunning them, and drew three cards.

La Roue de Fortune; La Prudence, reversee; Les Oiseaux et les Poissons, Protection.

The Past: The Wheel of Fortune. Fortune. Karmic Wheel.

The Present: Prudence reversed, the mirror looking at me.

The Future: Birds and fishes, protection

So. I had blindly spun the Wheel of Fortune. Prudence, looking in her mirror reversed. Someone watching me, very closely indeed. And in the future: protection. Was I under the protection of beasts?

Or I would I be seeking protection *from* them?

I took another card out, laid it crossways. *Le Trois de Baton.* Fire. Light into darkness, a trinity. Light shed on a situation.

All right.

The breathless underwater feeling faded. I took a deep breath and another deep drag, blew the smoke across the cards and stared into the swirls. I saw a wolf's head, a tiger slipping through jungle foliage. Fluid motion. Blue eyes staring at me from behind prison bars—or were they stripes? A tiger's stripes?

Tremont was trapped in something, here in this town where frog-goblins worked at the local bank, who knew what worked at the diner, and it wasn't safe outside after dark. The town that, even if it felt weird, was still one of the most welcoming places I'd been, if only because of him.

Fortune, or Fate, or my mother's gods had brought me. I was here to do something, but what?

I sat back, finished smoking. I sighed, swept the cards up with one hand, and felt the subtle shiver under my skin that meant, *don't stop yet.*

I picked out another card. *Deux de Baton reversee.* Surprise.

As if the card was the key to a door in my brain, the vision took me with startling swiftness, like it always did.

—there in the entryway, a thin girl with dark-blue eyes, dripping wet. Chest-clenching pain, the kind usually associated with cardiac arrest, the beast rising, choking. Long dark hair, a river of water across the floor, and she cocked her head, looking. Sudden shock of rightness—

Another flash.

—running, breath locked inside my chest, every single cigarette I've ever smoked rising up to haunt me, the sound of snarling behind me, the bag torn from my shoulder and I whirl, the need to save the cards suddenly greater than the need to outrun whatever was chasing me. The claws—

Darkness whistled through my head. I came back in bits and pieces, slumped on the floor, the cigarette in the ashtray, ground out. A taste of copper; I'd bitten my lip, hard.

I groaned.

Hungry.

The world shifted in between past and future like a candleflame in a draft, guttering.

It was getting harder and harder to come back after these little trips into the rushing wind of time. The flashes hardly ever helped, being unrecognizable until it was too late. Without the cards to give me a lattice, a framework for decoding, I might have ended up a homeless wandering beggar in danger of being locked up in psych wards for fits and muttering to myself, treated for epilepsy instead of for a seer's gift. If I hadn't been born to a woman with her own witchcraft, trained to use it by a grandmother grounded in folklore and folk magic, I might even have believed myself insane instead of just weird.

"Isabella?" A knock at the door, echoing tinnily through a long tunnel. "Isabella, are you all right?"

Tremont. He sounded frantic.

Ouch.

"Not gonna tango too soon," I croaked, regathered my breath. "I'm fine," I added, loudly enough to be heard through the door. That set off a cough, and I hacked for a good twenty seconds. I was really going to have to quit smoking soon. Like, tomorrow.

Maybe.

"Supper will be ready in ten minutes. Do you want to come down for a drink?" Tentative. Just outside the door, his fingers spread against it, tendons standing out on the back of his hand. The gilt mermaids carved shifted uneasily under his hand—

I shook my head. If I slid out of my body and started looking around the house, I might never come back. "Okay," I mumbled. "Hang on."

I tied the cards up in the black bandanna. My hands shook so badly I almost couldn't make a knot. I shoved them in my bag and put it over my shoulder, then hauled myself to my feet. My knees felt like water. I was hitting the wall hard. Too much weirdness, too much stress, not enough food; it all added up to one skinny little witch in a bad, bad way.

I made it to the door, fumbled with the lock, then stood staring vacantly, trying to remember if it opened in or out. Jeremy finally twisted the knob and opened the door cautiously. He peered in, looking for all the world like a kid on Christmas Eve at about eleven p.m., trying to peek to see Sandy Claus. His blue eyes widened, grotesque in that scarred face.

"My God, you're *bleeding*." He shoved the door fully open. "What the—"

I stumbled, the door hitting me on the shoulder. It was a glancing blow, but it almost knocked me over. Tremont caught my other arm, keeping me upright. His fingers were gentle, but I felt the strength in them.

He could snap a bone if he wasn't careful.

"Oh, no," he said. "I'm sorry, I'm sorry—"

He sounded downright horrified. The kind of breathless apology a shy man would give at a party right after he'd spilled his drink on you while staring at your cleavage.

I just shook my head and tipped forward. My forehead hit his shoulder. He was solid, he was *real*, and I rested against the hollow between his shoulder and his chest, right under his collarbone. He hunched over, his shoulders rounded, as if trying to make himself smaller.

It must have been uncomfortable. "Stay...still," I managed to get out, and he did.

As a matter of fact, he even stopped breathing for about thirty seconds. I gasped, getting my lungs under control, and managed to sigh when the faint movement of an unwilling exhale moved through him.

"Are you all right?" His voice rumbled comfortingly against my cheek. "Isabella?" Very soft, very tentative.

"Fine," I whispered. Leaning against someone who was moving through time in the normal way helped me stay inside my own skin. Besides, he was starting to smell really good. "Just had a bit of a spell, ha ha. I'll be okay in a second. Just let me get my bearings."

"Was it your cards?" The boy was quick.

"'Twas," I mumbled. "I saw you behind prison bars. Or tiger stripes."

"Mh." Another of those brief noises of assent he was so good at. "Let me see. You're bleeding."

I didn't want to move my head. But I did, tipping back and staring up at him. Blue eyes half-lidded, his scarred face, he lifted one finger to touch my bleeding lower lip. His hand dropped away. Hey presto, vanished. "Might need stitches," he said. "Isabella—"

"I'm okay." At least, I almost was. "I must have bitten it when I fell over."

"You fell over?"

"I was sitting on the floor," I said. "It wasn't far."

"Was it Calamus?" Something sparked in his eyes. "Did he trigger this?"

I shook my head, wished I hadn't, because the entire world spun out from under me. I wasn't quite ready to move yet. "No. It was just...when I get hungry, they get harder to deal with. The visions." My bag's strap tangled in my fingers, I hauled it up. Tremont held my shoulder, so motionless I almost wanted to check him for a pulse. My lip hurt. "My mother used to say I needed to eat to anchor myself here, or I just might drift off." I fumbled in my bag one-handed, holding it between my arm and my hip.

He smelled good. Was it cologne? It smelled too...well, glandular to be a cologne. "Don't fire me over this," I muttered.

"I wouldn't," he said hoarsely.

I found what I was looking for—a well-squashed emergency Snickers bar.

"You'd eat that?" He sounded surprised.

"Only about half of it. It's got peanuts, and it never goes stale."

"That's a matter of opinion," he muttered, and I made a weak little amused sound. "You should be more careful."

I ripped the candy bar open, dropping my bag, and sank my teeth in. Chewed, swallowed, grimaced at the sick-sweet taste of it. "Gah that's nasty." I took another bite.

"Coffee?" Tremont hadn't moved.

"Didn't you say dinner?" I looked up at him. He was still blessedly solid, still holding my arm, and I was shaken with the sudden urge to simply fold forward again and rest my head on his chest for another little while. "I'm sorry."

"Don't apologize." It was half a growl, and I moved restlessly. He swallowed, statue-still, right inside the door. "Dinner can wait. Did I frighten you?" He sounded just as breathless as I felt.

"Low blood sugar." It was the best excuse I could find. "Hypoglycemia."

A long pause. Maybe he was trying to figure out if he should believe that. "All right," he said quietly. "Let's blame that. Would you like to sit down? I could bring you a washcloth, for your lip."

No, I just want you to hold still so I can put my head on that nice chest of yours and stop the world from spinning. "All right," I agreed, and he finally moved. Very slowly, he shifted his grip on my arm, still careful not to hurt me. "It's okay. I can make it."

"Humor me." He guided my unsteady steps across the room to a chair. I sank down gratefully while he vanished into the bathroom, coming back with a cool wet washcloth. "What can I get you, Isabella? Coffee with sugar? A Coke? Trail mix?"

I folded the rest of the candy bar back into its wrapper and shoved it back into my bag. "I'll be okay in a second. Then I can come down to dinner and be social."

He knelt in front of the chair and dabbed carefully at my lip. The rough terrycloth stung briefly; Tremont flinched when I took his hand and pressed the washcloth firmly down. My gaze met his, and I wondered why my pulse was still galloping along.

His was too. His skin was warm, and I didn't let him let go.

We had a whole silent conversation, his eyes communicating; mine speaking back. But I'll be damned if I knew exactly what was said.

He probably wasn't very used to being touched. We held the rag to my bleeding lip for a minute or so before I could bring myself to look away, over his shoulder at the curtains moving on a slow, soft night breeze. The electric lights were bright and comforting, and I smelled approaching rain.

Maybe even a storm. I could just curl up in the gallery with a book and watch it on my lunch break.

I do like storms. When I'm not trudging through them soaked and cold and uncertain, that is.

Finally I let him go and took the washcloth, doubling it over and wiping at my lip again. "There," I said. "How's that? Any more blood?"

"It looks painful." He stayed kneeling, his gaze fixed to my mouth, one hand on the arm of the chair, the other one dropped. "You'll have a lovely scar."

"Ouch." I grimaced, experimentally, fresh scabs crinkling. The feeling was less than comfortable. "Well, I won't win any prizes. Certainly not the Miss Congeniality award. I've been awfully rude today."

"You fit right in." His tone was so ironic I laughed, a sad little sound. "Dinner's waiting, Isabella. Do you want my arm?"

"You can keep it," I said smartly, trying to decide if my legs would carry me. "What would I do with three of them?" What I *really* wanted, I realized, was to get close enough to lay my head on his shoulder again and feel that novel sense of...what?

Safety? The relief of leaning on something steady and unmoving?

His expression shifted again. Was that a flash of hurt?

I sighed. Poor guy. "Cheese and tripe. I'm sorry. That was a joke. Yes, I'd like to lean on your arm a little, at least down the stairs."

"We'll eat in the solarium," he said. "I thought you'd like it, all the ferns and palms. It's still warm, and it's right next to the kitchen."

Sounds great. Solarium, he called it. I'll bet he called the living room a parlor, too.

I waited, but he didn't move. "You'll have to move so I can stand up."

He subtracted the cloth deftly from my fingers and rose with fluid grace. He vanished into the bathroom again, and I made it unsteadily to my feet.

I had to stop doing this to myself.

Ever since Mom…went, I've been acutely aware of just how little time most of us have. When I was running from one thing to the next, not stopping even to eat, I didn't have to think about anything painful, did I?

Tremont returned, running his fingers back through his hair as if he wanted it to stay down. He halted beside me, offering his arm like Fred Astaire in an old movie. Or Cary Grant. "Here." He didn't look at me. "If you like."

I slid my hand through, grateful for the support. "Thanks." I meant it, tried to make it sound less tired and more thankful. "Really, Jeremy. Thank you. I'd have been all right, but still. You're a nice guy."

"I'm aiming for niceness." He guided me out of the room with short careful steps. He left the lights on, I didn't argue with him. It was his electric bill. "At least, for your sake."

Now that my blood sugar level was rising, I was beginning to feel a little less wild. The world had stopped guttering like a candleflame. I had my hand on his arm, and he reached over with his other hand and laid it across mine, anchoring me. There was that same feeling again, of my pulse speeding up at the touch of his skin.

"I usually don't crash that hard. Sorry if I freaked you out." I tried to sound as repentant as I felt.

"There's no need to apologize." He stared straight ahead until we reached the stairs leading to the kitchen; there, he spared me a single glance. "We'll go slowly down the stairs, no?"

"Lead on, Tremont. I'll keep up."

He nodded, stepped down one, waited for me, stepped down another.

"Oh, for Christ's sake," I said after about five of these, "come *on*." I dragged him down the rest of the way.

Calamus was already in the kitchen, holding a glass of red wine. His threadbare clothes were neatly arranged.

"Holy—" he muttered, and glanced at Jeremy, who stiffened slightly. "Miss Isabella," Calamus continued, formally. "Are you quite all right?"

I restrained the urge to crack a joke, for once. "Fine. Had a little accident with my blood sugar. I'm all right now."

He performed an odd little half-bow, his hand twitching as if he wanted to sweep a cocked hat. The wine swirled uneasily in his glass. "I apologize. You're a part of the household, and due my respect."

Good Lord. "It's *fine*, Cal. I'll promise not to be offended if you promise not to try to offend me. Okay?"

He shot an amazed glance at Tremont, who was content just to stand there and glower, his hand trapping mine in the crook of his elbow.

"I can promise that," the ragged man finally said. "Tremont seems to have taken quite a shine to you, young lady."

Jeremy tensed next to me. I don't know why, but I brought up my free hand and patted his upper arm, soothingly. "He's a nice guy. Hey, can we eat now? I'm starving."

"Your wish is our command," Tremont said, not sounding in the least sarcastic.

CHAPTER THIRTEEN

It was a nice dinner, steak and mashed potatoes and salad with vinaigrette. Garlic bread, steamed vegetables. I skipped the wine and stuck to milk. My lip stung with the pepper rubbed into the steak, and the vinaigrette.

Calamus had evidently made up his mind to be charming. He'd been to a lot of the same cities I had, and we traded down-and-out stories. One in particular, about wharfside rats in New York, made me shiver.

Tremont said next to nothing, but he listened with a great deal of apparent amusement, especially to my stories. Unfortunately, he also went still and tense when I told some of my only-funny-in-retrospect tales— like how I left New Orleans twice, or the incident with the wannabe-vampire coven in Mankato. I found myself sticking to lighter subjects after that, but the oddest things made him uncomfortable.

I was too damn tired to wonder why.

He filled Cal's glass when it ran dry, ate with his exquisite manners, and prodded the conversation when it looked like it was heading for dangerous territory. By the time we were all finished, Cal was three sheets to the wind and had loosened up considerably, and I was sleepy. I excused myself after dessert and was halfway to my feet when Tremont rocketed up. "Shall I walk you to your room, Isabella?" he asked, and Calamus snorted into his wineglass, trying unsuccessfully to hide it.

Jesus. I hope his other guests aren't all like this. "I'm a big girl, Jeremy. Thank you. Have a few more drinks." Smiling made my lip hurt. I felt a lot better, just sleepy. "I'm going to go sleep for about fifteen hours."

"Please do." He studied my face, a scrutiny I found I didn't mind. "Goodnight then, Isabella."

"Goodnight. Night, Cal."

"Pleasant dreams," Cal shot back. I shook my head and left them there.

I paused in the kitchen to fill a glass with water, and heard Calamus again. "A prithee—a pretty lady, Jeremy."

"Shut up." Tremont didn't sound amused. "You behaved yourself."

"Good for me. Only takes one threat. She's—"

"I said shut up." Silence crackled, and I carried my water glass away. The eavesdropping in this house qualified as an Olympic event, I decided. I wasn't quite sure yet if I was going to throw politeness to the winds and start sneaking around.

I was mighty close, though.

I found a pile of clean clothes in my room, put them away, locked the door and doused the lights. Fitful starshine pierced the building clouds, and I decided to wait until another night to use the salt. I also decided to have one last smoke and opened up the window, settling myself in the window seat with a cigarette and my cards.

I settled with a half-swallowed groan and heard movement below.

The cougar was back, filling a pool of shadow where only the gleam of its eyes and its stillness gave it away. "Well, hello." I squinted. It was definite, even though the light was bad.

The cougar had stripes.

Whoever heard of a striped cougar? Especially such a big one.

Ergo: not a cougar. What the hell?

It gazed silently up, not even flicking an ear.

"I've had a busy day," I said, softly, knowing the cat could hear. "I almost passed out from seeing the future again. I guess maybe it's not such a great talent, huh? My mother always called it fifty-fifty, curse and gift."

The cat, of course, said nothing. But I got the feeling he was listening.

"Something's going on here." The cat didn't move a muscle. "I don't know what, but I'm going to find out. Tremont's in some kind of trouble. I can feel it."

The cat cocked his head, the tip of his tail twitching. I took a drag off my smoke. "Nice eyes. I'm not used to shy guys. But I like him. It's a pity he's not a jerk, I'd be tempted to date him, job be damned." I took another drag, ashed into a convenient little brass dish I'd found on the nightstand. "But he's got major baggage. I wish you could tell me what's going on. I bet you know."

The cat flicked his tail again. I pulled my knees up on the window seat. "I like it here. I hope I can stay for a while."

The cat, of course, did not reply.

CAL LEFT BEFORE DAWN THAT morning. I found this out when I tripped blithely into the library at nine a.m. to start work. Tremont handed me a cup of coffee with cream and the news. "Cal said to tell you goodbye, and good luck."

"Well, wasn't that nice of him. Good morning to you." *Give me the caffeine and I'll let you live.*

"Good morning. Let's go down to the kitchen, you need breakfast."

"I'll be okay—" I began, and he fixed me with an utterly serious look, eyebrows drawn together and that sculpted mouth tight.

"Breakfast, Miss Harpe. That's an order." He looked determined, but his gaze sparkled with pure mischief.

I rolled my eyes. He was wearing the same musky, natural-smelling cologne. I tried not to be obvious about getting a good lungful of it. "Whatever, lord and master. Wish I could give orders with that kind of authority."

"You can ask for anything you want."

I thought he was making another one of those ironic jokes. "What, jump over the moon? No thanks. I'm a low-maintenance type of girl. All right, a nice little breakfast it is." My lip had bled overnight, and twinged a little when I washed my face.

I'm usually a quick healer.

He nodded, his hair falling over his forehead. "How are you feeling this morning?" His eyes strayed over my face, lingered on my bottom lip. I'd worried at my lip with my teeth overnight, and it had bled more too. Yuck.

"A little tired, but okay. My lip hurts."

"I don't doubt it." For a moment he seemed about to say something else, then shook his shaggy golden head. "Come. Breakfast first. I shall undertake to feed you regularly."

I tugged the crocheted vest down with one hand—black velvet bellbottoms, a blue paisley shirt, and the vest, barefoot and clean, my patented Woodstock refugee look. "Nice of you, Ward Cleaver."

Okay, so I said it *sarcastically*. As sarcastically as I could.

"I live to serve," he shot back, and I found myself laughing. Even before coffee.

I followed him down to the kitchen and we had breakfast—sesame waffles, hash browns, toast, and soy-substitute sausages. I raised my eyebrows at that, and Tremont spread his hands a little helplessly. "The house thinks you're a vegetarian, last night notwithstanding. How do you like them?"

They taste like dried tofu. Probably because they are. "They're all right. It's nice to be treated so considerately."

He nodded. "Yes." He took a swallow of coffee, his mug black with worn silver around its rim. "They want very badly to please you."

"It's funny that I haven't seen a single one of them." *Or felt them, or heard them. Not just funny, it's creepy.*

"Be grateful," he returned with barely a pause. "Besides, I like them to be discreet."

"They're not discreet, they're invisible. There's a difference." *Invisible servants. I bet there are a few East Coast society matrons who wish they could patent that process.*

"True," he agreed. "I like order. Predictability."

I bit into another carefully into another sausage. Pseudo-sausage. Whatever. "Okay. I get it, you run a tight ship. Jeez. How did I end up here? You probably even vote Republican."

He set his coffee cup down and fixed me with a quelling, blue-eyed look. "Isabella," he said, very gently. "I will allow you a great deal, but please, don't ask me about the servants. And don't try to bait me. I don't advise it."

I set my fork down to match, almost annoyed. Did he think I was stupid, or that I wouldn't notice the lack of light refraction in the household staff? I'd seen stranger things, but it would have helped to have him at least *address* the issue honestly. "I'm not baiting you. If I was, you'd know it. You seem kind of staid and starchy. I wonder why you picked me." *I'm a witch, Tremont. You think a few invisible things are going to bother me?*

Then again, the frog-goblin had really thrown me.

"You were the only applicant." His eyes hooded, their vivid blue strangely dark in the sunlight coming through the windows.

"Cal said you've turned down a lot of librarians."

"Most of them didn't come in response to the ad. You were the only one that seemed even remotely plausible. And..."

I didn't know why I wanted to piss him off. Probably because he was a decent guy. I didn't know how to handle decent guys. If he'd been a jerk I would have been on safer ground. "And what?" I pushed.

He made a little face, as if he was sucking on something medicinally bitter. "And you were polite, and well-spoken, and you occurred by just as I had finished making the promise to myself that I would hire the next person that came by. You were the answer to a prayer, Miss Harpe."

I made a face. He wasn't going to give. Whatever was happening here, I had to figure it out on my own. "I'm a regular angel in disguise. Hey, I need to get to work to earn what you're paying me, okay? I'm stuffed. I couldn't eat another bite."

"You're sure?" He studied me over the rim of his coffee cup. Now, with Cal gone, he was a lot easier with his scarred face. Then he would remember, and jerk his head forward a little so his hair fell down. It was the closest thing to a nervous tic he had.

"I'm sure." My chair scraped as I rose, an annoying *teeek* sound. He rose too, quickly, with those manners again. "You don't have to, Jeremy. I'm just going to put the dishes in the sink."

"Leave it. It's not your job."

"It's just some dishes." *What the hell is your problem, Tremont?*

"Please, Isabella. Leave it."

What, the invisible staff needs a workout? Fine. "It's your house. I presume I can get to work?"

He nodded. "I'll be along."

I retreated, biting my already-sore lip to keep from making a snide comment. This guy was really too much.

CHAPTER FOURTEEN

THE DAYS QUICKLY SETTLED INTO a regular rhythm. Up between seven and nine, run downstairs to the kitchen for a quick breakfast, trying to catch a glimpse of the mysterious servants. Then I'd go back to the library with a stainless-steel travel cup full of coffee and cream and get down to business. I'd break at one or so for lunch, usually a gulped PB & J and a glass of milk, and then it was more stacking, shelving, et cetera, until the holy four o'clock teatime. Tremont took his tea religiously, and I read for him between five and six. Shakespeare, Ovid, Dante, Lucian, Juvenal—and once he even had me read some Neruda.

I liked that.

He wouldn't say anything but, "That's enough, Isabella. Thank you," when six o'clock rolled around, and I got up, laid the book on the couch next to him, and headed back to shelving or whatever it was I was doing for another hour or two. He usually came down to ask me to dinner at about seven-thirty, and by then I was glad of the respite. He chided me for working too hard, and I agreed with him and kept on going. I didn't know how long I'd be here, so I wanted to do as much as I could before the wind started whispering my name again. My checking account balance started getting bigger and bigger, and I had a nice stash to tide me over when I had to leave next.

I thought I might even be able to buy another car if it kept up.

It didn't take me long to figure out that he watched me. I got used to it—he only stared. He never tried anything, and did his best to be looking elsewhere when I glanced at him. And it was his library, he had a right to be there.

I still hadn't used the salt. I didn't know why. My mother's voice had spoken so clearly, but she didn't speak again, and I decided to wait.

When the time was right, I'd know. Or maybe I was afraid of what would happen if I used it.

Jeremy's manners stayed. I asked him to quit getting up when I came into the room, but he kept right on with it, especially at mealtimes. About the only time he didn't leap to his feet was when I finished reading and laid the book next to him. He would sit, his eyes closed or fixed out the windows, immobile.

I liked that best of all.

Spring had folded into early summer by the time I started my nightly explorations of the Tremont house. I stayed in my room for an hour or so after saying goodnight, smoking, picking at my nails, pacing, trying to read.

Then I'd unlock the mermaid door, check the hall, and step out to begin my explorations.

The house was a lot bigger than it looked, even though it looked like a huge pile already from the outside. First floor and the basement didn't hold my interest much; the basement gave me the creeps and held no skeletons of any sort.

I was almost disappointed.

The only part of the first floor I visited regularly was the laundry room. No matter what time I ventured by there, the washers or dryers or both (there were three of each) were almost always running. It was a cheerful room floored with yellow linoleum and smelling of fabric softener and clean cloth, something I've always associated with safety. Sometimes, when I checked, my own clothes were in the dryer. If so, I'd wait for them, sitting on the table that held folded shirts (but never stacks of underwear). When the dryer buzzed I would fold my own clothes and carry them upstairs, I might also put the clothes in the washer in the dryer. I never saw a pile of dirty clothes, and I never saw another human being—though once, when I came into the laundry room, I saw a large basket on top the dryer, one of Tremont's black sweaters finishing falling into it, neatly folded. A breeze smelling of warm bread and fabric softener touched my cheek as I rounded the corner, and I saw a shimmer in the air, like heat above pavement on a summer.

"Wait!" I said, and the shimmer paused in the air, hovering in the long hall leading to the laundry room, uncertainly. The smell of fresh-baked bread was almost overwhelming. "I've been meaning to thank you." I addressed it as if it was a person. "You do a wonderful job with my clothes. I really appreciate it."

Great. If it's a brownie it'll probably never come back.

The shimmer quivered and sped away; I almost thought I saw the painting hung on the end of the hall move a little as whatever-it-was passed.

The laundry kept getting folded, so it probably wasn't a brownie. It was good to have at least one certainty.

If I hadn't been accustomed to a slightly more elastic version of reality than most, it might have given me some problems. As it was, I felt a sneaking sense of relief, and didn't visit the laundry room so much.

Instead, I prowled the second and third floors. I studied the paintings in the gallery for a whole week, moving from one to the next. He had a van Dyck, and a Raphael I was almost certain was legit, as well as a van Gogh I was less sure of. It would have taken me weeks to go through them all, but I ended up spending most of my time on the four Pollacks and a whole clutch of portraits of blond men and different women—most with a certain merry tilt to their mouths, as if they had just been told a joke—dressed in Puritan and then Victorian; then 20's flapper, Depression-era beauties, a war-era matron, and one large oil painting of a woman who had Jeremy's electric blue eyes and a shy, beautiful smile. She wore a very Jackie Kennedy white sheath and gloves, her dark hair pulled back from a sweet heart-shaped face.

The men were all very handsome, but they all looked grim. I liked looking at the women better, and looking at the woman in white most of all. I spent almost a whole night in the gallery, settled on the floor and wishing I could smoke while I watched her portrait, almost certain that if I waited long enough she would talk.

None of the portraits were labeled.

There was a reproduction of Canova's *Cupid & Psyche* in the gallery, and another Minotaur marble, one which I thought might actually be the real deal. The woman in white seemed to glance at the Minotaur sadly every once in a while, but that might have been just nerves on my part.

One rain-drenched night—the storms came in with distressing regularity, there was a fresh thunderstorm every three or four days and a shower every afternoon like clockwork—I waited only a half hour after bedtime before sallying forth. I had a dim thought of going to the gallery again, but instead I wandered through the third floor for a while and decided to take the stairs down to the laundry room and see if I could catch the shimmer again. I was beginning to find my way around, learning shortcuts—although some parts of the house were almost willfully determined to be confusing and I kept ending up more often than not at the end of the second floor hall that held my room.

I crept along the open hall on the second floor with its fantastically carved balustrade on one side, looking down into the immense checkerboard foyer with the ticking grandfather clock, when a rattling series of thumps shook the front door.

I actually let out a thin cry of surprise and flinched. My heart leapt up in my throat and hammered, preventing me from swallowing and also making me croak when I tried to inhale. Thunder crumpled wetly overhead.

The chandelier suddenly blazed, and I shrank back into the shadows of the hall. I'm surprised the walls didn't shake, my heart was thudding so loud.

I heard a slow, measured step I'd know anywhere, and the faint squeak of the door hinges. "Smith." Tremont's voice, low and cold. "It's the middle of the night."

"It can't wait." This voice was male, and pleasant except for the crawling sense of blind white maggots it evoked. It sounded like a social call, though Tremont didn't sound particularly social. "Trouble with the Pastes over on Seventh Avenue. You going to clear that nest out, or give me a few quanta?"

What the hell is this? I sank down to my knees and worked forward, too curious to think about little things like politeness and spying and eavesdropping. The din of rain striking the porch roof echoed against the marble floor.

This hall gave out onto the grand staircase leading down to the foyer, but a smaller part of it split off to a door that lead to another maze of halls and a stair that would take me almost directly to the laundry room. I peered through the balustrade, glad it was carved with flowers and vines; it was pretty, if a little overdone, and the shadows up here would hide me—I hoped.

"Since when are you interested in clearing the *vrkolak* out of town, Smith? Get out of here." Tremont didn't even sound like himself. He sounded like bad news, the words so cold and sharp that if I hadn't been looking down through the railing and seen his familiar shape—black sweater, jeans, heavy boots, leonine hair—I wouldn't have thought it was him.

"Still scarred, I see. Why don't you let the pretty girl out to play? We'd all love to meet her." The voice made me shiver.

There was no other female in the house, not that I'd ever met. There was a bright flash outside, a long pause.

"Maybe she has entirely too much taste to hang around with the likes of you. Guests at my house are sacrosanct, Smith. Get off my property." Tremont now sounded dismissive. Thunder overlaid the last sentence, almost as if he'd planned it for maximum effect.

My hands were icy. I looked down at my shadowed arms, saw goosebumps the size of dimes rising under the skin. *Vrkolak.*

I knew that word. Some people thought it meant *vampire*. It doesn't, it's a catchall term for just about anything nasty that will eat whatever it can, whether it be human or otherwise. Kine don't quite qualify as *vrkolak*, but my mother and I had met quite a few things that did—things that had very little trouble eating a witch if the mood took them, if said witch wasn't careful.

The world was a lot darker and stranger than anyone supposed, and if not for a witch's finely-developed sense of danger...well, some bad things could have happened to me. To my mother. To us both.

Vrkolak had once meant witch, or sorcerer, or night-wandering spirit. Now it simply meant two things: *not human* and *hungry*.

So whoever this was at the door knew about the strange side of the world. And by extension, so did Tremont.

Oh, come on, Isabella, a man who lives in a house with invisible laundry-maids and an occult library, who knows about witches and isn't bothered by them; of COURSE he knows about hungry predators. The question is, is he one of them?

I didn't think he was. My instincts weren't *that* off.

"Is she the cursebreaker?" Smith asked.

Wait a minute, Cal said something about that too. I barely breathed, didn't shift my weight, my ears prickling and tingling.

Tremont made a quick movement. There was a sound suspiciously like fist meeting flesh. "Get away from my house, *djambeling*," he said softly. "Or I will come out and hunt you."

He shut the door, not waiting for a reply, and stood in the empty foyer, one hand out, spread against the front door. His hand was big, but there was something strange about it; maybe it was a trick of the light. The darkness in his aura swirled, funneling around him. His shoulders hunched as the house reverberated under the lash of thunder.

It was a bad storm, coming down off the mountains and walking between the houses with bars on their windows.

The people here go mad after dark.

Was the town suffering an infestation of *vrkolak*? It wasn't unlikely—they tended to drift to urban areas, good eating. There wasn't enough wilderness to lose yourself in anymore, not if you wanted to eat what so many nonhuman species did—everything from rotten meat to the scent of certain emotions or perfumes. I'd even run across a snakelike thing in New York that fed on terracotta statues and was in the habit of quoting Keats and Whitman.

Another mystery laid over the first, one veil on top of another. Or maybe a part of the deeper puzzle. Just who was this scarred, quiet man?

"Isabella," he said, and I jumped guiltily. But he didn't say it like he suspected my presence. No, he said it like it was something private, as if my name meant something to him.

His shoulders straightened. I doubt I could have shoveled my jaw up from the floor at that point.

"Isabella," he said again, very softly, under another rattling roll of thunder. "I'm a fool."

Strangely enough, listening to the conversation hadn't made me feel guilty, but this did. My cheeks flared with heat there in the dark, and I prayed he wouldn't come up the grand stairs. After a while I heard movement, the chandelier's light falling away as if sliced. Dazzled by sudden darkness, I froze, listening to the rain fingering walls and roof.

I felt like I'd just been caught peeking through Tremont's underwear drawer.

A curse. A curse, and a scarred man in a house with invisible servants and a fantastic library. *How do I get myself into these things? Was I born under a lucky star or what?*

I made it up to my feet, my knees shaking. All this nightly wandering-around; I'd have to start napping in the afternoons to catch up with sleep.

I suddenly wanted very badly to go back to the room behind the mermaid door and pull the covers up over my head with the door firmly locked. This was too much even for me.

What was it about the way he said my name that sounded so...private?

I made my way on cat-soft, bare feet through the dark house. The statues watched me, especially when I passed yet another Minotaur bronze. Someone had liked the myth, apparently, though I couldn't tell why. A labyrinth, a ball of string, a princess scorned—or a prince sacrificed in the older versions of the story, before the monster-killers had begun to triumph. My mother had always preferred the older myths, and taught them to me almost before I could talk.

I reached the mermaid door without incident and gratefully locked it, staring at the now-familiar shapes of vanity, bed, rug...and the window, running with rivulets of water and occasionally lit with a photographer's flash of lightning. The mountains caught the weather in summer, like Florida with its afternoon drenchers.

I leaned against the door, my heart hammering and the sour taste of fear in my mouth. Then, again, I heard footsteps.

I swallowed. The steps paused at my door. I closed my eyes, my entire body one giant, listening ear.

What was Jeremy Tremont doing outside my door after that conversation?

A slight creak. My back was to the door, and I suddenly wondered if he had reached out, touching the mermaid's carved, fish-scaled hip. That would put his hand against my back, on the other side of a heavy wooden panel. My skin warmed at the thought.

My mother's voice echoed inside my head. *You should be planning your escape, my dear. This is too much even for you.*

Thunder, rain, silence; the crackling static of someone right outside my bedroom door.

I heard him under the steady sound of the rain, walking away. I listened until the sound of the rain melted them into an indistinct blur.

My throat was dry. My knees felt like melted butter. My eyes smarted, dryly.

I finally peeled myself away from the door and lit a cigarette. I had to brace my elbows on the nightstand, my arms shook so badly. I carried the ashtray to the window seat and popped the glass open just a little, not caring if the rain came in. Townlights glimmered through the falling water, now seeming more like hard bright little eyes than the welcoming pinpricks of civilization.

Lightning flashed, etching every dripping leaf and wind-tossed rosebush below. I gasped, choking on cigarette smoke.

Below my window in his accustomed place was the striped beast. I only caught a flash, because in the split instant of lightning he was already moving back under the shadow of a carefully trimmed evergreen hedge. *That's another thing. Who takes care of the frocking lawn, an Invisible Gardener? Does he do his work in the nude? Does it matter?*

The other thought was even more breathless and panicky. *Cougars don't have stripes.*

I lifted the cigarette to my mouth with a trembling hand.

Why don't you let the pretty girl out to play? We'd all love to meet her. The soft, maggot-writhing voice intruded again, touching off another spate of shaking. I was suddenly very glad I was inside 4444 Tremont. Invisible servants and weird scarred shy men I could handle. I could even take a stab at handling bankers that were really frog-goblins in human skin. They were probably more honest than *human* bureaucrats.

But things that sounded like the man at the front door and *vrkolak* I most definitely could not handle. The best way to deal with those was to push down the gas pedal and get the hell out of Dodge before they noticed you.

The storm receded as I smoked that cigarette, and lit another. My hands weren't shaking quite so badly.

Curse. Jeremy Tremont had a curse.

Well, I was a witch, wasn't I?

Don't get involved. Get out. Get out of here now.

Oh, it was too late for that.

If I left, for the rest of my life I would hear Jeremy Tremont saying my name in the vast empty foyer, softly, privately. As if he liked the sound of it.

I finally finished my lung cancer for the day, closed my window, and stumbled for the bed. I was gone as soon as my head hit the pillow. By the time morning dawned and I had to get up, I could almost chalk the dozy terror up to a dream.

Except for the fact that I avoided the foyer for a few weeks. Especially at night.

I WENT BACK TO THE headshop every week for more candles, and ended up the fifth time scoring some weed from a nervous, skinny kid with a shock of black hair and dark eyes. The ghost of acne still clung to his cheeks, and he jittered in place like he was always on a meth jag. The tingle in my fingers told me he wasn't a narc, so I went ahead.

I wasn't sure how Jeremy would feel about a joint or two— after all, it was his house, and he was so staid and starchy. Still, I went back to the house whistling an old Led Zep tune, carrying my candles and some sorely needed recreation.

For once, I hadn't told Jeremy I was going anywhere; the headshop was an hour and a half walk and I needed the exercise. The sky was overcast and the humidity high by the time I let myself in the front door, vaguely surprised to find him at the bottom of the grand staircase, alone in the huge marble-floored foyer. Just…sitting there, his chin in his hands, his blue eyes slitted, and I could tell by the set of his shoulders that he was angry.

Since my little adventure in eavesdropping, I'd grown a lot better at figuring out his moods. Neither of us spoke much, existing in a comfortable silence broken only by *can you pass the salt?* and *here's that book.* Except, of course, my afternoons of reading to him. Lately it was Trollope, Shakespeare (*King Lear*), Thoreau, and Neruda (in Spanish, of course.)

The silence between us after he said *that's enough, Isabella, thank you,* was always full of dangerous questions neither of us asked.

"Hey there." I said, hefting the paper bag of weed and candles. It had been sunny when I left at about ten in the morning, and it was two-thirty now, clouds drifting in from the north. Another big afternoon storm, thunder in the distance. "What are you up to?"

"Waiting for you." His irises burned, the endless blue of summer when the sky is infinite and hot.

My smile felt like a mask. "I worked through the weekend, I thought you wouldn't mind if I took a couple hours today. Is that a problem?"

He shook his head. "No problem, I was simply worried. I would have made the car available to you." He bit off the end of each word, and I put my hands on my hips.

Or tried to, paper crackled as I smacked the candles against my leg. *Good one, Isabella. Very graceful. Ouch.* "Look, Jeremy, you're pissed off. I can see it. Why don't you just yell at me now and get it over with?"

"I don't want to yell at you." His shoulders slumped, his mouth pursing again. "You said yourself you have to go when the wind calls. I was wondering if today was that day."

It was the most personal thing he'd said in weeks. My jaw almost dropped. "I wouldn't go while I owed you work. That would make me a thief." I couldn't quite let it go at that, though. "And I wouldn't go without telling you."

"Do you promise? It would save me worrying."

Here was a golden opportunity, so I picked every word carefully, consideringly. "There's all sorts of odd things happening here. I might leave if I find out you've been lying to me about any of them." *Say something about the midnight visitors, Jeremy. Say something about* vrkolak, *or the curse. Say something about the invisible servants. Say something about* me, *for God's sake!*

He made a little waving motion with his hand, brushing that away. "Barring that. Can you promise?"

"Barring that." A smile tugged at the corners of my lips, this one much more natural. What was it about him that amused me so much? I even secretly liked that unconsciously-arrogant tone. *Inside every shy man lurks a real he-man Tarzan, I guess.* "I promise."

He nodded. "All right." His shoulders were slumped as if he was tired and sore. Why? He'd been fine when I'd left this morning.

"I scored some weed." Now was as good a time as any to test his tolerance for herb. "You ever done any?"

His face changed slightly. "No." No hint of disapproval, just surprise. "Never."

"Well, never too late to try." I couldn't help myself. *Watch me be a bad girl, you starchy straight arrow.* "It'll relax you. You need a little R & R, you're pretty intense." I kicked the door shut behind me, gently, and cocked my head, shoving my hair back from my forehead. *I just walked right past where that man was standing. Smith.* A shiver traced up my back. "What do you say?"

"If it will make you happy." His hair was getting shaggier and shaggier. "After dinner, then?"

My God. "Better before, but okay. Hey, you need a haircut, buddy. When are you going into town?" I walked across the foyer, my boots clicking on the marble squares, and plopped down onto the stairs right next to him, lighting a cigarette. A crystal dish sat between us; I used it for an ashtray, wondering why he'd carried it there. "Or I could do it for you."

That earned me a sidelong glance. "All right," he said. "If it will make you happy."

"Great. Except if I did it, it would look like a weed whacker attacked you." I smoked in silence until I couldn't keep quiet any longer. "You keep it long to hide your face, don't you." It wasn't a question.

"I don't know. I just like it this way."

The sense of a door closing in my face was definite, inescapable. "All right. No haircut. It's teatime, isn't it. What am I reading today?"

"Blake," he answered, glancing sidelong at me. His eyes were very blue, and he was still tense. "Unless you're too tired."

"Nope." *Running around the house at night makes me tired, but I'm okay right now. Thanks for asking.* I took another drag off the cigarette, ground it out. "I'll go take my shoes off and get cleaned up. Meet you in the kitchen?"

"Would you like tea in the library?" We were back to stiffly formal.

Serves me right, too. "Fine." I hauled myself up to my feet, my bag bumping against my side. "Jeremy?" I gave him a sharp look, bending down. He tipped his chin up, his hair falling away. "Will you just admit you're upset?"

"I was worried," he mumbled, that blue gaze boring into mine.

The impulse to touch him hit me, hard and fast. I cupped his chin, tipping his face further so I could really examine him.

"Yeah," I breathed. "You look mad." *What am I trying to do here?*

As if I didn't know.

"Worried," he repeated, breathlessly. Ridged skin, supple leathery scars under my palm and fingertips. The contact was warm, and I smelled that musk cologne again. "Very worried. I came to the library to check on you and you were gone. I thought—" He stopped. "Isabella."

I let go, slowly releasing the pressure. "Okay. You pass the exam. I'll meet you in the library."

I brushed past, every inch of my skin alive and flaming. I'd actually touched him again, and I'd felt what he was feeling as clear and sharp as a jolt of horse to a junkie's system.

I'd have to be careful.

You're a very pretty girl.

I wasn't used to guys that didn't buy me a drink or ask me to dance. I doubly wasn't used to guys that were so shy as to be crippled when it came to deciphering the signals of female interest.

And what about that curse? And the frog-goblin, and the bloody teeth, and the *vrkolak*, and midnight visitors that sounded like slimy blind maggots crawling into your ears.

What was I still doing here? The kids at the headshop were normal enough. I'd seen a couple things that weren't quite usual at the thrift stores—a woman with long hair tinged with green, her hands knob-roughened, a squat man with high pointed ears. Nothing that felt dangerous.

At least, not during the day.

I made it to my room, washed my face, and took my boots off. Barefoot, I picked up my messenger bag and went downstairs for tea.

He had settled in the library, contemplating a silver teapot and two mugs. We'd fallen into habit very quickly, he and I, a nice cozy little domestic routine. I watched as he rose, his eyes on the floor now, blinking fiercely enough to look owlish instead of prim.

He had indeed been worried, worried *sick*. I wasn't sure I liked this intensity of feeling from him. You shouldn't ever date your boss, it causes all sorts of problems.

So here I was in the Twilight Zone, with a boss who had the hots for me and a library that seemed almost to want to run itself...although that was another story.

I dropped down into the chair opposite his. There was no fire today, and the open window to the witch's garden carried in a breath of lavender. Bees buzzed drowsily out among the flowers and herbs. "You can stop the gentleman thing, Tremont. I don't need you to stand up like a jack in the box."

"I like it." He lowered himself gently into his own chair. "Tea?"

"Is there any coffee? I only had one cup this morning."

"Right here." He poured me a mug of coffee, added cream, and I picked up a cream-cheese-and-cucumber sandwich. Today was a light tea day—yesterday it had been roast beef sandwiches, with horseradish and saffron. Just the sort of thing I'd been craving, actually. How about that for weird? "Are you feeling well, Isabella? You look...thoughtful."

I gave him a distracted glance. *Throw me a bone, Tremont. Give me a clue. Any clue.* "I've noticed the library seems to be putting books away for me, once I decide where I want them. Would you have anything to do with that?"

He shrugged. "We all want to please you." He selected a sandwich of his own, took a token bite, laid it down.

The green reek of approaching rain on the breeze didn't really soothe me. "You know, I'm beginning to feel more like a guest and less like an employee. As soon as I decide where I want the books, it's like they put themselves away. If I leave a stack out overnight they're gone in the morning, neatly shelved as the New York Public. Have you been coming along behind me?"

He shrugged. "Have another sandwich. I occasionally put a book or two away. That's all."

"It's strange," I said, watching his eyes. He examined the table, darted a quick glance to my hand. As if he didn't quite have the nerve to look at my face. It was too bad, I was just warming up. Whether he liked it or not, we were going to get some things straight. "Really strange."

"I know," he said. "Believe me, I know."

I pulled my legs up into the chair, wiggled my bare toes. A white cotton peasant top and jeans was by far the best work uniform I'd ever had. I had a long crocheted vest in black too, and a pair of purple glass mushroom earrings I'd got at the thrift store and had to disinfect. They swung against my cheeks as I turned my head. "Jeremy," I said gently but firmly. "It's about time for some answers."

"Have some more coffee." His eyelids dropped a fraction, that was all. The library ticked and groaned with the afternoon silence of older houses, all the wood singing its slow song of expansion.

You're not getting off that easy, bucko. I finished the cream-cheese sandwich with dainty little bites. "You're doing this cards-close-to-the-vest thing. What's so bad you can't tell me about it?"

"Can't," he said. "That's a good word."

I groaned inwardly. "Okay, fine. We're doing Blake today. Good fucking deal."

"Language," he said mildly. "Isabella."

"What's wrong with that word?" I said, leaning forward, putting my feet on the floor and setting down my coffee cup.

"Isabella," he said, but not like he disapproved. As a matter of fact, he was trying not to smile.

"Copulate." I let my eyebrows waggle a little. "Do you prefer *that* word?"

Jeremy choked on his tea. "Isabella—"

"Oh, come on, Jeremy. Set yourself free," I said. "Say it. Come on. Fucking *copulate*."

He almost sprayed tea over himself with a surprised chuckle. "Isabella! Really—"

"There you are, that's the Jeremy I know." I leaned back in my chair. "You were really worried, huh."

"Very." The laughter left, but it was better. He no longer looked so pinched and angry.

Now that we've got that established..."Okay. So who's cleaning up the library after me?"

"The library has decided to obey you. It only needs your direction to organize itself." He said it like it was a dirty secret, holding himself as if he expected a punch. Did he think I would run out the door screaming?

For God's sake, I'm a *witch*.

"Okay. That's a good answer. The library's cleaning itself up? Then what the bloody blue blazes do you need *me* for?"

"It needs your direction. Think of it like a dog, it needs your command to work properly." His mouth twisted briefly. He set his cup down with a click.

Now we're getting somewhere. I nodded. "You're talking about magick. With a *k*. Not the stage variety."

It would be hard for him to look any more miserable. "In a way."

"Okay. So it needs me to figure out where I want the books, then it takes care of it on its own. All right. Sure. Why couldn't it take orders from you?"

He was so still I felt tempted to snap my fingers a couple times. What did he think I was, *normal?* A nine-to-fiver? Would a nice normal girl *ever* have ended up here in Tremont? "Does it frighten you, Isabella?"

I made a big show of thinking about it. "No. Not at all. Well...maybe a little. But not much. I've seen a lot of magick in my time." Like my mother, for instance. I wondered what Jeremy would think if he saw me light the candles and pour out the salt and use the chant...I still hadn't used the salt, I was waiting for the right time. When it would roll along, I didn't know.

The telltale little flicker of heat under my breastbone was anger. How *dare* he act like I was a stupid, brainless little tart without the sense to know real power when I saw it? Did he think he could keep me from talking about it forever?

He nodded. "Drink your coffee." The faint note of command was annoying too.

"Is that why you can't get anyone else to work here? Because it scares them?" I persisted.

"It frightens them." A grudging nod. "Yes. That, and other things."

"Other things?" *Like maybe the curse? Or the things that come to your door in the middle of the night? Or the fact that this town isn't quite right?*

If I went down that road, though, I'd have to admit to sneaking around his house at night, wouldn't I, if I asked him about that? Embarrassment mixed with anger, I took a deep breath, fighting to stay calm. This wasn't going the way I'd intended. "And why doesn't it take orders from you?"

"Not right now, Miss Harpe." His blue eyes were level and completely honest. Or at least, they *looked* completely honest. What was he hiding, why wouldn't he *tell* me?

And we were back to *Miss Harpe* again. Great. Wonderful. Fan-fucking-tastic. "Okay. Not right now. Then when?"

"Please," he repeated, his jaw clenched tight. But his eyes were...pleading, almost. Dark and haunted, in his ruined face.

I took a deep breath, held it for three counts, let it out with a long whistling sound. Took another one, held it, let it out. For the third time.

As a charm to calm me down, it wasn't working.

I set my mug down and stood, slinging my bag over my shoulder.

"Isabella, *please*."

I shook my head, stray curls falling in my face.

"When you want to tell me what sort of thing is going on here, I'll be more than happy to listen." I stalked away.

"Isabella," he said, but I wasn't listening, and he didn't scream. He said it very quietly.

Why did it sound like a despairing cry, then? Add that to the list of things I couldn't figure out.

I made it to the front door and shoved my way out. I was tired and hungry, and I only intended to walk around the garden a little bit until I cooled down, seeing as how I was barefoot and breathing like an obscene phone call. It was a complete surprise to find myself outside the front gate, heading down the sidewalk, still barefoot. I got to the end of the block and sat down on the curb, looking at the blank-faced houses. My hair was a heavy, hot weight against my back—he wasn't the only one who needed a trim.

Clouds massed thick and dark over the town, thunder stirring sleepily against the mountains. I lit a cigarette, looking across the street to a manicured yard full of pansies and peonies and rhododendrons. The house was Spanish Revival, faux stucco and red tile a wee bit out of place this far north.

I suppose you'd only think that if you'd seen a real adobe though, not just imitations.

I rested my chin on my knees. Nobody home. Maybe they were at work during the day.

Was there a mill or something? This was a prosperous little place, more like a small city than a big town. It was a weird amalgamation of fifties America and the heavily strange with a good helping of current capitalism thrown into the mix. In the middle of nowhere, in the bustling town of Tremont, the Kiwanis welcome you. The goblins will hold your money and the *vrkolak* will show you to your seat.

I smoked that cigarette down, field-stripped it, lit another.

I owed Tremont four hundred dollars if I was going to leave tonight. But then, I'd promised, hadn't I? My word was good. It was about the only thing about me that was.

"Mama," I said out loud. "I need you."

Get out the salt then, light your candle, and ask your questions. It's always worked before. What are you waiting for? My mother's voice was deep and soft, the way it had always been. My mother, always seeming to be laughing at some joke nobody else had heard. She'd had my long curling black hair and my bright blue eyes, my cheekbones, my mouth. It was as if we were more sisters than mother and daughter, especially once I hit teenage time.

A full fifteen years she'd been gone, and I still heard her as clearly as if it was yesterday.

"He's a nice guy," I told her memory. "He really is."

That was the hell of it, right there. I wanted to help him. I liked him. If he was cursed, if he was having some kind of problem, I wanted to be the one to fix it.

Isabella Harpe, codependent fixer-upper. I really wanted to see him relax, to maybe hear him laugh a little more without the bitter taste to it. I wanted to show him that he was worth far more than locking himself up in the house. Even a cage with a beautiful library, crammed full of art and the finer things, was still only a cage for someone like him. He deserved galleries in Paris and New York and the theater, plays and indie films and maybe even a concert or two if I could get him to unwind.

Thunder rumbled. I sat very still, closing my eyes, took another drag off my smoke. Opened my eyes to find the world just the same, Tremont Avenue under a pall of weird green stormlight. It was going to be another doozy. What was it about this place that made the weather so funky?

A red Nissan went by slowly, the little old lady driving it gripping the wheel with fanatic determination. I took a deep breath. Did I imagine the shadow of butterfly wings filling the inside of her car, or the fantastic purple glint of her large egg-shaped eyes behind her hornrimmed glasses? Her white hair piled high atop of her head, she didn't look human at all.

I stared after the car until it vanished at the next intersection.

More thunder. The air was full of electricity. I could curl up in the gallery and watch the rain. I'd spent a whole night doing that, about a week ago, and woke up in the library with a blanket snugged around me on the leather couch. Tremont had insisted I take a nap in the afternoon. I couldn't tell who had pulled the blanket over me.

It's a house run by invisible people, unless he does all the cooking and while he probably does some, there's no way he does it all and the dishes too and spends so much time in the library. No way in hell. There's not a speck of dust in the entire house. So the Invisible People do it. For Christ's sake, Isabella, you even saw one of them, that shimmer in the air. You've caught little flickers at the corner of your eye, you know what you're dealing with here.

Major mega weird. Felt just like home.

I remembered that occult shop in Texas, the one with the stuffed alligators and the old woman sitting out front in her rocker, only she never rocked, just sat and watched. The store where you could buy a potion to get rid of a cheating husband, or a pill to make an unwanted baby go away, or a connection to make you rich and famous in return for what? A soul, maybe? *Remember how comfortable, how familiar it all was? And Roberto, telling me that I had the gift.* I sighed. *So I'm here in weirdness up to my eyeballs again. The world's stranger than even Mama thought.*

I'd worked there for three years, all told, a kind of apprenticeship in major-league weirdness. Not the kind, gentle, inevitable magick my mother had practiced, but a different breed. Something harsh and carnivorous and just as inevitable. Whenever I practiced my own, there was always a horrible price. Some acts were necessary, but I didn't have my mother's gift for controlling the aftereffects of my spells. So I'd just settled into drifting along, which was just as well. Skating the edge of weirdness didn't put anyone I cared about in danger.

Of course, who could I say I cared about? I spent most of my time moving from place to place, avoiding getting attached to anything at all.

The sky turned the color of an old bruise. Yellow-green, just like the light. It was going to be a big one.

I finished my second cigarette, lit another. When it started to rain I'd get drenched. And then...I would go back to the house, pick my way over the wet concrete, and go inside. Tremont would probably fire me, I'd just gotten up and walked away from him.

Maybe he didn't want me around for the job. What other use would I be? I wasn't a virgin, so sacrificing was out.

He was scarred so horrifically. What had done that to him? What was the curse?

I wasn't going to find any answers sitting here on the curb. I would have to get out at night and visit a tavern or two, talk to some people, find some things out. Isabella Harpe, girl detective. Then again, this town seemed pretty close-knit. Or maybe just defensive.

I could ask him outright about the scars. Would he tell me?

A cursed millionaire in a house with invisible servants and books that put themselves away. Books on magick, astrology, clairvoyance, sorcery, the occult. Grimoires and ephemerae, books of correspondences, books on how to call demons and banish them, familiar spirits, Holy Guardian Angels.

So what?

So what if he tried some of his reading material and got half his face taken off and a curse in the bargain?

"Well, that's certainly one way to think about it," I muttered, and spatters of rain flirted with hot pavement. An amazing bolt of lightning slammed down in the distance, where the purple bulk of the mountains loomed. *So what the hell am I here for?* I counted to twenty, and the thunder rolled by, a long amazing peal like a freight train at midnight.

Maybe he was just lonely. Stuck, alone in that house, for how long?

Another thing. He never left the house. Was it agoraphobia or something else? He had been just sitting there. Like he wouldn't—or couldn't—leave. Just sitting there boiling, angry, impatient, scared to death?

The rain just kept teasing another ten minutes or so as I sat and mulled over the same ground, over and over. When it came in earnest, it would be quarter-sized drops in sheets. I stood and dusted my jeans off. Two more cars came by—a Taurus and a Volvo, both new, their headlights on. Lights began popping on in the houses. The world went rolling on. No matter what was going on at 4444 Tremont, the rest of the town was doing okay.

I trudged slowly down the block and went back in through the massive gates. They stood ajar, just a little, and I wasn't surprised to see the windows blazing with light.

The ranks of roses hadn't bloomed yet, but the buds were ripening. I saw flashes of crimson on each and every one.

Ill-luck plants, Mom always told me, and for my mother to say ill-luck was dire indeed. *Flowers that drive people mad.*

I reached the cover of the porch. The rain chose that moment to break loose from the clouds and drummed down in solid sheets, lightning flicking off and on. It was going to be a hell of a storm.

It was a relief to have the tension finally broken. I opened up the front door and went in, shaking the damp out of my hair.

The foyer stood empty, lit by the great chandelier. The house was profoundly silent, once I'd closed the door, the bulk of the gray stone—quarried from the local mountains, I'd found out—turned the storm into a distant sound instead of a pressing reality. I glanced up at the shadowed hall behind its carved railing.

Nobody there. Not even a little shimmer in the air.

I made my way to the now-familiar kitchen, which was also brilliantly-lit and empty. I filled the kettle with water, and turned around to find a mug on the counter that wasn't there before. "Thanks," I said to the empty, listening air. "It's some storm, isn't it."

I put the kettle on the stove and was looking around for the teabags when a cupboard door drifted open, showing a shelf with an assortment of teas, each different kind in a neat little glass jars with a fitted lid. "Thanks," I said again, and selected some chamomile. I needed the calming. "I wonder where Tremont is."

No answer. Guess invisible servants don't talk much. I put the glass jar back up on the shelf, closed the cupboard door, and waited for the water to boil.

When it did, I poured myself a cup of it and dumped the rest out, leaving the kettle empty on a cool stove burner. I'd take care of it later, or the invisibles would. "Thank you." I said it gravely, formally, and had that sensation again, like the air itself was listening to me. "I'll be heading up to the library to watch the storm, if anyone needs me."

It was amazing how used to the whole place I'd gotten. I let myself into my library and glanced over, my desk sitting neatly in its expected place. The books all lay where I'd put them, except the stack of poetry tomes I had wanted to shelve tomorrow. Those were gone, probably all where they should be. Obediently.

Like a dog that needed my direction to work properly. He wouldn't answer why the library didn't obey *him*.

Or maybe it did. Maybe he just wanted a reason to keep someone here to talk to.

I went up to the gallery and settled on the leather couch, where Tremont usually sat. A plate of sugar cookies greeted me. I saw no sign of the interrupted tea. I nibbled on a golden, buttery cookie and listened to the thunder.

Lightning crashed down. The house lights didn't flicker. "Can you turn the lights down a little?" I asked, experimentally. "Better for storm-watching."

The lights faded. I could just imagine the dimmer switch twisting all by itself, and that gave me a bit of pause.

"Thank you." I stared at the rain running down the window. It was so much water that the glass itself looked rippled, and the bolts of lightning arcing took on weird shimmers. Thunder rattled the windows.

By seven o'clock I was tired, and I left the library and stumbled up to my room. I'd started thinking of it as my room, just like my library. I suppose you can get used to just about anything. Even I had sense enough to be happy when nobody stole my earnings for smack or gave me a sideways look when I got out my cards. As weird as this place was, it felt just like home.

No.

It felt like *home*. The first place that ever had.

I perched on the window seat and looked out over the garden below, the window slightly open so I could blow smoke out into the rainy air; the wind hit the other end of the house so I was safely in the lee. The lightning strikes were a little less frequent, but the rain still kept up. The town would be flooded if this continued. Thunder rattled, and I amused myself by counting the lightning strikes, watching the clouds shift, and trying not to imagine where Tremont was. I didn't know where he spent his time when he wasn't in the library or at meals. *He must work out sometime*, I figured, *he must have some kind of a life.*

Movement, in the rainlashed garden.

It was half-hidden under the roses, but I caught it when a glare of lightning lit the entire garden. It froze, and why the hell was a not-cougar out in a thunderstorm anyway? It streaked toward the house, a long low liquid shape that looked much bigger than it had at night. *Cougars don't have stripes.* I flinched, expecting to hear the sound of a furred body hitting the windows—or a wall—downstairs. The door to my bedroom was locked, and if there were invisible cooking and cleaning servants I didn't think a big cat—even an impossible, striped one— would trouble them in the slightest.

I lost sight of the animal as it came close to the house, and I was still peering down trying to catch a glimpse of its tail when Jeremy Tremont stepped out, away from the house, shirtless, with his hair slicked down and dark with rain. He was barefoot, and his jeans were soaked. I inhaled sharply, and saw the muscle flickering under his skin.

No wonder his shoulders looked so broad.

I was about to swing the window open and yell a warning down at him—something along the lines of *watch out, there's a cat*—when he stepped away from the house again, and tilted his face up to the rain. His hair fell back; the scarring ran down his shoulder and most of his chest, marred his back and disappeared down into his jeans.

"Gods," I whispered.

He flinched, as if he'd heard me, but maybe it was only because the rain was cold. He stood, half-naked, in the pouring water. Thunder roared.

Jeremy Tremont threw his head back. His mouth opened, but any sound that he made was lost in the thunder that rose to a crescendo. His face twisted into a mask of suffering, his body bent away from the house as if chained but searching for escape. My skin went cold and tight, prickles running down my back and my nipples going hard and pebbly.

I dropped the cigarette in a red ceramic thrift store ashtray and ran for the bedroom door.

It took too long for me to run down the stairs and find the piano room on the ground floor, with its double doors leading to the gardens. It can't have taken as long as I thought, because the last incredible roll of thunder was just fading by the time I wrestled the French doors open and hurled myself outside, where a bucketful of water hit me in the face.

Tremont dropped to his knees, his head still flung back and the cords on his neck standing out.

I grabbed his arm. His skin was cold, slick, and rough with scarring, slippery-wet.

His head snapped down; his eyes, burning blue, glowed through all the running water. I hauled on his arm, feeling for a moment the sheer solid resistance of his weight. If he decided to fight me, I wouldn't be able to drag him.

Instead, he made it to his feet. I found myself on wet, muddy grass, having stepped off the small flagstone patio. There were other plants here, almost beaten flat by the rain—pungent rosemary, I was suddenly irrationally grateful it wasn't roses. I pulled his arm, and he came like a docile child, stumbling a little.

Then I saw the blood along his side, a nasty set of scratches. My heart leapt into my mouth, and I was about to say something to him, but he shook his head.

I got him inside, yanked the French doors closed and bolted them, and turned to find him standing with his head down, water dripping off his hair and fingers and jeans, puddling on the pristine hardwood floor. The Steinway in the center of the room made a slight sound, its strings reverberating to the vibration of thunder, and I jumped.

"There's a big cat out there." It was the closest to a question I could come up with, given the circumstances.

"Or something like one." His fingers flexed, he coughed a little, as if his voice didn't want to work quite correctly. "Absolutely."

I didn't feel gratified that he agreed. "You're bleeding."

He stared at the floor. "You left." Harshly.

Almost accusingly.

"I went down to the end of the block and had a smoke." I was trying to figure out if his eyes would really glow, or if it was just some trick of the light. "What were *you* doing?"

"I..." He trailed off, his eyes roving my face. "I don't know," he said, finally, and crumpled. I caught him—he was heavy enough I stumbled too, my bare feet slipping on the wet floor. He caught himself, making a harsh, tearing little sound of hurt. He almost closed his arms around me, flinched back.

"You're bleeding," I repeated, stupidly. "What the hell *happened?*"

"Nothing." Another one of those guttural sounds, too deep to be a cough, more like a rumbling bark. "I was going too fast."

"What about the cat?" I started ushering him over the slick wooden floor. "Come on."

"You're safe." He shivered, shaking so hard I could barely get him to put one foot in front of the other. My hands slipped on wet skin. "Leave me here."

"Bullshit," I said. "You're half-naked and you can't even walk. What were you doing out in the rain?"

"The weakness will pass. Stop." His hair dripped onto my shoulder, and my feet ached with the cold. "Please."

"Come on." I started hauling him up the stairs. I didn't even remember coming down them, I must have been going pretty fast. It was a miracle I didn't fall and break my fool neck. "What were you doing out in the rain, Tremont? I'd like some answers, you know."

"Can't," he said. "Was looking for you."

"Half-naked?" My voice hit a pitch of disbelief. "Jeremy—"

"Isabella. Please." It was the weariness in his voice that made me stop.

I took a deep breath. We reached the top of the stairs and I dragged him down the red-carpeted hall. My bedroom door was open. I ushered him in and steered him toward the bathroom. He was shivering, huge uncontrolled shudders. Bright spots of crimson pattered on my floor.

"What happened to you?" I wasn't sure I'd like the answer.

"What are you planning to do?" he returned. "Pack your bags and flee?"

Not that it's any of your business, except you're paying me. "I'm going to dump you in a warm shower, to get you to stop shivering," I said. "And I'm going to ask the servants—whatever they are—to bring up some dinner, because I'm starving and you probably are too. And to bring you some clothes, because your jeans are ruined. Why were you out there without a shirt on? And shoes? Huh, Jeremy? Then I'm going to bandage you up, and you're going to tell me what's going on. That's my plan and I'm sticking to it."

His eyelids fluttered, and his eyes rolled back into his head. I shook him. He managed to come back, looked wonderingly at me, and I finished hauling him into the bathroom and flipped the light on, made it to the bathtub. He was dripping instead of pouring water onto the floor now. I twisted the knobs and flipped the little lever that turned the shower on. A gurgle turned into cold water, and soon enough into hot. Steam rose.

"Can you do this or do I have to wash you?" I made it as businesslike as possible. "I've had to hose drunks off before, so I know what I'm doing."

He came back to himself with a galvanic jerk. "No. I can do it."

"All right." I tried not to feel disappointed. "If you're not out in ten minutes I'm coming in to check on you. You dig?"

"Thank you." He grabbed onto the tiled wall, his eyes sliding shut again. "Isabella."

There he went, saying my name in that oddly intimate way again. "Yeah, you're welcome." I left him to it. I didn't close the bathroom door all the way.

I tiptoed to the bedroom door and addressed the thin, expectant hush in the hallway. "We need dinner, and I need some cold water in a pitcher, with two wineglasses. And he needs some clothes pronto, because I don't think he wants to sit around in a towel. I'll also need some bandages and peroxide and Neosporin or something like it, and scissors to cut the bandages, and anything else you can think of."

I was talking to the hallway. Gods.

Was I losing my mind? Weren't you only supposed to be insane if you never doubted your sanity?

Case closed, I was as rational as it was possible to be under the circumstances.

Good for me.

The rain was still coming down steadily, but that amazing crash of thunder had been the last hurrah. Lightning still flickered, but it was far away above the mountains. The rain was merely heavy now, instead of cosmically flooding.

I had to get out my duffel bag. There it was, the bottle of venomous green *Fee Verte*, still half-full; the French sugar cubes were probably stale and battered since I hadn't had any for years. I found the silver absinthe spoon too, it looked like a perforated cake wedge and I wondered if the invisible servants would bring up a pair of honest-to-God absinthe glasses.

I wouldn't put it past them.

I arranged everything on the table just so, my pulse beating thinly in my throat and chest and wrists. Then I sat down, holding the bottle of almost-glowing green wormwood alcohol like an altar boy's dish, and waited.

The shower stopped. I left the bottle on my nightstand, and as I passed the open door to my room I saw a covered tray sitting on the floor outside my door. "Great. Can you put it on the table, and put his clothes on my bed with the bandaging stuff?"

The feeling of listening air returned. No shimmer, though. I knocked on the bathroom door, two quick raps. "Jeremy?"

"Wait." He sounded a lot better. I waited for maybe twenty seconds, pushed the door open.

He had a towel around his waist and another one around his shoulders, and was scrubbing at his hair with a third. The steam in the air drifted in shaggy, huge shapes with teeth and claws, glowing eyes. Hunger showing me below the surface of the world again.

I stepped close enough to feel the heat coming off him, and helped to dry his hair. Tried not to look at his naked, scarred back or the muscle moving under his skin. He was brushed with gold, the hairs on his arm were fringed with blond. He'd probably turn into a nice golden statue in the sunlight. Except for the scarring.

I tried not to think of Speedos and failed miserably. "Here you are," I said, my fingers gentle through the towel on his hair. He submitted without a sound. "That's going to tangle. Come on."

He followed me unsteadily out into the bedroom. I spotted a pile of darkness on the bed. "There are your clothes. Get your pants on, and some warm socks, but leave your shirt off. I want to look at those scratches on your side. I'll be back in a minute."

With that done, I carried a peasant top and a fresh pair of jeans into the bathroom. I didn't use the shower, but I did use the toilet and also washed my face, braided my hair into a single rope, mopped at the end of the braid with the towel.

When I came out, Tremont was sitting on a footstool, and he had bandaged his side himself. He was just in the process of pulling his sweater over his head, and I saw the glaring white of the gauze against his skin. Low on his left side, wrapping almost all the way around. He made soft, clenched sound of pain, and his head jerked up. He saw me, finished pulling his sweater down, tried to stand up.

"Forget it." I gathered up the towels, my clothes and his ruined, sodden jeans from the bathroom floor, and tipped the whole load down the laundry chute. The washers and dryers would be busy tonight.

Did the invisible servants *like* the work? That should have been my first question.

I retrieved the bottle, and collapsed in the chair that the footstool belonged to. I had to brush past him to do so, and I patted his shoulder.

He flinched.

I settled myself in the chair, held up the green-glowing bottle. My hand shook a little, the liquid slopped inside. "This is absinthe. I think we both need a drink."

His eyes widened. "How did you—"

"I have my ways," I said mysteriously. "But I don't think my legs will hold me up. Bring me the pitcher of cold water over there, and the two wineglasses. At least, I asked for them, they should be there."

He gave me another look I couldn't decipher, then pulled himself to his feet, wincing slightly. The tray on the table did hold a silver pitcher, so cold its outside was frosted with little condensation feathers, two wineglasses, and a lovely little fluted-glass sugar bowl piled with fresh white cubes.

I tried not to think about it. My hands moved by themselves, uncapping the bottle, I had to slide down to sit on the floor, propping my back against the chair. Jeremy folded himself down slowly after his second trip, bringing the sugar bowl. A little water in the glass first, then the spoon over the top; the sugar cube set just so on the spoon, then the absinthe over the top of the sugar. After I measured out a healthy dollop I switched to water, melting the rest of the sugar cube and causing the *louche*, the cloudy green transformation into the liquor of the gods.

I lifted my cup, studied the swirling cloudy green inside. The smell was bitter and laced with anise, I could taste it already.

Any substance, taken in the proper frame of mind, becomes a sacrament. My mother's voice was amused, as always, but held an edge. Absinthe was dangerous for witches; for some reason we're particularly susceptible to thujone.

Bitter green licorice freshness filled the air. "Here." I passed Tremont his glass. Crystal, fluted, and lovely; I would have bet that the glasses were probably worth more than I made in a year, even telling fortunes. "This is important. It's bitter, so drink slowly, and enjoy it."

He took the glass, his fingers avoiding mine, and took a deep cautious sniff of its contents. His nose wrinkled slightly, but he said nothing. He held his breath for a long moment, took a sip. I followed, rolling the sugared chill in my mouth. My tongue went numb, a burning calm slid through my stomach, and I began to anticipate what would happen when I finished the drink.

I was beginning to think that I would be able to handle this. Maybe.

We finished the absinthe in silence. I took two sips for every one of his, and was beginning to feel pleasantly mellow by the time he took the last drop of his. I ceremonially put the cap back on the bottle and regarded him through the haze of lassitude turning my body to warm liquid. "Well," I said. "Hmmm."

"Forgive me." He paused. "Isabella." Intimate and possessive, like he tasted my name each time he said it. That wonderful deep voice of his, stroking the word that belonged to me since birth.

I waved my hand, slowly. The familiar green cast crept over the world, a shifting veil that mercifully made my talent for telling the future into an indistinct blur. I gave a sigh of relief. "I was angry, Tremont. It's not the end of the world."

"You don't know that." His shoulders hunched, and he looked ashamed of himself. Even through the scars, it was easy to see.

Once you looked closely enough.

I reached over, took the cover off the tray. Eggplant and couscous for me, steak sandwich and salad for him. There was fried tofu, and a bowl of strawberries. Still steaming. My tongue was numb, but I enjoyed looking at the jeweled food glistening on the plate. "Eat, and we'll talk."

"Whatever you say, Isabella." His eyes half-closed. He waited until I began, then picked up his plate and started in on his sandwich.

"So what were you *doing?*" I asked around a mouthful of couscous, suddenly too hungry to be polite. Sometimes absinthe destroyed the appetite, sometimes it enhanced.

He finished chewing before he replied. "Looking for you. It was almost dark, and you...you were gone."

Just like a man. "So I was upset. Big deal. I was down on the corner, smoking a cigarette or two. I just had to think, that's all."

"I was afraid you would be hurt. Or you would vanish." He took another wolfish bite of his sandwich.

"I owe you work, for what you've paid me. Besides, I promised. I just don't want to be lied to, or put off. So the 'servants' are invisible and you're talking about magick-with-a-k. Why couldn't you say so and save us the trouble, huh? What else are you hiding?" I stopped, took a deep breath.

"More than you can imagine." He made that hurtful, bitter little sound again. The one that tried to be a laugh.

Relaxation came in waves, easing away the tension headache gathering behind my eyes. "You have invisible servants, and a whole library packed full of every occult book that's been published since the 1500s, and you can't—or won't—leave the property unless the situation's dire." Very slowly, laying out each piece. "There's something to do with you and a really big cat. Some kind of curse, and this town isn't quite right. Things live here that make Twin Peaks and Collinsport look like a summer resort."

He took another bite of his sandwich, chewed, swallowed. "I have tried to remember that you are unusually perceptive." If the drink affected him, he didn't show it.

Then again, he wasn't a witch.

What *was* he?

"Goody for me." The green mistiness over the world intensified, and my shoulders unloosed. Gods above, but I was hungry. "So?"

"If I could *tell* you, don't you think I *would?*" His eyes glittered with something uncomfortably close to anger.

At me? Or at something else? And lying next to that fury was something dark, hopeless, and wounded.

Maybe the drink *was* working.

"I don't know," I told him, honestly. "You don't seem to like anything other than riddles."

He sighed, and his shoulders dropped. "I'm sorry." Quietly.

"Gods *damn* it." I eyed him, wishing I could just reach out and shake him until his head bobbled. It might not have helped the situation, but at least I would have felt better. "Why can't you just tell me?"

"It's..." He set his sandwich down, took a deep breath, and looked at me. "It's...part of...." Sweat sprang out, bright sparkles standing out on his gold-brushed skin. "...the..." His fist clenched, his Adam's-apple bobbing, choking on a single word; cords stood out on his neck and his cheeks reddened. "The c-c-c-c-c—"

"The curse," I finished flatly.

He relaxed back into the chair. The sweat gilded his forehead.

"Jesus." My appetite fled. "So a curse. Was it an old gypsy woman, or a fairy scorned, or—"

Thunder boomed, rattling the windowpanes. "I was born this way. My father..." His throat worked while I watched. "I can't," he said finally. "I'm sorry."

"Wait a minute." I began to get the picture. Oh. Of *course.* "You can't tell me, I have to guess?"

He nodded, staring at his plate like he'd lost his appetite.

"Oh, my dear sweet gods," I said, slowly. "Jeremy Tremont, are you *serious*?"

He put his plate down. "I've said too much already," he said formally.

"Sit in that chair and finish your dinner." The mellow feeling was still there, or I would have yelled it. "It's raining, so I'm not going anywhere. Neither are you, goddammit."

Amazingly enough, he meekly picked up his plate and started to eat. I took another bite myself, though I'd lost a lot of the urge to eat.

It had been a long day.

Maybe it was just the thujone relaxing me enough to see it. I stifled a burp, tasted anise again. It reminded me of drinking with my mother in a small hotel room in the south of France, listening to the waves beat the shore and hearing her wonderful low voice tracing out fairy tales that we could both see in the colored smoke.

Oh, Mama, I miss you. You'd have this whole thing sorted out in no time.

"Hey," I said, and he looked at me. "You just did what I told you to."

He nodded. "I did," he said around a mouthful of steak. So much for those exquisite manners. He must be starving, to eat like that.

"Is that part of the terms of the curse? Can you tell me that?"

He nodded. His eyes were back to normal. Was that relief on his twisted, uneven architecture of a face?

And here I was thinking I could figure out his expressions so easily.

"So...was *that* what you ran the ad for?" I was not liking this at all. "And I just breezed in."

"You're it," he said softly. "The only one. The only *applicant* I can even consider."

"So what happens if I can't figure it out?" I was failing miserably as girl detective lately.

"It's not like you don't have the stories to guide you, if you would just *look*," he said bitterly. "But what happens to you? Nothing, Isabella. I wouldn't harm you. You go your way, with enough in your pockets to make you comfortable for a long while."

"Back up," I said. "*Harm* me?"

"I never would. Never." His eyes glittered angrily, as if I'd accused him of something.

"Why is this even a consideration?" The absinthe made me dopey and relaxed, and I felt only a kind of relaxed interest in this whole conversation. Good deal. Good fucking deal. Maybe I just had to be stoned to deal with this place.

The idea had its merits, but it was expensive to get decent green venom imported.

Then again, I could afford it if I stayed here, couldn't I? And there was always the weed to consider, but I get paranoid when I smoke too much.

Rain began smacking at the windows again. The animals would start going by two by two if this kept up for very long. I couldn't say that I cared.

He shrugged, looked at the fireplace. Blue eyes shone oddly, reflective. A gray-green-gold shine, for just a moment, like a cat's eyes at night, when streetlamp glow hits just right.

Thunder, quiet compared to the thunderous silence between us. We were finally getting somewhere.

All I had to do was figure out where.

"All right." I leaned back in my chair. "What *can* you tell me, then?"

He gave me a look that could only be interpreted as relieved.

The only way to get a useful answer is to ask the right question, Bella my love. I could almost *see* my mother through the thinning veils of green smoke, her long dark curling hair and dark eyes, her quiet private smile. I'm a lightweight when it came to alcohol; most witches are. We have some sort of genetic propensity to getting out of our heads anyway, it's a wonder we even *need* substances.

I met Jeremy's gaze, trying to see what lay behind that flat shine. His ruined face was now impossible to read, but if I watched his eyes closely enough, I would see something there, wouldn't I?

I did. I saw whatever he was feeling at that moment, printed clearly as if on a page.

Too bad it was in a different fucking language, one I had no hope of ever deciphering.

He spoke, calmly and evenly. "I can tell you that you are safe here, in this house, and that you may invoke my name in the town and be sure of safety, at least during the day. I can tell you that you are needed here, and that your...talents are no cause for concern. They are, in fact, appreciated here in a way you probably won't ever understand. I can tell you that you have all the time in the world to make your decision. I won't rush you."

Aha. Now we get to it. "What decision?"

He shrugged.

"Oh, great. Can you tell me anything *helpful?*"

"Believe it or not, I have."

I held up a finger. "I'm safe in the house, I'm needed here, and you're not freaked out because I'm a witch. And I've got time." Four fingers. Four "useful" things. "Which one of those is supposed to be useful?"

He continued eating, as if he was starving. I suppose he probably was. Another shrug. If he had grunted, it would have made him perfectly male.

I imagined the scarring running down his back, into his jeans. "What were you doing out there? And what's with your side? How did you get hurt?"

"I wasn't careful enough. I told you, people here...they go crazy after dark. That's the best I can explain it."

I closed my eyes. *What's the right question here?* I mentally reviewed the entire damn conversation. It was easier than it normally would be, because I was relaxed enough to just let the tape reel.

After a moment I opened my eyes. "Okay, Jeremy. So I think I know the real question. What happens to *you* if I can't figure it out?"

He set his plate aside and regard me steadily. "Do you really want to know?"

"Why am I sure I won't like this?" My voice was a little unsteady. Absinthe or no absinthe, this was one of the weirdest conversations I'd ever had.

And I've had some doozies. There was that one time in the back of the bus in Arkansas, for example, with the thin dreadlocked girl who wasn't…quite…solid.

My fingers began to itch. I wanted to pull the cards out, but it seemed a bit rude to do it right in the middle of dinner. Besides, I kind of already knew what they would say. *Get out the salt. Get out the candle. Ask your questions, it's always worked before.*

It happened again as I studied him. Darkness slid over his aura, something with teeth and bright flashing eyes, something low and striped and beautifully lethal.

This time I froze, the absinthe turning me into an utterly relaxed, utterly useless mass. I watched the blackness slide over him, slide away.

His face twisted a little, came back. "What do you see? When you look at me like that, Isabella? Your eyes are very dark."

"Nothing," I said, and it hurt me. It really did hurt me to lie, a swift piercing pain right behind my sternum. "Nothing at all."

He looked down at his plate, his blue eyes suddenly shut as if a door had slammed behind them. "Isabella. Please."

Quit saying my name like that. "What happens to you if I don't know the right thing to do?" I persisted. "What if I can't figure out your curse? What happens to you?"

He shrugged, looked down at his lap. "Nothing much. It would actually be a relief, I think."

"Great. I think you need another drink. You don't sound relaxed at all."

"Thank you." His shoulders hunched again, as if expecting a blow. I wondered who had done that to him, made him so afraid. "For coming back, and for dinner."

"Not to mention how I dragged you in out of the rain," I added judiciously. "Okay?"

That earned me a brief, precious smile. "Of course."

"So what's the deal, Tremont?"

He made it to his feet, a little less gracefully than usual. I saw a shadow of something cross his scarred face—something like pain. "Thank you, Isabella. I am afraid I must leave you now."

"Oh, no you don't." *Just when we were making progress. You are so goddamn male it's not even funny.* Had I ever thought him prissy? "You have to tell me, Jeremy. What happens to you?"

"Nothing much." He shook it off, picked up his plate and his wineglass—it was empty, how had he managed that?—and put them back on the tray. Sure. To make it easy for the invisible servants to pick up. I guessed it would make anyone messy, having invisible servants—but he wasn't messy. He was unerringly precise. "I have to go, Isabella. I've strained myself, and my control isn't perfect, more's the pity since I would love to spend more time with you. Forgive me."

"Sure. Go ahead. Leave me alone on a night like this. Fine. Big fucking mystery, everyone's in on it, just don't tell the new girl. Bully for you." I didn't sound sharp, I just sounded drunk and vicious. What a coincidence. I *was* half-drunk and probably vicious. "Great. Go away and leave me alone then."

His face blurred for moment. A flash of teeth, the scars turning to stripes. "You may even thank me someday. I'm saving you trouble." He moved slowly to the door, his footsteps heavy but silent, and paused. "Who, after all, would want *me?*"

He delivered that last parting shot over his shoulder, closing the gilt-mermaid door behind him with a quiet click.

"Well," I announced to the empty air. "That was certainly the biggest waste of time and effort since First Woman tried to domesticate men."

Who, after all, would want me? That one little sentence seemed the most useful one he'd uttered. I felt a completely uncharacteristic desire to laugh like a maniac and throw something breakable at the door just to finish off in style.

It was nice to just sit and bask in the fading mellowness. When I sobered up completely I would probably be furious at the way he'd just dismissed me. The bastard.

It even started to seem funny. Jeremy Tremont, scarred face, million-dollar house, and a library to die for, full of the kind of books that were full of people like me—weird people sitting on the edges of life, telling fortunes and drifting from place to place. Oh, I had a gift, to be sure. A gift for picking junkie boyfriends and scaring people with tarot cards.

It was nice, I decided, to be somewhere and be treated like an ordinary person. It was nice to avoid the whispers behind cupped hands, the bunco cops, the sniggers and stupid questions. So that was one mark in favor of staying.

Who, after all, would want me?

Something else itched under my skin and my eyes and drove me to distraction. Real power stirred the air here, and if I'd learned anything in three decades plus of walking the earth, it's that real power doesn't have a master. It goes where it likes and does what it wants, and if you can align yourself with the wave you can go an incredible distance.

Turn the wrong way on that wave, though, and you'll spill.

And let's not even talk about the sharks.

I took a long drink of water. So was I going to ride the wave here, or go back to the wading pool?

Who, after all, would want me?

"I would, you idiot," I whispered to the empty air, then shook my head. Useless to sit around dithering.

I stacked my plate neatly on the tray and walked into the bathroom, fetched the container of salt. I got a plain white novena out of the cupboard I'd put the candles and incense in. Then I took the small cedar box with my mother's ashes in it out of my duffel that had been living in the closet, its cavernous empty space now quarter-full of clothes and scented with patchouli instead of rose sachet.

I set the candle on top of the box, my pulse hiking with anticipation. Now wasn't the best time to do this.

No, half-drunk and mazed with high emotion, it was the *only* time to do this.

I lit the candle with my trusty Zippo and turned off the lights. Cracked the salt container open. Carefully, I sat down cross-legged—facing candle, facing north. The direction of earth, of mothers—and the traditional direction of the dead.

Each time I did this, it got easier. Because I knew it could be done, and because I knew what to expect.

It also became harder, because I hated to do it. I had tried to bury this part of myself a long time ago. This type of thing was dangerous while still feeling the absinthe.

I could walk right out of my body and never return.

"Candle, candle, burning bright." I dumped a mound of salt on the floor in the east. I had to reach behind me to get the south. "In the watches of the night." West was next. "Give me answers, let me know." Carefully, I poured a mound of salt out that was bigger than the other three, for the north. "I need you now, an answer show."

The candleflame sparked and guttered. Then, with a dry whispering sound, the flame turned bright blue, like an acetylene torch. Sibilance filled my head, a whispering, hissing, dry heat.

I settled myself, stared at the candle. At the flame, which was now three inches high and sweetly blue.

Oh, Mama. I miss you so much. You'd have this all straightened out in no time. You wouldn't need this kind of magick to make everything better.

"Candle, candle burning bright, give me now the gift of sight." I took it slow, enunciating each word calmly and quietly. The trick was to let the chant do what it wanted, without losing control of it. A fine delicate line to walk, between keeping a grip on the vision and letting the vision do what it needed to do.

Like riding a bicycle—only infinitely harder.

I kept chanting, looking at the blue flame. It burned up straight and tall, a blue door, a window, a low door set in a hill. A star, glimmering over the hill...a star, a star that had heralded my mother's...my mother's dying...

Candle, candle burning bright, give me now the gift of sight—My lips shaped the words, pushed them softly out, my body folding away as I rose, a collection of velvet drapes and jeweled nerve endings. The subliminal *click* happened.

I was no longer inside my own body.

I was Somewhere Else.

This space billowed with thick gray cloud, tinges of green fading like crackles of lightning. I floated on the tide a little while before I felt the tugging, directionless and vital, that would bring me an answer.

An answer to what, though?

I plummeted inward and upward, my eyes fluttering behind closed lids. Aware of my body, damp hair against my back, my fingers loosely curled together in my lap...but also gone, moving through the clouds at the speed of light, and falling into ...

Into...

—running, breath locked inside my chest, every single cigarette I've ever smoked rising up to haunt me, the sound of snarling behind me, the messenger bag torn from my shoulder and I whirled, the need to save the cards suddenly greater than the need to outrun whatever was chasing me. Chasing me with claws...

A nightmare, human form and animal pelt, like the stories of the Kine my mother used to tell, those who had a beast inside them. Those who could use the beast...if it did not use them.

But this was something unnatural, unholy, where the Kine moved with power and precision and grace. Mom had always told me how beautiful the Kine were.

I fell. My messenger bag, clutched to my chest—somehow it had only slid down my arm, not fallen completely away. I hugged the bag and screamed as I went down, my tailbone hit with a resounding thump that clicked my teeth together, and if my tongue had been there, I'd've bit it clean through.

The thing leapt for me—

—but fell, halfway. Thunder rolled. Claws and teeth and snarling, striped muzzle, the ruff around its cheeks clearly visible in the moonlight—

"Jeremy!" I screamed. "NO!"

Neither snarling, thrashing thing took any notice. I scooted backward, losing skin on my palms, smelling damp earth and rainy wind, and scrambled to try and stand.

The half-human thing chasing me let out an amazing howl of pain and defeated rage. I shivered, clutched the bag to my chest. "Jeremy—" I whispered, and I turned to run.

Behind me, I heard a tiger's chuffing roar, and a deathstrike cry.

Chapter Fifteen

KNOCKED AWAY FROM THE VISION, a clean *crack* like a baseball bat getting a good piece of a fresh new ball. Contact, my head snapping aside, and I thumped back into the meat that carried me around on a daily basis. The candle, snuffed, sent up a thin curl of smoke, and the salt was gone. How that happened, I didn't know.

I never know, but it always happens.

Thirsty and aching, I put my mother's ashes safely away and drank most of the Evian stashed on the night table. I scrubbed at my face, roughly, and it took me two tries to get to my feet. I made it to the bathroom and sighed at myself in the mirror—high hectic color in my cheeks, my hair working free of the braid, coal-black curls flying anyhow.

I looked like I had galloping consumption. Great-grandmama would have told me so.

"Shit," I whispered.

Then I mixed myself another huge wallop of absinthe, put the bottle away, and crawled into bed. I started to drink with a faint feeling of something not right, and ended with a haze of green smoke over the world and completely shot nerves. As a sedative, the booze wasn't helping. I just wanted to walk around and find some munchies. Explore the house some more, maybe have a chat with the painting of the woman in white. I had the unsettling feeling that tonight she might talk back, helped along by the mild hallucinogen in the bottle I considering finishing just for the hell of it.

I got out of bed, scratching languidly under my T-shirt. The gilt mermaid door was somehow locked—the invisibles looking after me, maybe—but I slipped out into the familiar nighttime quiet of 4444 Tremont.

I made it down the stairs and turned slowly toward the kitchen when I heard voices.

"—came as soon as I heard." A woman's voice, soft and clear. Another midnight visitor. The green smoke around me lit with sparkles; I sighed softly.

"Not necessary." Tremont's voice. I tried to decide if this qualified as eavesdropping. After all, I was half-drunk and wanted something to eat, right? "Cal shouldn't have said anything."

"A witch, here, after so long? It's news, Jeremy. This town has been attracting *vrkolak* for a long time." The woman sounded concerned. "You've got a population of hungry *s'lin*, *kalaks*, and Kine. Not to mention other things."

"The locus is safe," another male voice said. This one was vaguely hurtful, full of cold sharpness. "Tremont's a Protector, Mhari. He knows his duty."

"Don't preach duty to me, longshanks," the woman retorted. But there was amusement and affection in her tone. "Well, Jeremy? What is it? Stay or go?"

"You're welcome in this house," Jeremy said, a bit stiffly. "You know that. As long as you follow the rules, I have no quarrel with you."

"But *her*, Jeremy. A witch girl. From what clan? What coven?"

She's talking about me. I'm so popular with these people I haven't even met yet. A half-drunk giggle drifted upward from my stomach; I clapped my hand over my mouth. My arms and legs were heavy, I was moving through heavy oil.

"You're not an Aradian, so it's not your business, hmm?" There was a jagged edge to what Tremont's words. His mellowness must have worn off—if he'd ever had any to begin with.

How had I gotten to know him so well that I could tell his mood just by hearing his voice? But I couldn't tell anything else about him when it counted.

That's because you're too close to the forest to see the trees.

It was a very deep, possibly useful thought, but not very helpful at the moment. I stood, frozen and irresolute, in the hallway. Whoever they were, they were in the foyer, the massive black-and-white foyer under the tinkling chandelier. In the dark, with the ticking of the grandfather clock to keep them company.

"If she's witchblood, Aradian or not, she might be my business." The woman's voice had cooled perceptibly.

"Don't, Mhari," the other man said. "Leave him to his curse. It's only polite. And it's against the Rule to interfere."

"I can't wait to meet her." Her tone took on a shade of maliciousness I didn't care for.

I began ghosting down the corridor to the kitchen.

"You tried to leave the house in this form," yet another voice intruded. This one had a strange ringing quality, a crystal bell struck with a padded hammer. I couldn't tell if it was male or female. "It didn't kill you?"

"No," Tremont said. "I was...distracted, thinking of protection. Maybe that was why I could go...I had to Shift, found something out there and got hit low on the side. Nasty cut, but already healing. After I came back, I tried to go outside. In this form."

"What was out there?" the bell-like voice asked.

"Same thing that always is," Jeremy said shortly. "Darkness."

"Darkness," the woman said, echoing him. It sounded like she was shivering.

"You know where to find your customary rooms. I suppose this means I'm going to be inundated with well-wishers." Jeremy sounded resigned.

"Of course." The woman—Mhari—laughed, and it wasn't a nice sound. "I'm sure she's charming. And some of your guests might want to look at the library, too."

"Don't make me care enough to kick you out, Mharian Alaraia." Jeremy's voice stroked the name, pronounced it like a different language. It was small consolation that it wasn't like the way he said mine, like he was hungry and the sound was food.

I edged into the kitchen, and lost track of what they were saying. It wasn't right to eavesdrop.

Since when, sweetheart? You've been hoping to catch him talking to someone else for months now.

I turned the kitchen light on and found the kettle, filled it in slow motion, put it on the stove. Then I opened the fridge and was poking around when a slight sound alerted me to the fact that I was no longer alone.

Well, look at this.

I peered up over the fridge door and found myself face-to-face with a woman slightly younger than me, with short sleek hair—a young Judy Garland with a Sassoon cut.

She wore a white linen shirt and a long, rustling red skirt rainbows slid away from, light pooling on the floor, a belt made out of silver medallions whispering to my addled senses.

Well. Let's see what this is. "Hi there. I thought I was the only one up."

"Not in this house." She laughed. There was no malice in the sound, but there was a great deal of carelessness. Tossing her head back, her short hair moving enviably well, she regarded me out of large dark sloe eyes. "So you're Jeremy's new librarian."

I felt two things the instant I laid eyes on her. The first was an almost stupefying dislike. Something about her rasped against my edges in just the wrong way.

The second, contradictory thing was an odd kinship. She looked vaguely familiar.

"Mr. Tremont hired me recently, yes." It's hard to sound professional when you're coming down from an absinthe drunk. "Isabella Harpe. Nice to meet you." The fridge bathed me with cold air; I closed the door slowly. Now it wasn't a wall between us, and I sized her up.

Perfect velvety skin, the kind of paleness that never takes a tan well, and her face was a marvel of architecture, every bone and curve flawlessly balanced.

Familiar, too. Had I seen this woman before?

"I'm Mharian." Her eyes sparkled with mischief. "But you can call me Mhari. What do you think of it here?"

"There's enough work to keep me busy." I didn't quite answer.

Her dark eyes lit up with the kind of delight a mouse sees in a cat. "And Jeremy?" she persisted.

Don't you dare, bitch. He's mine. The thought rose like bad gas in a mineshaft; I hurriedly pushed it away and looked over at the kettle, which was just now starting to chirp. "Nice boss. Nice guy. Bit dull but okay, as bosses go. He's got enough sense to let me take care of the library." *Chew on that, sister.*

Was she an ex-girlfriend? Likely, the way she talked to him.

She studied me intently, a new and interesting beetle crawling under her handmade shoes. "So what's your Power?"

What? "Womanpower," I replied smartly. "My mother was an Original Feminist." *In other words, one hell of a witch.* I bit back a giggle. Hardwood was cold against my bare feet.

I realized I was still drunk-stoned to the Nth degree. Wonderful.

She opened her mouth to say something, and just then Jeremy Tremont strolled into the kitchen. His blue gaze flicked over everything once, and it seemed to my absinthe-fuzzed brain that there was something different about him. Something darker.

For the very first time, he looked fully awake, and completely alive.

"Alaraia," he said, almost curtly. "Guillame's found a room."

"Oh, he's no fun," she replied breezily. "I've just made a new friend."

"Mhari." His tone was one I'd only heard once before, a warning. "Not tonight."

She actually half-turned and *pouted* at him. "You never let me have any fun either."

"It will be a great relief to me when you grow out of being spoiled," he said, flatly. "This is my house. Go up to your room."

She turned back to me and grinned, pearly teeth bared. "I will definitely see you later." Something ancient and ill-tempered bloomed in her dark eyes for a moment before she whirled and did a tripping little dance-step out the door.

I blew out through my pursed lips, not quite whistling. The kettle began to boil in earnest. "Tea?" I congratulated myself silently on my diplomacy.

"If you like," he answered. His throat moved as he swallowed, probably holding down other words through sheer force of will just like I was. "I'm sorry I had to leave you, I wasn't feeling well."

"I guess not. That's the first time I think I've ever seen you be rude." For a moment, I toyed with the thought of telling him I'd heard another conversation, one between him and a man with a voice like squirming filth.

It wouldn't be worth it, no matter how satisfying it was likely to be.

"What, leaving you, or just now?" He sounded tired, and his ruined face even more drawn than usual.

I don't know why I did it, but I padded across the cold floor and touched his shoulder, as if I had every right to. As if we weren't weird boss and witchy employee, but something…else.

I also found words, nice soft conciliatory ones, for once. "You look pretty hashed. Are you okay?" Because it seemed, to my absinthe-addled brain, that he wasn't okay at all.

Unfortunately, he didn't take the cue. "What are you doing here in the middle of the night? You're usually a sound sleeper."

Oh, if you only knew how little I sleep here, Tremont. I pulled my hand away, quickly. Backed up a step, two. "Alcohol sometimes makes me hungry." I blinked at him, wondering what the noise was, realized it was the kettle. "Oh, yeah. Tea."

"I'll make it. I don't want you to burn yourself." He didn't sound disapproving at all, it was just a statement of fact.

"I wouldn't burn myself—" I began, but he slipped past me and took the kettle off, found two cups, a couple of teabags—they looked like chamomile—and proceeded to make tea.

"Are you still hungry?" His hair glowed under the kitchen lights, a tangled sunburst.

I nodded. "I'm craving shortbread cookies. And jellybeans. How's that for weird?"

"I thought you didn't like sweets." Something in the set of his shoulders had eased.

"I normally don't. Sour alcohol makes me crave sugar. Yum."

I didn't see how he did it, but he set down a little china plate with—what do you know—shortbread cookies, dusted with rock sugar, glittering harshly under the kitchen lights.

My mouth turned dry. Maybe I wasn't hungry after all. "Is this real? Or am I eating fairy-food, you know, sticks and dust?"

"I have nothing to do with fairies." An absolutely straight face, as if he knew what he was talking about. "They tend to avoid me. We had a pixie at the house once, and we couldn't find anything for a week. Damn fairy sense of humor."

I shuddered at the thought. Pixies had *teeth*. "But the household help. Are they fairies? Is it rude to ask?"

"No," he said, just that. Then, abruptly, "Thank you. For bringing me inside the house. I would have...well, it was painful, and I was disoriented."

Do you turn into a bloody big cat? Is that part of your curse? He'd probably tell me he couldn't tell me. Part of the curse. "I'm sorry I walked away. I thought I was going to start to yell at you, if I stayed." Unanswered questions, unsaid things, crowded us both, filling the kitchen, brushing the stovetop, sliding against the darkened window.

"I frustrate you." he said. "I can't help it. I dislike the thought of you wandering around unprotected."

It was obliquely warming and utterly frustrating at the same time. Did he think I was helpless? How did he think I'd *gotten* here? "I'm a big girl, Tremont. I've gotten out of some dicey situations before."

"Like?" he asked, leaning on the breakfast bar. He looked genuinely interested.

I took a shortbread cookie. "I got run out of a town once, when I was young and stupid. It taught me not to read cards on the street in a one-stoplight burg. I barely escaped being tarred and feathered—or burned as a witch." *An empty-eyed preacher and a bunch of white-hooded men, too.* I still had the scar on my hip from wriggling through the broken window, fleeing into the dark for the first time. "I jumped *that* ship just in time. I had to leave a bunch of stuff behind—including my rose necklace. I kind of miss it." I shrugged. "But better a necklace lost that my life. You dig?"

He looked down at his hand, resting on the counter. "Certainly." Harshly, the word stuck in his throat.

I looked up from my tea mug. "Are you all right?"

"Fine." He found the window fascinating. At least, he stared at it, maybe seeing our reflections in the darkened glass. "Really. I just...don't like the thought of you...dealing with that. Alone, I mean."

Isn't that nice of you. "Yeah." I took another cookie. Time for a subject change. "Hey, so we've got guests."

His mouth tightened a fraction. "Yes. Mharian is dangerous, she's too young to really have any restraint. Guillame will restrain her, but still... And Koren is here too. Koren is strange, but they won't hurt you."

"They?" I almost felt like I could understand this. Maybe I had to be permanently drunk to deal with this place.

The idea had its merits.

"They," he replied. "Pronoun of choice."

"Okay," I said. "Thanks for telling me. Have a cookie."

He did, biting into it reflectively. He looked a lot better. More relaxed.

"So what do I do while you've got them here?" I braced my elbows against the counter, looking up at him. *I like you, Tremont. I really do. I wish you'd talk to me.*

"Just take care of the library, Isabella. And I have your time from five to six, don't forget."

I shrugged. "What if I'm busy?" I was pushing, I knew it.

He simply looked at me, his blue eyes shuttered and bright. "It's the only thing in my day that gives me any pleasure, Isabella." He stopped, closed his mouth firmly, obviously wanting to say more.

That's not my fault. Still... He'd been nothing but pleasant and patient, but that wasn't the overriding factor. He was hiding things from me—but hadn't I hid things from people? All my life?

Everyone I had ever met, except my mother. And even then, some things just weren't spoken of.

Still, I hadn't had to lie to him. He knew about magick, and about gifts that could be curses. He probably knew more about curses than I ever would, and that's saying something.

Which brought me right back to his particular curse—the one he couldn't give me any pointers on.

Great.

"I wouldn't stop." My voice was oddly thick. "It's what you hired me for, after all." I set the remains of my fourth cookie down on the plate. Funny. I'd lost my appetite.

"Maybe." He was still examining me in that flat, disconcerting way. "You're free to go. I can't keep you here."

I could have sworn you didn't want me to. "If you want—"

"I just said you're free to go." Still looking at me. All it took was a playground and someone shouting *I double dog dare you to go!*

I slid down off the barstool. I hadn't even touched my tea. "Maybe I stay because I want to. Have you ever thought of that?" *Of course not. You're a man.* "I'm going to bed. I've had enough fun for one night."

The shocked pause was worth it. "Goodnight, Isabella." That particular, caressing weight on the syllables of my name again. "Sleep well."

I stalked out of the kitchen, back to the blue-and-white bedroom. I closed the gilt-mermaid door, and I pointedly left it unlocked.

If something wanted to bust into my room in the middle of the night—something with stripes and long teeth—let it.

Let it.

CHAPTER SIXTEEN

THE NEXT AFTERNOON, WHEN JEREMY said, "That's enough. Thank you, Isabella," I laid the book beside him on the leather couch.

It was Jacques Cazotte, *Le Diable amoureux*, and I enjoyed reading in French. I even halfway understood the language, thanks to my mother's patient tutoring and a summer we spent in Cannes, attached to a movie star's retinue. She read cards and did other things, physical and not so physical, for the man, who achieved phenomenal fame.

He broke with my mother, leaving us stranded in Nice after a drunken rage, and she simply shrugged. *Let him make his own luck*, she said, and within a year he was an alcoholic has-been.

That had been an education.

I ran up to my room to get a pair of Doc Martens I'd found at the thrift store. Then I made it down the stairs and out the front door without seeing a soul.

Our guests hadn't shown their faces, and I could only guess that they were sleeping in.

Jeremy had said almost nothing beyond polite greetings, and asking me if I wanted more coffee.

I hadn't asked a single question. Once I caught him looking at me, as I shelved books in the Western Occultism section— three copies of *The Magus* and a copy of *Dei Occultia*—his eyes blue and very sad, golden hair tangling over his face.

I headed down Tremont Avenue, humming. The walk didn't seem so long without rain pouring down, and there was no sign of an afternoon storm.

Instead, the day was hushed and hot and breathless, summer burgeoning in every branch and root.

When I saw the KwikMart and the L'il Drop, I felt a traitorous little bubble of excitement under my ribcage. I asked the teenage girl in a red polyester vest behind the Mart's counter to call me a cab. She gave me a strange look, but complied.

Of course, I could have given her a strange look in return, because her eyes were bulbous and refractive, like a fly's. Now that I was looking for the weird, the little tricks that hid it from normal people didn't work.

I waited outside, on the tiny sidewalk that attempted to make the front of the store more palatable, smoking a cigarette. A cab showed up in record time, driven by a strange rat-faced little man, hunched almost to a C behind the wheel. "Where ya goin?" he cawed, as I slid into the backseat.

"I'd like a tavern—one where I can ask a few questions and find a few friends." My fingers itched relentlessly. I held up a twenty-dollar bill. "One where I won't get hit on the head with a tire jack and carried off to Mexico."

He let out a wheezy laugh, greasy black hair curled tight against his head. He flipped the ancient meter-handle down.

Jimmy Cassidy loved to watch old reruns of *Taxi* and *Hill Street Blues*. *Starsky and Hutch*, too, but *Taxi* was his first love. He was a passionate fan of the theory that Andy Kauffman lived on.

"I take you to the right place," the cabdriver husked. "Good food, good drinks, good people. And answers, some of the time, eh?"

"Sounds good." I settled back in the seat.

The sun slid a little lower in the sky.

I wondered if Tremont knew I'd left the house yet. I wondered what he would do when I came back. I always felt the need to poke and pry, to push and slide past the rules.

Maybe it was my mother's genes.

The streets flowed smoothly by. We went down, farther into the valley. I'd been lucky, coming across the north part of town instead of through the middle. Tremont's house was on the very northern fringes.

Suburbia-R-Us, with a healthy dose of the Addams Family.

The cab bumped over the railroad tracks, and the industrial section of town rolled by the window. Not long after that, we pulled up outside the Belus Tavern, where a jolly neon sign proclaimed *Come In Out Of The Night.* As a motto it was a strange one, and I felt a shiver of unease.

I clamped my elbow down, reassured by the bulk of my bag against my side.

"Dat be fourteen dollars and twelve cents," the cabbie informed me.

I tossed the twenty over the seat. "Thanks." Then I wriggled out of the car and stood looking at the Belus.

It was a ramshackle old clapboard building, looked like a house had been renovated to make it. There was a breath of ozone—power, again.

My instincts were still good. If there was an opposite pole to Tremont's house with its quiet gardens and polished wooden floors, this was it. Decaying warehouses frowned on the other side of the street; a row of clapboard houses, plenty with boarded windows, stared back. Train tracks sliced along the back end of the warehouses, like a bad iron dream through a sleeping brain.

I tried to remember if I'd ever heard a train, at Jeremy's house.

Not a single whistle.

The cab bumped away. That greasy-haired little ferret of a man made me nervous, and the tufts of hair on the back of his hands didn't help.

The tavern's parking lot, dusty and cracked, was crowded with pickup trucks and three motorcycles. One of them was a spit-and-polish Indian, I admired it from a distance. My fingers tingled.

That was where I'd end up tonight.

I took a deep breath. My tiger's eye necklace, and Mom's pearls, were tucked under my black T-shirt. My turquoise bracelet clasped my left wrist.

I would need all the luck I had for this.

I walked up to the front door of the tavern. *Always Open,* a sign on the door proclaimed, and Darlene the waitress's warning rang in my head. *A hole to hide in after dark.*

I checked the sky. The sun sliding down, low and fiery, behind the western mountains. I had maybe another hour of dusk.

Night fell quickly out here in the sticks.

A jukebox was playing inside the tavern, tinny thumping drifting out through the swinging door.

I hope I know what I'm doing. Working on instinct again. The same instinct that had led me to Jeremy's house in the middle of a rainstorm.

I opened the door, and walked in to find some answers.

CHAPTER SEVENTEEN

THE BELUS LOOKED LIKE EVERY other tavern in the world, dark and grimy and full of cigarette smoke. A rustling intensified as I let the door swing shut, and the jukebox burped out some Patsy Cline about walking after midnight.

I've never liked country, even dear old Patsy.

I let my eyes adjust, noting that there were a fair amount of people in here, mostly men, a few barbags. *Why am I doing this?*

Too late now, it's done.

I headed for the bar, ignoring the whispers. There was only one empty spot, a stool between two heavyset, balding men both dressed in red flannel and baseball caps. Their shoulders were too big to be human, and they both had strange leathery skin in an unhealthy shade of blue. I leaned between them, smelling bar-breath, beer, and cigarette smoke, floor wash and the human smell of desperation with a darker tone.

A *much* darker tang, one that wasn't human at all.

It brought back memories of other unpleasant places so sharply I wondered if I was going to just turn around and leave...but it was a long walk back to Tremont, and pride wouldn't let me call and ask for a ride. Or call another cab.

I'd paid twenty bucks to get here, and goddamn it, I was going to get some satisfaction out of the night or else.

The bartender was a heavy, graying man with a soiled apron on. He stared, his jaw partially agape. I wouldn't have minded, except for the fact that if I looked closely, I could see a third eye set off-center in his forehead, blinking in unison with his other two. Plus, his mouth wasn't open because of my stunning looks. It just wouldn't shut completely because of the teeth.

"Hello." I ran my eye over the tavern's offerings. Pretty slim. "Can I have Michelob, please, in the bottle?" *Ugh, I hate beer.*

"Shore thing," he finally said, after a long measuring look. The guys on other side stared straight ahead, at the dusty flyspotted mirror behind the shelves of bottles arching behind the bartender.

He popped the top on my beer and gave it to me, and I gave him a fiver. He dug in a drawer for two dollars of change, and I waved it away, turned around and scanned the bar.

Now that I had a sense of the place, I had to admit it was dusty, and old, and creaking, and full of hicks. Hicks staring at me. Hicks with extra body parts and weird skin and gods knew what else.

I cast my senses out through the room, looking for the little tingle that would tell me where to land. It came—and something else arrived, too.

The feeling was so sharp and immediate I almost dropped my beer. They should have been laughing raucously by now, going back to their business, sneaking little looks at me. Instead, the pool tables set to my left, in what would have been a different room when the building was a house, were full of men.

One of them bent over a pool table, sighting. He drew back, let the cue ride, and the *thock* of the white ball meeting another one resounded, a crisp, authoritative sound. He straightened, letting the cue slide down through his fingers to touch the floor.

Here it was.

He took a swallow of beer, dark hair shining sleekly in the warm yellow light of the fixture over the table, and turned, slowly.

Nice. Very nice. Lean, in jeans, a belt with a silver buckle, good shoulders under a black T-shirt. A bladed face, proud nose, eyes maybe a little too far apart but other than that, very good. Motorcycle boots, and I would bet dollars to doughnuts that he had a black leather jacket hanging around. One that creaked when he moved, just a little, or one that *had* creaked until he'd broken it in.

The way he moved gave him away. He wasn't strictly human. Probably Kine.

I made eye contact, slid away from the bar to my left towards an empty, rickety one-person table, no more than a strip of plywood. That would take me out of his line of sight, so if he came looking for me I'd have the upper hand.

I hopped onto the barstool in front of the dinky little table, under a huge, glaring moose head bolted to the wall. The entire place was decorated with dead animal heads, neon signs, and antique beer ads done on thin sheets of tin.

The effect was lunacy and hunting, badly mixed.

I put my back to the wall, took a sip of my beer, didn't grimace. Instead, I lit a cigarette, and waited.

They watched me covertly, but the sound of the pool balls hitting each other resumed, breaking the tension. They went back to their drinking, and soon someone fed some quarters into the jukebox and it started to wail something about the midnight hour.

I smoked one cigarette all the way down, took a few hits of beer. It actually wasn't bad, for overpriced pisswater.

I lit another cigarette, and smoked it down all the way.

I was thinking that it would be a serious bust, but when I tapped another smoke out of the pack and was picking up my lighter, someone spun the wheel on a silver wolf's head Zippo and provided a golden flame.

Well, what do you know.

I brushed my hair back and lit my cigarette. Then he lit his own, and studied me for a moment.

I was relieved. For a moment I thought I would have to bag it. I've never had to wait longer than three cigarettes for a man.

Pure bad-boy eye candy. The type of guy I liked—if he had been human. "Thanks."

"Pleasure." Nice voice, a little raspy. There was something in his eyes like fever-shine. Yep, this was it. "I don't want to ask the obvious question."

The obvious question would be, *You're not from around here, are you?* That won a smile from me, and he set his beer down on my table and pulled up another barstool. The jukebox was spitting out the Dorell's 'Midnight Rider.' I tried to figure out what species of nonhuman he was.

He had to be Kine. Which was probably good.

"Good." I pitched my voice just high enough to be heard over what was now a roar of conversation. The sun was sinking, and the place was filling up. "Isabella." I offered my hand.

He took it, and showed me white, sharp teeth in a smile. His hand was warm and rough. "Raphael. Local, and charmed."

It was far more polished than I'd expected. I took my hand back, took a drag, blew it out. "Likewise. You play pool?"

He shrugged. His gaze was hotly intent, though. "Shouldn't Little Red Riding Hood be home in bed?"

I copied the shrug. "If I see her, I'll tell her so."

He measured me again, that shine in his eyes never fading. "What do you need?"

Bingo.

"Answers," I said. It explained everything, gave away nothing.

He looked away, over the bar. Nobody paid attention. As a matter of fact, once he sat down with me, people lost all interest in me. Someone laughed, a shrill cry of amusement. There was a general shout from the other corner of the room.

"Three games," he said. "You win, you get to ask a question. I win, you have to answer me one."

A familiar jolt of excited heat went through me. "Three games, three questions. If I win, you *answer* my questions," I corrected. If this was the opposite pole to Tremont's house, then I could get very hurt here.

Hurt or dead. Nothing like a little danger to spice up the day.

He measured me again, favored me with another sharp white smile. "All right. Come on, I've got a table."

"I know." I slid off the barstool.

I PICKED MY CUE WITH care, chalked it, and watched him set up. My cigarette fumed in a red plastic *Red Bull* ashtray. He took the triangle off, set the white ball down, and looked at me. "Ladies first."

I let my smile fade a little. *Good. Let him think I'm an amateur.*

I learned how to play from Pinkerton Stamm in New York, one of the greatest hustlers in that hustling city. He called me Luckyfingers, a name that brought much ribald punning until I started to sink the balls one at a time, sometimes two. Pinky taught me how to stand, how to ride the cue, how to whisper a ball into rolling the right way. How to narrow your focus until you *felt* the cue ball hit, felt the mass of physics and geometry take shape under your fingers, until you could get out of the way and let your body do what it had to.

There's still talk in New York of Pinky's five-hundred-G bet against Clifton Sharpe, who was run by the Trottino family. The Trottinos had been looking to take a piece of Pinky for a long time, but he was cautious. He never gave them an inch until one day they showed up with a foreclosure note on his pool hall.

Pinky took *that* personally.

So he matched me up against Clifton Sharpe, best of seven games. Sharpe was good, but I...I was magic. That one night, everything fell into place, and Pinky walked away from that deal without so much as a scratch. But the price was paid.

It always was, when I used my gifts.

He died of throat cancer two years later. He died happy, in the pool hall, as he was lining up to sink the 8 and win a game.

It was the only match he ever really lost.

After Pinky died, I left New York. The Trottinos made noises—if I was so lucky, they wanted a piece of it. I didn't want trouble, so I skipped town, vanishing into the night like a ghost. Among the hustlers, there grew a tale that I had cried out and exploded in a puff of smoke at the exact moment that Pinky died. I wasn't sure if I was supposed to be Pygmalion's goddess or the devil in female form in that one, but it didn't matter.

I sighted, pulled back, and let fly.

I dropped two solids off that first punch, and surveyed the table. Raphael watched, smiling faintly.

I took the easy shot— "Lemon in the corner pocket," I called my shot, and the yellow rode in on rails. "Jade in the center." And tapped the green in.

The next shot was kind of tricky. "Slut in the corner." I smashed the red ball, ricocheting it off the back wall. It rode the side, spinning, and dropped neatly as a penny into a beggar's purse.

I glanced at Raphael. He was still smiling. The poolroom had begun to get quieter.

I smiled, too. Then I smoked him, dropping the grape into the pocket and moving to stripes, smashing ball after ball until I shot the Magic 8 to round it off. "Game," I said. "One answer. I'll rack, you pop the cherry."

"Pleasure," he said again, and I rescued the balls and racked them neatly. I took the triangle off, picked up the cue ball, and looked at him.

"For luck," I said, kissed the cue ball, and set it down very gently.

I settled back on a barstool and lit another cigarette.

He sighted, leaning over the table, and the balls scattered. A solid and a stripe both dropped. He glanced at me. I shrugged.

He chose stripes, and set himself up, stroking the wino—the purple stripe—into the corner pocket. "Ivy in the rear." He stalked to the other side, popped the green stripe into the rear pocket. "Turk on the run, center." The orange spun crazily, lingered for a second on the brink, dropped in.

He studied the table. I saw two shots at least, but he reached out, tapped the ball with his cue, and gave me a brilliant, unsettled grin. "Jape's neck, Miss Pretty. Take your chances."

I shrugged. "If you really want to throw."

If he was thinking that he was being kind to a poor little girl, I would gladly take him to the cleaners.

I sized up the table for a moment, heard Pinky's voice. *Bitch of a third shot, but you can take it, Luckyfingers. Start with the slut, she's easy.*

I dropped the red ball first.

I sank every one of them and only had a moment's worth of trouble on the third shot—two rails and the grape, to knock it into the hole and set myself up to take out the poorboy. I actually wasn't sure about that one, and felt jarring relief when it dropped.

I cleared the table again. Pool's one of my better games. I really excel at poker—but then, low-level telepathy is an advantage in card games.

I can't bowl worth a damn, though.

I sank the Magic 8 and glanced at Raphael. He wasn't smiling anymore.

"I'll let you pop the cherry on the last one, too," I said quietly. "I'm serious."

"So am I," he said.

Looked like he meant it. I racked them, took the cue ball and kissed it again, set it down.

Raphael stalked to the edge of the table. The poolroom was now completely silent.

He picked up the cue ball, hefted it, lifted it to his mouth and pressed his lips against it, his gaze holding mine.

A flutter of excitement, way down deep in my belly. *I've got him interested in more than the game.*

Good.

"Luck," he said, and set it down.

He popped the cherry like he meant to shatter the balls, a fast hard break careening across the table. He dropped a solid on that, in a side pocket, and proceeded to smoke through, dropping everything solid except the Magic 8, leaving the stripes in play. Charitable of him.

When he got to the 8, he looked up at me and smiled broadly. I perched on the barstool, ankles demurely crossed.

He tapped the 8, gently, with his cue stick. "Jape's neck again, Miss Pretty. Clear the table, and we'll take a walk. I don't suppose you'd go for double or nothing?"

"My mama didn't raise a fool." I slid off the barstool again, glad I'd worn boots. "You sure you want to throw, angel?"

"Of course," he said. He inclined his dark head. "A lady must always have her way."

I let the corner of my mouth curl up. A crowd choked the entrance to the poolroom, and I bent over to sight on the 8. I heard a low whistle.

I smiled, pointed. "Turk going to church." The orange stripe dropped in. "Wino on the run, back door." Purple stripe, dropped. "Bumble on the west hive." The yellow stripe vanished.

I could swear nobody was even breathing. Then again, maybe some of them weren't oxygen-dependent.

I dropped the cherry and the streak, sank the bluebell and the shamrock. I studied the lone eight-ball, set near the back pocket from where I was. I glanced at Raphael, reached out with my cue, and lightly tapped it.

"Jape's neck," I said. "You can have an answer, angel. I think that's fair."

Hushed tension crackled over green felt, even the jukebox silenced.

Raphael laughed, leaning easy and hipshot against another table. "Good game." He chalked his cue, lazily. "Lucky fingers on you, Miss Pretty."

"So I've been told."

His back was broad under the black T-shirt, straining with muscle. He was tenser than he looked.

He ran the cue a couple of times, stood up, laid his stick on the table. It was a clear easy shot. "I give. Let me get my jacket."

The room erupted into applause. I smiled, feeling the flush begin deep in the pit of my belly and rise to my cheeks. Nicely done. He was the playboy now, instead of a sore loser. He could always say that he'd *let* me win.

Especially if he was a shapeshifter.

He picked up a broken-in black leather jacket tossed carelessly over a stool—I had to hide a smile—and led me through the now utterly jam-packed tavern. A feral current slid deep and tense through the wooden structure, full of murmurs and shifting bits of darkness. Some of them still looked human, others...well.

I'd got what I asked for. Now we'd see what the price was.

Outside, the mountains had swallowed the sun, their edges dyed with scarves of red and purple. "Dangerous time to be out, if you're a stranger in town." Raphael stepped off the pavement into the parking lot, shrugging into his jacket

"So I'm told." I'd won two straight answers and could bargain for the third if he got sticky. It was a good place to be in.

"What's your first question, Miss Pretty?"

I studied his profile while he lit another smoke, the brief flare of flame caressing his high cheekbones with a golden tinge. I might have been actively flirting with him if I'd been sure he was human.

"Tell me about Jeremy Tremont," I said, quietly.

He stopped, turned on his heel, and took a long step, crowding right next to me. Three or four inches taller than me at the moment, but that fever-shine in his eyes and the heat rising off his skin told me it wasn't permanent. He could get taller, if he wanted to.

Shapeshifters.

I set my jaw, didn't step back. Kine use little dominance games like that to establish who's in control, the males moving up on the females and herding them; it could be anything from a test to a mark of possession. The important thing was not to cower submissively.

"You're asking about the Protector." A nice deep chest-grumble of a voice. "Either you're brave or foolish, but you're not stupid."

I waited a few moments, looking up at him through lowered eyelashes. "That's not an answer."

"It was hardly a question." He didn't shift his weight, holding still. "You don't even know what you want to ask."

I couldn't argue with that, so I said nothing.

He laughed, a long, low sound. "Come on, then. I'll take you for a little ride, and I'll tell you about the Protector. What about your second question?"

"Why isn't it safe after dark?"

He found something in that genuinely funny. "Oh, you're something else, aren't you. I can't believe he let you out of the house." Looming over me, looking down, he inhaled sharply, let the air out again. "Tonight it might be safe, just for you."

I followed him to the motorcycles, dark and venomous-gleaming under an indifferent streetlight standing. As I'd suspected, his was the Indian.

"Nice chopper," I said. "You don't do helmets?"

"Bad for your brain. If you're riding with me, you're safe enough."

"Is that so." I made a show of admiring the bike's long, clean lines and sinuous curves. "What's your question?"

"I'll ask it after I answer yours." He swung a leg over and twisted the key. Then he kick-started it. The engine roared and settled to a boneshaking purr.

Just like a big striped cat.

"Come on, Miss Pretty. You've spun your wheel and won, let's see what you plan to do with your jackpot."

I slid onto the back of the bike, and put my arms around his waist; I snugged myself against his back, knowing that he would like the feeling. "All right, angel," I breathed against his ear. "Let's see how low you can fly."

He eased the bike forward. It banked like a small airplane coming out of the parking lot, then he tensed and gunned it. I was ready, holding onto his waist, and I put my head against his leather-clad shoulder.

You pay your money and you take your chances. I'd done it now.

CHAPTER EIGHTEEN

RAPHAEL'S SMALL HOUSE ON THE same side of the tracks as the Belus had a weedy yard littered with engine blocks and other things. A glass windchime hung on the leaning rickety porch, jangling in the breeze as he brought the chopper to a stop. It was full dark, and frogs croaked madly in some hidden marshy pocket. There was no storm in the air, but the night drew close, velvet curtains full of teeth.

He cut the engine and waited. I slid off the chopper, lingering a little bit. He regarded me, popped the stand down, and dismounted with the type of grace Gene Autry used to display. I glanced over the house.

Painted yellow, a slightly crooked front porch, but that was the only thing wrong with it. Two stories, a cute saltbox. "A lovely cottage."

Proprietary pride lifted his chin a little. "It's not the Tremont place, but it does. You're the librarian."

"Is that your question?" Maybe I added a *little* bit of flirtation; to imply you don't notice a Kine's attractiveness if they deign to speak to a human is impolite.

"No, not at all. Come on in. You want a glass of wine, don't you?"

I tipped my head back a little. "Among other things."

He led me up the porch and into the house. It was unlocked. Either he was confident or...something else. But really, who would steal from a Kine? Not that it looked like he had much to steal, and they're ferocious trackers. The best of them can follow you even over running water and bare rock; I've heard of Kine bounty hunters bringing in human-or-not criminals, though it was whispered they don't deal with witches or psychics.

Inside, it was furnished in kind of a fifties retro. Must have gone with the leather jacket. A small spotless kitchen, a dining room with a glass-topped table holding an unfinished jigsaw puzzle, and a living room with a battered leather couch and a red easy chair.

I settled myself on the couch at his nod, and he brought out a dusty bottle of wine. It was a zinfandel, very sweet; I took a sip and nodded. "Very nice."

He shrugged, dropped down in the easy chair, stretching out his suddenly-longer legs with a crackle. "You want to know about the Protector."

I settled back, crossed my own legs, and gave him my full attention.

"A long time ago, this land—here between the mountains, this valley—well, even the Indians avoided it. They said bad things walked here, and evil bred between the trees. The shamans kept it clear, with drums and other things. But when the white man came...well, there wasn't much here, some hurried through as fast as their horse or their legs could take them. They were the wise ones." He took a sip of his wine. "There's a locus under this town, Miss Pretty. Do you know what that means?"

No self-respecting witch wouldn't. "A meeting of ley lines."

He nodded. "Got it in one. There's nine powerlines—ley lines—meeting under this town."

"Good gods." I took another drink. "Nine. Wow." *That makes this the magickal equivalent of the Niagara Falls power station. All that energy—no wonder all sorts of things live here.*

I should have figured it out, that's why it felt like thirteen o'clock around here all the time. Lines meeting exponentially amplify each other, and that's a turbocharge for the weird side of the world.

"Guess where the node it is."

I had a sinking suspicion I knew, but just raised my eyebrows.

"Right at the north edge of town," he continued. "4444 Tremont, the Protector holds the gate to the locus. A hell of a lot of power, there for the taking." His eyes glittered for a moment, anger or lust, I couldn't tell. He dropped his gaze at my chest. I was used to that, let it slide. Whatever he could tell me would be useful, worth a little bit of ogling.

Unless he was thinking about picking his teeth with my ribs instead of measuring my bra size.

"Tremont's ancestors came here after the shamans couldn't look after it anymore. Part of a long line of meddlers, they built themselves right over the locus. Now, there aren't a lot of humans—even the deadmind ones—that want to live here. The power makes 'em edgy. Some of the darker psychics come, but it tends to destabilize them." His faint smile intensified, as if he liked the idea. "The fact that you're not laughing out loud in disbelief tells me that you're not a deadhead, Miss Pretty."

I shook my head. "No. I'm not." A disparaging term for people who couldn't or wouldn't exercise psychic powers. I'd heard it before, with a derogatory little snort most times.

"Jeremy Tremont's the latest in a long line. He watches over the locus, parcels out the extra power in easy-to-use quanta—um, packages. He...it's his job to protect the locus. Can you imagine, if a Fallen shapeshifter or a *kalak*—or even a zombie—got into the locus and stayed for a while? This place has been a feeding ground for strange stuff since before the white man even dreamed of getting down out of the trees." Raphael's voice had taken on a singsong quality. "Tremont's young, and very strong. But he's paying for his father's sins."

Like most males, he liked to hear himself talk, and would probably give me more than I'd bargained for if I just listened.

"It's rumor, I'll admit, but it's all I've got. The story is that Tremont's father made the mistake of trying to force a young woman—a cursebreaker—to stay with him. He killed her— ripped her to shreds—when she wanted to leave. I heard she was scared, but that didn't matter to Grant Tremont. I heard he killed her, and the backlash—murder that close to the locus— well, it killed Grant, and it scarred Tremont so badly that nobody thought he'd survive. A few of us were cautiously hopeful—the ones that think the locus should be free. But no, he survived, and holed himself up in that house. He only comes out to thin the ranks of the scavengers and nasties every once in a while.

He's a good fighter, and as long as he's alive the locus stays firmly in control of the Protectors."

"Who watches the watchmen?" I murmured, and watched his face change to something bright and interested. *So his father was married to a 'cursebreaker'. Is it a catchall term for a witch, or is it something to do with Jeremy's curse? Ten bucks says it's the latter.* The pieces were beginning to slide into place.

"Exactly," he said. "What gives *him* the right? There's a whole lot of us that want to see him gone and the locus freed."

"Sure. Okay." *And you'd like any leverage you can get on him. No wonder he's lonely.*

Raphael took another long swallow of wine. "And that answers your second question." He set his jelly glass down. "Night is when we take off our masks. Most of us aren't what you would call human, and the few humans here have learned to respect as much. There are also a fair number of people who work in-town—our economy's always good, because of the locus—and they're outside the city limits before dark, or else. You? You're a witch, unless I miss my guess, and you're a pretty piece. Tremont's got you in the house because it's the only way to make sure you don't run foul of something with sharp teeth. Also, he has to breed to carry on the Protectors." The chair creaked as he shifted a little. "There are plenty of factions in this town who bow and scrape to Tremont's face who would gladly do him some harm if they could."

"So I'm at risk because I'm a witch living in the Tremont house. And he might possibly want to...to breed me?" *I don't believe that. He wouldn't.*

"Well, human females with a little magic on them are few and far between for most of us." Raphael's smile widened a little. "We tend to play a bit rough. Still, there's nothing like a skingirl for a bit of fun."

This was altogether something more than I'd expected. "Well. Thank you. What's your question?"

He looked at me over the rim of his glass. His eyes glittered, fevershine. "Would you care to have dinner with me? Next week? And I think I can get some time off work, maybe show you the town during daylight. What do you say?"

Charming. "Sure." *Keep him happy.* "You seem like a nice guy."

That made him laugh again. Then he set his wineglass down and flowed upright. "Come on, Miss Pretty. We'd better take you home to Tremont. He'll be having kittens right about now. But he hasn't left the house, so you can't be what we think you are."

Oh, you're a nasty one, aren't you. "Kittens," I said, lingering over the word to give myself time to think. "I go where I want and do what I please. If he doesn't like it, I'll skip town."

Raphael's expression plainly shouted doubt. "Trust me on this, Miss Pretty. You should have left before dark fell your first day. Now you're here, and he's got his hooks in. You're valuable, even if you're not what most of us guessed you were."

I strangled the flare of irritation that called up in me. "I do what I like," I repeated. "He'd better know that. And what did you think I was?" *There. That's the real question.*

"He wouldn't have let you out after dark if you were his cursebreaker. And I probably wouldn't let you go if you were, either." Raphael shrugged. "You like Italian? Later, I mean. For dinner."

My, he was a fast mover. "Sure." *I don't have any free questions left from this guy. I'm lucky he doesn't think I'm anything important other than a potential breeder.* I swallowed dryly, gooseflesh brushing my back and thighs. "How about tomorrow, you and I go for coffee downtown. If you want."

"Absolutely." His dark eyes glittered, and I wasn't imagining it: he was taller now.

Chapter Nineteen

He drove me through the town, my hair streaming behind me in the wind. He smelled like night and leather, and I was a little disappointed when the ride came to an end just down the street from Tremont's house.

"I won't go any closer." Raphael braced the bike with one long leg. "Be here at noon tomorrow, we'll go for coffee. Don't break my heart."

I swung down from the chopper's seat, dusted myself off as if I needed it. "I'm a good girl. I don't go around breaking hearts." *I'm pretty sure whatever you're looking to get out of this isn't a heart.*

"That's a good thing." Pure bad-boy eye-candy. Jeez. And he'd been a perfect gentleman.

Damn.

I leaned over, resting my hand on his leather-covered shoulder, and kissed him on the cheek. Closed, a locked door, not much for empathy to fasten on. Nothing but shaven skin and a faint lemony aftershave that I didn't like as much as Jeremy's musky cologne. "Thank you for a good game of pool. And for being a gentleman."

"Well, the big bad wolf has to show his softer side once in a while. Since you're not the cursebreaker, I might as well try my chances." He quirked me a smile. "Run along home, Miss Pretty. I'll see you soon."

"Noon, tomorrow, right here. I'm glad I'm not this cursebreaker thingie."

He started the chopper. "Me too. Walk safe. You should be all right."

I nodded. "Goodnight, angel."

"Goodnight, Miss Pretty."

Engine-purr faded as I stood there, watching until he made the turn at Fourteenth. It was three blocks to the house.

What can happen in three blocks? I'd lived in too many cities not to know.

I got going, my bag bumping against my hip. I couldn't wait to get home and ask the cards about Raphael. I hadn't noticed any swords—but then, it could be figurative. And the vision could just as easily not apply to him. A heart, covered and blind, that's what the vision had said. Knight of Swords.

What about Tremont?

Breeding. My gods. I simply couldn't imagine Jeremy coldly plotting *that.*

If the things in this town thought I was this...cursebreaker...what would they do?

I did intend to break the curse. It was the least I could do. Would it work if I wasn't what they thought?

How did Raphael know that Jeremy hadn't left the house?

A cursed man, whose father had killed his mother? No wonder he was so grim.

Pacing, thinking fiercely, my hands swinging loose and easy and my bag bumping my hip—and something brushed along the edges of my senses.

Something hard, and cold, and snarling with rage.

I didn't even pause, just hitched into an unsteady run. My head snapped up, and I pounded down the pavement. My boots slapped the concrete, copper adrenaline filling my mouth.

The iron gate loomed in the distance, ajar. I ran, heart pounding and my chest on fire, and I slipped inside just as a low growling echoed behind me. Running feet velveted with fur, claws clicking against concrete—I squeezed through the gate, my lungs protesting and black flowers blooming at the edges of my vision.

The driveway was slick and perfect, as always, but it was *right behind me*, snarling and growling, scrabbling on pavement.

I put my head down and sprinted for the porch.

The growling faded into a deep, rasping laugh, a motorcycle engine gunning. I leapt up the porch steps, reached the front door, and whirled, looking behind me.

Nothing. The driveway and the rosebushes were their usual selves, the darkness broken by the carriage lights along either side of the drive. I shoved my hair back, sweat standing out on my skin.

"Jesus," I whispered. "*Vrkolaks.*"

The gate moved, slightly, as if brushed by a heavy wind. Then, slowly and deliberately, it slid shut, latching with a click.

I had never seen this kind of deliberate, flagrant power. Not even in the *bodegas* and the bookstores I'd worked in, where Power was spoken of every day and recipes were exchanged, spells bartered, potions and poisons brewed.

Sure, I'd seen heart attacks and strokes induced, I had seen people barter away their souls for privilege and power, I had even seen my own gifts work in startling and unexpected ways, always with a price to be paid.

But this? A whole *town* full of magicians of every species, and predators of every stripe? A town thrumming with nine ley lines?

My fingers, cold sausages, clenched tighter and tighter. The darkness pressed against the gate, the iron groaning slightly. I dug around behind me for the doorknob. If it was locked I would sit against it and pray for dawn, or just start screaming.

It was about even, fifty-fifty.

It was that slight creaking that convinced me. Metal doesn't make that sound unless something leans on it. *Hard.*

My cold, sweating hand finally found the doorknob. I twisted, and the door opened inward. I almost fell, gained my feet, whirled, and pushed it closed. Stood with my forehead against the wood, my sides flaring with deep heaving breaths. Carved mahogany, cool and wonderful against my suddenly hot, salt-slick skin.

"Gods," I said, to the door. To the dark silence inside the house. I finally peeled myself away from the door, turned around, and ran straight into Jeremy Tremont's broad black-sweatered chest.

I will admit it. I screamed, a high thin breathless sound.

He caught me by my shoulders, and waited. I gasped back the last half of the scream, staring at him, blinked. "J-J-J-J—"

"Where were you?" His voice was a low rumble, deep in his chest.

Light, then, searing through my eyelids as they reflexively closed. Someone had turned the chandelier on. "*Hey*—"I burst out, but it was useless.

"*There* she is!" a female voice spat. "The little *bitch!*"

Tremont's grip on my shoulders shifted a little, softened. "Language, Mharian. This does not concern you."

"But you're—" she began, and he turned his head just a little. I heard an undignified squeak, and looked up, blinking furiously.

He had half-turned, pulling me with him, and was now looking at Mharian, who stood at the bottom of the grand staircase. Behind her was a stick-thin, sharp-eyed man with gray-threaded black hair. He had a curled mustache that looked like something out of the Three Musketeer days, and his clothing carried the theme to a ridiculous extent—dusty jeans and a blue poet's shirt, the laces tied neatly at the throat.

Just the way he stood shouted he was ready for a fight.

Mharian wore a long white robe, belted with silver chain, and she looked *furious*, her short hair standing straight up, an angry catlike ruff. I expected her to start spitting and hissing at any moment.

"This does not concern you," Tremont repeated. I could only see a slice of his face—his chin, the arc of one ruined cheekbone, the edge of one eye. Still, something about his tone. The chill in the words could have flash-frozen boiling lava. "Thank you."

With that, he looked down, his face changing in an instant. My teeth chattered, adrenaline jittering all through me.

"Are you all right?" he asked, quietly. Each word edged with pain and fury. But for all that, he was trying to be gentle.

I wouldn't have known if I hadn't been so used to him.

"F-f-fine," *I'm lying. I'm not fine.* "I'm okay. Thanks."

"I was worried about you," he said, shortly. "I won't ask you where you went."

"Good." I had the odd sense of being pulled like taffy between two conflicting emotions—anger that he would act so goddamn condescending, and genuine relief at seeing him.

Knee-loosening, gut-deep relief.

I felt *safe*. "I went out for a drink." My lips were numb. "I ended up at a tavern. Met someone, had a nice conversation, came back."

Mharian stood, anger, on the staircase. "Jeremy, you can't *possibly*—"

"I told you to leave it, Mharian." He gazed at her again, and I saw the stick-thin man lay his brown hand on Mharian's shoulder.

The stick-man's ears poked up through his mat of gray and black hair, coming to sharp points. *Oh, my gods. But I bet it's useful at Star Trek conventions.*

I didn't like the thought. It had the sort of screamy breathy panic that I associated with rabbit-fear, freezing while the hawk dives for you, claws outstretched.

"Isabella." Jeremy turned his attention back to me. "You're shaking." I caught a blast of some dark emotion, his or mine, who could tell?

A low grinding agony, a feeling so overwhelming I wasn't sure I could name it.

I took a firmer hold on myself. "I'm okay, Jeremy. Really. I promise."

He nodded. "Very well." But he didn't let go of my shoulders. His hands were very gentle, and burned through my shirt.

"I'd skin her alive for causing this much trouble." Mharian turned on her heel and stamped up the stairs past the stick-man. He gave Tremont a curt nod, then turned to follow the cat-woman. I wondered just exactly what she was, and considered bursting into tears.

I drew in a shuddering breath. "I'm sorry," I said, all in a rush. "But you didn't tell me. You haven't told me *anything*."

"Now you know." His face stilled, became awful. "Or do you? What were you told?"

"That th-th-there's a locus under the house, and that you're a Protector, and that your family moved in and took over the locus—"

"Ah," he said. "We were asked to, actually."

"By who?" I fired back. *Or whom. Is it whom? Who cares about grammar, after the night I've had?*

"By the ones who used to guard this place, but were no longer able to. Would you like a cup of tea?" His nostrils flared just a little, something black and awful crossing his scarred face. It was something that should have scared the bejesus out of me.

It didn't. I seemed to have used up my night's allowance of terror.

I caught a complicated blast of feeling from him—fear, pain, unwilling *need*.

"I guess so." I wasn't used to feeling someone else's emotions so clearly and being so utterly unable to decipher them.

"You were quite foolish. I'm thankful you're home."

"Me t-t-too," I said. "Raphael dropped me off three blocks from here, and—"

His fingers bit my shoulders. "Rafe Dietrich? Did he hurt you? *Did he?*"

I took a single step back, shaking myself free. Stood, staring at him and trembling.

"I'm sorry," he said, immediately, and it was the Tremont I knew. Shaking with something close to violence, but still a shy, mordant, familiar man. "Isabella—"

I could break and run up to the bedroom, pack my bag, and be gone at dawn. He wouldn't try to stop me, despite what Raphael said. I could hitch my way out of this town and forget the whole fucking thing posthaste.

Or I could take a deep breath, and look up at him, and stay.

If I left, how much longer before I ran across something even *I* couldn't charm my way out of? Roaming from town to town, telling fortunes, ending up lonely and alone in some hotel room, dying without even a terrified sixteen-year-old at my bedside.

I pulled in a whispery scream of a breath. "Are you going to try to breed me to something?"

That terrible darkness passed over his face again. His hands curled into fists at his sides.

I didn't move, nailed in place. If I broke and ran, would he come after me?

It passed. Sweat gemmed his forehead, highlighting the thick ropes of scarring. "I wouldn't presume, Isabella. Why would I?"

Why would he be so kind—and so painfully shy? I finished the sentence inside my head. *Well, that makes sense. But I know he wants me. At least, I think he does.*

"To the others, I suppose it looks like that. It's part of the *vrkolak* inheritance in my family, the...the need. The c-c-c—" I saw his throat swell with the word, and supplied it for him.

"The curse," I finished.

"Yes." He looked grateful. "That."

I took another deep jolting breath. Sweat dried to a crack-glaze on my back, and my heart was slowing down a little. "What *can* you tell me, Jeremy?"

"Nothing." He made that bitter little sound again, the one that tried to be a laugh. "I'm barred from giving you even the slightest scrap of information. It has to be...decided on faith."

"Great." *Isn't that just par for the course.* "I'll take that tea, Jeremy. I went to—"

He shook his head. "Tell me later."

I'm not sure I'll want to. "I went to a tavern called the Belus. Have you ever been?"

"Are you trying to drive me into a rage?" His fists shook, his teeth locked together, the words forced out in small sharp chunks. "If you are, this is the way to do so."

I took another deep breath. "Jeremy." The gods only knew why I did it, but I stepped closer and touched his shoulder. A thunderous charge, a power transformer humming under my hand and the black cashmere. His shoulder was rigid, and a muscle jumped in his jaw. "Look," I said, and my voice sounded very small. "You can't expect me just to stay stuck in here when you can't tell me anything. I have to find out on my own. I found a friend, and—"

"I doubt Rafe Dietrich is a friend to anyone," Jeremy snapped. "He's dangerous."

"Well, he was good enough to me, and I'm meeting him tomorrow for coffee on my lunch break."

Tremont said nothing. I had finally struck him speechless.

"And a week from now he's taking me to dinner. I'll find out what I can about your curse."

He shut his eyes. His jaw worked.

"And then I'll see what I can do about that curse of yours."

"No," Tremont said. "Isabella. *Please.* All I can do is ask."

I was beginning to calm down a little. "I'm glad you're here. I thought something chased me."

"Something?" Taut and harsh, like the rest of him.

What could I say? *I almost thought that you'd changed into a big cat and were chasing me.* Had I really thought he would do something so petty or vindictive? He seemed to go out of his way *not* to frighten me, not to show me any more of his own obvious weirdness than he could possibly manage. Did he think I would turn tail and run if he admitted to knowing a little bit of sorcery?

I had to ask. "Are you dangerous?"

"Sometimes." His eyes still closed, he leaned away from me. "Not...not to you."

"Well, good." Did I believe him?

He was as calm and even-tempered as I'd ever seen a man get, most of the time. "Did you know I'd left the house?"

"Do you know what it's like to sit here and wait for someone to deliver your dead body? I can't afford to leave here, that will alert them, and place you in even more danger...I could have torn this damn place down."

Well, that puts an entirely different shine on things. "I'll be all right," I said. "Really. I know what I'm doing."

"Do you? Raphael is dangerous. If he thinks you're..." Something eased in him, the hard dark rage relaxing just a fraction.

My lips were dry. If I could just sit down and talk to him, I could probably figure all this out. "Is that offer of tea still good?"

"Are you sure you want to?" The way he said it surprised me—each word bitten off, hard. It only made his voice more beautiful.

"Maybe," I said.

"What is it that you want me to say, Miss Harpe? I've said all I'm *allowed,* I can't do any more." He opened his eyes finally, looked at me. "Will you allow me some faith, some benefit of the doubt?"

I opened my mouth to reply, shut it. He was right. He'd been good to me. Better than a lot of others.

What about this cursebreaker thing? Do I just not have to worry until I actually do break this bloody curse? But how can I without... An idea struck me with an almost physical force.

"I'm seeing Raphael for a while," I said. "That's final. But after I squeeze him for the information he has, I'll do my best to break your curse. Okay?"

His shoulders sagged. Tremont shrank right in front of me. "No," he said, finally, and there was a new tinge of bitter sarcasm. "But I accept your terms. I can hardly do otherwise. If you told me to jump from the roof and sing on the way down, I would be compelled to do so. I hope *that* eases your mind." He sounded bitterly sarcastic.

"Not really." I sounded just as sarcastic. How on earth had we ended up *here?* I wanted to help him. "But we can start with that cup of tea, and while we're having that we can talk. I have a better idea of what I want to ask you, now." *Like, am I this cursebreaker? And if I was, why wouldn't you let me leave the house?*

He shook his head. "I will have to decline, my dear." His voice was thick, a glimmer in his blue, blue eyes. "I am not safe right now. Not even for you, no matter how much I want to be."

What the hell does that mean? "Jeremy—"

He shook his head. "When you're done playing with Dietrich, we'll have that cup of tea, Isabella."

Then, to cap off the entire goddamn night, he turned away and left me standing there in the foyer, feeling—of all things—cheated.

Why? I'd paid my money, played my game of pool, and gotten some answers. More than I had before.

Okay, that's it. Time for bed and some heavy brooding.

I trudged up the stairs, heading for my bedroom. Even though I knew, miserably, that I wasn't going to be able to sleep.

CHAPTER TWENTY

THE NEXT MORNING WAS A total, utter fucking disaster.

First of all, Jeremy wasn't in the library when I came down all freshly-scrubbed and contrite. I passed a bad night tossing and turning, got up early, and found the place deserted. The coffee tray was there, of course, but I hadn't realized just how much I'd grown used to him in the mornings, his occasional quiet word or ironic observation.

Then, after I'd stubbed a toe, spilled coffee on my gray silk Chinese-collared shirt, knocked over not one but *two* stacks of books, and uselessly gone up and down the stairs to the second level four times, forgetting something crucial each time, Mharian strolled into the library.

Her hair still stood up in an angry ruff, and she stalked across the first floor straight for my desk, where I was sitting staring at a pile of ephemerides that refused, no matter how hard I glared, to get any smaller. I had just poured myself a fresh cup of coffee and was considering hurling the cup through the window, as well.

She halted right in front of my desk, long slim woman in a long slim black skirt and white blouse, her belt now drips and scallops of silver chain. I gave up wondering exactly what she was. In this town, who knew, and who cared anyway? It was kind of cool being the closest thing to normal in a whole city.

No. Not really. Not cool at all.

Mharian stared, sloe eyes wide and sharp with displeasure. I stared back, contemplating the wisdom of just going back to bed and pulling the covers over my head.

I was tempted to do that a lot lately.

Finally she let out another small spitting noise, just like a cat. "If you hurt him, I'll kill you." This she pronounced with all a three-year-old's certainty.

Oh, you don't even want to start with me, little girl. I set my coffee cup down with a precise little click. "What the hell are you fucking babbling about?"

There, I'd been deliberately rude. Maybe Jeremy would fire me.

The thought, oddly enough, didn't make me feel liberated. Instead, it touched off a burst of panic that I swallowed, narrowing my eyes, staring her down.

Her pale cheeks flushed. She really did have great skin, damn her. "He's my *friend.*" She enunciated clearly, as if I was an idiot, hands on hips and eyes glowing like dark coals. "And he's an *honorable man.* Any woman would feel *lucky.* Blessed, even. You hurt him and I'll *kill* you."

I was forcibly reminded of grade school, the way she talked. Was it just me, or did she seem slightly developmentally off? She looked just a little younger than me, and I'm no spring chicken.

Don't be ridiculous. Almost thirty-two isn't over the hill. You're just coming into your own. The disagreeable smile that brought to my lips probably wasn't the most tactful thing in the world. Neither was what I said after that.

"If you have some sort of complaint about me, go visit the boss." I realized all my wandering around the house hadn't shown me Jeremy's bedroom. I wondered where he slept. "He's bound to be along sooner or later."

"It's not like he can stay away."

My skin prickled—another thunderstorm, charged air rippling through the library.

The hem of her long black skirt ruffled, she leaned forward like a horse at the starting gate. "Are you stupid? Don't you know what's going on here?"

Lady, if I knew what was going on here, I'd be halfway to fixing it. What do you think I'm trying to do? "Going on?" I made my eyes big and innocent. "I'm just a glorified housekeeper, shelving books and reading to the master of the house. Nobody tells me anything." *Nobody except Raphael.*

"He's *in love*, you dolt." Her cheeks flamed with color, her eyes glowing, she actually looked very pretty. Like Judy Garland in Technicolor, all vivid and beautiful.

I felt my own sallow drabness come back to haunt me— just an aging hippie witch bouncing from place to place. *You're a very pretty girl*, Tremont had said, and I knew other people had said it too. But I wasn't feeling very pretty right now, and that's usually the kiss of death for any kind of beauty.

Irritation rose to a furious pitch. She really did scrape me the wrong way all the way down to my genes. "Good. I've already got a guy I'm seeing, a nice guy with a motorcycle who tells me more in half an hour than the rest of this goddamn place has told me in months. And anyway, my personal life doesn't concern you, sister. So just...*back...off!*"

Her flush drained like spilled wine. She raised her right hand.

My fingers folded around a copy of Trelawney's *Curses And Their Makings*, a heavy leatherbound monstrosity I could probably chuck at her if I needed to. The way I was feeling right now I would have loved to smash her in the face.

And that frightened me. I *never* got this angry. Bad mood plus whatever this woman did that rubbed me so raw equaled one Isabella Harpe shaking with too much anger. For someone with my talents, that kind of anger can be lethal.

Something in me—that oddly enough had Jeremy's deep beautiful voice—was trying to tell me to calm down.

I had to blink twice before my eyes returned the verdict: yes, I was seeing a red, crackling, spitting haze around the fingers of her right hand.

"I should teach you a lesson, you dirtblooded amateur." Her eyes now glittered coldly, and her voice had changed, become more adult. "About respecting your betters."

That did it. My temper snapped. I pushed myself upright, knocking my chair over; it thudded on the carpeted floor. I carried the book with me, my hands locked around it—if I pointed, or snapped my fingers, one of my own curses might fly free. "Get the hell out of my library." Each word scraped past my teeth.

For a moment, she looked uncertain. The red haze writhing over her fingers hummed, a low malicious sound.

"*Mharian!*" From the second level. It was the chill hurtful voice of the man with elf-ears; I had the impression he was leaning over the railing on the second floor. "What in the name of Underhill do you think you're doing?"

Neither of us looked up.

"She needs a lesson." Mharian's hair fluttered on a slight breeze that came from nowhere. I knew this feeling, having seen a few witch's duels in my time. She was getting ready to do something very nasty and possibly painful to yours truly.

My fingers dug into the leather of the book's cover, my feet braced against the library floor. If she tossed that red crackling static at me, what would happen?

I was almost mad enough to want to find out.

I inhaled deeply. "Look." My tone was calm, reasonable, and made the entire library rattle uneasily. "I don't know who you think you are, but my life is none of your business. Calm down and leave me alone, I'm having a *really* bad morning and I do *not* want to take it out on you."

For some reason, that just drove her into fresh cold fury. Her skin was almost translucent now, and I caught a glimpse of something moving under her skirt. Something that definitely did *not* look like human legs.

"Mharian!" The slim brown Spock-eared man appeared, catching her raised right wrist. "Are you mad?" He cast one passionless glance at me. "If you cause trouble here..."

"Let go, Guillame." She sounded a lot more adult now. "I'm going to kill her."

"If you try to harm her, Tremont will be well within his rights to—" He glanced back at me.

I stood stiffly, my fingers locked around the book. Cold sweat gathered under my arms and at the small of my back; I was sharply aware of my heartbeat suddenly smoothing down, easing. Whatever was about to happen was very close, and all I had to do was relax and see my way through it. The library resonated like the inside of a bell, stroked softly by the vibration of faroff thunder.

My gaze locked with Mharian's. She knew, too. It had gone too far to stop. Some things, once they've achieved critical mass, just have to roll until they lose momentum.

She pushed the brown man away and made one smooth, complex movement with her right hand. The crackling red sparking haze bulleted toward my face, a burst of warmth from my nose. My arms jerked, bringing the book up, and I shouted something shapeless. Whatever it was, it did the job, because the red stuff veered away at the last moment as if I'd hit it with a baseball bat.

Glass shattered, cool morning air flooding in. Crisped leather and charred paper exploded. Mharian let out a short, cheated scream.

I would have fallen if I hadn't fetched up against something hard and warm. Stacks of books on my desk fell over, a low shattering growl rumbled inside my bones.

The warm wetness dripping from my nose was blood.

Great. The silk was going to be ruined.

The brown man caught Mharian's wrist, twisted *hard*. Her mouth made a soft *O* of surprise as she went down to her knees. "I should have known," Spock-Ears said grimly. "My apologies, Tremont."

What the bloody blue hell is going on? Did I just do that? Whatever happened had subsided. It was a good thing, too; my blood sugar and pressure had both just bottomed out. Dealing with shit like this will do that to you.

Jeremy's hands clasped my shoulders. He set me back on my feet. Somehow my entire body recognized his hands. And that musky cologne washed over me, I just couldn't smell it very well through the warm copper of blood in my nose.

Wait. There was no *way* he could have gotten behind me without me noticing, there weren't any doors behind my desk.

"What's going on here?" The growl was coming from him. I knew because the words rose out of it seamlessly, colored with a rage that threatened to smash the maplewood desk to splinters.

It was a singularly interesting moment. Guy with elf-ears holding catwoman in an armlock, her arm torqued inhumanly far up. Behind me, Jeremy Tremont, boiling with a rage so intense a hot draft touched the library, the desk groaning, more books falling, paper ruffling, my coffee cup chattering and steaming.

If that spills, I'm going to have to clean it up.

Elf-ears, catwoman, scarred millionaire. And one witch with a nosebleed. *How do I get into these situations? Mom? Grandma? Anyone want to tell me?*

"She's a dirtblooded little *bitch!*" Mharian gasped.

The temperature dropped about twenty degrees. Jeremy's hands were gentle, irresistible, as he turned me to face him. I didn't think I could—if I was feeling his rage this clearly with no skin-to-skin contact, what would meeting his eyes do?

Shudders spilled through me as if an animal had me in its teeth, shaking, shaking.

"Isabella?" There it was again, that oddly possessive tone when he said my name.

Need a sign for library rules: don't spill, don't talk loudly, and don't throw red lightning at the librarian. That should about cover it.

"I'm okay," I heard myself lie, shakily, staring at his broad chest as more blood dripped, spattered warmly on gray silk. "Where did you come from?"

His right hand cupped my chin, forced my head back; his skin was warm and very dry. My gaze met his, and I found to my profound relief that he looked just the same. I barely even saw the scars anymore, I just saw his eyes and the betraying little movements around his mouth that would give away what he was feeling. Right now his irises were incandescent blue and his mouth was so tight I could have snapped it in half. He was holding onto his temper by the thinnest of margins.

It should have frightened me.

"You're bleeding." He said it softly, but his gaze flicked over my shoulder and the dart of unrestrained fury took all the starch out of my knees. Mharian blurted out another soft sound of pain as wood groaned. I heard something splinter. Was *he* doing that?

"It's my own damn fault." I searched for something else to say. "Do you have a Kleenex?"

He blinked, looked back down at me. I felt a little gratified for having distracted him.

Then his gaze rose over my shoulder again, and Mharian let out a tiny shocked sound. I didn't blame her, I *never* wanted Jeremy Tremont to look at me that way, as if I was a cockroach that needed squishing badly. I never thought a scarred man who was so shy and diffident could look so damn *lethal*.

The shyness actually made it worse, because I understood that he didn't get angry often, if at all.

Well, he was furious now.

"She's young," Guillame said. Was that *apology* in his cold, hurtful voice? And just a small helping of fear? "She doesn't know any better."

"In my house, she should know better." Jeremy's words scraped along my skin. His hand was still on my chin, warm and comforting, and if it hadn't been for him holding me up with the other hand curled around my right arm I might have decided to faint. Checkout time at eleven, too much fun in the last few days. "I *told* you. My librarian is *off-limits*, she is *not* to be touched. You are not to even *breathe* in her direction."

"Jeremy." I leaned into him, trying to get his attention. "*Jeremy.*"

Silence rang and bloomed, fell victim to the deep heavy growling. It *was* coming from him, but it didn't seem to frighten me. I'd probably gone beyond fear at the moment. Finally, he looked back down at me. The growl lessened, faded, stilled. "Isabella."

"Leave her alone." My throat was dry as desert sand, my tongue oddly thick. I haven't had my voice shake like that since the first car accident I'd predicted in high school. "It wasn't her fault, it was mine. Leave her alone."

"You broke a window with a *salieris* curse?" One eyebrow quirked. "Come now, Isabella. The rules are simple, you are *not* to be disturbed."

"Why, because you think I'll hit the road if I see a little weirdness? Come on, Jeremy. Get off it and get me a Kleenex." I hoped Spock-Ears would get the drift and take Mharian out of here. Tremont didn't look happy. He looked, in fact, murderously angry, and I should have been afraid of him. Especially after last night.

I wasn't. Instead, I was relieved to see him. One could say I was damn near overjoyed.

He was about to look over my shoulder again, so I had to take drastic action. I let my knees give and pitched myself forward into him, hoping he'd move his hand on my chin or I'd look really stupid.

It worked. He let go of my chin and caught me, and I was suddenly in an almost-familiar place, with my forehead resting in the hollow under where his collarbone met his shoulder, breathing in that musky cologne tainted with the smell of my own blood.

"Don't move," I said, hoping I sounded faint. It was truth in advertising, I *felt* a little faint, but not for the reason one might think—having red lightning thrown at me and windows breaking. Not to mention everything else that had happened since my Oldsmobile blew its radiator.

No, it felt *really* good to lean into him, to feel his arms close around me, and to close out the rest of this weird, weird world.

I don't know how long I stayed there, but I did notice he was breathing kind of strangely. He would take a deep inhale I could feel ruffling the top of my messy, loose hair, and hold it in like he was doing a joint. Just when I thought he would pass out from oxygen deprivation, he let it out softly, and repeated the whole process.

And me? The shakes evened out until I wasn't shuddering like a bug in a zapper anymore. I took in a few deep breaths of my own, let them out as sighs. For the first time since last night, I was starting to feel all right again. More like myself.

Cool air blew in through the shattered window. I smelled boiled coffee, charred leather, and the wet heavy freshness of morning. I also smelled *him*, and was acutely aware that I was probably getting blood on his ever-present black sweater.

That made me move. I didn't want to, I wanted to stay right where I was. But I had a curse to figure out and some damage control to do, so I raised my head and found out he definitely *did* have his arms around me. And newsflash number two was that I had a cascade of mostly improper thoughts that I'd never had about a boss, or a guy so shy he could give the Elephant Man lessons.

I said the first thing that popped into my head. "Do you have a Kleenex?" *I've got a bloody face, you know. Good one, Isabella. Really going for the romance here, aren't you?*

"Oh. My God, I'm sorry. Here." He dug in the back pocket of his jeans and produced—of all things—a nice white linen handkerchief. I've spent my life making do, I realized it was nice to be around someone so anal-retentively over-prepared. "Would you like to tell me what happened? I'll throw that little bitch out as soon as dusk hits, or earlier if you like."

He was so mannerly, it was almost a shock to hear him say 'bitch'. I wiped at my nose, grimacing as dried blood cracked. The second shock was the restrained violence in his tone.

"Not necessary." I decided the best way to deal with it was to pretend not to notice he was angry. He'd probably calm down.

I hoped.

"It was my fault," I continued. "I was having a bad morning, and I snapped at her. I was rude." I glossed over the fact that she'd threatened to kill me. It was the type of thing a kid would say, and the rest of her was just as childlike. "She acts like an eight-year-old."

"An eight-year-old with entirely too much power. Guillame should have been with her." He studied my face, forgetting to shake his hair down to cover his scars and fall in his eyes. "You're pale."

"I didn't sleep well. And you weren't here this morning." I tried not to sound petulant.

That stopped him for a full fifteen seconds. It was the first time I ever saw Jeremy Tremont's jaw drop. He finally managed to yank it back up while I congratulated myself for distracting him from that scary, unpredictable rage. "You...I mean, I thought...I..."

I had a completely reprehensible urge to grin like a maniac. Go figure. "I'm used to having coffee with you in the mornings, you know."

He stared at me like I was speaking a different language. Cool air touched my face, I wiped harder at the dried blood under my nose. I wanted to wash my face. I wanted to take another shower and put the silk to soak in some cold water. I wanted to go back to bed and forget about all of this.

Most of all, I wanted to step up close to him again, rest my face against his chest, and feel that damnable *safety* again. "You know, you have this really odd way of making me feel safe. It's nice. I bet nobody's ever told you that before." I scrubbed harder at the dried blood. Was I *blushing?* Gods above and below, I was.

He looked like I'd hit him with a hammer, or like I'd just told him there was ratshit in his Cheerios. I had a funny sinking sensation in my chest.

I decided to keep talking. Silence was dangerous. "Anyway, it wasn't Mharian's fault. She got angry, I was in a snit, you see the result." I took two steps back, not wanting to look at the damage. "I've got to go clean up. I'll pick up down here as soon as I change my shirt and wash my face, okay?"

He looked around like he had to be reminded of where he was. Still said nothing.

My chest was definitely hurting now. I'd been half-believing...what? I knew he was attracted to me, and counting on me to break this curse of his, but I'd thought...

"Great. Lovely." I backed up another step. He just kept staring at me like I'd grown another head. "Okay, I'll see you later, then."

I bolted. All the way up to my room I tried to console myself with the thought that I hadn't done anything stupid, that the man was my boss, and why on earth was I adding more trouble to a situation that was already weirder than Detroit on Devil's Night?

Like I said, the morning was a complete, utter, fucking disaster. It almost made me regret leaving Jimmy Cassidy.

No. Not really.

Chapter Twenty-One

YOU'D THINK THAT WITH THE morning's events I would have forgotten about my coffee date with Raphael. But no, I'd paid for any information he could give me, and I intended to get the most I could for that coin.

Besides, I needed to get out of the house. I didn't even go back to the library. I figured the morning's fun and games were enough for one day. If there were shredded books and broken glass, I didn't want to see them.

Having invisible servants had to be good for something.

The idea that maybe I was avoiding facing Jeremy again occurred to me with depressing regularity as I got dressed.

I wore jeans and a blue peasant blouse, and a cute pair of cotton espadrilles I'd actually paid full price for. I could afford new shoes, and *that* was a nice change.

The day was very warm, and when Raphael showed up, motorcycle growling, dark hair flying, I was beginning to feel a little better about the whole deal.

He didn't look so handsome in daylight. Some men need dark bars and a little alcohol to make them seem more attractive. He was okay, there was just something...missing...in the clear light of day.

I was so glad to see someone who would at least *talk* to me, I showed it by barely waiting for him to stop before I climbed on the back of the bike, and away we went.

He took me to downtown Tremont proper. It was a nice little main street, with some parts blocked off for pedestrians, shops and boutiques and only the persistent breath of weirdness even in the middle of the day to remind me of where I was. The buildings were turn-of-the-century, good bones under the cosmetic excess of the twenties and fifties, very little new construction but lots of new paint and redone elegance. The roofs were steeply pitched—well, this close to the mountains it must snow a lot in winter.

The thought of Tremont under six feet of snow made me shiver and tighten my arms around Raphael's waist. Or, maybe, it was the thought of curling up in front of the big fire in the library with a book and a pot of tea, and Jeremy's companionable silence.

He parked in a small lot facing the back end of a laundromat, the blank brick wall suspiciously free of graffiti, and put the kickstand down as I slid off the back of the bike. His dark hair was ruffled and his jacket creaked just a little as he moved; I'd had enough presence of mind to braid my hair tightly so only a few black curls fell in my face.

"So, Miss Pretty," he said, half-twisting on the seat as I fiddled with my messenger bag, getting it to hang just right. "Little bit eager to get out of the house?"

"Every girl needs a holiday." I felt my mouth tilting, for the first time, into a smile. I blew a curl out of my face. "I had a little problem with one of the guests this morning. It was an intriguing experience."

"They come fast and thick in Tremont town." He'd shaved, and his hair was a soft mess. Some essential hardness was missing in him now. Night would be when the predator in him came out. "I didn't think you'd show."

"Why?" I quit fussing with my bag long enough to give him a lopsided grin. "I promised not to break my angel's heart."

The grin made him smile. He dismounted, his jacket open and showing a plain white T-shirt. If he'd had cigarettes rolled into his sleeve, he could have done a fair James Dean impression, except for the fact that his hair was a chaos of darkness instead of a slick almost-pompadour. The feeling that I was looking at the antithesis to Jeremy Tremont's careful precision returned. It was a little uncomfortable. Jeremy wouldn't hurt me; did that mean Raphael would?

"Your eyes just went dark, Miss Pretty." He produced a cigarette, which made me dig in my bag for mine. Sunlight poured down, he lit my smoke for me, and we started walking.

It was the most natural thing in the world. "What's going on in that head of yours?"

I suppose last night might have given him a healthy respect for my intellectual capability. "Just thinking about how I ended up here, that's all. An odd place for the wind to bring me."

All the shops had iron grilles or doors rolled out of the way, just like Babe's Café. There were padlocks hanging neatly, too. I suppose a normal person or a tourist wouldn't have seen them, but once you did, they wouldn't go away. Several of the shops had names that weren't quite what one would expect. Like the Siren's Green, a music shop. Or Grimbolding's, a small boutique that apparently sold little statues of twisted ceramic and fluid stone. One of the places—a bar called Stoker's Corner—exhaled a cold breath of malice onto the sidewalk as we passed its open maw. I thought of being down here at night, with all the shops shuttered and that chill exhale.

The businesses were doing well, thriving, in fact. How many tourists simply stopped in this Charming Little Mountain Town to buy a few trinkets and hurried on to find a hotel?

"You've been here a while." Raphael's voice cut through my woolgathering. I had to pay attention to him.

If he was Kine, he was capable of doing a lot of damage in a very short amount of time. The Trottinos had employed a Kine enforcer once, without knowing it; I'd seen him in action during a bar brawl. It was a good thing they considered it beneath themselves to beat up on humans most of the time.

"Couple of months." I frowned. I'd arrived just as spring did, we were now past May Day and into the beginning of summer. "Or a little more." The sunlight was delicious, on my shoulders like a benediction. My earrings shivered—cheap imitation silver drops.

There were people on the street, but I didn't look too closely. I didn't want to. Still, I caught glimpses: a man with long black feathers on his muscled forearms, a woman in a fluttering pink gauze dress that clashed just a little with the bright blue of her skin and the long primrose fall of her hair. The world wavered, but Raphael remained normal each time I looked at him.

So he wasn't wearing a shield of magic to keep normal people from seeing something. Then again, it was almost unnecessary, most normal people don't *want* to see the other species that lived among us.

Even I didn't really want to see sometimes. This wasn't like other cities, where you maybe caught glimpses every few days or so.

No, this was a constant reminder, itching behind my eyes, throbbing in my fingers, making me want to pull my cards out.

Just how many Others live in this town? No wonder *vrkolak* came here, everything else did too and anything hungry would love the chance to get in on the act.

"Nobody's ever put up with Tremont this long." He gave me a curious glance, ditching his butt in the gutter. I did the same.

My, my, Raphael, I do believe you're fishing. "Tremont's strange." I made my tone light, teasing. "But I'm used to strange men. He's easy to please, all I have to do is put the damn books away and make sure the plants are watered. Not that he pays enough for putting up with this weird place, but a girl's got to eat, and at least here I don't have a slimy son of a bitch trying to put his hand up my skirt because he signs my checks." I had to stop to take a breath.

"Bitter, party of one?" Raphael chuffed out a short laugh, walking alongside me with that hipshot lazy grace, between me and the road like a gentleman. Bustling downtown Tremont, Main Street USA. Just don't look under the curtain or behind the iron gates. "There's the coffee shop. Don't worry, it's human."

"Should I be worried?" I gave him a big-eyed, mock-serious stare, and he laughed easily. The laugh sent a thread of pleasant heat through me. I could almost pretend I was walking down the street with a normal man.

Then he made a quick movement, and presented me with a little parcel wrapped in brown paper. "Hope not. Nothing to worry about, especially if you're with me. I take care of my own, Miss Pretty."

"Oh, I can believe that." I mentally reviewed everything I knew about Kine. Would I be agreeing to more than coffee if I took the present? *But I'm not one of yours, angel.* "So you're trying your luck, then?" I took the package. It was small, and very heavy.

"Definitely. If you were Tremont's cursebreaker, he wouldn't let you go walking. Especially with me. We don't see eye-to-eye, His Majesty and me."

My espadrilles made a shushing sound. "And why is that? Thank you, for the present."

"Open it later. It's a surprise." He held the door open, and I was suddenly acutely aware that I hadn't had lunch and that he was wearing a citrusy cologne. I didn't like it as much as I liked Jeremy's, but maybe I was just being picky. I moved past him, a little closer than necessary, and he went very still as my shoulder brushed his coat. The kind of stillness that folds over a man when he's acutely aware of a woman near him.

It reminded me of how Jeremy would freeze, even when I only reached past him for the sugar or a book.

I gave my head a little shake, pushing the thought away. "Why don't you two see eye-to-eye?"

"He's a douche," Raphael said. "Closes himself up in that house and bars access to the locus. It's maddening, really. If you could drop him a little word about this being the twentieth century, I'd appreciate it."

"I don't think he'd listen." The coffee shop was brightly lit, painted warm gold and orange, and the two teenagers behind the counter were, indeed, blessedly normal and oblivious. Although how they *could* be, working in this town, was beyond me. I gave Raphael a wide, if somewhat unsettled smile. "I'll buy you coffee, angel. Why don't you tell me what else you'd like to reach Tremont's ears, then we can settle down to getting to know each other?"

IT WAS LATE AFTERNOON BY the time I looked up from the chessboard and noticed the fall of the light. "I'd better get back," I said, and Raphael groaned, sliding his hands back through his dark hair. His eyes twinkled merrily, and for a moment—just a moment—they were a little too far apart again, and they glowed with a light that wasn't a reflection from the counter.

"Come on, the game's getting good," he said. "Two more moves and I'll have you."

We'd taken over a corner with comfortable chairs and a chessboard, and a murmured request had brought out a paper bag of cheap plastic pieces. I hadn't done too badly.

Chess isn't one of my favorites, it takes a cool calculating hatred to play well, and I'm not good at that. But I've had enough practice not to embarrass myself, and Raphael had let slip a little more than he'd probably intended.

For instance, there had been a fair amount of talk about my being at the Tremont house. *We all thought everything was over, and you'd be snapped up in no time. Imagine our surprise when you started going shopping.* Here Raphael had laughed, moving his bishop as I took a sip of my cappuccino. My hands still ached for my cards. As soon as I got home, then.

Funny how I'd started thinking of 4444 Tremont as *home.*

"You've been saying that for a half-hour." I took a swallow of cold cappuccino. The crumbled remains of a croissant lay on a plate between us, but I'd done all the eating and he'd done all the talking.

"Only because you take too much time between moves." His eyes met mine, interested and amused, and there was a shadow in them that made my heart pound. His teeth were very white. "Just finish out the game, sweets."

I shook my head, hauling myself up to my feet. "I've got other appointments today, angel." Was I too late to read to Jeremy? Maybe, from the way the light came through the plate glass windows.

"I'll take you home, then." But he made no move to hurry, picking up the pieces one by one and slipping them into the bag.

"I'll call a cab. No reason to have you ferry me around." I let my lips curve. "Though I do enjoy it."

"Have dinner with me." He looked up from the table. "I'd be more than happy to take you home, Miss Pretty."

Why do you keep calling me that? Irritation worked at my good humor; I pushed it away. It was only lack of sleep and an unsatisfying morning that made me snappish. Try as I might,

Raphael wouldn't tell me about the Tremont curse—but the other things he told me were just as interesting. "Next week?" I hazarded. "Thursday?" It was my day to see to all the little errands of living—going to the drugstore, shopping for clothes, that sort of thing.

"Seven sharp, on the corner. You're sure you don't want me to take you home?"

"It's not my home," I reminded him. "Just somewhere I'm staying until the wind calls my name again."

"Hope that won't happen before we can finish this game," he said, and gave me a very wide, white smile. I was suddenly struck by the uncomfortable thought that I wasn't fooling either of us. But there was a tone of uncertainty—he had taken it for granted that if I had anything to do with Tremont's curse I wouldn't be allowed to spend time with him.

You don't know Jeremy, I thought, my lip threatening to curl. Go figure, I was actually a little miffed on Tremont's behalf, even though he probably wouldn't have cared what a Kine thought of him.

"I hope so too." I leaned in close to give him a peck on the cheek. He went still again, and I could have laughed. Whatever else Raphael was, he was male, and that gave me an edge.

He wasn't invulnerable to my charms, at least. Not like a certain scarred man I could name.

"Thank you, angel," I breathed in his ear. "You've saved my day. It was going badly until you showed up."

He let out a long soft exhale that sounded more menacing than it should have. "Nobody's ever said that to me before." His grin was just as self-deprecating and charming as ever as I straightened; his hands deft among the pieces on the chessboard. "Thank you, Miss Pretty."

"See you next Thursday."

"You can count on it." He looked back down at the table, and I left.

Outside, the air was very soft, the sun sinking in the sky and turning bloody. I'd spent longer than I'd thought in the coffee shop, time drifting away. I was too late to read to Jeremy or do anything else. He probably wouldn't want to talk to me either. I kept my gaze deliberately averted. People hurried to their cars, others walking more slowly, unconcerned. All the hurrying people were normal; the ones that didn't...

It only took two blocks out on the street before a familiar, very old car braked to a stop, pulling close into the pavement and taking advantage of an empty parking spot. I sighed, bending down to look in the passenger-side window. Sad, equally familiar brown eyes met mine.

It was Lewis, and the antique car.

I tried to feel annoyed. Instead, all I felt was relief. I was in the front seat with him before you could say jacksparrow, pulled the door closed and pressed the ancient lock down, then looked over to find Lewis staring at me.

"Jeremy sent you, didn't he." It wasn't a question.

He shrugged, hit his turn signal, and pulled smoothly out into traffic. I lit a cigarette, trying not to look out the windows.

I didn't mind the strange so much when I was skating its outer corners, but to be in a whole town full of it?

"I wish you could talk to me." My own voice startled me. "I've spent an entire afternoon playing chess and being stuffed full of trivia about this place." I lapsed into silence, smoking and thinking furiously.

There are several factions here, Raphael had told me, his face abstract in the middle of the game. *There's the Kine, of course; they want the locus open. The s'lin and kalak don't give a damn as long as they get to eat, but Tremont thins their ranks every now and again and they have no love for him. The earthfolk want the ley lines to continue running smoothly, the refugees from other places just want peace and quiet and the chance to fleece the human tourists, and then...there's the Hungry Ones. They don't care much either, as long as they can hunt and feed—but Tremont thins them out too, when the pressure gets too bad. They hate him as much as anyone else. The earthfolk and refugees don't care much for him, for all he keeps the peace, and the Hungry Ones actively work against him. Still, he rules the town like his father did, and all from his manor in the north.*

It wasn't so much the disdain in Raphael's voice as the thought of Jeremy, stuck in the silent house, hated by everyone, that got to me. That part of the pattern was clear, at least; Jeremy was truly alone. If he'd inherited his family's stand at the gates of whatever power in this town everyone was so hungry to possess, I couldn't see him doing less than watching over it with fierce commitment. Prissy and silent dedication, but dedication nonetheless.

"That's the difference," I murmured, and Lewis gave me an inquiring look. I shook my head; more black curls had fallen in my face.

Lewis didn't reply. He never did. Instead, he piloted the car through the thinning traffic and the purple of swiftly-falling dusk. When I saw the double iron gates I heaved an involuntary sigh of relief, and Lewis gave me a dark, sad glance. I tried not to look at him either, wondering what he'd turn into when it got dark.

He goes out to thin them, Raphael said. So Jeremy *could* leave the house.

Stone and windows rose up in comforting solidity, all three stories of it, and I was barely out of the car before it took off again, heading out through the gates with its tires whispering on the perfect black asphalt. The roses were still freighted only with buds, and that was strange—whoever heard of roses not blooming when it came into summer? But the buds were full and fat, and each one was still tipped with crimson. Just another strange thing in this strange place.

I should have left ages ago. The wind hadn't whispered my name. Whatever was going on here, I was meant to figure it out. If I couldn't, who could?

I was a witch, after all. Who better to untangle a curse?

I made it into the house while the sun was still in the sky, red and purple scarves painting the vault of heaven. The front door wasn't locked, and I didn't feel like trying one of the side doors. Instead, I shut the heavy carved wood behind me and leaned against it, my knees gone suspiciously weak. My bag was heavy with whatever Raphael had given me; I couldn't wait to unwrap it.

I hadn't had a home, ever, that I could recall. Each place I landed was only a stepping-stone to somewhere else, somewhere new and different.

Nobody was waiting on the stairs. I climbed them anyway, and made it through the maze of halls until I reached the library.

I pushed the double doors open, and walked through the familiar bookshelves. The section on curses was on this floor.

The library was eerily silent. I usually had music playing—and I remembered now that Jeremy never balked at any of it, not even when I went on a Led Zep kick and kept singing *hanging from the gallows pole* over and over again while I shelved. In fact, he seemed almost to like my singing, and my taste in music too. Though I had caught him wincing once or twice when I twisted the volume knob up.

He'd never complained about a single thing, even my smoking. And I'd just gone on, blithely unconcerned, while he suffered under the lash of an entire town's contempt—a town he did his best to protect from chaos.

I heard a slight sound and whirled so fast my braid whipped out.

Jeremy's hand fell back down to his side. His face was set and white, his eyes bright blue, his hair mussed and falling over his forehead. He said nothing. Had he just appeared out of thin air?

I wouldn't put it past him. I swallowed, set my shoulders. "Hi," I offered, inadequately.

He simply stood there, staring at me. He was taller than Raphael, and his shoulders were a little wider. I knew just how strong he was. How could I *not* know? He'd held me, I'd felt the power running through him. How could I have missed that, his power or his grace? Under those scars muscle rippled. All the way down his chest, disappearing into his jeans.

I wondered what it would feel like to touch them, to slide my hand along the roughness over his ribs.

"I know I missed reading to you," I rushed forward. "I'm sorry. I just...this morning. I had to get *out*. See, I'm back before dark, and I thought I'd look around the curses section and maybe take another stab at figuring out what to do to help—"

That was as far as I got before he took two steps forward, caught my shoulders, and kissed me.

I more than met him halfway, and it was like lightning. His hands on me, one at the small of my back scorching through my shirt, the other sliding under my messed-up braid to cup my nape. His mouth was warm, he tasted like night and musk and mint, and I leaned into him shamelessly, almost melting. I've been kissed before, but never so thoroughly. My heart sped up, pounding all through me, and in the middle of the sudden urgent drag of desire I felt a curious comfort.

I made a little sound of protest when he broke away, and he smiled, smoothing his thumb over my cheekbone. I barely saw the pleats and wrinkles of ruined flesh, only the light in his eyes and the shape his mouth made. That smile floored me. It was unexpectedly sweet.

"I trust you," he whispered. Darkness was gathering in the library as the sun sank from the sky, night creeping into town. "Do you understand?"

No, I don't. "I had coffee with Raphael today," I whispered. "He told me some very interesting—"

Jeremy let go of me, abruptly, and stepped back. His hands dropped to his sides, and I had to stop myself from lurching towards him. The light was fading too quickly, no storm tonight for once, but maybe there would be bad weather right here in the library. Would he look at me the way he'd looked at Mharian?

"He's an enemy." His beautiful caramel voice turned bitter again. His shoulders slumped. "My enemy."

"And he's most definitely not my friend, either." I was tired, I was upset, and by every god there ever was, I wanted something I couldn't even name to myself. *Trust me to find a guy I really like living under a curse in the weirdest town on the continent—and that's saying something. Why can't this be a little simpler?*

If it was simpler, probably, I would have been long gone by now. I felt my own shoulders sag under the weight, my skin prickling with the charge of magick in the air. Like that coven of witches in El Paso, their eyes all full of that flat silver sheen, their voices high and piercing-sweet as their goddess walked among them.

The memory made my bones ache. I had barely gotten away that time, another escape. They were getting narrower and narrower these days. "Look." I tried to sound conciliatory. "I'm trying to figure this out. I...I don't want anything bad to happen to you. If I can help you, I will. Don't you understand that? But you've got to let me help in my own way. All right?"

"It's dangerous," he said. "Why you can't..."

I waited, but nothing else came out of him. Instead, the darkness intensified. I could barely see even the glimmer of his eyes, the bookshelves to either side blocked out any light coming in through the windows.

Finally, he spoke again. "Will you read to me tomorrow, Isabella?"

I don't know why I felt so grateful. "Of course. You just pick me something other than Latin. Nothing's changed, Jeremy." The lie tasted sour as nicotine on my tongue. Everything had changed. He wasn't just the slightly weird scarred boss I'd thought was so harmless.

There was nothing harmless about Jeremy Tremont.

"I was afraid of that." Bitterness, again. Didn't he know any other way to talk? "I'll have dinner sent to your room, Isabella. Goodnight."

"Jeremy—"

It was too late. He was gone again, his step oddly soft on the carpeted floor. I bolted for the end of the aisle, but he'd vanished, and the library was full of uneasy shadows. I thought I heard the window behind his desk—the same window that had broken this morning—latch shut, and might have smelled a brief breath of night air, but that was ridiculous. He didn't leave the house, did he?

Maybe not in that shape, at least. *Do you turn into a big cat, Jeremy? Do I smell like a tasty snack when you've got four feet and whiskers?*

"Gods above," I whispered. "I'm being ridiculous. It's time to get something to eat and go to bed, I've had enough fun for one day."

I didn't even admit to myself how my lips burned, how my cheeks were hot, and especially didn't admit to the low ache in the very bottom of my belly. I'd be tossing and turning in my bed again tonight unless I took matters into my own hands. I almost wished Raphael was a normal man, it would have been nice to take the edge off.

I laughed. It didn't sound right, the sound fell into the dark well of the deserted library. It was as bitter as any of Jeremy's little barks. "All right, Bella," I muttered, as if I was my mother.

"Down, girl. Go get some sleep. It's not as hopeless as it looks."

Chapter Twenty-Two

It wasn't as hopeless as it looked. It was, true to form, worse.

I didn't see Jeremy for a few days, though I knew he was around; the papers on his desk were rearranged every morning, different books opened and set in different places. Despite asking me to read to him, he didn't show up, and I spent Sunday and Monday shelving books and muttering imprecations. I spent both days and Tuesday ransacking the curses section from one end to the other and stretched my limited Latin, not to mention the little bit of French I still had from Nice and Cannes, to their limits, and I checked every translation I could.

I found curses to founder horses and ships, I found curses to spoil milk, I found curses to kill enemies and lay kingdoms low—now *there* was a thought, not that there were any kingdoms left anymore. I found curses to send locusts against crops and curses to brew storms, not like this town needed any help with that.

I finally remembered Raphael's gift and rescued it from my purse. The crackling, heavy brown-paper package held what might have been a little joke: a statue of a tiger, carved out of fluid supple oiled wood. I set it out on the front porch, unwilling to have it glaring at me in my room. If this was his idea of a nice present, I could do without.

The entire town felt stuffed to the brim with nasty in-jokes. Little *secrets*.

I didn't see the mysterious guests, but just before I drifted off to sleep at night I would hear voices in the halls, Mharian's unsubtle chilling laugh, movement. I was existing in an alternate universe from the rest of them, and I can't say I was unhappy. I needed the time to think.

Trays were delivered to the library promptly, and Tuesday delivered to my bedroom door with those queer thudding knocks. I didn't leave my room all day Tuesday, busy poring over a stack of books I'd kidnapped from the Curses section and lugged down the hall. Breakfast, lunch, tea, dinner, all delivered, and I sat in my window seat as dark fell again, smoking and paging through Ramiriez-Jouberte's *La Sorciere et la Maleficience* while carefully tapping my ash into a fresh ashtray. The window, half-open, let in a soft breath flavored with dusk and lavender, the astringency of rosemary, and a faint heady smell I was too cautious to call rose-scent.

I frowned at the book and glanced up, with the sudden undeniable sense of being watched.

I looked out, into the familiar shapes of the gardens below my window, and saw a familiar, low, liquid form. The striped cougar.

Cougars aren't striped.

"Well, hello!" I said, a little louder than I'd meant to. The cat stalked back and forth in the gathering purple gloom, its tail twitching. It looked as uncomfortable and restless as I felt. "I've missed you."

That made the cat pause. He turned in a tight circle—*why do you call it a 'he', you don't know, it could be a girl cougar.* The sense that it was male was just too strong.

He settled on his haunches, looking up at the window. I would probably be framed in light, the bedside lamp on once it started to go dark. He cocked his head, his eyes shining blue-gold, and I was again forcibly reminded of Jeremy.

"Yes, I've missed you. I've missed Jeremy too. I think he's avoiding me." The words tumbled out; I hadn't spoken to anyone in three days and had even missed his silences. "Why, I don't know, unless it's something to do with that damnable curse." I tapped my cigarette into the bowl, eyeing the cat. "I wish you could help me. I wish *anyone* could help me."

The only person likely to give you any information is Raphael, I told myself again. *I'll go to dinner with him. I will.*

No, I won't.

Yes, I will. I have to.

The cat's eyes met mine, suddenly huge and eloquently sad. How such a wild animal could express such human sadness, I couldn't guess. I inhaled deeply, trying to see if I could smell that faint breath of rose-smell again. The wind shifted, and I smelled rain. Were the storms coming back? Had the last few days just been the eerie breath before the plunge?

"Gods," I whispered. "I want to help him so badly, and I don't have a single goddamn clue."

The cat shook himself, rising to his broad, padded feet. He looked up, his face barred with stripes, and I had a sudden vision of a scarred face lifted to the rain, mouth open in a rictus of agony.

Jeremy's not Kine, Raphael is, I would know if Jeremy was a shapechanger, wouldn't I?

Wouldn't I?

It was too late, the cat was gone, melting back into shadow. I took another deep breath, smelled familiar musk. Whether it was my imagination or just my frantic desire, I couldn't tell.

Time was running out. I was meeting Raphael for dinner on Thursday, and that would mean being out after dark, playing this dangerous game all the way to the finish. The thought made my stomach rebel, though I couldn't have told anyone what I'd had for dinner. I barely noticed the food anymore.

I was in such a bad temper, I tossed *La Sorciere* to the floor and dug in my bag, bringing out the familiar black bandanna and my cards. No matter how many times I shuffled and threw them down, it was always the same.

Three blank white cards, *Le Chevalier de Epee* and *l'As de Coupe.* Again, and again, and again, no matter how I mixed them up.

I didn't get out the salt, either. That was all I needed, another useless vision of being chased by a beast I couldn't see, beasts fighting...

I picked up the first blank card, staring at it. "Jeremy," I whispered, again. "You've got to throw me a bone here, I'm being more than usually stupid. Nobody's giving me *anything* useful!"

Believe it or not, I have, Jeremy's voice echoed in my head.

I gave it up, put my cards away, and sat staring and smoking in the window seat. A curious fatalism settled over me: if I was meant to break the damn curse, surely it would have been more obvious—

That's when it hit me right between the eyes.

If anyone had been watching I would have looked like an idiot, because I stiffened and sat upright, spilling my messenger bag onto the floor. Dear gods above, could it really be so *easy*? Yeah, sure, I was a witch—but I was a woman too, and the easiest way to free a man from bad influences was to exercise another influence on him. Two birds with one stone, and a broken curse.

"Hot damn," I said, grinning at my own ghostly reflection in the window. "Finally. A magick I know how to work."

I was so pleased with myself that I went to bed, and slept all the way through the night without a disturbing dream.

THE NEXT EVENING, I STAYED in the library as it got dark. I turned the lights up and settled myself behind Jeremy's desk with my bare feet propped among his papers. I didn't have to wait long—almost as soon as he could be sure I'd left and gone up to my room he appeared, stepping out from between rows of bookshelves and stopping, his face indecipherable, as he saw me in his chair.

I didn't give him a chance to vanish. "Don't run off again, Tremont. I want to talk to you."

I almost held my breath. *He said he had to do what I told him, I hope I don't have to be clearer than that or pronounce everything thrice.* My heart lodged in my throat. The light shone in his hair, and there were dark circles under his bright blue eyes.

He looked tired.

He folded his arms carefully, leaned against the nearest bookshelf. Just like a feral cat will sit and look at a human offering food. *Hungry,* the look said, his scarred face settling into itself. *Starving, in fact. But I have my pride.*

"I've m-missed you," he said. The slight stutter told me volumes. He shook his hair down over his face.

Oh, my gods. Why didn't I see this before?

"Likewise," I told him. "Look, I'll take that cup of tea you promised. Please."

He nodded. Then he indicated the way to the kitchen with a graceful sweep of the arm.

"No." Something fuzzy right under the border of my conscious mind took shape. It wasn't completely hopeless. I was going to do something I hadn't done for a while, and fear began to prickle under my skin. *This is a lunatic idea.* "I want to go up to my bedroom. They can bring the tea up there, please. The...invisibles."

He nodded unwillingly, his jaw set, his eyes hard and glittering.

I made it to my feet, stretching—nonchalance makes you stiff after a while—and I was very conscious of the carpeted floor against my feet, the way my tank top slid against my skin, my hair tangling every which way. I hadn't seen fit to drag a comb through it for a couple of days. I approached him as carefully as I would approach any other stray, moving very slowly, holding his gaze with mine.

That I wouldn't do to a dog or a cat, but I was afraid if I looked away Jeremy would vanish, and I'd lose my chance to get things on the right track.

I stepped close to him, reached up to touch his cheek. He flinched, stood still, not even breathing. Scarred skin rough and warm under my fingertips.

"Give me a few minutes to get cleaned up." The bottom of my stomach dropped. Maybe a reaction to the sudden release of tension. It was always better to have *something,* some plan of action, than to flail around without a clue. "Okay?"

He nodded. "As you like, Isabella." His voice was husky.

I left him there and climbed the stairs. I looked back once.

He stood, his left hand raised, touching his cheek. Right where I had.

Bingo.

Okay.

I TOOK A FIVE MINUTE shower, not washing my hair, and I changed into a nice little white peasant top and a pair of black leggings. I left my feet bare, and I brushed my teeth.

Seduction needs toothpaste.

When I came out of the bathroom, there was a tea tray sitting on a table next to the fireplace. It was a little too warm for a fire, but the invisibles had obliged anyway.

I lit a single jasmine-scented candle bought on a whim, and set it on the mantel. My hands trembled just a little.

Do you know what you're doing?

Yes. I know this territory.

I turned all the lights off, and opened the gilt-mermaid door. The firelight and the single candle made the room a dim cave. There was an almost-full moon, its silver benediction dappling the windowsill. No storm, again, just the scary breathlessness in the air. Were we just enjoying the center of a hurricane, or the sudden hush that falls right before one?

Any peace is short-lived. That's called life.

I didn't have any way of measuring, but I suspect it was *exactly* fifteen minutes later that Jeremy Tremont knocked at the doorway. "Isabella?" He sounded uncertain.

"Shut the door. Lock it." *Come into my parlor, little boy. Let me show you how it's done. Let's break a few curses, shall we?*

He stepped inside, shut the door slowly, turned the lock. "Am I—" he began.

I knew that tone, he was about to say something bitter again.

"Come on in and sit down." I was sitting on the rug in front of the fireplace, the tea tray moved back. There was enough space for him if he wanted to sit next to me.

He paced into the room, stood watching me for a moment. Then he lowered himself next to me, gingerly.

"Pour us a cup of tea, if you want," I said, and lay down on the rug on my side, propping my head on my hand. "Let's talk."

He nodded. "As you like. Is that jasmine?"

"Isn't it nice?" *Rose candles are more traditional for this, but I bet you wouldn't like them. You won't say you've missed me too, not again. Oh, you silly, silly man. Why couldn't you have just told me?*

I knew why. Scarred, left alone, hated...no wonder he didn't know how to handle a girl, especially a witch like me.

"It is." He poured tea with two shaking hands. *That* was promising, and I heaved an entirely mental sigh of relief. "Green tea. The house attributes some strange tastes to you, Isabella."

I shrugged. Took the cup he handed me. "Tell me about your mother," I said, neutrally. *Just call me Freud.* Firelight licked us both, warmed my back.

Of all the things he probably expected, that had to be one of the last. "My..." He coughed, slightly. "Well. My mother." A long pause, and he took a couth sip of tea. "My father loved her very much. She was a little unhappy here, but she understood we couldn't move, that my father had...responsibilities. She got sick. I'm not sure. But I think someone slipped her something. We had some people from the town working here, but my father turned them out of the house. She died at the end of a long illness, and my father could do nothing. He died shortly after."

"How long after?" I had him off-balance now. He wasn't retreating, he was too distracted. Unwilling to break the truce between us, maybe, or just miserably compelled to stay in the room because I'd told him to?

I shoved that thought away.

"About two and a half minutes." His ruined face was haunted now, his mouth turned down in a sort of frown. "The...the shock was too great."

No wonder you're so messed up. "How old were you?"

His shoulders hunched, and I saw the ghost of the child he might have been.

"Ten. The...family inheritance became mine. It almost killed me. Calamus was here, and Guillame. A few others. Another Protector came—Jude the Bellwright, he trained me, taught me. When I recovered, I found out that...the scars started to come."

"The scars." *So there's more of you out there. I wonder if they all have curses?*

"Oh, yes," he said. "The scars. Marks. The inheritance. I was told, but I didn't...I didn't understand."

I felt my heart twist. I took a gulp of scalding-hot tea. I dipped my fingertip, traced the top of the cup. The words trembled in my mind, took shape. Just a simple spell, one I'd done so many times it wasn't even a spell, more like a little *push*.

He was so painfully shy, gods alone knew what he'd been telling himself the past few days. He was probably all tangled up in a ball of guilt, just like a man. Making everything complicated.

"So you're not quite what I'd think of as human, right?" *Duh, Isabella. You've figured that one out all by yourself. Are you Kine, Jeremy? I'm on the right track, but I need your help.*

He shrugged. "Protectors generally aren't. That much power, it's hard for a human body to handle. Human enough. But not quite."

I nodded. "Okay," I lifted my finger from the rim of the cup. The spell was complete. "I think I can guess what you want, now."

"I doubt it." His perfect mouth twisted a little. "I won't—"

"Oh, just shut up. Look. I think you need something from me, right?"

No answer. Which probably meant I was right. His jaw set and he looked away. The urge to smile visited me again. I throttled myself.

"And I think I know what it is," I continued. Now was the time to sit up, and I did. Slowly. I didn't want to spook him yet.

"I doubt it," he repeated. But the way he was staring at me was as good as a billboard.

I smiled, holding his blue gaze with mine. I had let my hair down, and it swung forward as I made it up to my knees and leaned over, brushing his shoulder with my curls. My face was inches from his, and he froze.

"You have no idea," I said, in a very low voice, "what I know, or don't know. You can't even ask me because of your curse. I'm not stupid, Jeremy. I have a faint idea of what's going on around here, even if I'm not this cursebreaker."

"Isa—" he started, but I leaned forward a little more and pressed my lips on his.

I even slipped him the tongue.

He froze again, not even breathing. I took advantage of that to slide into his lap, with my legs on either side of him, and locked my ankles behind his back. That meant I could put my arms around him too. It was a little awkward, but I did it. I was slim enough that I fit into his lap with room left over.

He was still barely breathing. I took my time, flirted with his tongue, slowly, and he softened a little and kissed me back. His mouth was warm, and flavored with tea, and he made a small sound, as if he was drowning.

He was a little clumsy, which I could understand. I didn't think he'd had a lot of girlfriends. But it was still like lightning, the jolt that went through me at the touch of his skin. He must have been driven almost to madness in the library when he first kissed me; right now he was more controlled.

I wasn't sure I liked that, I didn't want him having second thoughts or freezing up now.

I've done my share of seducing. It hasn't been too hard. Still, I was beginning to get a bit nervous by the time I felt his hands flatten against my back, and I moved a little on his lap to gauge the situation, so to speak.

Either he was half-dead, or he had better self-control than I thought. *Oh, come on, please.*

Just as I thought that, though, the situation started to improve. I wriggled more, to confirm, still using my seduction kiss—the gentle one. The soft, hopeful one.

Yep. He'd risen to the occasion all right.

Thank the gods. I was beginning to think I was unattractive.

I broke a little, to take a breath, and noticed that his eyes were shut. I worked my fingers into his hair, ridges of scar tissue under my fingers and palms.

"See?" I whispered. "I'm not stupid, Tremont. I know what I want." I moved slightly, again, and he gasped. He was sweating, his throat working. This was good. This was very, very good. "So it's up to you," I concluded. "Bed, or floor? My personal vote goes for the bed—" I considered him, moved in and kissed him again, my tongue sliding against his, used my teeth a little on his bottom lip, then broke away. "—but I'm willing to be overruled."

"Isabella," he gasped. It sounded like a prayer.

Yep. Definitely what I wanted.

"Bed? Or floor? Answer me, Tremont." I moved again, pressing my hips down and rocking. He made a low, hopeless sound.

"Bed," he whispered. "More comfortable for you."

"Good," I said, and slid my hands under his shirt.

It took a great deal of effort and coaxing on my part to get him to the bed. He froze several times. That was okay—it gave me a chance to work on his belt, and his zipper, and to get the sweater off over his head. He actually ripped my shirt—he was a little stronger than I'd thought—and I'd chosen the leggings because they were easy to pull off. I pushed him down onto the bed and followed him, decided to get a bit rough. I bit his lip, tensed my fingers, and drove my nails into his shoulders.

It worked.

He let out a low growl and rose up, and we wrestled for a bit. I was starting to sweat now too, I closed my eyes and imagined...

Well, I tried to imagine leather, and night air, cigarette smoke, bourbon. The feel of smoothly muscled skin under my palms—but the funniest thing started to happen.

I started to realize who I was seducing.

He tasted like musk and green tea and desperation. He was a little rough, not much, I could tell it was just clumsiness and not being accustomed to this yet. And he kept his eyes closed, and whispered my name in a rough broken voice every once in a while.

The strangest thing of all? I wasn't locked up inside my head, participating in this coolly and with the faintest touch of condescension.

I started to mean it. To mean every sigh, every kiss, every stroke against his skin.

When he finally, gently, slipped into me, I simply closed my eyes and gave myself up. I used him, certainly, but I let him use me at the same time, and...well.

I'd thought I would do this, see if it worked, and if it didn't try something else. I hadn't counted on his gentleness, or his responsiveness to me, or...or the way that he kept saying my name, like a prayer. Like...well, as if...

No, I wasn't prepared for that.

There was a whole lot about this that I wasn't prepared for, and seducing Jeremy Tremont was not the first on that long list.

CHAPTER TWENTY-THREE

Thursday morning dawned cool and still, with the promise of heat riding the morning air like the far off ozone of approaching lightning.

I woke curled against someone's back, my cheek against his nape, his golden hair webbed over my face. One arm curled under my head, because I'd lost my pillow, and my other arm thrown over him, hugging. I was as close to him as I could possibly get, skin to skin, and I yawned sleepily, tried to blow the strands of blond hair out of my face. The blankets were warm, and he was even warmer. It was nice, first thing in the morning. I usually kicked the covers off halfway through the night and woke up chilled.

I didn't realize he was awake until I noticed how rigidly he lay, stiff as a board.

I yawned again, sighed, tasted morning-mouth, and slipped my arm free of him. I rolled over, reached for the pack of cigarettes on the night table.

"Smoke," I said. "D'you mind?"

"No," he almost-choked, and I lit up, shimmying to sit up and pull the sheet up my chest, balance the red ashtray on my knee. He still lay facing the other way, the broad expanse of his back with its river of scarring. Was it different? I couldn't tell, I was too busy waking up.

He did have some nice muscle definition, though. Very nice.

I smoked the first cigarette of the day in complete silence, looking at the morning sunlight falling in through the window. "Dibs on the bathroom," I finally said. "Why don't you see if you can get us some coffee?"

He made a sound that was either desperation or agreement, and I padded into the bathroom.

We'd see if that measly curse could stand up to Isabella Harpe.

I used the toilet, thought longingly about a shower, brushed my teeth. Then, suitably fortified, I came back out into the bedroom. I found a white *Che Lives!* T-shirt draped over an antique blue-velvet chair, struggled into it, stepped into a pair of sweatpants.

I dropped down on the bed next to Jeremy, who hadn't moved. "Hey. Are they bringing coffee?" *Just see how well I'm dealing with the invisible servants, Jeremy. Look, I'm a tough girl, I won't break.*

He nodded, his golden head moving on the pillow. I patted his head, threaded my fingers through his hair. "Jeremy, are you going to look at me?"

"If you like."

Hold the phone. He didn't sound happy. As a matter of fact, he sounded bloody miserable, and that dispelled my postcoital glow in a hurry.

"Is it that you don't like me anymore?" *Don't let it be that.*

He made some kind of noise, again, a sound like he was hurt.

"Jeremy?"

"I've been waiting for you to wake up."

"Can you look at me, please?" Yep. Postcoital glow definitely gone, dammit. "Or if you want to leave, the door's over there. It won't be the first time a guy's ditched me. You can if you want."

He rolled over, then. Sat up in one fluid motion. My jaw nearly dropped.

The scarring that had run down his face and chest was less, somehow. Now his mouth and chin were both free, and the clear skin extended up his cheek. "Jesus," I said, blankly. "Did...did that—"

"I don't know. Is it worse, or better?"

I felt my lips twitching up into a smile. Relief burst inside me. "The scarring's smaller. But worse or better, I can't tell. It's not your face I'm interested in."

That made the corner of his mouth twitch. Then he laughed, and it was that same bitter little sound. "What is it exactly, Isabella? I have nothing to offer you. This house is a cage, this town isn't much better. And I—"

Oh, all the gods save me from men. "So we ditch it and move onto the next place. What's with you, Tremont? You don't like me or something?"

He looked down at his hands, resting in his lap. "I can't leave the house, Isabella. I'm a Protector. My duty's here. And...well, I'm afraid. What if..."

"What if you turn into a giant cat?"

He gave me a look of such complete surprise I started to laugh. There might be hope yet. "What, you think I'm *stupid?* Come on, Tremont. You turn into a big stripey Hobbes if you leave the house, right?"

"It's not that simple. I... The coffee's here."

He levered himself up out of bed. I spent a few moments in artistic appreciation of his bare ass before he pulled his jeans back on and made it over to the door.

Who would have thought such a starchy guy went commando?

When he came back he had a breakfast tray. "Coffee?"

"Coffee and answers. You going to give me both?"

"As many as I can." His golden hair was tousled, and something about the set of his mouth was a little more relaxed. Or so I hoped. Otherwise I might have started to feel less attractive, again, and that wasn't good for my mood.

"Still cursed?" *Ha, ha. One measly curse can't hold up to Isabella Harpe.*

"Yes," he said, shortly.

Oh, crap.

"Well." I pursed my lips. He set the tray down on the small table near the fireplace, poured me a cup of coffee, added a little cream, and brought it to me. Refused to look directly at me, and avoided my fingers when I took the cup. Then he poured himself a one and stood by the tray, his head hanging.

What now? I searched for the best way to handle crashing disappointment, settled on politeness. "Come on over. Unless you can't stand to be near me."

"I think it's more that I want too much to be near you." He raised his golden head, blue eyes bright and intent. I felt a little rumpled—okay, a *lot* rumpled. He made a small, stoppered movement, as if he wanted to touch me, even all the way across the room. "It's been torture, being so close and being unable to..." He stopped. His hand dropped back down to his side. "And then, when I do get near you, I can't think of what to do."

I examined the scarring on his body, fascinated. It was definitely less. I'd done *something.*

Small victory, perhaps—I'd been so *sure*, and a few bells and trumpets might have been better than just-plain disappointment. "So what breaks the curse? I thought for sure that would do it."

He let out that bitter laugh again, watching me. His shoulders were rigid. "Your experiment's only half successful, then."

"It wasn't an *experiment.*" I was hard put to contain the irritation. "I don't experiment with my body, Tremont. Now come over here, please, and *talk* to me."

He obeyed, striding across the room, muscle moving under his skin. He dropped down on the bed next to me with that swift economy, and I touched his shoulder before I could stop myself. His skin was warm, and I polished his scarred shoulder with my palm.

It felt good.

He dropped his head, staring at the pillow. "I'm sorry." His wonderful voice was so low I had to lean forward to hear him. "Why would you want to...why would you even *look* at me, Isabella? What brought you here to my door?"

"Luck, and my mother's gods, probably. And I like you, Jeremy. You've been kind to me, even if you did it for your own reasons. There are things you've done that you didn't have to do, even if you were cursed. I just..." I paused. "What breaks the curse?"

"You wouldn't want to do it, even if I told you." He shifted his gaze, looking down into his coffee cup as if it held the secrets of the universe.

"God*damn* it, Tremont, will you just *tell* me what *breaks* the goddamn curse?" I lost my temper, and he sighed. It was a strange sigh, almost relieved.

"I'm a coward," he said obliquely. "Isabella Harpe, will you marry me?"

My jaw dropped open. "Um," was my incredibly deep and profound response. I followed it up with the equally profound, "Oh..."

"You see?" He set his coffee cup down on the nightstand. "You wouldn't."

"You don't know what I'll do," I outright snapped. *Hell of a thing to just spring on a girl.* "Last night proved that, at least."

His mouth quirked slightly, as if he couldn't help himself. "Are we having another fight?"

I swore at him, a colorful term I'd picked up in the middle of Illinois, working with another traveling carnival. His blue eyes widened, and I felt gratified for all of about three seconds. I sighed, rubbing at my forehead. "No, I don't think this is a fight, Jeremy. I just...wow. What a question. You just...you can't just spring that on a girl, you know."

"I didn't have my parents to teach me how to approach a woman." His mouth still quirked up at one corner. What would it take to make him really smile again? I was failing miserably, just when I should be doing better. "Though I think perhaps my father wouldn't have been much help. He never did know how to handle my mother."

"And you feel..." I made a vague movement, coffee splashing in my cup. "About that?"

"I can understand." Something on his scarred face that made my heart leap and do the can-can. He watched me closely, unblinking. "I can honestly understand."

"So if I agree to...to marry you, then that breaks the curse?"

He pursed his lips and nodded, once.

"Hoo boy," I said. "Whoa. Wow."

"You..." He swallowed. Hard. "You're beautiful, Isabella."

I've heard that before. From men with leather jackets and hard shiny eyes, men with needle habits or an attachment to the bottle, boys with lazy movements and cigarettes hanging from their lips.

Boys I could predict. Sooner or later they would leave me, in pursuit of the next high, the next girl. I was a temporary stop, and that absolved me of all sorts of responsibility.

I looked down at my hands. I wanted to see what the cards would say about this. Probably something too true for me to handle, unless they served me the same three-blank-cards-and-confusion routine again. All the years of using my gift for others—now I wanted to use it for myself, because I was uncertain.

My mother's gods had a sense of humor, at least.

I took a deep breath. "You really want me to..."

"I want you," he said, harshly, as if his throat was blocked. "I had finished making my promise to take the first applicant that walked in the door, or commit suicide. There's a way to do it, lay it down. I didn't want the...the burden anymore. But you... I doubt," he said finally, "that I have ever seen anything as beautiful as you standing just inside my door, dripping from the storm I'd called up in my frustration and anger. I wanted to touch you, Isabella, but I couldn't afford to. I have been afraid." He sounded bitter again. "I have been afraid all my life."

He stared down at his wide, graceful hands. The calluses on the tips of his fingers and across his palms, the blunt fingers—no doubt he was seeing something else in the lines across his palms.

"Afraid of me?"

He nodded, his golden hair falling forward over his face. "Someone like you would never...I'm boring and stiff and not very fun. You're like lightning, Isabella, you're so...and there's no way you would consent to staying in this mausoleum of a town for the rest of your life."

"Whoa," I said. "Wow. You really..."

"Jude warned me that I would love without hope. The curse stoppers all tongues in the house. You have to decide on faith."

Oh, great. I took a long drink of coffee. I needed the caffeine. And it had cooled enough now. "So, um, next question. You sound like it's your first time."

"Only once, Isabella. That's what it means to be a Tremont. Double or nothing."

"If I..." I licked my lips. "If I didn't want to get hitched, what would you do?"

He examined his knees. "If you leave me—it's your right to do so—I will simply fade. I don't mind. I've seen enough and done enough to know that there isn't any forgiveness in the world."

"Fade? You mean *die?*"

He shrugged. "I suppose."

"Hoo boy." I couldn't come up with anything better to say. "Jeremy."

"You don't have to decide right away. Take some time—I mean—"

I put my coffee cup down on the nightstand, reached over, and took his hand. He didn't look at me, still staring at his lap. "Jeremy. Look at me."

He looked up. A scarred man waiting for execution.

"Are there still things you can't tell me?"

He pursed his lips, nodded, his hair falling forward.

My heart fell, splashed into my innards and paddled around. God*dam*mit. Always a catch. Always a goddamn motherfucking catch, like everything else in my life.

I swallowed dryly. "Okay. I'm going out to dinner tonight. I'll find out what I can, then I'll decide. Fair enough?"

"Raphael is dangerous. If he guesses what you are to me..." He searched my face. "Please, Isabella."

"I know. If he thinks I'm this cursebreaking thingahoochie he'll eat me for lunch. But I *have* to find out what I can." I tried to disguise the hurt and disappointment in my voice, failed. "You want me to make a decision like this without getting all the angles? Wrong answer, Jeremy."

"Please," he said, still looking at me with his blue eyes wide and wild in his scarred face. I was right. The scarring was fading.

What would he look like without it?

It didn't matter. I didn't care.

"Oh, for God's sake. Can't you trust me, Jeremy?"

His look made me blush, my cheeks scorching. And other places, too. "It's Raphael I don't trust."

"I'm not going to do anything but find out whatever I can about completely breaking your curse. I *have* to, Jeremy. If there are things you can't tell me, he probably can, God knows he's been a fount of helpful information so far. I won't make a decision like this without being informed. Those goddamn terms and conditions." *Like, do you have to eat me on my wedding night?*

That was exactly the wrong thing to think. After all, I'd just slept with him. But...*but*. There was something he couldn't tell me, still.

And if it was anything like the rest of this place, it was a doozy.

He nodded, with no real hope. "Isabella," he said, slowly. I waited.

He said nothing else. I bit my lip, studying his face. I ran my fingers over his cheek, feeling the roughness of scarring, a little bit of rough golden stubble. He leaned into the touch, a slight movement that made my splashing heart do some more acrobatics. If this kept up I wouldn't need an exercise program, I could get all my cardio from just hanging around him.

"So what precisely are the scars from?"

He shrugged. "It's inherited, passed along the Tremont family line. One of my ancestors survived an attack that left him...infected. He decided to strike a bargain with a sort of *vrkolak*. It's...well..." His mouth twisted a little. He looked ashamed. "It's passed down through the male line."

"Wow," I said, still tracing the scarring. He shuddered a little, his eyes half-lidded, blue burning out from under his eyelids. "Are you okay?"

He shuddered again and I stopped, my fingers resting against his cheekbone. "You don't have to stop." Harsh and throaty, full of something I recognized.

Desire.

I found out I was smiling. "You're a good guy, Jeremy."

That look was definitely going to stop my heart one of these days. "Do you like good guys?"

"I'm starting to." And I was.

"Will you read to me today?"

"Of course, if you promise not to vanish."

He acknowledged it with a wry fleeting smile.

I had to grin in response. "I'll read to you. I promise I'll be careful... I should take a shower and get to work."

"You could take a day off." He sounded hopeful.

"I want to get the Blavatsky shelf back in order. And the Psychometry shelves too. Somehow that always seems to get disarranged. I tore the Curses section apart looking for clues." I had kind of forgotten that I was touching him. Okay, I hadn't forgotten, I just hadn't stopped because it felt really nice to be touching him. "And I haven't seen any of the...guests. If they show up, I should help them."

"They know their way around. Especially Guillame and Koren. And anyway, I told them to stay away from you. I didn't want you hurt or frightened again. I was tempted to—"

I didn't want him thinking about that, because his eyes turned hard and my heart completed its exercise regimen by lodging in my throat and stretching out. "If I did take a day off," I interrupted, tracing his cheekbone meditatively, "what would I do instead?"

Now I found out what really made him smile. I found my heart thundering away in my chest.

"I have a few ideas."

"I'm sure you do." My breath caught. "Starting with what?"

CHAPTER TWENTY-FOUR

I ENDED UP SPENDING MOST of the morning and into the afternoon with him in the blue room, neither of us saying much, just enjoying each other's company. I finally got up and took a shower, and he met me in the library—which was curiously deserted again. I didn't blame the "guests" for staying clear; Jeremy probably had been ultra-scary about it. Just like a man, no tact at all.

Jeremy sat with his eyes closed as I sat on the other side of the couch, reading Milton. He did something that he had never done before—stopped me at five-thirty. "Isabella?"

I blinked at him, looking up from the book as I sat cross-legged. I felt sleepy and languid, my entire body a little sore and unstrung. It had been a long time since I'd enjoyed myself this much. "Hmm?"

"Now that you're here...if I stopped guarding the locus, my scars would come back but I could leave," he said, slowly. "If I did that, would you leave right now with me?"

"What?" I didn't think I'd heard him right.

"If I left here right now, laid down my duty, and remained scarred, would you come with me? We could see the world." He hunched his shoulders, nervously.

I looked down at the book, back up at him. "You've got a responsibility here." I said, slowly. "Those things just don't go away. You'd come back to it. I know you well enough to know that." *And believe me, having to come back to this place would be an awful chore. I'm not sure my heart could stand the excitement.*

He sighed. "I suppose you're still determined to go through with this dinner idea."

"I like Raphael," I admitted. "And he's useful."

"Useful for what? The only thing he's ever done is cause trouble. I'm warning you, Isabella. If he finds out what you are, he'll kill you at the very least."

Goddamn it, he's the only shot I have for finding out I can agree to this whole thing! "He hasn't done anything to me yet," I said, a little sharply. "I judge people on what they *do*, not what they might do. You should be grateful for that."

"I am." He leaned his head back on the couch. "Believe me, I am. You can read, or go now. As you like."

I looked down at the book, and continued reading. "*These two, Imparadised in each other's arms—*"

AT SIX O'CLOCK I LAID the book next to Tremont. He had his eyes closed, and his hands shook slightly. I left him sitting there and paced away, made it up the stairs and to my room. Or the room he'd given me. Either way. I was thinking of this entire house as mine now, and that was a little...disturbing. I'd already half made up my mind to stay.

Even if he did have to eat me on the wedding night. His father had married, though, right?

But what happened before that? You don't know, and you don't know what to believe—Raphael's version, or whatever this curse will let Jeremy say.

I chose my black sundress. The weather was warm enough, and it had a strappy top that showed off my arms and shoulders. I was proud of my smoothly-muscled shoulders, and the tattoo on my left shoulder was a nice one. It should have been, I'd paid enough for it. The phoenix marked in red and gold had been in my dreams for months before I'd finally broken down and gotten inked.

I wrapped a black scarf around my neck and stepped into my boots. "A vision of loveliness." I regarded myself in the mirror over the vanity. My hair was a mass of curling blackness, my eyes indigo accentuated by black eyeliner. I looked ready to go clubbing.

I put the strap of my messenger bag over my head, settled it just right. My entire body twinged, reminding me of what I'd spent last night—and this morning—doing. Or having done. I smiled at the thought.

If I could completely break this curse of his...

What would he do if I did? He probably would give me some cash and send me on my way. A marriage ceremony, maybe a wedding night—*no eating the bride, please, it's bad manners*—and then what? *So long, Isabella, thanks; I can look in the mirror now without flinching?*

I knew from my mother's stories just how little most men thought of marriage, and my grandmother had accumulated marriages like other people collect china figurines. The form, the ceremony could be the important thing, and then, curse broken, there would be nothing for me to do but drift on with my life.

"I hope not," I said to the mirror, and watched my own lips moving. "I kind of like you, Jeremy Tremont."

I hadn't had a chance to look at the cards again, and I put my hand in my bag, touching the black bandanna. *They would probably only tell me how badly this is going to work out.*

Stop it. You're put on earth to help people. It'll be nice to have a scarred millionaire owe me a favor. There's nothing that says I can't marry him and keep on wandering. Maybe all he needs is someone willing *to marry him.*

All I had to do was pump Raphael for a little more information. Who, after all, was I trying to kid? *I'm not meant to marry anyone,* I told myself. *I'm too weird to marry anyone, even though he could give me a serious run for my money in that department.*

I pulled my hand out of my bag.

Three blanks, *Le Chevalier de Epee* and *l'As de Coupe*. Same thing all over again.

Happiness was always short-lived. Loving someone only meant disaster. If I'd gained no other wisdom in my life, I'd at least gained that. So what if my heart had started to hammer every time I looked at him? So what if I had genuinely enjoyed myself this morning? So what if the way he held me—my head on his shoulder, his fingers in my hair—made a funny warm feeling start in my stomach? So what if the way he kissed me made me feel like lightning was shooting all through my veins?

So what if I kind of really liked him more than I'd liked any boyfriend? So what if he was funny—albeit with a mordant black sort of humor—and sharp and easy to be around?

"I guess I'll just break this fucking curse and get on with business," I said to the mirror, to the room, to the whole goddamn house that had started to feel just like home. Home with a bunch of roses that hadn't bloomed yet, just stayed tight little buds with splashes of color painting their tips. Home with a scarred man that I'd kind of...sort of...grown very fond of.

Kind of sort of fallen in love with.

"Shit," I muttered, and wiped away the salt water welling up in my eyes. I dug for a pair of sunglasses, and jammed them on. Then I left the door to the blue room wide open and made it down the stairs and out of the house without anyone noticing.

Or at least, if anyone was watching, I didn't see them.

CHAPTER TWENTY-FIVE

I PICKED UP THE WOODEN tiger on my way out, and dropped it in the gutter just outside the gates. I tried to feel guilty—after all, it had been a present. But...I felt curiously light, as if someone had taken a weight off my shoulders.

I was committed now.

I smoked a cigarette on the corner before Raphael's motorcycle made its loud appearance. I wasn't crying anymore, but I did feel kind of...what? What exactly was I feeling?

The day was warm and just starting to get dark.

He brought the bike to a stop, the beginning of the evening deepening the sky behind him.

Summer solstice was very close. That would be nice—celebrating in a rose garden, maybe with a joint and a bit of lemonade, talking to Jeremy about the Year King.

Get your head out of the clouds.

The fevershine in Raphael's eyes made them flat coins. Was it just my imagination, or was he looking less and less attractive the more time I spent with him?

A strange panicked feeling started under my breastbone, died away.

"You don't look so sure today, Miss Pretty. Found out more about Tremont?" Lazy and cocksure, one long leg keeping the bike propped up, the leather jacket on his back even though it was a good balmy seventy-eight degrees. The sound of the bike's engine filled the evening along with cut grass and exhaust, heady summer smells.

I summoned up a smile, confidence returning. "I just don't often wear a dress. This is a special occasion."

He regarded me from head to toe with a great deal of interest. It was so unlike Jeremy's shyness that I felt a momentary chill.

"It certainly is," he said, meditatively. "Maybe we can finish that game of ours." He looked a little thoughtful, a little suspicious.

I wasn't quite prepared for the way I kept comparing him to Jeremy. "Maybe we can. It's not every day the cutest guy in town takes me out to dinner." I rested a hand on my hip; I did everything but bat my eyelashes at him. "And Italian at that. Where are we headed, angel?"

The corner of his mouth curled up. He started to look a little handsomer. *What's wrong with me?* My skin roughened with chill. It was an instinctive response, maybe. He was Kine, could he smell what I'd spent the morning doing?

That was a distinctly uncomfortable thought. I was glad I'd taken a shower.

"Want me to take you to heaven, then, Miss Pretty?"

It was less finesse than I'd grown to expect from him, but if I'd still been charmed, it would have worked. As it was, I smiled, and climbed on the back of the bike. "I've never needed heaven, angel. I like it on earth just fine."

I told my internal voice of reason and caution to take a hike. I *needed* to find out what Jeremy couldn't or wouldn't tell me.

"Enjoy it while you can." The bike leapt forward. I held on, laying my head against the broadness of his leather-clad shoulder.

I closed my eyes and thought of Jeremy, saying my name softly while he stroked my cheek, ran his fingers through my hair. I tucked that thought away.

Specifically, I had to find out what exactly broke his curse, what the thing he couldn't tell me was—and what I really wanted to know, nobody could tell me at all, which was if he'd still want me around when he was *uncursed*.

We flashed through the town, people stopping and looking after us, shading their eyes. The strangeness bloomed.

For example, on a corner, a woman walking her dog. Except the woman was covered in fine short reddish fur, and her dog had warthog tusks. Or the man crouching against a wall, his bald head bright blue. He was painting something on the bricks.

What about the woman walking in a long tattered green dress, her bare feet on the concrete, with her long brown hair that held tiny yellow leaves and flowers?

Now that I *knew* this place was Weirdness USA, it was hard to ignore. Some layer had peeled back, exposing reality underneath. There were a few humans, but they were hurrying along the sidewalk, obviously intent on leaving town—or getting home—before dark. Green skin, blue skin, furry skin, pointed ears, fangs—and several of them turned to look after me on the back of Raphael's motorcycle, clinging to him.

Cities are savage anyway, the psychic energy of so many people crammed together in one place swirling around and feeding all sorts of things. Human predators—and not-so-human, the *vrkolak*. But this city had something electric, a subliminal hum that I couldn't believe I hadn't noticed before.

Then again, if my mother's gods had brought me here, I wouldn't have. They were more than capable of blinding me until I was in too deep to get out without accomplishing what they wanted me to.

Hell, I was capable of blinding myself; I'd been trying to talk myself out of falling in love with Jeremy Tremont for months now.

So what was I doing?

Raphael drove fast but carefully, and finally pulled into a small seedy parking lot between a pawnshop and a record store, weeds growing in the pavement's cracks. I slid off the back of the bike and he cut the ignition and put the kickstand down. "Be careful, Miss Pretty," he said to me. "They're going to assume you're mine if you're with me after dark. Just keep that pretty mouth between us, all right?"

"I've never been good at playing the little woman," I said, quirking a smile at him. He didn't smile back, just lit a cigarette, the flare of the lighter causing a sharp shadow to cloak his eyes for a moment. "But I'll try to be good, just for you."

He gave me a lopsided grin that would have made my heart flutter last week. Now it just made me think of Jeremy's bitter smile, and suffered in the comparison. "I'll take care of you, Miss Pretty. I promise."

There's a lot "taking care" of me could mean.

"You'd better, angel." I tossed my hair back. "I can get mean over a dinner table as well as a pool table. Or a chessboard."

"I can't wait to see that." His appraising look might have made me blush.

If I hadn't been thinking of Jeremy.

What was *wrong* with me? I tried not to think of other men when I was on a date, it was bad manners.

He swung himself off the gleaming Indian and stood. Same black T-shirt, jeans, belt with a silver buckle. Same height—two or three inches taller than me. But he was bigger now. *Much* bigger. The fevershine in his dark eyes glittered briefly, and darkness slid over him.

Not over his aura—over *him*. Something with teeth.

He was Kine, and I didn't know enough about them to be entirely comfortable with the way he suddenly seemed far too big for his size.

He walked beside me, pacing down the shadowed sidewalk. He said nothing, smoking his cigarette, his boots making crisp sounds. Shapes hurried past—a man with hooves instead of shoes, a woman trailing scarves of scarlet light, a low liquid dark shape too big to be a dog. When that came by, Raphael slid his arm over my shoulder, and we walked with strangely synchronized steps. The thing that might have been a dog passed us by, but Raphael kept his arm over my shoulders. He was too warm, heat roiling off him like standing next to a stove, and I half expected his fingers to scorch the bare skin of my upper arm.

"You see?" he said in my ear. "Best you stay with me, Miss Pretty, and just watch. The dark side of Tremont's out tonight."

"Can't wait." *How do I break Tremont's curse, what's the price for that act of magick? Will he still want me around when it's done?* That was all.

Wasn't it?

"So how did His Highness act when you got home the other day?" Raphael asked. "Was he having kittens?"

"He didn't seem too invested in the event, one way or the other," I lied sweetly. "He's only upset about potentially having to find another librarian."

"That would be one hell of a bother," Raphael agreed lightly. His boots sounded heavier than mine. "Wonder if I should apply for the job?"

"It's not vacant yet. And how much do you like being cooped up inside, stacking books?" I shook my head, my hair tangling and sliding against his arm.

"Point," he conceded.

We passed the pawnshop, an Indian grocery, a small bookstore that looked promising. An antique store—no, a junk shop with pretensions. *Secondhand Rose* was painted on a sandwich board set out in front of that one. Right after that was a small Italian restaurant—*Bella Nocta.*

Not a very auspicious name, but at least it wasn't Stoker's Corner. I had to suppress a shiver at *that* one.

Just a cute little storefront, the plate glass painted with the name of the restaurant in gold and an Italian flag painted in mid-flap underneath it. Round tables inside covered with red, and candles beginning to glimmer.

The place swirled with viscous darkness, hiding the human shapes, showing fantastical things like feathers, or horns, or a long fall of hair made of flame.

I didn't like it, but I'd promised. "Is this our stop?"

He looked a little disappointed. "You still want to do this, Miss Pretty? You're not safe out here after dark."

"I'm with an angel." Our silhouettes blurred together in the window. "What can go wrong?"

I looked up at him, seeing only the curve of one cheekbone, a slice of his eyebrow, part of his mouth. None of them looked like they fit together just right.

Maybe it was the fear spiking under my skin, coloring everything. Maybe it had something to do with Jeremy, and me.

Raphael held the door open for me, and I took a deep breath and stepped inside.

CHAPTER TWENTY-SIX

THE SUN FELL BELOW THE horizon at about the time the proprietor—a chubby black-haired man wearing a stained white apron—poured me a glass of red wine. The man had a pair of fleshy bulbs quivering on his cheeks. That made me a little nauseous, but I pretended I didn't notice. At least the food was good.

I had Portobello-and-cheese ravioli, and Raphael ordered a pasta primavera. There was fresh fragrant garlic bread. All in all it wasn't too bad, except for the people staring at me. And I mean 'people' very loosely.

Raphael and I made conversation. I didn't ask him about the gelatinous mass that sat in the back of the restaurant, beady little yellow eyes on stalks waving like seaweed. Or about the man with maroon skin and two ram's horns sprouting from his forehead, curving back around his ears. Or the woman with the sharp catlike face and crackling red hair that looked like liquid flame. I didn't ask him about the thin man at a lone table, who wore travel-soiled clothes like Indiana Jones's. This thin man had a gray face, and slurped at his pasta like he was starving. He would stop every once in a while to tip back a pitcher of beer— and I mean that literally, a *whole pitcher*. He hefted it to his lips and took long swallows.

It must have been one hell of a thirst he was trying to kill.

No, instead I asked Raphael about himself. This amused him.

Men like that sort of thing, no matter their species.

"So what's your day job?"

"Nothing very interesting." His gaze flicked over the interior of the restaurant, came to rest on me. "I work at the motorcycle shop. That's how I can afford the chopper."

"It's a nice one," I agreed, relieved to be discussing something normal.

He smiled, and for a moment he looked much younger. "Would you believe she was just a shattered hulk of rusted junk when I found her? I spent most of a year and a half fixing her up."

"A marvelous rescue." I tried some of the ravioli, found out that it was good. "She rides so smoothly."

"You're making me blush," Raphael said. "I've still got a bit of work to do with her. She's a little temperamental."

"What woman isn't?" I laughed, and he smiled benevolently across the table.

Even the woman with the fiery hair was watching me. She out of all of them didn't bother to disguise it.

"You don't seem temperamental, Miss Pretty. You seem very easy to get along with."

"I've had a lot of practice."

He shrugged, took a forkful of pasta. "So how did you get here? I never asked, but it must be quite a story."

"I left the big bad city when my boyfriend stole the rent money for drugs." It didn't even hurt to remember. "Then my car blew up. I walked into town and fell into the librarian job. Same as everything else in my life. I blow from place to place, stay until the wind changes and calls my name. Which I think will happen soon. I'm beginning to feel restless." I looked at my wineglass, hearing myself recite the same old lines, almost forgetting where I was. "So when the wind calls my name I'm going to fly. It's what I do." I took another ravioli.

Raphael leaned back in his chair. "So you're planning on leaving? Tremont won't let you."

"He doesn't have a choice," I said, calmly. "I've left stranger places than this behind, angel. It's all the same to Tremont, what I do. Besides, it's bad luck to keep a witch where she doesn't want to be."

Raphael's mouth curved up. Outside it was getting darker, and I began to hear a faint, faraway sound. Like a drumbeat, pressing against my skin. I listened for a few moments until I was sure. The drumbeat echoed my heart, but it wasn't my heartbeat

My palms were damp.

This town had a pulse. And it was waking up.

"How long has the town been asleep?" I hadn't intended to, it just came out.

Raphael took a long pull off his beer. "About thirty years. Since the last cursebreaker died."

"Oh yes. The famous cursebreaker."

"Tremont's mother. She was a gentle soul." Raphael shrugged, his wide shoulders moving under the T-shirt. His eyes were glittering a little more now, and the darkness on him intensified. His aura was snapping and crackling at the edges, little fingers of blackness waving like poisonous tentacles. "A pity."

So it was his mother. "Jeremy said she was poisoned," I looked down at my plate, cold all over.

I'd just said something I shouldn't have. The sudden knowledge chilled me all the way down to the bone.

"I heard Grant tore her into pieces when she tried to leave him." Raphael shrugged. "Guess there's two different stories."

"I guess so."

The restaurant began to fill up. Some of the people even looked normal. I didn't examine them too closely. Raphael ate slowly, with good manners. I focused on my ravioli and didn't drink any more wine. I needed a clear head for this.

Why did I ever leave the damn house?

"So why does the town sleep?" I might as well, the damage was already done. "It sounds like...like there's a pulse."

"There certainly is," he said, his dark eyes slitting, the fevershine quicksilver-bright.

I shivered. *I should have brought a coat. No, scratch that. I should never have agreed to this. Why did I?*

Because you were thinking with your hormones rather than with your brain, Isabella.

"The town sleeps because the locus sort of goes dormant when there's not a cursebreaker." Raphael's smile, wide and white, was full of genuine good humor. "Tremont can hand out energy, but the locus itself is sleepy. When it wakes up, the energy's a lot freer, and it attracts a lot more of the nasties. A cursebreaker amplifies the effect, it's a way to bind the Protector to the locus." He leaned back and picked up his beer again. Took a healthy gulp. Little murmurs of conversation swirled around us.

Outside, the sky was indigo, darkening to black. "So what exactly is a cursebreaker supposed to do?"

Raphael smiled. "Ask Tremont. He knows. I think I do, too. How's your ravioli?"

"It's good," I said. "How's your primavera?"

"Not enough meat," he said, deadpan, and I laughed again, despite myself. *Play nice with him, Isabella, and go home as soon as possible.*

If you can. If he lets you.

The sound made the entire restaurant break out into another buzz of conversation. I didn't look around, took another breadstick. "You're not the only carnivore in town."

Another one of those slow sleepy smiles. I flushed. I was thinking guilty thoughts. Guilty, adrenaline-laced thoughts.

One moment I was sure he was going to hurt me, and just playing with me like a cat plays with a mouse. The next, I was certain I had him fooled. One moment, he was attractive, the next he wasn't as handsome. Then his profile would call up the same half-unconscious flare of desire I used to feel for Jimmy Cassidy. Which brought me back around to Jeremy, and feeling even guiltier.

It was a special kind of purgatory.

"Nothing like flesh to make a man happy." Raphael played with his beer glass.

Now *that* was a little more than I'd expected from him.

"I guess so." I had thankfully finished most of the ravioli. *How soon can I be over with this and go home?*

Always blowing from place to place, dust in the wind, I'd never longed for a physical place when I thought of the word. "So why would Jeremy tell me you're especially dangerous, angel?"

Raphael blinked. "Now why would he say that?"

I shrugged, felt the phoenix tattoo on my left shoulder shift, and my entire body went cold. *Trouble.* Bad trouble, heading straight for me. "I think he thinks you'll besmirch my fair reputation." I tried a laugh. It sounded shaky. "Are you a love 'em and leave 'em type of guy?"

Raphael no longer smiled. Instead, he looked thoughtful, and just a little angry. "Really. You came here anyway, even though he warned you?"

"I wanted to." *Now I want to go home.*

"I don't think you're ready to play in Tremont City, pretty." Raphael stretched. "I think we're done."

I nodded. "I think we are."

He shrugged, the fevershine glittering and obscuring the iris and whites. His eyes hadn't looked like that during pool, or our little tete-a-tete in his yellow saltbox.

"Pity," he said. "It's fun. I enjoy the chance to make Tremont sweat a little. He's always been a self-righteous little punk."

I felt my face change. I flipped open my bag and started digging in it.

"Don't," Raphael said. "An honor and a pleasure, Isabella."

I wish I hadn't told him my name. I tipped my head gracefully, accepting the thanks, and Raphael paid for dinner.

CHAPTER TWENTY-SEVEN

OUTSIDE, THE NIGHT HAD TURNED sultry. So why did I feel so cold?

The pulsing intensified. I walked next to Raphael, my messenger bag slung across my body, and recognized the feeling. I've endured two riots, and I know that breathless chill.

Something was building up, a different type of storm.

We were almost at the motorcycle when someone fell into step on Raphael's other side. "What a lovely evening." A male voice, strangely mushy, as if he had a mouth full of something. I didn't want to see, looked down at my feet, my skin suddenly crawling. "And a nice little piece you have there, Dietrich."

"A lady," Raphael said, quietly, and there was a sliding, shifting menace under the words that brought out all my gooseflesh. The dark intensified, pressing between streetlamps.

"So selfish." The footsteps were soft and squishing slightly, shoes filled with Jell-O. "Is that a witch?"

I couldn't help myself. I looked.

Then I just as quickly looked down. Nothing that had that soft gray skin and those bulbous pink watery eyes should be wearing a faded *Glory Lives* T-shirt and a pair of chinos. Nothing that had those large, bare, painfully shredded feet should be able to keep up with Raphael's stride and my own long steps. Nothing that had that large, bald, greasy-looking head and lipless mouth should be looking at me so avidly, peering around Raphael's bulk.

The Kine made a sudden movement, and there was a snarl. The gray thing scurried away. I didn't jump, or flinch, of which I was exceedingly proud. Instead, I slipped my arm through

Raphael's, slightly sickened by the heat shimmering out from him.

"Well," I said lightly. "You're defending my good name."

"More like your skin." A definite edge to the words. "Not for long, Miss Pretty. I think you've miscalculated."

"What do you say I call a cab?"

"I don't think so. In fact, I think you'd better come with me. I have something to show you. You're curious about Tremont, aren't you?"

"I guess." I would have tried to pull my arm away, but I couldn't do it without seeming rude. And since politeness was the only thing that seemed to defuse Raphael, it was all I had left. Besides...it wasn't so bad. He'd just gotten rid of something big and squooshy and gray, hadn't he?

Never let them smell your fear, my mother's voice said clearly inside my head, just as it always did when I was in danger. *You took your chances, my daughter. You wanted answers, now you're going to get them.*

You're going to receive all the answers you ever wanted.

Caution thrown to the wind, I asked the million-dollar question. "So what breaks the Tremont curse?"

Raphael stopped. Looked down at me, slightly flushed under the shadow of shaven stubble on his cheeks, and the darkness in his aura retreated a little. "You want to break Tremont's curse?" His mouth stretched up into a kind of smile.

"If I can do it without hurting anyone or selling myself into slavery, I thought I'd give it a try. He's been good to me."

"His father tore his mother apart. He'll do the same to you." Raphael glanced up the street, pulled me with him as he started walking again. This time I had to almost trot to keep up, my skirt swinging, my boots clopping against the pavement. Even my feet were sweating. I wanted a cigarette.

What other lies have you told me? My skin was alternately cold and hot, a trickle of sweat sliding down my spine like an icy-chill finger. "So what does break the curse?" I persisted.

"I'll tell you later."

We reached the parking lot. The Indian sat, pristine and glowing under a circle of sodium-arc light. "You want me to show you, or do you want to go home? Last chance, Miss Pretty."

This is the time curiosity is going to kill me, I realized, and opened my mouth to ask to be taken back to the house.

"Show me," I said. "I want to know everything."

What the hell did I just say? Am I insane?

No, I wasn't.

There was no way he was going to drive me back to the Tremont house. I might as well get what I could out of this before I found out whatever nastiness he had planned.

"Fair enough." He led me to the bike. I was shivering continuously now, and my nipples were hard as pebbles under the thin cotton of the dress. He didn't even look. I was actually grateful.

I think I might have started screaming if he had tried to flirt more with me.

He started the bike, and the harsh purring of the engine now had teeth. "Come on."

I was glad again that the sundress had a wide enough skirt; I wasn't flashing an incredible amount of thigh. Somehow power-hoochie did not seem like the image I should be presenting right now. Instead, something like *bitter* and *stringy* and *lots of bones* was what I wanted to project.

He's not going to let me go, which means escape. I have a better chance of out where there aren't all those other...things...around.

I slid my arms around his waist just as the heartbeat of the town—still audible under the sound of the bike—paused.

Raphael turned his head slightly, listening.

Then the heartbeat came back, even stronger. Something had changed in the night, and I wasn't shivering anymore. "Well," Raphael said over his shoulder. "Tremont's felt it, and left his house. The nightsiders are going to start scurrying for cover. I guess it's official, now."

"What's official? He's felt *what?*" I asked, but he shook his head, lips clamping shut over his teeth. He popped the clutch and turned the bike, starting forward, slowly.

I held on. There was nothing to do but wait for whatever the night had in store.

CHAPTER TWENTY-EIGHT

WE FLICKED THROUGH THE STREETS, through pools of shadow, through glaring pools of streetlamp light that got farther and farther apart. Into the industrial section of town again, over the archetypal railroad tracks. The faint drumbeat of the pulse was further away now, but oddly just as present, an impossibility all its own.

Raphael finally pulled to a stop outside a wide, sloping, abandoned warehouse. There was a low expanse of weeds and shrubs on one side, and twisted wreckage spreading out around the building—a junkyard. Tremont: where appliances came to die.

I winced, wishing I hadn't thought of it that way. Raphael cut the engine, and the night around us was suddenly full of the buzz of crickets and the stealthy sounds of things moving.

The electric feeling intensified. Definitely riot material. It was beginning to seem more and more like I was the spark that would detonate it. I slid slowly off the back of the bike and might have bolted, but Raphael was suddenly off the bike himself. I froze like a rabbit, searching for something to say that would defuse the situation.

When he turned to me with his eyes full of silver and that darkness sliding over him I swallowed the words. Danger exhaled from him, something blind and furious. The time for answering questions was apparently over.

Being Jeremy's girlfriend was a punishable offense in this part of town. Or maybe I'd broken just enough of the curse to be considered a murder material.

"Be a good pretty," he said, reflectively. "Stand right there. I like that, seeing you with the light in your hair."

I stood still. If I broke and ran now, he would come after me. I knew that the way a mouse knows that a cat will spring, eventually. If I was still lucky—and that was looking vanishingly unlikely—I would find out how to break Jeremy's curse and be alive come dawn to do it.

If I was lucky.

"Not so many questions now, hmm, Miss Pretty?" When I'd met him, he only topped me by two or three inches. Now he topped me by at least five. He'd gotten taller. And wider around the shoulders.

Knowing and having the evidence right in front of you are two very, very different things. I had only met two or three Kine in my life, and each one had scared me badly. They aren't like normal people—they're faster, stronger, and generally a lot smarter. Nature blesses them with unthinkable vitality and physical and mental gifts—and curses them as well. They lived in packs, prides, clans—a Kine without a family is a dangerous thing; especially if they started Changing shape with the moon's wax and wane. If that happened, they'd fall further and further into a kind of psychotic state—the Kine called those poor beasts the Fallen.

They had to have iron control to deal with the Change, when the Beast was allowed to come out and play.

I wondered how good Raphael's control was, this close to a full moon. And if I stank of fear, what would *that* do?

No wonder he was a closed door. Kine were generally very resistant to telepathy, unless it was among themselves.

Charm your way out of this one, Isabella.

"It won't hurt much," Raphael said, softly. "And you'll be in service to a greater cause. You'd like that, wouldn't you, Miss Pretty?"

"What cause would that be?" I sidled nervously away when he reached for my arm.

"Freedom," he said, but he looked a little startled. Of course—he'd been counting on Kine pheromones and their particular hypnotism to keep me still. I was a witch, and so less affected by it; especially now that I wasn't half-charmed.

I skipped back again, stopped dead when he fixed me with those bright, quicksilver eyes.

"Democracy. Capitalism. All those mom and pop apple pie words. We take you and Tremont has to open the locus. He can't risk a single scratch to your pretty skin."

Then he moved again, quicker than I could follow, and his fingers clamped around my upper arm. "I couldn't believe it," he continued, dragging me toward the warehouse. "It threw me, it really did, when he let you out to play. I almost thought you were just another failed candidate, just a witch passing through. You almost had me believing he didn't give a good goddamn about you." The skittering, slithering sounds in the darkness intensified.

Tremont City was taking off its masks—and getting ready for a town meeting, in a nice little junkyard warehouse.

I was pretty sure I was number one on the agenda.

"But I took the precaution of sending a messenger to him, to yank his chain, and he leaves his hallowed walls. He's looking for you, pretty. He's got to be desperate, to do a stupid stunt like this; he's going to run right into our trap."

Raphael had sent someone to taunt Jeremy into leaving the house. *I've been outplayed by a guy who turns into a walking carpet. Great.*

I tried pulling away, but he just clamped down, bands of iron around my arm. I let out a short pained sound and he clucked his tongue, like chastising a child.

"Don't do that, pretty. My control's not good this close to the Moonfall. You don't want any accidents, do you? You're a nice bargaining chip, and I'd hate to have to break any bones."

"You know," I told him, desperation making my tone sharp, "you're not turning out to be a very good date."

It was empty bravado, and we both knew it. "Who said this was a date?" A genuine, wide, and terrifying smile stretched his lips. "I said *dinner.* You've had yours. It's only fair that I have mine."

CHAPTER TWENTY-NINE

THE WAREHOUSE WAS A GIANT, cavernous space inside, Power sparkling and stirring into the visible spectrum. This must have been a meeting place for a long time. It reeked of Kine and things I had spent my life avoiding, skating on the thin edge between the normal world and the place where magick lived.

Vrkolak. Hungry Ones. So many names.

Raphael held my arm. Held? No, gripped as if he wanted to break it. I would be bruised, if I lived through this. A sort of platform was cobbled together out of old pallets and bits of broken wood, and he hauled me up to the top of it. I was glad I'd worn my boots—sandals would have been torn away.

"Don't do this," I began. "You're better than this." If they hurt Jeremy, if he walked into a trap thinking he was going to save me—

"You don't get it, do you?" He whirled me to face him, his eyes glittering and his face suffused with ugliness. "You're a *bargaining chip* now, Miss Pretty. You're the only way we have to make Tremont open up the locus and make it free. *Free!* For everyone, not just the ones that the Protectors give their rubber-stamp to. You're our leverage."

Great. I'm a hostage to a magickal IRA. "Leverage?" *Keep him talking, Isabella.* "Why don't you just ask him?"

I don't want Jeremy to come here. He'll get eaten alive, they'll surround him and hurt him.

Which meant I had to get creative.

"We've asked," he said. "He keeps saying the Protectors are here to make sure Darkness and the *vrkolak* don't overrun everything. That controlling the locus is his job, and that he won't hand it over."

"What about you? I mean, what makes you any different? You just want to control it yourself." I tried to pull away again, testing the footing, and the entire platform rocked. He shook me as casually as he would a dishrag, my head snapping back and forth. *I hope he realizes it's a trap and goes home. Please let him be smart enough to do that.*

"I told you not to do that, pretty," he said. "Do it again, and I'll break something. Moonfall's almost here, and I'm not as careful as I should be." He showed his teeth, a feral grimace. I swallowed blood—I'd bitten the inside of my cheek.

Clicking and hissing sounds filled the dimness. The doors flew open, crashed against the walls like splintered teeth grinding. The crowd flowed in, filling the warehouse.

I shut my eyes, hanging limply from Raphael's grasp. *Gods of my mother, protect me,* I prayed, without any real hope.

Now I realized what I should have known all along. I wasn't trying to find out about Jeremy's curse.

I was trying to run away from him.

Be still and watch. Open your eyes.

I obeyed.

The crowd filled the space, spilled into the street. There were horns and strangely-colored skin, a contingent of the squooshy gray things with torn and battered feet, low shaggy shapes pacing back and forth, huge dogshapes that had no shadows. A whole contingent of Kine threaded through the crowd to take up stations around the platform, like guards. Mostly men, one woman with a long fall of brown hair, all of them crackling with the heat and the glittering eyes that matched Raphael's.

Ah. So it's the Kine running this. They want to take Jeremy's place as controllers of the locus.

Great. I slumped against Raphael's grip, my arm starting to throb. My fingers felt swollen.

"Oh, look," someone said—a tall maroon-skinned humanoid with a ruff of feathers around his round head. "Rafe's got a new pet."

"Smells like a witch," someone else said—someone I couldn't see. "Bad luck to eat a witch."

"Maybe for you," one of the gray things piped up through its mush-filled mouth. A ripple of amusement went through the crowd. "Looks tasty, doesn't she?"

"I called this Meeting to address the question of the Protector." Raphael gave me a contemptuous little shake, and my teeth clicked together. My bag—I slid my free hand into my bag, but Raphael shook me again and I had to stop. I ran over everything I was carrying.

Kine were sometimes allergic to gold. But nope, I had nothing that would help.

Raphael kept going. This was his moment to shine. "We have his cursebreaker, and we can make him open the locus. Power for all."

A new ripple went through the crowd. "Cursebreaker," someone said, very softly.

"How can we be sure?" This voice was hypnotic, soothing, but full of ice.

"He's left his house," one of the gray things replied. "Why would he do that so close to a Moonfall if he wasn't looking for her?"

"We sent a messenger." The Kine woman's voice was throaty and oddly sweet. "He didn't deny that the girl's his cursebreaker. He's coming."

A fresh spate of rustling and murmuring greeted this revelation. I sagged in Raphael's grip. *Oh, Jeremy.*

"The locus." A huge dog settled back on its haunches. Its muzzle wrinkled at it sniffed. How its mouth could make recognizable sounds I don't know. "It's awake. And it follows her heartbeat."

"So it's true." The maroon-skinned, feathered man folded his arms. "Well."

Another buzz of conversation.

"Give uss the curssebreaker," came a low, evil voice from the very back of the room. "We will ssee what Tremont will do when sshe sstartss to bleed." Several of the people—not-people, whatever they were—rustled, glanced over their shoulders at the voice.

Vrkolak. Whatever it is, it's hungry. Oh, gods. I shivered. Raphael shook me again. I had the unpleasant thought that I might pass out soon.

"Oh, for Nona's sake." A tall woman with long green hair stepped forward, her voice full of running water and creaking wood. "Are we so weak we have to torture those even weaker to reach our goals? Look at her. Not even a mouthful." Her hair had fluttering leaves in it, little yellow flowers. She looked so familiar, but maybe it was only terror that made me think so.

"I would think you would hate her, Willow," Raphael answered. "Humans have never done you any good."

The woman gazed at him with eyes full of clear green darkness. "She's a witch, Raphael. There is a difference. Why do we need more Power? There is enough and to spare."

"There's never enough," one of the Kine said. "Not while the Protectors bar access."

"They keep the Balance, and keep chaos at bay," Willow murmured, clearly audible even through the crowd-noise. "Surely that counts as useful."

"They don't hunt *you*, dryad," the soft evil voice interjected, and there was another rustle though the crowd.

"They're despots," Raphael said.

"Would you do any better?" A harsh, crackling voice like dry sticks being rubbed together, coming from a dry sticklike thing that looked like a praying mantis. "There you are with your tribe, holding a hostage. When you hold the locus, what will *you* do?"

Yeah! I wanted to cheer. *Ask him that again while I figure out how to get out of here!*

"We're wasting time," Raphael said. "I've always opposed Tremont. You know that. I'm trying to do what's best for *all* of us. We need to send someone to negotiate with him, since he killed our messenger—"

His fingers loosened for one split second, and I dropped, going limp. My arm tore out of his grasp and I rolled off the platform, diving between two Kine who both snarled and leapt for me. They collided, and I felt a burst of nasty satisfaction as I scrambled up and tore between two of the huge dog-things, who leapt to their feet.

The room exploded into motion. I dashed for a side door, the *Exit* sign over it dark and lifeless. My ankle twisted, but I ignored the flare of pain. I hit the door hard, hoping it wasn't locked; it flew open and I tumbled out into darkness, sharp bright jabs jolting up from my ankle at every step.

Howls and screams burst behind me. A pile of junked cars blocked the view of the crowd gathered before the warehouse. I ducked around another pile of smashed metal, hoping it would throw off pursuit. The light wasn't good out here, the streetlamps were only lit out in front, with the crowd and the sidewalk.

I aimed for a belt of scrub brush I'd glimpsed from the parking lot. Chances weren't good that I could hide until daylight, but it was all I had.

I was going to take it.

I leapt over a three-foot concrete divider and plunged into scrub and weeds. None of it was big enough to hide me, and I was gasping for breath already. *Not in good shape. Too much wine and ravioli. And cigarettes. Mama was right, they'll kill me.*

Someone grabbed my shoulder and pushed me down. I would have let out a scream, but a strong brown hand clamped over my mouth. "Hush," she said, the words full of wind and dripping water. "Stay still."

It was the woman with long green hair—Willow. She knelt next to me, exhaling a breath of wood and growing leaves. "It's summer," she whispered against my cheek, "and the power of trees is at its peak. Stay still until they have passed." She leaned close, and her long green hair falling capelike across my bare shoulders.

I crouched, trying to breathe quietly, my side and my ankle throbbing. Rushing feet, howls under the almost-full moon masked behind a spray of cloud. Thick ruthless electricity against every pore, making it hard to breathe.

It took a long time, as all the things gathered there scattered into the night, hunting. I remembered legends of the Wild Hunt that I'd heard all through my childhood, and a fresh fit of shivering seized me.

A snarl, something pausing to look in our direction, snout lifted, white teeth gleaming. I stopped breathing, despite the burning in my lungs. Willow whispered, just a breath of sound, wind in the treetops. Her hand still clamped over my mouth, bark-rough and cold.

The snarling passed.

Still she waited. Sweating and chilled at the same time, the world around me full of damp bark and fresh green leaves. I couldn't smell myself at all, which was disconcerting.

Soft squishy feet padded by, paired with low wet breathing. "Nothing here," one of the gray things said.

"Keep looking," another replied. "She *must* be somewhere close."

"Witches," the first gray thing said. "Tricky things."

"Must have had help. You're right. She'll be going toward the locus. Tremont's out, and hunting."

"Bad for us, if he catches us."

"Very bad. He doesn't forget."

"Or forgive."

They squish-paddled away. Willow waited a few more minutes. Then she took her hand from my mouth. "There," she said softly. "Nobody left to see you, witch-kin."

"Th-thank you—" I started to stammer, she touched my cheek. Her fingers were rough, barklike, but now warm.

"A good deed, done for a tree. You honored me." Slow, thoughtful words. "It's been a long time since anyone spoke to me. So many trees simply sleep now." She shivered, a sound like branches groaning. "Now go. Go carefully. Hope that *he* finds you before the Hungry Ones do."

"Raphael," I couldn't even finish the question.

"He is not Fallen yet," she said. "But it is very close. Go *now*. You don't have time to talk."

"Thank you," I said, but she rose. There was a rushing of wind through thin branches, and she disappeared.

Thunder rattled over the distant mountains.

We would have a storm tonight after all.

Chapter Thirty

I crouched for a few moments, trembling. My ankle hurt. The trembling locked me to the ground like a scared rabbit. Even I have my limits for weirdness.

If I went into shock completely, the world would fade into a gray blanket and I would stay there shaking until someone arrived to pick me up and do whatever they wanted to me.

Get up. My mother's voice, faint and staticky, like a radio at the very edge of a station's range. *Get moving. Now, Isabella! Get up!*

Even after so many years, hers was the voice of obedience for me. I made it upright. Took two drunken steps. Another. The crumbling dry dirt underfoot shifted and held, and the weeds smelled like freedom.

I could do it. I could walk. I just couldn't chew gum at the same time, ha ha. Funny me. Funny Isabella.

I took a deep breath, oriented myself. If I got far enough north, I could figure out where the house was. My sense of direction was still good.

North is in the bones, my mother always said.

I made my way through the belt of scrub brush and to a deserted street. There was an alley offering some handy cover, and I stood there in the shadows, holding on to the wall, my fingers flexing as if they intended to drive themselves into the brick.

It took far more courage than I would have thought to step out onto the street. I walked quickly, chin up, hoping to bluff my way through whatever trouble I encountered. Lots of urban living proves it—if you walk like you're a badass, people will generally assume you *are* one, and leave you alone. I forded pools of streetlamp light, my mental walls thinning, using every erg of skill I'd gained in three decades of surviving an inhospitable world.

Hopefully I would feel them before they felt me.

The far-off thunder flirted a little closer. Static popped and sparked in my hair, the entire seething hill of Tremont thick things hunting in dark corners and deserted streets.

It took concentrated effort not to shrink into the shadows. That would be a dead giveaway. I simply hurried on, tangled hair falling over my eyes. I stuck my hand in my bag and touched the black bandanna over my cards. Reassured, my fingers also found a pack of cigarettes, and I thought longingly of lighting up.

If I make it out of this I'm going to smoke a whole pack. Then I'm quitting. I was handling this pretty well, all things considered. That faint, distant heartbeat just kept drumming away. If I aimed for it, I could probably cut through backyards and alleys, find the house, and go to bed.

It was a wonderful thought.

It took me perhaps an hour to find and cross the railroad tracks, carefully, using a dilapidated little side street and cutting through a small backyard to do it. The houses were all dark. If I'd been smart enough to be inside tonight, I would have bolted the doors and prayed for dawn too.

My bladder felt hot and uncomfortably full, so I found a little greenbelt on the other side of the tracks and gratefully relieved myself, wiping with a handful of grass. Then, feeling ten pounds lighter and not quite as nervous, I started working my way through a tangle of streets, edging northward. This was going to take a while.

My ankle throbbed. Several times I had to duck into an alley and crouch, waiting, until they passed. Nothing on the street right now would be normal or human. I trembled against brick walls and behind dumpsters while the huge shadowless dogs ran, miraculously missing me. I had to shimmy under a laurel hedge once to avoid a squad of those gray things. If I hadn't had so much experience hiding in cities, always looking for those little slices of forgotten ground, I would never have made it.

As it was, I was incredibly lucky.

I had been walking for maybe two and a half hours when the very threshold of my sensing-range brushed against something hot and spiked, and I immediately looked around for cover.

Nothing, no comforting alleys or side streets close enough. The street was full of little boutiques, so there were no yards to hide in. The only thing that could possibly provide any safety was a scarce number of parked cars.

My nape prickled. I threw myself to hands and knees, crawling under a blue pickup truck in front of a dark pet food store. *Why are there people parked here at this hour?* There had to be houses back from the main road, and that parking would be at a premium here. Plus there were a few restaurants—but the streets were deserted.

I just don't care, I told myself practically. *Cover is cover.*

Thunder kept rumbling, greasy growls across a hot muggy sky. I huddled under the pickup, hoping there was no broken glass, and waited.

Something moved from shadow to shadow down the street, flitting between pools of darkness. Fluttering and black, it moved like a bedsheet caught in a high wind, flapping. *A kalak.*

An honest-to-god nightflyer.

I stayed very still.

The *kalak* crossed and re-crossed the street, drifting, avoiding the streetlamps as much as it could. *Kalaks* were smart in a fight, but generally stupid otherwise, being opportunistic scavengers preying on psychics too weak to defend themselves. This one looked a little bigger than most, and I prayed it wouldn't find me.

I didn't feel up to offering much of a fight.

It finally fluttered away, and I waited until I couldn't sense it anymore to wriggle out from under the pickup. I had just gotten to my feet and dusted myself off when I heard the roaring of a motorcycle engine.

Down I went again and slithered under the truck, scraping my knees painfully in the process. The sundress was never going to survive, it was already grimy and sweat-soaked. *Don't let them smell me. Please, just don't let them smell me.*

If I craned my neck just right, I would be able to see them. I hoped they wouldn't see me, or smell me, or even hear how loudly my heart was pounding away. I rapped my head painfully on a gearcase or something—the truck was jacked up high enough so that I had a good chance of looking out and not being seen if I rolled toward the curb a bit. Which I did, wishing I could see more than just one narrow slice of street.

They roared down the avenue, Raphael at their head, a fleet of seven exhaust-snorting motorcycles holding lithe, deadly Kine. I huddled, my hip bumping a tire.

His dark hair a shock of wildness and his eyes were scorching silver, Raphael snarled, a stripe of drying blood across his face. The Kine woman, with her long brown mane flying bannerlike, dropped back a little and glance around, her face alight with predatory glee. Then she sped up and rejoined the pack.

None of them looked back. At least, not that I could tell.

Raphael turned one way, with three of them, and the other three banked the opposite direction. Engine-racket faded, and a long howl lifted from what I guessed was the south.

A high, chilling sound, sawing at the edges of my hearing, answered by something else howling in the east. The second howl had more gravel in it, a distinctly older voice. I covered my ears with my hands and tried to make myself even smaller, wishing it would all just go away.

I waited until the shaking passed, breathing deeply, and scrambled out from under the pickup again. I could just stay there until morning, but by then I'd be too stiff and sore to move...and the longer I froze in one place, the greater chance of being found.

I forced myself to walk away.

I made it to the next parked car, and the next. I was almost beginning to feel a little more confident when a long low shape melted out of the darkness and strode for me, light tipping its pelt in gold.

A golden furnace glow, behind black iron bars. Definitely catlike, and the stripes were oh-so-familiar.

A tiger. The paws looked a little too big, the blue-gold animal eyes were too conscious. Too *present*. And it was walking on a city street in blithe disregard of its own unreality. It appeared too suddenly for me to hide, without a single breath of warning.

Thunder settled, turned over in the sky above the town. It had sighted what it was after, and was adjusting itself for the leap.

I swallowed, my throat clicking dryly. The heartbeat of the town still pulsed.

The tiger stopped six feet away, and regarded me with its blue-gold eyes. It cocked its head, and I was forcibly reminded of Jeremy. Again.

My knees buckled, and the tiger-not-cougar paced forward, slowly, each paw placed precisely.

"Jeremy?" I whispered.

CHAPTER THIRTY-ONE

THE TIGER SANK BACK TO sit, staring at me. The stripes were the pattern of scarring on a man's face.

He gazed out of the tiger's eyes and blinked, once, deliberately.

The breath whooshed out of me. I staggered, and that brought him forward again.

His shoulders reached my elbow. He carried the massive head proudly, whiskers of solid gold and a sensitive nose. Impossibly vital, the beast burning like a flame.

A Kine. No, just something so close to it that it doesn't matter...he can't leave the house, though! He said...unless... My brain stuttered drunkenly. *Unless he has to leave the house as a big giant tiger.*

"Oh," I said, in a queer little *I might just pass out now* voice. "Jeremy."

Familiar heat soaked into my skin, radiating from him. Thunder rumbled again, restlessly.

The tiger slid under my arm on one side, nearly knocking me off my unsteady legs, then curved around me just as a cat would. He ended up on my other side, between me and the road. I put my hand up, blindly, fingers sinking into the savage sliding pelt. "Gods," I whispered. "I'm glad to see you, Jeremy. I'm so sorry."

The tiger took one step, glanced over his shoulder. His whole attitude shouted, *well, come on.* His fur slid under my arm. I felt every individual gold-tipped hair.

I took a trembling step, another. The tiger paced next to me, my hand lost up to the wrist in fur. Warmth rose up my arm and into my shoulder, hesitating before pouring down into my body. It was such a relief I didn't care about the tears soaking my cheeks.

"They're hunting for me," I said. The tiger's ears flicked back, just as Jeremy would listen to me read. "I...Raphael. He took me to a warehouse...it was a meeting. He wanted to use me as a hostage to get access to the locus."

The tiger growled, a single low note almost as frightening as approaching thunder. My fist clenched in his fur, and it must have been uncomfortable. I tried to let go, couldn't make myself. "I'm pulling your fur." Hot salt tears dropped onto my collarbones. My bag bumped against my hip and my ankle throbbed with each step. I heard that pulsing again, under the surface of my skin, and it was a lot closer now. "There was a woman—Willow. She helped me hide once I got away. I think— this is crazy—but I think she's the willow tree I parked my car under when it blew up." I couldn't get enough air in.

We reached an intersection, and the tiger led me left, along a dark narrow street with blank-faced houses on either side. I stumbled, my stomach twisting with relief and fresh nausea, and he stopped until I could right myself.

"This is crazy even for me," I said. "I'm used to being the weirdest thing around. But this—"

I had never realized how much I wanted everyone else to be normal.

Jeremy said nothing, of course. Of course. He was a *tiger*, for God's sake.

"I was trying to find out how to break your curse. Or I was trying to run away from you. I'm not sure which. I'm not too good at dating nice guys. But I think I'll give you a try. Okay?"

The tiger's ears flicked again, and he made a sort of low chuffing sound. It sounded so much like Jeremy's bitter little laugh that I had to laugh too.

My laughter had a low screamy quality to it that I didn't like, but I couldn't stop. My sanity depended on laughing, even while tears rolled down my cheeks and my nose filled up with saline. "Jeremy," I said, between giggles, "I really like you. I think I'm really fond of you..." I trailed off. "I think I..."

I was a coward. Crying harder, laughing at the same time, the words stuck in my throat. The tiger patiently padded along, turning me right at the next intersection, then immediately left. Something strange was happening around us—the town shivered and blurred, ink running on wet paper. The heartbeat stuttered, and I began to feel truly sick, my stomach revolving.

"I love you," I finally whispered, too quiet to really be heard. But tigers have excellent hearing, don't they? "I'm sorry. Please, I'm sorry."

The tiger stopped, twisted to look back at me. It blinked again, and bumped against me, almost throwing me off my feet. He was trying to *comfort* me, I realized, and the thought made me break out into fresh tear-soaked hilarity. I gulped, trying to get a hold of myself, and the tiger led me forward again.

We rounded one more corner to the left, and another impossibility confronted me. We were on Tremont Avenue, three blocks from the house. The nausea vanished.

"How did you *do* that? It's a great trick. We were all the way across town!"

The tiger's head bobbed, and it made that little chuffing sound again. I would know that laugh anywhere. I didn't even care about the bitterness in it.

Relief crashed inside me, and I grayed out. I came back to myself sitting on the curb, fresh scrapes on my knees. Had I fallen? I couldn't tell. I was hyperventilating, and the tiger produced a grinding sound.

I couldn't tell if it was a purr or a warning growl.

I hauled myself upright again. "Come on, Isabella. Get inside the house, *then* you can have a nervous breakdown. I promise. I swear I am *never* going out after dark in this town again. Not even for dinner."

The tiger rose too, its ears pricked. His weight shifted, a movement I felt all through my own aching, battered body.

"What is it?"

His lip lifted, exposing gleaming teeth. I could imagine very well what they would do to me. The grinding intensified.

Definitely a growl.

Thunder rolled and rattled. I was getting very tired of the weather here. If this kept up I might not like thunderstorms anymore.

I peered up the street. "Come on," I said, nervously. "Let's get inside."

The tiger rose to his feet and, with great deliberation, put his head down and pushed me in the direction of the house.

"Why don't you come too?" High and breathless-panicked. "Come on, Jeremy."

He pushed me again, and I nearly lost my balance. He was too strong to really be gentle. I stumbled, righted myself again.

"Okay," I said, and took two steps, looked back at him.

He folded himself down on his hindquarters. His head dipped down, raised again, a nod. As if he was saying, *go on.* The pounding of the town's heartbeat filled my fingers and toes. It echoed my own heartbeat. I wasn't sure I liked that. If I left Tremont, would my heart stop?

"All right." I took another few shaky steps towards safety.

Toward home.

When I looked back, my heart fell into my stomach and splashed. I tasted bile.

He was gone. The street was empty. The faint buzzing of motorcycles rasped against each shuttered house.

"Oh, no." I could almost make out the streetlamps in front of the iron gates from here. I started walking as quickly as my trembling legs and throbbing ankle would allow.

CHAPTER THIRTY-TWO

I MADE IT A BLOCK and a half before having to lean against a low stone wall blocking off someone's yard to rub at my ankle. A few stinging drops of rain hit the sidewalk. I couldn't wait for the storm to break—well, actually, I could. I wanted to be inside when it did, curled up in bed with the covers pulled firmly up over my head.

I wanted to stay under the covers for at least a week. No, a month. Listening to the pounding pulse that was this goddamn weird place living and breathing.

I can deal with the pulse. It's the men I just can't stand.

The low purring sound of a well-maintained motorcycle, creeping along, broke the breathlessness. Then…it stopped.

Nausea slammed into me again. I bent over, my arms crossed over my stomach, biting back a moan. Shallow sipping little breaths, trying to shove the roiling of my stomach down where it belonged. It didn't want to go.

I straightened and glanced down the street again, idiotically hoping to see the tiger. My heart exploded, I tasted bile again. *I should just puke and get it over with.*

There was the Indian, lonely and naked under a pool of orange streetlight.

Why did—

I had no time to think. Raphael glided towards me deliberately, taking great swinging soundless strides, his face a mask of rage. His lips peeled back from his teeth, and then...

Then he began to *change.*

Flesh ran like hot wax. Bones cracked, tendons snapped as his head dropped down, his arms lengthening, claws gleaming where his hands used to be, his jeans ripping with loud tearing sounds that would have been hilarious in another context.

Dark glossy fur sprouted along his face, his chin jutting forward. His eyes were fearful silver holes, and his teeth burst out, misshapen. A low awful noise, partly pain, partly fury, threaded between the thunder and my own hyperventilating, and I realized something was very wrong.

He's lost control, and this close to a full moon you know what that means.

I could guess. *He's no longer Kine. He's Fallen.*

I swallowed, tasting blood. I had bitten my lower lip again, almost clean through. I stood there, dreamily watching my death pound its way toward me on feet that melted out of his boots and became twisted, heavy paws. Claws *skritched* against the pavement, and his eyes were silver lamps with a tinge of green now, scorching holes in the night. The heartbeat of the town pounded in my ears, smacked against my skin.

I whirled, the spell of fear broken. It was another block and a half. I wasn't going to make it. The vision from a circle of candles and salt rose under my skin, and I began to scream. Pointlessly, it was wasted breath, but I couldn't help it.

The sound of claws scrabbled behind me.

One block left. One small block left to the iron gates.

I wanted to look back, didn't dare, just put my head down and sprinted, feet pounding, my ankle screaming with agony, my breath coming in great gulping, seizure-painful gasps. I ran. I *ran*.

The gates were open, and I pelted through onto the paved drive, hair flying, eyes watering, thunder roaring above. Raindrops flicked down, smashed on the pavement. It was the first light wave of rain before the storm truly started. I was so *close* to the house.

Too late.

Breath locked inside my chest, every single cigarette I'd ever smoked rising up to haunt me, the messenger bag's strap broke and I whirled, the need to save the cards suddenly greater than the need to outrun whatever was chasing me. Chasing me with claws.

It was now a nightmare, not a man. Human form and animal pelt, like the stories of the Kine my mother used to tell me, those who had a beast inside them, those who could use it...if it did not use them.

The Kine moved with power and precision and grace. I'd seen that fierce beauty with my own eyes.

They were never ugly. Unless they Fell.

Raphael howled. His breath, hot and dry, a volcano exhalation, freighted with a horrifying stench, rotting from the inside.

This was what all the Kine feared, a creature that had lost their precious control.

I fell, my bag clutched to my chest—somehow it had only slid down my body, not fallen completely away. I screamed as I went down, my eyes straining as if they were going to pop out of my head. My tailbone hit the driveway with a resounding thump, my teeth clicked together hard, and if my tongue had been there, I would have lost a chunk of it.

I saw stars, tiny pinpricks of light.

So this is how I die, I thought, wonderingly. *So close to the—*

Lightning sizzle-flashed. The thing that had been Raphael leapt for me—

—but fell, halfway there. Thunder banged and crashed. Something large and fluid and striped had caught the half-human thing chasing me. Claws and teeth and snarling, striped muzzle, the ruff around its cheeks clearly visible in the moonlight.

"Jeremy!" I screamed. *"NO!"*

Neither snarling, thrashing thing took any notice. I scooted back, losing skin on both my palms, the wind freshening as the storm broke. Amazingly, I found myself upright, and my ankle gave one last vicious flare of pain before I forgot all about it again.

The Fallen Kine let out an amazing howl of pain and defeated rage. Teeth flashed. Blood flew, dark in the streetlamp-starred night. I shivered, clutched the bag to my chest.

A tiger's deep bass roar, and a deathlike scream.

My ankle, finally giving up, snapped under me and I fell again, fully erasing the skin on both palms. I didn't care.

Blood, black in the dim light. Rain steamed against two smoking, writhing beasts.

No. One snarling beast.

"Jeremy…" A faint, hopeless whisper.

The tiger limped away from a fallen heap of fur that had been Raphael. Death glazed the silver eyes, but even so, he stared, a terrible accusing glare.

His throat was gone. Blood pumped across unforgiving concrete of the driveway, steaming in a sudden stormchill.

The tiger took two staggering steps. Blood smoked out from his belly. A bad wound. There were other stripes of dark fluid in his pelt. His throat, his muzzle, he favored his left hack leg, heavily hop-limping sideways.

I made it to my knees. I had to try three times to push myself up again. Lightning crackled, my hair catching raindrops.

The tiger let out a low moaning sound, his head dropping. I limped over to him, my ankle screaming viciously every time I put any weight on it, great red spikes of pain. *Jeremy.*

The tiger wavered.

"NO!" I screamed, and made it to him in a limping rush. "Come on, Tremont!" I sank my fingers into his ruff and pulled, as if he was a kitten, with hysterical strength.

It didn't budge him, but he did raise his head wearily. Blinked away the blood falling into one blue-gold eye. Made a tired, inquiring sound.

"Come on." I pulled at him again. "Come on. The house, Jeremy. We've got to get inside."

His head dropped again. How many hundred pounds of muscle and fur, trembling?

"Jeremy, I can't bloody well marry you if you don't get inside that house!" I screamed, and there was an amazing flash of lightning. That got his attention.

He took one faltering step and stopped. I yanked on his fur again. *"Come on!"* I screamed, my voice breaking. *"Come on!"*

Step by step, we staggered. I glanced over my shoulder, at the gate.

Closed now, it seemed a thin curtain against what lay behind. Yellow eyes, pink eyes, eyes burning green. The gate groaned. Bits of iron began to peel off and fall, ringing and chiming, on the driveway. An amazing howl of rage lifted in the near distance, under the thunder.

I let out a hoarse sound, half -scream, half-sob. *"Come on!"*

We made it to the steps. I hauled on him again, fingers slipping in blood and water. Raining for real now, gunshots against the porch roof. Soaked in a matter of moments, chilled clear through.

The front door opened, soundless, graceful. A thin, short-haired girl—Mharian—stood silhouetted, her hands on her hips. I was too busy pulling on him to care.

In theory, it would be impossible for one small human female to drag a tiger that comes up to her chest *anywhere*. However, I managed it. I *had* to manage it. Of course, he probably helped.

I pushed past Mharian into the foyer, black and white squares shiny in the warm electric light. Fur melted under my hands and Jeremy tumbled to the floor, hitting hard and making a low sound, something like a tired grunt.

"What did you do to him?" Mharian's face twisted up with concern. She really did look like a Judy Garland cat with a boy's haircut, and I suppressed a wild braying laugh only by sheer force of will. I pointed at the door.

"Close that," I snapped. "And get your Spock-eared friend out here. He needs *help*."

"Isa...bella..." Jeremy whispered, and I dropped to my knees beside him, pushed at his shoulders with my bleeding hands.

"I'm here," I said, and he looked up at me, his blue eyes almost black with pain. His right eye was swollen shut and crusted with blood. Covered with blood and water, his hair dark and streaming against the tiles.

Hitch-gasping with useless sobs, I got my arms around him, and he curled weakly into me, his legs lying limp. I couldn't see his scars. I didn't want to see them. They reminded me too much of stripes now.

"Isabella," he whispered. His belly was a mess. Ragged skin, raw wet redness of exposed and torn muscle, the glaring white of bone from one rib peeking out. He had one arm clamped over the wound, hiding it. "Are you...are you..."

"I'm here," I choked, suppressing the urge to throw up with one last desperate effort. Mharian said something over her shoulder. I ignored her.

"Hurt?" he whispered. "Are you hurt?"

That tore something inside me. I felt it give, like cloth ripping. "No, I'm an idiot, but I'm not hurt. You...you just lie still. You're going to be okay."

"Marry...me?" he asked, his left eye closing too, and I let out a sharp sound, as if I'd been hit.

"Of course, you idiot," I said. "Now just rest. You're going to be okay, I promise." I looked up at Mharian. "Call an ambulance! *Do* something!"

"I will." Her green skirt fluttered, the silver belt glittering in the electric light from the chandelier. She looked far older now, her eyes dark with something terrible and serene at the same time.

"What hap—oh. Oh dear."

It was a passionless, androgynous voice, ringing like bells being stroked together. I looked up to see a tall, slender humanoid figure with long curling brown hair. A lipsticked mouth, small breasts, a long blue silk dress that was designer if I'd ever seen one, and a face too strong-jawed to be female.

A drag queen? Here?

Why wasn't I surprised?

"Get down here and anchor him," Mharian snapped, sounding more like a battlefield general than a spoiled brat of a girl. "Guillame!"

"You rang?" The stick-thin, nut-brown elf-eared man appeared, tying the belt of a shapeless green silken robe. "Mharian, are you—"

"I'm going to heal him. Help Koren anchor him, he's fading." She pushed her hands down on the ruined mess of Jeremy's abdomen. Thunder boomed again, rattling the entire house. The heartbeat of the town was very close, it thudded in the walls. It matched my own heart, pounding high and wild behind the cage of my ribs.

"Mharian," Guillame began, but I never did hear the rest of it, because I slumped down over Jeremy, shielding his body with mine, and passed out.

CHAPTER THIRTY-THREE

WHEN I WOKE UP, I was in my bed, a wet washcloth on my forehead. It smelled like lavender.

My entire body ached. My ankle sang with pain. My palms hurt. I'd pulled something in my leg. My ribs twinged. I was clutching my messenger bag to my side, its broken strap wrapped around my hands.

The drag queen coughed a little, politely. "Good evening," he—or she—said calmly. "My name is Koren." The voice was exquisite.

I found the right pronoun with an effort. *They.*

Their face was exquisite too, the blending of male and female working perfectly in tandem. Long nose, strong jaw, lovely skin, the kind of eyelashes little boys have, thickly fringed.

"Jeremy," I husked. I blinked at this beautiful vision, whose crimson lipstick was still pristine. They smelled of baking bread and crushed mint—a hell of a perfume. Their long curling hair fell artfully forward over their lightly muscled shoulders.

"He's sleeping. As you should be. Mharian is a healer, and she did well with him. He will survive."

I closed my eyes, scalding relief all through me. "Good." I hadn't killed him with stupidity. The price was paid, and we were both still alive.

Koren took the washcloth from my forehead, wringing it over a white enamel basin. Then the coolness was replaced, and the smell of lavender intensified. "The roses are blooming," Koren said. "Do you know what that means?"

I shook my head slightly, trying to keep the washcloth on.

"It means that the curse is broken. He's free." Their fingers realigned the washcloth. "You must love him very much."

For all the good it does either of us. The darkness behind my eyelids got deeper and deeper. I was going to go back to sleep. I was tired, and I hurt all over. I wanted a cigarette.

I don't think I'll ever smoke again. "Good," I repeated, hoarsely. "My work here is done."

Their bell-like voice laughed, a merry, pleasant sound. "Oh, no, young one. Yours is just beginning. Sleep now."

As if they had cast a spell on me, I did.

WHEN I WOKE UP AGAIN, it was the middle of the day. Something told me I'd been asleep for a long time. Koren was gone, and so was the washcloth. I lay very still for a few minutes, watching the reflected sunlight fall across the ceiling. The house creaked, singing to itself as all old houses do, and the town's heartbeat slid along under mine.

If I left, would mine stop? Or would it just hurt, a nameless ache in my chest?

The roses are blooming. He's free.

Great. So he was free. Where did that leave me?

Out of luck, that's what. His curse was broken, probably no thanks to me thrashing around and getting myself in trouble. I didn't have the faintest clue what to do now.

I didn't have the faintest clue of what I'd *done.*

I rolled up out of bed, grimacing, and padded across the hardwood floor. The black sundress was filthy, and I peeled it off bit by bit. Dropped it on the floor right outside the bathroom.

I was a goddamn mess. Hopelessly tangled hair, huge circles under my eyes, a huge dark bruise on my cheek and my lip bitten through and swollen again. I was going to have to stop doing that. More fresh redblack bruises across my shoulders, and the dark print of Raphael's fingers on my left arm. Those particular marks were deep and awful, and would be sore for a long time. My palms were scabbed over, and my ankle was swollen. It hurt to put any weight on it.

I took a long tepid shower, cursing as shampoo and the soap stung my raw hands. Gingerly braided my hair after I got out, then spent a little time looking in the mirror.

Yes, my own familiar face was there. Under the bruising, I was still there. My mother's cheekbones, my mother's lips, my forehead.

You're a very pretty girl. How long would I be able to say that to myself?

I managed to get into a *Tragic Diamonds* T-shirt and a pair of jeans, and sniffed at my sodden boots. I pulled a pair of socks on, worked my feet into the boots.

The house was utterly silent. If I was at work in the library, I would have Mozart playing. Or Tchaikovsky. Or maybe some Grateful Dead. I would be stacking books, or facing a shelf, or shelving new acquisitions. It would be teatime soon, I guessed. I'd gotten used to the schedule here.

I knotted the strap of the messenger bag together. I would leave the clothes. I didn't need them. I didn't need anything but the one thing I was leaving behind, the one thing I couldn't stay for.

I dug eight fresh hundred-dollar bills out of my messenger bag. I owed him for a week's pay.

I took down the camel coat I'd bought last week. The nights would get cold in the mountains before I got to the next town. When I got past them I'd head down the coast for California. Finally, I'd visit Los Angeles.

Maybe that big of a city could even swallow me.

I left the money on the unmade bed. I owed him more than that, but what could I have paid for almost killing him? Not enough. I had a little over five thousand dollars cached in my bag and more in the bank, but they could have it. It didn't matter. I had enough of a stake to get me to California.

Sunshine. Maybe the seashore. A clientele of movie stars. And a chance to forget the way my heart was already tearing itself in half. The drumbeat that was the town—or the locus, I didn't know which—still resounded strong and steady under my ribs and in my fingers.

The roses are blooming. He's free.

If he was, he didn't need me anymore.

I made it out of the gilt-mermaid door and down past the library, found myself in the front hall. I had to take the stairs one at a time, my ankle hurt so badly. I needed rest, and ice, and some arnica to take the swelling out.

Too bad. I was going to walk until I dropped, or hitch a ride. I could get over the city limits by nightfall.

I had to.

The massive chandelier in the entryway tinkled gently overhead. Creaks and murmurs all around made me suspect we had guests. Lots of guests.

Of course people would come. His friends, probably. Calamus too. They would be glad his curse was broken.

The black and white marble squares were pristine, no sign of blood or water. Good. If I had to see his blood again, I might get sick.

I walked across the foyer, my footsteps shushing quietly. He wouldn't miss me. His curse was broken.

I put my hand on the doorknob. Just one little twist, and then just one step outside. Then one more. How hard was it? It wasn't hard at all. Why couldn't I do it?

I squeezed the doorknob hard as I could, twisted it. Heard a soft, sliding sound behind me.

His hand came over my shoulder, flattened itself on the door. "Good morning," he said in my ear.

A wonderful, velvety voice. A voice I'd pay to hear on the stage.

I shut my eyes. My hair dripped a little; I couldn't get it dry enough with my injured hands protesting. "I left the week's pay on the bed," I said. "I'm no thief."

"I know." His heat, coming through my coat. I would sweat outside until I took it off, or until nightfall. By nightfall it would be cold, I'd be far enough away. "Have I done something to offend you, Isabella?"

"Koren told me the curse is broken." I twisted the doorknob a little, a little more. "Congratulations."

"The roses are blooming." Warm breath against my cheek. "Isabella, what are you doing?"

"You don't need me anymore." I was wearily amazed that he wanted me to say it. "If the curse is broken, and you can do whatever you want—"

"Why don't you come and have some tea, and I'll explain?"

"I'd rather leave now, please," I said, politely. If I had to turn around and look at him, I might cave in. I might agree to something I couldn't do. I might find out that the scars were gone and that—

"Don't." His tone was extremely quiet. "You *belong* here. With me."

It was official. My heart was breaking, cracking inside my chest. "Jeremy, I was just here to break the curse. That's all. You don't need to be nice to me anymore."

"It pleases me to be nice to you. Turn around."

White-knuckled, I clung grimly to the doorknob.

"Please," he said, softly. "Then you can decide."

"Jeremy," I began. He leaned in. Almost touching me. That soft, forgiving heat of his choked off whatever I wanted to say. My knees shook, and my ankle throbbed fiercely.

"Turn around," he said.

I let go. Turned, very slowly, because he didn't move, just stood there. I didn't have much room. This left me staring at his chest, covered by a black T-shirt instead of a sweater.

"Look," I said to his chest, too much of a coward to even look at his chin, "sooner or later the wind's going to call me, and I'll have to leave."

"We'll cross that bridge when we come to it. You promised to marry me."

"I thought you were dying," I said, inconsequentially.

He shrugged. A fluid movement, muscle rippling under black cotton. It was probably too warm for a sweater. "I did too. Why won't you look at me?"

"Isn't it obvious? I'm too scared."

He laughed then, and his hands cupped my shoulders. He pulled me forward, hugging me. My tired, sore body collapsed into his. It felt good. "Always so honest."

My ankle gave one last scream and subsided, mostly because he'd picked me up. My legs dangled, and my messenger bag did to. I let out a surprised sound halfway between a yelp and a scream and grabbed his shoulder, slipping my arm behind his neck to steady myself, and looked up.

The scarring was gone.

My mouth went dry.

Oh, my.

Blue eyes, and that savage golden hair. Sharp bladed cheekbones, and a chiseled mouth. A classical, aquiline nose. He'd never be a model, but he had 'bad-boy' written all over him. The kind of face that usually made my knees go weak. A strong face.

A *nice* face. It was a good thing I wasn't standing up.

"Do you think you can stand to look at me?" Wryly, one corner of his mouth quirking up. He turned on his heel, carrying me as if I weighed nothing.

Of course, if he was almost-Kine, I probably did. He could handle even my deadweight easily.

"But—" I began.

"But nothing." He was carrying me up the *stairs*, for God's sake, like some sort of mad movie hero. His boots made reassuringly crisp noises against hardwood, muffled occasionally by carpeting. The whole house was quiet, holding its collective breath. "You promised, Isabella."

"You don't have to be nice to me. I just broke the curse, that's all."

"You don't even know what you did." He turned at the top of the stairs, and strode down a hall I'd never seen, even on my midnight rambles, hung with red velvet and graced by the scarred marble bust of a Roman emperor in a niche.

He pushed a door open, and carried me into a plain, severe bedroom that I knew was his by the absolute lack of decoration on the walls and the crimson bedspread he unceremoniously dumped me on. There were no mirrors. A slice of a painfully clean white bathroom glowed through a door, and the huge bay windows looked out on rows and rows of blooming blood-crimson roses. A wide wingback chair covered in scarred leather stood next to a stack of leatherbound books in front of an empty fireplace. Other than that, the room held no furniture. Just a bare wooden floor, a bed, a chair. And books.

"We're really going to have to talk about your whole Spartan aesthetic," I managed, and pulled my legs up, hugged my knees. My ankle and my legs ached relentlessly. So did my face.

"We can change it to whatever you want, I don't care." He dropped down on the foot of the bed and looked at me, shaking his hair over his face again, that quick habitual movement he used to hide behind. "Now, what the *hell* is going on with you?"

I hugged my knees even tighter. "Look, I know you're probably grateful and all, but I can't stay. I'm a wanderer, I go where the wind blows, and I can't promise that I'll—"

"What is it really? Actually, no. Don't tell me. I'll tell you something. Do you know the only thing that breaks the Tremont curse?" He reached over, took my boot, and pulled on it gently. I had to let him, letting go of my knees, and while my swollen ankle throbbed, he worked my boot off and dropped it over the side of the bed.

"I haven't a clue." I stole tiny sipping glances at his profile. He started working on the other boot with sure, deft fingers.

"I couldn't ask for anything from you, even anything that you would give freely. I couldn't even tell you about the curse. But you broke it anyway." He dropped my second boot over the side of the bed. Then he gave me a long, considering look, his eyes bluer than the sky. "It's a family curse, and somehow things always work out. But you never know." He sounded quiet, and a little uncertain, but not bitter.

Not anymore.

"You never know," I echoed numbly. "But, Jeremy—"

He shook his head. "I can do anything I want, now. I have a duty here, but if you want, I'll leave. With you."

"But—" I began, and he peeled my sock off. He made a low sound when he saw the swelling and bruising around my ankle.

"Ouch. I'll have Mharian take care of that."

I let out a sharp, dry laugh. "You're not listening. I have to go. I've done what you wanted me to do—"

"I love you." He stared at my feet. One sock off, one sock on. I needed a pedicure in the worst way. "I've loved you ever since you walked in my front door, dripping from head to toe and more beautiful than anything I've ever seen in my life. My heart literally stops every time I see you. You don't know what it's like, to sit in the library and watch you all day, and be unable to *tell* you without being throttled by a goddamn family curse."

I sneaked a glance at face, found out that he was still staring at my feet. He reached over, slowly, and peeled the second sock free.

Then he looked up. His gaze met mine. Blue. Very blue. I had the curious sensation of all the air in the room deserting me.

"You really..." I was trying to breathe, and it wasn't working.

"I really do. You've broken the curse, Isabella, and you've promised to marry me. Now why would you run away from that?"

"I...um...I..." Was my utterly profound and ridiculous response.

He dropped my socks over the side of the bed and moved, up on his hands and knees. He stalked forward just like a tiger would, and my throat was dry.

"Is it that I can turn into an animal?" he asked, his face inches from mine. "You saw what happened to Raphael, and you're afraid of me?"

"No." I lost even more breath. I didn't think I could be afraid of him if I tried. I just couldn't. I remembered him sitting with his eyes closed through so many quiet afternoons, listening to my voice, book after book.

I knew him far too well to be frightened ever again.

"Part of being Tremont, and having a cursebreaker, means that I *don't* lose control like a Kine would." His lips were inches from mine. It really wasn't fair that he had such beautiful eyes. And the mouth—his mouth—"You have no idea what it's like, to fight the beast. With you, I won't have to. You're my safety valve. I'll turn into something worse than an animal, Isabella, something like Raphael, if I lose you. If you're hurt. And if you die...I'll follow you. That's the terms and conditions, so to speak. So if you don't want me—"

"I didn't say that," I said. Sky-eyes, without any shadows. Something funny was happening to my chest—my heart was going a mile a minute. And my abraded palms, stinging with sweat. "Um, Jeremy—"

"Do you mean you've changed your mind, and you don't want me?" He leaned forward a little, almost nose-to-nose.

I gave up. I cupped his face with my raw hands. His skin was smooth, not scarred, and he didn't resist me when I pulled him forward.

His mouth met mine, and I kissed him as if I was drowning. It wasn't as good as I remembered.

It was better. Even with my bottom lip hurting, it was better.

He kissed me softly, hopefully, his hands gently cupping my shoulders. I lost track of time. Worlds could have collided while I kissed him, and I wouldn't have known.

He finally took some mercy on me and my poor abused body, and I sat on his bed, breathing heavily while he watched my face, his eyes dark and wounded.

Waiting. How long had he been stuck in this house, scarred and silent, waiting for me?

"Do you really want me to stay?" I whispered.

"I really want you to stay," he whispered back. The smell of him, clean healthy musk. "Please, Isabella. *Please.*"

"Kiss me again," I said. "Convince me."

He didn't need me to ask twice.

By the time that kiss was finished, I had his shirt off, and I hissed out a little when he pulled my T-shirt over my head. He touched the bruise on my arm, gently, and I bit my abused lip again. "How did—"

"Raphael," I said, and a swift silent snarl crossed his face. I shivered, adding hurriedly, "I'm not ever going to do that again."

He brushed his fingertips over my cheek. "Good. My heart couldn't take it. We should wrap that ankle of yours, and—"

"Later," I said, reaching up to touch his face again, and drag his mouth up to mine. "Much later."

He evidently agreed, because he was already working on my jeans, and I couldn't seem to stop kissing him.

THAT EVENING, AS THE LIGHT began to fail, I lay sleepy and content in his arms. He held me gently, as if afraid of hurting me, and lifted my hand up so he could see the abrasions. It looked awful. "Ouch," he said, ruefully, and kissed my palm.

"It's not that bad." I felt like I would never get enough sleep again.

The wind was up outside, sighing through the trees and ruffling the rosebushes. Early evening light poured through the bay windows. I listened closely, but the wind wasn't saying anything. It was just a normal, regular, reassuring breeze.

And thank God, no thunder.

"So what do we do now?"

He yawned, a faint rumbling in his chest. Just like a big cat. A big, sleepy cat.

Don't think about that.

"I suppose we have a nice quiet ceremony and order some more books. And anything else you might need."

"But what do you *do*?"

"I keep chaos away and you help me keep the locus under control. Since you're the cursebreaker and all." He yawned again. "Plenty of work. It won't ever be boring, especially with you around."

"What if I want to leave?" *Oh, God, Isabella, don't ruin the moment.*

But I had to know.

"Then I'll go with you. But the further I get from the power lines and the loci, the less power is available to me. I'll just be like an ordinary Kine then. I need a power source to be a Protector. The good news is, there are loci everywhere."

He didn't sound like it was any big deal. "Okay." Sleep was coming up fast. "I guess. Do you really like me, or are you just happy I broke your curse?"

"I really love you, Isabella," he said, quietly, stroking my hair. "Just rest."

I did.

CHAPTER THIRTY-FOUR

WE GOT HITCHED IN A small ceremony in the library. I wore white lace gloves and a Barbarella T-shirt. Jeremy actually wore a suit. He's a bit stuffy about that sort of thing. Everyone else had roses in their hair. Cal wore a lei made of roses that he had carefully stripped the thorns from, a project that took a good four hours and kept him out of everyone's way. Jeremy wore a small bunch of lavender in his buttonhole.

I wore a crown of white roses Calamus brought.

Koren, licensed as a priest (Episcopalian, I think, although they never said) did the ceremony. They looked lovely in a long blue cassock. There were a bunch of other Protectors there, all different shapes and sizes. It's kind of mind-boggling to see how many different species are living alongside humans, and the normal never even guess.

After the ceremony there was a big party, but I opted out and climbed the stairs to the blue bedroom. The music from the DJ's booth—the DJ was a short childlike creature with six fingers and big bulbous insect eyes that had introduced himself as Doyle Starlight—made the floorboards shake, and I heard a drunken cheer resounding from the great dining room. Neither sound could drown out the omnipresent soft drumbeat of the locus. Every so often, mostly when it was quiet, I would notice that sound again.

Talk about weird.

The party spilled out into the rose garden, and I smiled through my window, watching Calamus juggling balls of orange flame. Mharian on the patio, her head on Guillame's shoulder, swayed gently. Several couples danced, and a small group of kobolding occupying themselves with four kegs and an arcane drinking game. Pale floating globes of light illuminated the rose garden, and several of the guests were playing a sort of tag among the nodding rosebushes, dodging the globes and singing in a chorus of voices that competed with Doyle's thumping bass.

The invisibles would have their hands full cleaning up after all this.

I sat in the window seat, smoking a cigarette, and was still there an hour later, watching the party, when the door opened softly and Jeremy padded in.

He dropped down across from me, I offered him a cigarette. He shook his head, looking down at the roses. They hadn't quit blooming yet. The heady smell of roses drenched the air, but I had stopped smelling it after the second week. It was a relief. The air was constantly dyed with it, a heavy physical presence.

Only these roses smelled weird, like vanilla and roses and sandalwood all mixed together. It was lovely, but even beautiful smells get boring after a while.

"So," I said. "It's done."

He shrugged. His profile was clean and classic,, not a trace of scarring remained. A handsome man, a very handsome man. How had I lucked out? "Or just starting, whatever way you look at it."

I smoked my way through the cigarette and ground it out in the ashtray. A shout went up from the rose garden—someone had won the game. Doyle's music shifted to something with a little less driving beat, but it still thumped and rattled. I grimaced. "That's the last one ever. I've quit."

"Really?" He looked pleased. "Do you really want to stay here, Isabella?"

I looked at him in the gathering twilight. Nightfall, and I was safely in the house. You couldn't have paid me to step outside—not without him.

I wouldn't stay here forever, no. But for right now...

"Yes." I looked out at the rose garden. "I'll stay. Of course I'll stay."

When I left, he'd go with me. It would be fun to travel with him. He'd like seeing new places, telling fortunes. I couldn't wait to see him working a carnival. Maybe I could be a tiger-tamer, if he didn't mind using his powers for cash. We could work our way across the country that way.

Or any way, really. We might not even have to work.

It didn't matter. The important thing was, he'd go with me. Wherever I went, at least I wasn't alone now.

A freshening breeze rattled the rosebushes, and the distant brass rumble of thunder began. Heat lightning played through the clouds.

Something about the locus made storms more frequent here, power playing havoc on air and cloud. The partygoers started to stream inside, Calamus still juggling as he walked, Mharian fussing at people to get indoors before the rain started. Doors opened, closed. They would party inside all night, and the invisible servants would have one hell of a time in the morning. Although I guessed that it was a nice break in the monotony for them, they didn't have much to do with just Jeremy and me in the house.

I had a whole box of astrology books to put away tomorrow. "Another storm."

"Yes." He didn't look at me. It was a lifelong habit, I'd learned, not to stare at what he couldn't have. So he didn't have to see the disgust on people's faces, to see the fear, or the hatred.

He looked at my hands, instead, or at the curve of my knee. There was a new expression on his face—a blind, sweet hope I ached to see.

"Come on, Tremont." I slid my fingers through his, pulled gently on his hand. "Let them party if they want. Let's go to bed."

I didn't have to tell him twice.

Finis

ABOUT THE AUTHOR

LILI LIVES IN VANCOUVER, WASHINGTON, with two dogs, two cats, two children, and a metric ton of books holding her house together. However, referring to her as "Noah" will likely get you a lecture. You can visit her online at www.lilithsaintcrow.com.

ALSO BY LILITH SAINTCROW

The Dante Valentine Series

The Jill Kismet Series

The Bannon and Clare Series

The Strange Angels Series

Tales of Beauty and Madness

Romances of Arquitaine

Selene: A Saint City Novel

SquirrelTerror

Trailer Park Fae (forthcoming)

...and many more.